SAKURU

By **TODD DOWNING**

FIRST EDITION

ISBN: 979-8-9861181-7-8

Cover design by Todd Downing
Editing services by Dan Heinrich & Raechelle Downing
Special thanks to Trish Heinrich

WWW.TODDDOWNING.COM

Stilt first appeared in *Zingo Magazine* #1, © 1983

Cuda, Creep, Tigress, KML029 ("Camel") and Van Pezzoni first appeared in *Tales of Zingo* #1, © 1984

Deep7 Press is a subsidiary of Despot Media, LLC
1214 Woods Rd SE Port Orchard, WA 98366 USA

WWW.DEEP7.COM

For Randy, David,
Bron, and Mark—
the original Shihodo boys

And for Steve and JD—
the second wave

Sākuru (サークル) : *circle; a group with common interest.*

Shihōdō (四方道) : *"the way of the four directions" ; A study of martial arts incorporating influences from a variety of regions and philosophies.*

FOREWORD

The *SAKURU PROPERTY* (formerly *Shihodo*, formerly *Inner Circle*, formerly *The Underground*) has been in development in one way or another since about 1982, when a martial arts vigilante called Stilt appeared in the underground comic publication, *Zingo Magazine*. Stilt began as a doodle at a friend's kitchen table, and ended up leading a motley crew of martial arts action heroes in various graphical incarnations. For reasons only my fellow writers know, good characters become an addiction, and these made up a crazy roster inspired by too much 1980s Japanese animation and an obsession with Frank Miller's *Daredevil* and *Wolverine* runs.

While I exercised my humor in the *Zingo* comic strip in local Bay Area newspapers, Stilt and the Shihodo gang occupied a series of epic, dystopian science fiction graphic novel projects, which, for a variety of financial or timing-related reasons, were never ultimately published.

Finally in 1991, after moving to Seattle—away from my contacts in the Bay Area comics world—I decided to take a break from writing an action-horror series and novelize the script for the most recent manga-style graphic novel that artist Mark Holmes and I had attempted. Completed in 1992, it was as epic as ever, edgy as hell, with all the hallmarks of so-called "cyberpunk" literature of the time, but a decade past Gibson's Neuromancer and swimming in borderline toxic twentysomething attitude.

Nonetheless, it made the rounds to the publishers, and secured an option from the new author imprint of a major publishing house. Unfortunately, the line editor ended up leaving—taking their catalog of optioned works with her—and within a couple months she'd disappeared into the dark recesses of another publisher in New York.

I moved onto other projects, becoming an artist in the videogame industry, occasionally flirting with the resurrection of the Shihodo property in one form or another. But for the most part, that was that.

One of the great double-edged swords of being an artist is that you get to return to your back catalog and look at older work with a fresh perspective. So it was that more than a quarter century later, I was combing through some old, unpublished writing and ran across the original *Inner Circle* novel files. The fact that I'd begun a sequel back in 1993 pushed me toward the decision to do an overhaul, strip out the outdated terminology and leave the action, adventure and social commentary.

The process has been a rewarding one. As the original novel had been set in 2020 (which at the time was thirty years in the future), it was entertaining to see which of my future prognostications had come to fruition by then. Turns out the economic stratification of the classes that bloomed in the Reagan era had become exponentially worse, the corporate arcology culture owning much at the expense of the working poor and inner city neighborhoods. I nailed the ascent of professional MMA as a mass-market spectator sport, and many of the issues plaguing law enforcement in the 21st century. I got close with genetic constructs, nanotech and DNA information storage. But I failed miserably on the flying cars (damnit, where are our flying cars?), and the ubiquity of voice and touch-screen media interfaces. I mean, when this story was first written, there was barely an Internet, not to mention an Internet of things or Cloud.

You can't win them all.

I knew the story had solid bones. I just needed to give it a face-lift, bring it back to being more about the characters and society, and less about the kewl flash.

The irony of a more than quarter-century upgrade to a futurist story first written in Word for DOS is not lost, trust me.

I hope you like this shiny new old discovery.

- Todd Downing, Port Orchard, WA
   Winter, 2023

ORIGIN

North Korea, 2034

THE EXPLOSIONS were blinding, like the halogen flash of a strobe unit set to an intermittent pulse. A new target appeared in the crosshairs of a video reticle: a boxy warehouse structure with a lone smokestack erupting from the roof. It rushed toward the monitor at high speed and disappeared in a flash of white.

Colonel Meredith watched the scene from the forward base at Cheorwon, peering over the shoulder of a young drone operator as the screen lit up in saturated color.

"Target neutralized, Colonel," she announced.

"Good, good."

A gray-haired man of fifty-four, Meredith was in the midst of overseeing multiple operations within a hundred kilometers of the border. Most were the usual: air strikes, strategic drone sorties and the like, but one particular mission—or at least the weapons being used in it—was to remain "off the books".

It didn't matter that he found the use of such weapons unethical at best and an abomination at worst. His approval was irrelevant to the process. It was merely his job to ensure that the chaos unleashed would be returned safely to Pandora's Box when the mission was complete. But then that notion was somewhat contrary to the very premise of the Greek myth.

A young sergeant appeared in the doorway to Meredith's left and caught his eye. The colonel turned, and the soldier snapped to attention.

"Colonel Meredith, sir. Sergeant Holmes, reporting as ordered."

The colonel approached, gesturing "at ease", and Sgt. Holmes relaxed as much as he dared, which wasn't a lot.

"Status," Meredith demanded.

Holmes cleared his throat. "Well the control center has been neutralized—"

"I can see that, Sergeant," Colonel Meredith pointed at the array of monitors and various remote drone pilots and control personnel in the room. "I mean the strike team."

Holmes swallowed dryly. "Dead, sir."

Meredith frowned, turning away from the soldier to glance at the screens once again. "All accounted for?"

"All except...Erikson, sir. We believe he set the charge."

The Colonel spun on his heel, suddenly inches from Holmes' red face. "Did you recover a body?"

Sergeant Holmes looked confused. "Um, sir...there's no way anyone could have cleared the initial blast. He must have been vaporized on ignition."

If Meredith was close before, Holmes could now see every vein in his eyes, every pore in the skin across his nose and cheeks. He smelled of Havana cigars, expensive Bourbon and cheap aftershave. The Colonel spoke in a measured tone that struck fear into the soldier's heart more than any screaming tirade. "Sergeant, you'd better bring me back a body. One piece or a hundred."

The message was focused and clear. Holmes blinked and tried to look anywhere but in the Colonel's bloodshot eyes.

But Meredith wasn't finished. "Uncle Sam is not going to appreciate an experimental military weapon waltzing around enemy territory un-monitored."

Holmes found his opportunity to get the hell out of there. He snapped back to attention and saluted. "Yessir!"

Col. Meredith turned to the wall of monitors, and Sgt. Holmes quickly disappeared through the door of the command bunker.

The UN field hospital was set up within a secluded, wooded area in Mt. Kumgang National Park. It was understaffed and not well-protected, as it was the first and thus far only service of its kind in the combat zone. Once again, the US had strong-armed the Security Council, essentially invading North Korea under the guise of "leading an international coalition to enforce sanctions", and someone in the Japanese government, having concerns with regard to civilian casualties, arranged for this small gesture until more formal plans could be made for civilian refugee evacuation and medical care.

Dr. Mariko Tokura, a slender medic from Kyoto, moved from stretcher to stretcher as more wounded poured into the camp. A tall woman of thirty-eight, she wore military fatigues under a white lab coat, stethoscope clamped around her neck as she triaged patients.

A young corpsman called to her from the new batch of casualties as they were unloaded from a UN armored personnel carrier being used as an ambulance. "Lieutenant Tokura!" he hailed in Japanese.

Dr. Tokura turned and strode toward the APC, curious. "What is it, Corporal?"

As she came upon the body, she knew this day would irrevocably alter the rest of her life. The unconscious soldier was a huge man—close to two meters tall, muscled like a war horse. It seemed like his entire vascular system was twice normal size, veins standing out proudly under suntanned skin. He had severe burns over half his exposed flesh, and his left ear was missing completely. The combat body armor he wore was charred and shredded.

Tokura found his dog tags and turned them over in her hand, wiping away the soot with her thumb.

ERIKSON, DAVID A

"American?" she frowned.

The corpsman squinted into the distance. "There was an American force assaulting the missile control center near Kosan. That's over fifty klicks from here. Our patrols go nowhere that far inside the border. I wonder where they found him."

Mariko Tokura looked over the wounded soldier's body, noticing for the first time a piece of mechanical hardware strapped to his chest under the broken armor. She reached toward him, tracing the outline of the metallic protrusion with a lithe finger.

"What's this he's wearing? Looks like some sort of—"

As her fingertip brushed the corner of the module, a light blinked on and Mariko recoiled in surprise. There was a faint click, followed by a hiss. The soldier's eyes blinked open suddenly, and both medics gasped in unison.

Dr. Tokura stared wide-eyed at the soldier as she realized what the electronic module on his chest was, and by extension, what he was.

"Corporal?" she said softly, but with grave urgency.

The corpsman looked equally scared. "Yes?"

"Back away quietly."

The American soldier's eyes locked onto them, swollen and red from hemorrhage.

Mariko stepped back instinctively, but a giant hand clamped around her wrist, and she found herself trapped. Her fight-or-flight instinct manifested in tunnel vision and a spike in respiration and blood pressure. The hand encircling her own simply held on as if holding her in place was the easiest feat in the world.

The red eyes—probably hazel before the drugs and injuries had exploded them—glared at her, and the soldier's jaw began to move. Somewhere within him, a deep baritone voice welled up. "Please help."

Mariko looked down at the man. Clearly she hadn't heard him right. Had he said *please help?*

The distant thrum of a Blackhawk helicopter told her the Americans had probably located their stray and would be there soon to retrieve him.

"What...what can I do—?" she stammered in broken English.

"Take a blood sample," the soldier urged. "Before they find me. Take it to the UN. Let them know."

Then he released her, and she beckoned to the Corporal to bring a syringe and vial for a blood draw. The mystery had gripped her now. She was far more intrigued than frightened. "Let them know what?"

The swollen red eyes shut, and the soldier relaxed, offering his left arm as Mariko swabbed it, prepping the needle.

"Our program violates just about every treaty and international law," he said quietly. "We're not supposed to exist."

The syringe was inserted, and Mariko drew a full vial of blood from the patient, without another word passing between them. When she was finished, he opened his eyes once more, finding her kind but worried face in the humid morning air.

"Get out of here," he ordered. "Don't look back, and don't let anyone detain you. You never saw me. We never spoke."

Frowning, Mariko pulled away and stood, nodding at the Corporal as he cleaned up the disposable packaging from the medical instruments. They walked quickly to the APC and shut the doors, driving away as the American helicopter came down in the meadow next to the mobile hospital, its long blades whipping at the sky.

Erikson swung his legs over the cot and waited for the familiar click-hiss of the drug harness to dispense another dose of "juice", a cocktail of adrenaline, steroidal compounds and who knew what else. The stuff that made it possible to survive an explosion the way he'd just done. The stuff that made being a world-class predator animal a question of simple instinct.

But no sound came. Whether damaged by the explosion or disabled remotely by Command, the harness was offline. As he watched the men leap from the belly of the Blackhawk, he realized that there was only one thing left to do.

He closed his eyes and smelled the pine on the morning breeze.

The SEAL team was quick and clean. As Erikson sat upright on the edge of the field cot, eyes shut, a Mk 14 Enhanced Battle Rifle popped a single round through his skull. UN medics froze in a state of borderline panic as the soldier slumped sideways in a seeping puddle of red. Without so much as a nod of acknowledgment, the team simply gathered Erikson's body and carried it back to the chopper, which bore them away into the golden morning.

Blue-helmeted UN soldiers ran to see what the commotion was, but the mystery soldier was already gone—as was Mariko Tokura.

San Francisco, 2065

THE **NIGHT FOG** sat over the city like a blanket of gray watercolor. Blinking lights on the Transamerica Pyramid and aircraft strobes atop the Bay Bridge would have to suffice for stars. The air was thick and smelled of moist steel, concrete and stale urine.

Cracks in acres of warm cement released the musty vapor of the post-6 p.m. rain. The sky was underlit by a sickly, radioactive orange glow, a great mass of nature's vengeance threatening to let loose again with another downpour.

But it wouldn't.

Not until tomorrow afternoon at 4:16 p.m.

At least, that's what the schedule said. It was known to be a couple minutes off from time to time.

Glass and steel spires of fifty corporate headquarters lined a back-lit sky, dropping on mammoth metal legs to the streets of the financial district below. They looked a lot closer together here, at ground level: a giant maze of mirrored Lego blocks stacked up against a smoke-colored backdrop. Catwalks of cement and girder and bullet-proof panes connected some of the closer buildings every few stories, looking for all the world like horizontal sutures across a gaping vertical wound. One would only hope it were enough to keep a sky full of blood from bursting through onto the corner of Clay and Battery.

The spot was on the west side of Kitayamacorp San Francisco headquarters, and would shortly play host to something its corporate owners definitely wouldn't approve of. Yet this was the chosen meeting place, since it was off the beat of the SFPD. External security could be dismantled with some hacking courtesy of inside assets and a simple, focused EM pulse. Hi-def cameras sat dark, a dozen automated security bots stood frozen at their charging stations. The area was an empty concrete quad in the shadow of the arcology spires above, motion-sensitive lighting dormant.

Everything looked gray here. Or black.

The Lexus AV-50: That was the kind of black you only saw in a well-calibrated graphics monitor. A shade without hue, absorbing all light around it. It matched Bug's leather trench coat, his Italian slacks, his tight gloves. And his sunglasses too, which Dennis Murray presumed were the new Nikon multi-optics that gave the wearer a choice of light spectra to choose from, allowing almost perfect vision in near-darkness.

Actually, Dennis thought, *those are kinda badass.*

A man whose facial features and rich pigment revealed ethnic elements of African and Mediterranean, traces of Latino and plenty of cosmetic surgery, Bug was well-known in the illicit pharmaceutical industry. Dennis figured him somewhere in the higher mid-tier of whichever corporation was manufacturing his product—not low enough to have to sling that product on the street, but not high enough to register on most federal databases as a kingpin. Bug was comfortable middle management.

Dennis shuffled his trainers in the dust and smiled confidently. He needed this deal. And right now he was as close as he'd ever been. Sure, it took some time and capital. But the end result would be well worth the investment.

"Let's have it," Bug ordered.

Dennis waved a muscular hand, skin freckled and weathered from years of surfing and manual labor in the sun. This was someone who hadn't grown up in the corporate apartments of the Financial District, sheltered behind UV-blocking windows and blessed with what the working class called an "arcology tan". Growing up, he'd actually played outdoors.

A tall indigenous Mexican in black jeans and an Army jacket stepped forward, cradling an armored briefcase like a newborn child. As he approached the Lexus, two men who resembled great iron golems stepped forth from Bug's rear flank.

"Hold it," growled the one on the right. "Open it there."

"Easy, Biggs." Bug smiled, his upper lip curling under to unmask acrylic dental implants, a recent acquisition. "Don't scare the kid, bruh."

The one called Biggs couldn't have asked for a more appropriate name. He was six-foot-four and at least three-hundred-twenty pounds of solid, muscled flesh. His hairline receded gracefully up his temples and he wore a smile reminiscent of Frankenstein's monster. The dark overcoat covering his mammoth pecs had to have taken fifteen meters of fabric to make.

Like the moguls of old, it seemed Bug had a penchant for Viking mercenaries. The silent thug on his left could have been the wiki entry for Nietzsche's *Übermensch*. Johann was about Biggs' height, and weighed at least three-hundred pounds, dressed fashionably in a French silk suit and tie, short-cropped blond hair poking up wildly around his head like a halo in a Renaissance painting. His goatee was only slightly darker than his hair, and a mirrored optical implant stared out from where his left eye should have been.

Dennis fished out a disposable nic-stick and pressed down on the filter to set the microbattery cooking. "It's all there," he mumbled, putting the short cylinder to his lips and inhaling odorless vapor. "Half a mil."

The young Mexican popped the lid on the case, and it was Bug's turn to smile. Sure, it was all there. About half in actual unmarked paper currency, and the balance in prepaid plastic chip-cards.

"No it ain't," Bug said, flexing his fingers within their tight leather skin.

Dennis coughed in surprise. He glared at Bug with fiery blue eyes, eyes that were still his, still natural. What the hell *was* this? His closely-buzzed platinum hair ruffled in a warm gust of wind off the street and he straightened, stepping away from the hood of the Acura coupe. His other slinger, a wiry Caribbean woman with impressive dreadlocks, shifted uncomfortably and folded her arms.

"The fuck you mean it's not there?" Dennis grunted.

Bug's smile grew even wider, if that were possible. "Decipher me, Denny. That's only five-hundred."

"Half a mil's the price, man. You said."

"That was yesterday. This is today." Bug stepped forward and shrugged his padded shoulders. "Inflation, you know?"

"Bullshit."

"It's seven-fifty now."

"Bull. Shit."

"Hey, you don't want the stuff, babe, you don't gotta take it. I ain't got time to sit here and negotiate with you."

Dennis threw the smoldering nic-stick on the damp ground and shook his head from side to side in a show of anger. "What the hell, man? I ain't ever *seen* the stuff. How am I supposed to come up with another two-fucking-fifty?"

The Caribbean slinger cringed, kicking at the ground with the toe of her boot. "Gonna have to raise the street price, Denny. Ain't nobody gonna like it."

Dennis sighed, folding muscular arms defensively across his blue T-shirt and glanced at the giants flanking Bug. The only other backup his supplier seemed to have was a long-haired Thai kid standing patiently behind the open driver-side door of the Lexus. Probably had a gun, some kind of SMG, hidden just out of sight.

Bug didn't take chances. Everyone knew it. And now Dennis was becoming genuinely worried.

"Whassup, Bug-man? I move good units for you. Why you messin' with my cash flow?"

Bug continued his misplaced grin. "All good, bruh. I think you'll find the price worthwhile when you see the product."

"Yeah, well show me the stuff. I wanna see what I'm laying down my goddamn life savings for."

Bug gestured to his thugs. "Yo, Biggs."

As the giant strode forward, the young Mexican flinched involuntarily, and Bug broke into a laugh. "Denny, you gotta get yourself some boys with a backbone, man."

Biggs smiled politely, closing the lid on the case, and removed it from the custody of the Mexican's arms. The young man glanced back at Dennis, who shuffled his feet, sweating.

This was *not* going well.

Dennis squinted anxiously and watched as Biggs turned toward the Lexus, and half a million dollars in seed money disappeared behind the massive thug.

Above and behind the alley, the round silhouette of a tiny parabolic mic dish lay submerged in the shadows atop the first catwalk. A minuscule green LED on the earpiece was the only indication that audio was being recorded.

The chiseled face was Asian, pale-complected with a few days stubble, and it shifted beneath the reflective chrome-plating of a sleek, protective visor. A lock of dark hair fell across the field of vision and was silently tamed with a black-gloved hand.

"Did you get that?"

A large body shifted next to him, a mass of muscles and worry. The figure was bald, with dark skin and a goatee that showed some gray at the corners of the mouth. Chestnut eyes scanned back and forth. A faint blue glow indicated the small phone cam in his hand was live and recording everything in the alley beneath them.

"It's goin' down. Where the hell is Pezzoni?"

"Shh. Wait. Here it comes." One gloved finger gestured down into the alley, and their attention returned to the scene below.

The Mexican kid had switched places with Dennis. The metal briefcase sat upright in the dirt next to the Lexus. Bug stood his ground as Biggs returned from the car with an identical case. Biggs popped it open in front of Dennis and he flinched.

Bug stepped forward. "You're jumpy tonight, *amigo.*"

Dennis wondered if Bug's eyewear had picked up his spike in body temperature with the thermo filter. Nervously, he peered inside the open case. Countless plastic capsules filled with crimson liquid met his eyes.

"What is it?"

"Brand new, bruh. It's Jet. Pure-strain, straight-to-the-brain and insane."

Dennis looked skeptical. "What about the Indigo Ice, man?"

"Indigo's gone, *amigo.* Shit was glorified meth. They ain't making it no more. Jet is *now.*"

Dennis frowned. It didn't make sense. A successful drug operation didn't just stop making a profitable product and replace it. If anything they'd diversify. Some big fish was behind a move like this.

"But seven-fifty..."

"Cost-effective, Denny, I guarantee you. Built from the molecule up. Hooks after one time. High lasts a day, man. Twice as long as Indigo. They won't believe what they can do. And they'll all be back for more. It's more expensive 'cause it does more and lasts longer. Costs more to make, too. Only one lab on the Coast."

Dennis wasn't happy. He should have been, but a subtle chill down the nape of his neck told him Bug was up to something. "How long has this been out?"

"You're the first."

"The fuck I am."

"Can't fool you, Denny." Bug grinned with the entire lower half of his face. "Been out for a week."

"On the street?"

"On the street."

"Who's slinging it?"

Atop the catwalk, the visor twitched. "Oh shit."

The dark torso leaned in close. "What."

"Windy."

The back door of the Lexus opened, and a woman stepped out, approaching Bug from behind. She was barely twenty-five and absolutely stunning—a retro scifi pinup come to life, a genetic tapestry of Eurasian extractions. Platinum white hair seemed to explode from her head in a great tangled sculpture of mousse and styling spray, and tiny rainbows of light winked playfully from the fiberoptic stars scattered randomly throughout.

Her face was vampire pale and made up to emphasize sparkling green eyes and pouty lips. Geometric earrings glowed with channeled available light, and her leather jacket and miniskirt outfit were the height of fetish scene fashion. Black fishnets encased slender white legs, and calf-high black boots tapered down to a sharp point from three-inch heels.

She had it, she *knew* she had it, and she worked it to her advantage.

"What's taking so long, Bug?"

Bug did not look at her, but watched Dennis as *he* looked at her. "Just business, baby. Get back in the car."

The visored face slid further into the shadows, and the gloved hand removed the earpiece. "Goddamnit, I told her not to show."

The black giant followed his partner's lead. "The hell is Pezzoni, man? He said he was gonna be here, but he's not picking up—"

"Well he isn't here. Screw Pezzoni. What do you see?"

The large man gave a worried glance that showed the ravages of street life and the loss of loved ones behind his dark eyes. He didn't want to lose another. "We can't take 'em, Stilt. It'd be suicide."

The man he called Stilt shifted his gaze from target to target, long years of martial arts training flooding his senses like an automatic wave of combat instinct. "Driver," he said, nodding at the Thai behind the open car door. "FN P90 bullpup."

The other man squinted. Sure enough, the very edge of a wide gun strap dangled just below the bottom contour of the driver's side door. But the exact make and model? Really? How the hell did he know that?

The answer was as accurate as it was unsatisfactory: *He just did.*

His giant partner knew how he'd been able to glean the information, and he often wondered if the process involved mirrors and assistants hidden behind a curtain. It certainly seemed like magic, in the greatest Vegas tradition.

In reality, Stilt had spent his formative years under expert tutelage, trained to notice the most minute movements in the human machine, the slightest twitch or glance or shifting of weight.

He was fluent in body language.

He could look at a wrinkle in the front of a coat, like Biggs' or Johann's, and: "Viking, crazy hair. Nine millimeter. *Nunchaku*, right lapel. Cyberoptic."

"Forget it, man. We can't take these guys."

"Blond boy spike. Classic Colt .45 auto. Rear belt."

"Stilt, come on."

"Rasta girl. Glock 9, rear belt. Left-handed."

"Stilt. No."

"Bug. Nine millimeter auto. Left lapel. He's itchy for it."

As they looked on, Windy leaned in close and stuck her hand in Bug's waistband.

"Business? We trading stuff? Can I play?"

Bug glanced down at the smiling young woman, unamused. "Wha'd you say?"

Stilt was right. The fingers of Bug's right hand clenched repeatedly into a fist. He wanted trouble.

The woman snapped her gum and winked. "Aww, come on, Bug. Just make your little deal and let's go have some fun."

Bug frowned, turning completely away from Dennis. "Listen, bitch. I'll be done when I'm done. Don't tell me my business."

Dennis eyed the case of the brand new drug. "Come on, Bug. You gonna let me have the stuff? I can get the extra two-fifty in a couple days—"

Windy smiled and leaned in close. "C'mon, Buggie. Let him have the stuff."

Bug's back stiffened and his jaw clenched tight. "Don't fucking call me that," he ordered.

Giggling, she pursed her lips. "Aww, Buggie-boo."

Dennis winced. *That* certainly hadn't helped.

Until now, Bug's focus had been completely on Dennis and his posse. But now he turned to face Windy, fury evident in spite of the shades obscuring his eyes. "Bitch, you open your mouth when I say, and it ain't for talkin'! You get me?" His face drew within inches of hers.

Windy dropped her smile, suddenly very worried. She was usually able to manage a client's emotional state like a master puppeteer, but Bug had recently become...unpredictable.

Dennis studied the case of drugs in Biggs' tree trunk arms. The other case, full of his money, lay on the ground next to the open rear door of the Lexus and he found himself counting paces. "Come on, man. Yes or no? If it's no deal, gimme my money." He was sweating hard now.

The distraction of the lovers' quarrel continued unabated.

Windy chimed sweetly. "I-I'm sorry—"

"Shut it!"

"Sorry..." She caught herself too late. The word was muttered under her breath, but it was loud enough that Bug noticed.

His right fist launched out and met her face with a hard leather *crack*. She fell with a gasp, sprawling in the soft gravelly dirt.

Stilt stood upright in the shadows, hands suddenly tense as he watched Bug turn toward Windy and reach toward his left lapel.

"Stilt, come on, man. We can't do it."

"You coming or not, Cuda?"

The giant stood and looked down at the alley just as Bug pulled out the nine-millimeter pistol Stilt had promised was there, lowering the barrel toward Windy's fallen frame. There wasn't any time to argue.

"Aww hell," he groaned.

And they jumped.

"How many lives you got?" Bug yanked back the Browning's slide mechanism and extended the barrel at Windy, who was just staggering to her feet.

The sudden crash of automotive window glass and the crunch of metal echoed through the concrete canyon. Bug spun to face the noise.

The tall, skinny Asian wore a dark gray workout *dogi* over a black bodysuit and baggy pants, his long, dark hair pulled back into a functional ponytail. His feet were encased in *tabi* boots with rubberized grips on the soles, and some kind of polished metal shades covered his eyes. The bronze giant wore an open navy blue nylon jacket, but no bodysuit underneath. He was content with gray canvas baggies and huge Nike high tops.

The tall one gestured emphatically in the direction of Bug's fallen companion. "Windy! Get outta there!"

Astonished, Bug glanced at Windy as she disappeared down the side alleyway into the darkness. That was all he could register in the flurry of motion as he ducked behind Biggs and dashed toward the Lexus.

The Caribbean gangster whipped a pistol from behind her back. Cuda leaped from the trunk of the coupe, spinning a kick in midair that caught her full-face, knocking her instantly to the ground. Stilt hopped from the crumpled roof to the hood, whipping what looked like two aluminum rods from twin scabbards on his back.

Dennis whirled around, grabbing for his pistol, and found to his horror the round-end of a large, chrome stick whistling toward his face with uncanny force. He felt his nose pop, stars erupted in his eyes and he dropped to the ground.

Then the shooting started.

A dozen cops in full riot gear rushed in, pelting the Lexus with small-arms fire. Johann pulled the rear door shut, and the Thai ducked inside, revving the AV's engine to life.

Cuda's hand actually touched the briefcase full of cash, before Biggs ripped it away and used it as a bludgeon. Cuda landed two meters away, blood gushing from his nose.

The front door slammed, and the Lexus soared into the air with a deafening blast from the repulsors. It climbed quickly, zigzagging through the scattered catwalks between the towers of the Kitayama arcology, clipping the left front fender on a cement bulwark.

The alley was suddenly bathed in the light of fifty halogen spots.

"Hold it right there, asshole!"

Cuda's head snapped up, and he found himself staring at the wrong end of a police-issue Glock and a chrome badge with the prominent letters *S-F-P-D.*

"Shit."

Glaring back at him from the other end of the gun was the bloodied face of the Caribbean woman with the impressive dreads. "Oh, you got pretty too," she said, noticing his own bloodied face. "No no, don't get up."

Cuda turned his head over on the pavement. He could see Stilt, thrust up against the side of the wrecked coupe, undergoing a fairly serious weapon search. The two pieces of titanium alloy had been connected into a seven-foot-long *bo* staff, and now lay in the dirt as the young Mexican and a riot cop patted him down.

Cuda glanced forward and saw the shiny black boots of a cop in riot gear approaching. "Whassup, man? What's goin' down?"

The cop squatted down and smiled. He was white, because of course he was—most SF cops were. It wasn't that fact that most bothered Cuda. There hadn't been any serious charges of civil rights abuses by the SFPD in more than a decade, but just the same, he wasn't altogether comfortable laying face-down in the dirt with the boots of a white riot cop so close to his head.

"*You* are, *amigo*."

"Wha'd we do, man?"

"Oh, obstruction, aiding a known felon, assaulting a police officer, assault with intent maybe, willful destruction of property, just for starters. Your long-haired buddy over there, we'll get him for assault with a deadly weapon. You guys screwed up pretty bad."

Cuda laid his head back on the side that didn't hurt and sighed as he felt the cuffs go on. The cop stood. "Harris, McAllister, see to Murray. Looks like his nose is broke. And Tracy, get over here and read this asshole his rights."

A muscular redheaded Amazon in riot gear strode up to Cuda and smiled. He *hated* that. Too damn courteous while you were roped like a steer face-down in the dust of a dank alleyway.

"Comfortable?" she smirked.

"Yeah. My safe-word is 'bananas', by the way."

"Funny guy," she said. "You have the right to remain silent..."

Yeah yeah. "Thanks. It's been awhile, but I think I remember the deal."

"You know the part about us using whatever you say against you in a court of law?"

"Yup."

"And if you can't afford an attorney, one will be appointed?"

"Yeah. Got it down."

He watched as Stilt was lowered hastily to the ground and cuffed behind his back. The lanky man turned his visored eyes toward Cuda.

"Don't say a goddamn thing, Cuda."

Cuda laughed, inhaling a nostril full of wet dust. "No, I really had fun, man. We oughtta do this again real soon."

Asano's fingers trembled weakly on the acrylic keys as he finished the last bar of Sakamoto's *Solitude*. The final melancholy chord echoed through the spacious penthouse and was a long time fading away. Asano leaned back, shifting his foot from the sustain pedal on the giant black Yamaha grand. With his eyes closed, his face became a shattered maze of scars and hospital patchwork that, even years after the accident, stood out grotesquely from his otherwise handsome, angular Asian face.

Once, a long time ago, Asano might have cared about that face. Not anymore. The fortune, the cars, the status—they meant nothing. The music was his escape. The *dojo* was his diversion.

Reality...*that* still hurt. And it had to be avoided at all costs.

That was why he'd accepted the Tigress' invitation to come play the States. The only reason. Not for music sales, not for publicity—good lord, he'd practically been a hermit for the past three years.

Escape. That was it.

Asano blinked watery brown eyes and turned to look out the enormous window, gazing over the city: the night fog soft and aglow with tiny rectangles of corporate light from the neighboring skyscrapers; the steady pulse of the warning lights atop the Golden Gate; somewhere, out over the bay, a solitary AV banked and turned south toward the peninsula—he could see its running lights surge through the mist.

His mind reached out toward the Bay, and he imagined himself able to just float away on a western breeze and never return.

And then his phone chirped, and he was back at the piano bench, in the penthouse suite, in the K-Corp Marina building. For all his freedom and luxury, he may as well have been in a prison cell.

A female voice announced: "Incoming call from Susan Kitayama."

"Answer," he told the empty room.

He rose tiredly and ambled through the plushly decorated sunken living room to the kitchen, straightening a silk Armani shirt, cuffs hanging loose and unbuttoned. *"Moshi moshi."*

The voice at the other end was soft and feminine, and sounded of expensively-educated corporate professionalism. "Asano? It's Susan Kitayama." She spoke in fluid, New World Japanese. "I'm sorry for calling so late. I just wanted to find out if your accommodations were satisfactory."

"They are more than satisfactory. Thank you," he answered in the old dialect. The two accents were different in some inflection and syntax, but remained similar enough to comprehend each other.

Silently removing the lid from the ceramic teapot on the counter, he put it beneath the hot water dispenser in the sink. The sensor triggered a stream of steaming water into the vessel, rattling the metal tea-ball chained to the handle. "The suite is quite luxurious."

"Practicing hard for Friday?"

"Yes. Just getting in a bit of Sakamoto before bed." He set the warm pot on the counter and left it to steep. A few wandered steps and Asano found himself back in the living room, staring out over the city once again.

"Well, don't be up too late. Artists need their rest too. I'll check back with you in a couple of days. Do let me know if you need anything."

"I will."

"Alright then. Good night."

"Susan?" Asano added hastily.

There was a pause, and the soft voice answered: "Yes?"

Asano closed his eyes. "Thank you. For the chance to come back. You have been most kind."

"You are most welcome, Asano. I'm at your service. Now get some sleep."

"Good night," he said.

"Good night," she said.

The signal dropped, and he looked down at the screen: 1:04 a.m.

The pale LED *dojo* lights blinked on in sequence, and Asano entered the small practice gym. The rubber feet of his nylon *tabi* socks made a sticky ripping noise on the floor.

He moved past the rack of *shinai* to the far wall, hefting a *kenjutsu* practice sword from its peg mounts, turning to face the target dummy that stood like a padded chess piece in the center of the room—about six feet tall, with two thick arms sprouting from the sides like a lower-case "t".

He clutched the braided grip of the *bokken* with both hands and extended the tip toward the dummy as he stepped into his attack stance. Closing his eyes, breathing steadily, he felt all of the anger and shame of the past ten years well up in his chest, and he forced the energy out through his arms, his hands, through the wooden sword to his target.

He struck, and the pain of shattered auto glass seared his face. He struck again and heard the plaintive squeal of tires, and the scream of brakes pushed beyond their limit filled his ears to bursting.

Stepping back, he inhaled, eyeing the target as it swayed on its weighted base. Then he leaped into the air and swung like hell, the blunt wooden blade of his sword slicing out and up in a graceful arc. He heard a ripping sound, and a *pop*, and when Asano landed, he pivoted defensively to face the dummy. The *bokken* had separated one of the padded arms from the thick body, and the dummy had toppled to its side on the padded floor. Not pausing more than a moment, he sprang once again at his target, striking, striking, mercilessly.

Sweat flew in heavy drops. He smacked down hard with the sword, and a large chunk of closed-cell foam flew past his head. He swung again and again, each time hearing the peal of rubber on asphalt and the mighty crash of metal and plastic, of flesh and glass.

Suddenly he felt very tired. He let the *bokken* slip from his fingers to clatter stiffly to the floor.

Asano looked down at his hands and noted that they were shaking. Clasping them together in a desperate prayer for solace and peace, he raised his eyes to the vaulted ceiling and let himself cry.

Lani...

He wept bitterly, and he slumped to his knees. And after only thirty seconds, he collapsed over the mangled practice target in exhaustion.

And slept.

02

Captain Cheryl Bonner was not amused. Not even a little.

The atomic-green paint that covered the outside of her dim office window gave her naturally kinky hair an eerie, mutant halo. She turned at the desk, her russet skin awash in the same sickly tint. Fifty years, half of it on the force, was carved into the features of an otherwise motherly face.

All six-foot-six of the impossibly-slim Kai Tokura slouched quietly in the vinyl chair before her, his visor reflecting the radioactive glow in a psychedelic neon effect. He didn't speak. He didn't move.

"What is this? Number four? Listen, Mr. Tokura, I'm not sure we won't be pressing full charges this time."

Stilt looked up at her. "Lock me up, then."

"I'd like to, believe me. You just broke the nose of a long-time associate of mine. Murray's the best undercover cop and federal task force officer I've ever worked with. You took him down in the middle of the biggest bust this year."

"He drew on me."

"He's a *cop*."

"He didn't ID himself."

Cheryl scowled. "According to all of the cops at the scene, he didn't have a chance. You just jumped out of nowhere and started handing everyone their asses! You lost us half a mil in capital, almost a year's worth of foreplay and maybe even the whole bust. So help me out here—what should I do?"

"Lock me up."

"*Then* what?"

"Then the problem gets worse."

"Christ, Tokura, you're a major component of the problem! You can't just think you can walk into the middle of a police maneuver and beat people up!"

"Looked like a drug deal to me," offered Stilt.

Cheryl wasn't having it. "The SFPD isn't in the habit of making our joint ops with the DEA a public affair."

Stilt glared at her. "So give us a contract."

"Fuck you."

"Fair enough," Stilt muttered.

"Shut it," Cheryl hissed, "before I lose control of my trigger finger and accidentally shoot you in self defense."

Stilt turned his gaze back to the green window, while Cheryl circled the room like a hungry shark. She tested him with sharp verbal jabs. "Why should we give a contract to three guys from the Sunset with nothing but a metal *stick* between them? Huh? You don't pack heat."

"We don't need to."

"Oh yeah, you're tough guys. Martial-fucking-arts masters with a stick and some attitude. Think that's gonna save your ass?"

"Always has."

Cheryl laughed and leaned a slender buttock on the acrylic wood-print desk. "Oh please." She paused, and Stilt looked back at her.

Through the dim green glare of the window and her starched blue fatigues Stilt couldn't see anything but a hard-ass, a stubborn police captain with the power of a deputy contract over him. It was all he and Cuda needed, and it would have been so simple for her to run it through the system.

Last time, she'd suggested he try out for the police academy. He'd practically laughed in her face, citing at least a dozen reasons why he'd rather do literally anything else than become a cop. To become a cop, in his estimation, was to give in: to become a fascist, a bureaucrat and a bigot, a hireling in an everlasting corporate war. Sure, upholding the law was important, but for the most part, private citizens were far better at securing their neighborhoods than the police were.

To a large extent, metropolitan police forces had been established to protect the property of the wealthy, and not much had changed. They existed to pay lip service to the old concept of "protect and serve". In reality, most officers took a second payday from whichever corporate player required their services in the realm of civil law.

No, if the police wouldn't give Stilt, Cuda and Pezzoni a contract, the Irving Street *Yōgosha* would have no choice than to keep doing what they were doing illegally. And one of these days, they'd lock him up, and then they'd see how much they really needed him. How much they needed the Shihodo boys.

They'd see. Sooner or later. Probably later.

Suddenly the ancient office door swung open and the young Mexican peered in. "Captain. Pezzoni and Kapp."

Cheryl frowned. "Alright, Ricardo. Let 'em in."

The officer backed out of the doorway, and Stilt turned with anticipation. He was glad to see Pezzoni. The Italian kid was barely twenty-six, but between his days as a gang member and a Guardian Angel, he'd seen enough violence to last at least three lifetimes.

He was stocky and muscular, clad in a customary uniform of denim and leather, his black beret propped to one side over short cropped raven hair. His eyes were chestnut brown, and a scar traced the contour of his left cheek, from nose to jaw. A tiny dagger rested on his broad chest at the end of a silver chain, and a well-chewed toothpick bobbed back and forth between his lips.

Cuda was right behind him, the black Goliath dwarfing every object and occupant of the room. Stilt may have been slightly taller, but John Kapp was as broad as two Kai Tokuras. His smooth, bald head caught the green falloff from the window, and a thin beard hugged his broad lips and chin, fading to the shaved portion of his head just below his temples.

Pezzoni smiled anxiously. "Hi, Cheryl."

"Captain Bonner," she corrected.

"Captain Bonner." Pezzoni glanced nervously at the floor, up at Cheryl, back at the floor. "Can he go yet?"

Cheryl laughed again, and it was a vicious sound. "Can he go yet?" She slid from the desk, turning toward Stilt. She began to speak, halted suddenly, then paced around behind him. "Mr. Kapp."

Cuda straightened. "Yes."

"You tell your brother over in Oakland he owes me one. He swears you're a good guy, so I'm gonna save some admin time and let you go for now. If he wasn't the fucking Chief, I probably wouldn't have thought twice about packing both of you away. And don't get the wrong idea—I'm not trying to kiss up. It's out of the goodness of my heart that all three of your asses aren't precious commodities down at County."

Van nodded humbly. "Understood, Captain Bonner." Ass-kissing was a practiced skill, and it had been good to him.

She turned back toward Stilt as he stood from the chair to tower over her. "And Tokura, this is the last time. You stay in town. Murray and LeGrande may still press charges, and you'll have to own up to that."

As they moved toward the door and began to file out, Cheryl thumbed the end of a nic-stick and leaned against the desk again. "You boys stay clean. If I get one more complaint about any one of you, I'll have your balls for breakfast."

Stilt cracked a half-smile.

Pezzoni almost bowed as he swung the door shut behind him. "Thanks, Cheryl," he whispered in departure.

The trio walked silently to the fourth floor elevators, passing bustling offices full of cops in blue fatigues, scummy-looking undercover agents and their street quarry. No one looked at them. They looked at no one.

Finally, as they assembled at the closed elevator doors, Stilt pressed the down arrow and nodded at Pezzoni. "Thanks, bro."

Pezzoni started at the numbers on the display, frowning. "You weenies. Both o' ya."

The Warfield marquee lights on Market Street boasted all night dancing to some of the hottest acts in the world—mostly touring DJs and loosely-defined "bands" offering a range of post-EDM and new aggro.

At 3 a.m., the second set by ELDX was just ending, and Windy found herself in the cool night air under the lit sign with the people she called her friends. This was Mecca to the alternative artist community, and to those like Windy it was a sanctuary. A sea of black leather and crazy hair, neon bangles and spikes—safe and friendly and accepting, regardless of race, creed, fashion, gender expression or sexual orientation.

A contingent of her friends exited the club, still sweating from the last set: Vance, the thin Bengali with a blue rooster crest and round glasses—one lens green, the other red; Pete, a big Maltese teddy bear, bearded and boyish; Cat, with her auburn-purple bob cut and sweet round Asian face, and everyone in black leather.

Windy pulled her jacket a bit tighter against the crisp night breeze wafting down Market. She raised a slender hand and waved at them. "I'm out. See ya."

Vance winked, but it looked more like a nervous tic than a planned gesture. "Later, doll."

Cat noticed Windy's solemn mood and stepped toward her, ears still abuzz from the concert. "Whaddup, Win? It's only three. Whatcha got planned?"

Windy looked down, then glanced thoughtfully at the marquee, red and yellow flashes painting her face in neon glow. She didn't want to go home. Not with Bug out there, looking for her. Then she realized it wasn't Bug that frightened her, but the prospect of being alone. Of course, she couldn't turn to her friends for help. They were adequate for relationship advice, or sharing some indica and watching lame influencer vlogs online. But when it came to dealing with running afoul of a powerful criminal element, it was something she'd have to take care of herself.

She'd been on her own from age ten and had never relied on anyone but herself, and she wasn't about to change. Smiling, she reached into her bag and fished out a nic-stick. "Think I'll go find me a stud. I kinda feel like prowling tonight. How 'bout you?"

Pete grinned with sparkling acrylic dental implants. "Boinking."

Cat slugged him. "Shut up."

Vance twitched again, closing the bottom snaps on his motorcycle jacket. The thing was a work of art, a demented patchwork of alien-looking fabrics and psychedelic patterns. A sprayed stencil on the back read *Neopigs* in a bright rainbow hologram. He shrugged and shoved calloused hands into the front pockets of his jeans. "I think a little trip to the land of Ned, then I'll sit naked on my fire escape and tell people to go away."

"So the usual," Cat winked.

Windy grinned and hoped she wouldn't cross paths with Bug. She hoped he hadn't heard Stilt. She hoped he'd been scared enough to stay out of the city tonight.

But she kind of knew better.

"*Später Tagen,* guys." She waved and turned away from the flashing marquee lights, striding into the night with her friends waving casually goodbye.

Vance yelled after her. "Set to kill, Windy! Serious Ned!"

The tram was unusually crowded for this time of night. Stevedores on their way to the docks, Market Street swing-shifters on their way home to the hoods. As Windy skipped onto the running board, a short, balding brogrammer gave her a salacious looking-over, then quickly buried his gaze in the evening *Chronicle* on his tablet when she returned his stare. The crisp breeze ruffled her hair, tossing a couple of the glowing stars from her white mop.

Her eyes began to tear up, and perhaps not because of the wind in her face.

She jumped off at the corner of 16th and Van Ness, and walked a short distance to Hustle City, the four-block segment of South Van Ness Avenue where no drug or sexual perk was impossible to find, at least for the right price. Men, women, teens of every color and persuasion, offering everything from a gram of dust or a shard of Indigo Ice to a quick blow in the corner alleyway. Suits avoided this area like a bad investment, and certainly had no reason to go there when they could afford 10K-per-night escort services.

Every homeless or down-and-out immigrant from across the globe eventually found the way to Hustle City, making it a United Nations microcosm—for all the wrong reasons. San Francisco had become the land of opportunity for any refugee who realized that selling drugs or sex was certainly better than having one's brains blown out by the local government death squad du jour.

The cops didn't even try to keep an eye on the strip. So long as everyone had their shots, the SFPD turned a blind eye to the activities in Hustle City—especially given the fact that a lot of cops moonlighted as pimps. And thank God for the shots. As Windy passed row upon row of strutting escorts and addicts with disposable hypos, it didn't even occur to her that, a generation ago, these people would all be dead or dying.

Robust antivirals that included a new—and particularly effective—HIV vaccine had finally changed that outcome. And Windy went blithely on her way, enjoying the sexual freedom it brought, ignoring the miracle of modern science.

A slender Vietnamese man with closely-cropped black hair and a gray paisley vest approached her and smiled. "Walk you home?" he asked, in flawless English.

Most prostitutes in Hustle City were good enough at what they did to earn four figures or a good fix every night. The ones that did the best knew six or seven languages fluently, and the rest knew at least "Do you want to do the Wild Thing?" and "Fifty cash for a blow." Even fewer of them knew "Put that gun away," or "Give me back my money, asshole."

It was rumored that a Sioux trans-femme by the name of Gabrielle could make a deal in fifteen languages and pulled in enough in one night to buy a month's worth of Indigo. It was also rumored that she knew about eighty different ways to kill a person with her left thumb, and therefore had never been scammed.

Windy looked the guy over with an experienced eye. Years on both ends of the hustling game had given her a kind of X-ray vision when it came to people. She started at the snake-skin cowboy boots, following the seam of his tight black jeans upward. Nice legs, nice ass. His crotch was padded, or he had an implant, but that didn't matter when all she wanted was to invite him to "eat out".

He also smelled good, and that was often half the battle.

"Whatcha on?"

"Indigo. Party for a gram."

Windy smiled seductively. She happened to have a gram of Indigo Ice in her bag, a "free sample" she'd filched from Bug's pre-bust meet-and-greet before everything had gone to shit. "I think I can handle it. Your place?"

The man smiled handsomely. "Right this way."

They sauntered arm in arm, the hustler and the Jane, down the remaining blocks of the strip, hanging a right on Twenty-fourth Street. As they ducked and strode through the black shadows, skipping over puddles and drainage grates, Windy found herself happy for the first time all day. She'd have some fun, a place to sleep, and maybe she'd see Bug later, after he'd cooled off. Maybe not.

They turned the corner into Orange Alley, and were promptly blinded by the headlights of a black Lexus AV. Windy gasped, turned to run, and found her way blocked by two immense shadows. She shifted, letting the beam of the headlights illuminate their faces.

Biggs and Johann.

Spinning toward the car, she made out the haloed silhouette of Bug as he stepped in front of the bumper. Quan, the young Thai, shut the driver's door with a muffled *thump* and pulled back the bolt on the submachine gun.

Windy swallowed. "Shit."

The gigolo cleared his throat, stepping back from the car. "She's all yours, man."

Bug nodded. "Biggs, give the gentleman something for his trouble."

The man approached Biggs, and the broad giant pulled a plastic card from his coat. He handed it to the slender hustler, and the man turned back to face Bug.

"Pleasure doing business with y'all." Then he was gone.

Windy was terrified.

Bug stood completely still for about a minute, staring at her from the brilliant outline of the headlights. Then he moved forward.

Windy brought up her automatic defense: a sweet voice and disarming smile. "Hey, Bug. What's—uh, How are you?"

Bug moved closer, slowly. He didn't speak.

"Bug, hey, baby. I didn't know those guys, hon', really."

Closer.

Windy was frantic. Her eyes began to well up as he moved within arm's reach. She felt his hand clamp down on her arm like a rabid animal taking a bite.

His voice was unnervingly calm. "Let's go for a ride."

03

IT was 8:13 a.m. in Los Angeles, and Creep found himself in a pit facing a reject from the WWE. The juggernaut was huge, a great blob of genetic steroids and carbs bursting from a flimsy black leotard. His pasty skin glistened with sweat and he growled convincingly before lashing out in a clumsy right hook.

Creep ducked and rolled away easily, his long, silky blond hair flowing out behind him as he sprang to an attack stance.

David "Creep" Maddock was a Brit, with crystal blue eyes and a flair for wry Eastender wit that usually ended up pissing off any opponent he faced. This instance was no different. He quickly shook the stray hair from his eyes and skipped from foot to foot in a wiggling war dance. He was covered in hair from head to toe—short, auburn fur with tufts of longer golden hair that made him look like Lon Chaney Jr. in a heavy metal band. *Hypertrichosis*, they called it. A glandular disorder that had caused as much grief as celebrity in his life. Although a genetic cure existed, the media attention given to his unusual look far outweighed the scars of childhood trauma. He had made it work for him, even to the point of augmenting it with canine dental implants and reinforced fingernails he kept sharp. Both augmentations nonetheless passed the Arena's "no cybernetics" rule.

"Come on, mate. Give us a kiss."

The great pale colossus frowned, swinging out again with an animal grunt. Creep ducked away, rolling to his left on the padded floor. As he spun he could see the chain-link dome above, and the dimly-lit theater seats go whirling by. Again he leaped to an attack stance, though he still held back from any offensive action.

"Come on, you can do better than that."

From above, a familiar voice rang out. It was harsh and parental, and Creep knew it well.

"Maddock!"

Creep pretended not to hear. He circled his opponent, grinning wickedly, blue eyes gleaming. "Whatsamatter, mate? Knickers too tight?"

"Maddock!"

Again, he pretended not to hear the call. "Got a wedgie, do ya?"

The large gladiator found he'd had quite enough of this game. "Fuck you!" He swung both fists out in a neck-snap combination, and Creep dropped to the floor.

"You can't hope to win."

The next thing Creep's opponent saw was the padded floor rushing up against his face as the hirsute fighter knocked him off balance and launched him over forward.

"I'm much better."

The voice rang out again. "Goddamnit, Maddock!"

Creep shot an icy glare in the general direction of the sound. "What!"

"You know damn well what!"

His opponent staggered dizzily to his feet and stumbled off to the showers, clumsily pulling the Lycra leotard out of the crack of his ass. Creep continued to lounge on the floor where he'd dropped. "I was only—"

"Creep. I told you. You're losing tonight."

Creep smiled, shielding his eyes from the glare of the arena lights as he searched for the angry source of the voice. He found the tall, lanky outline of Jonathan Fox in the third row. "And I told you, that's bullshit!"

"Don't pull that naive fucking act on me, Maddock. It's. Not. Your. Turn. Yet."

"Says you?"

"Yeah, says me. And the Arena board of directors. Don't forget the reason you have a career is because of me. I've fed and clothed you since you were a pup, or whatever it is you are."

Creep looked away. "Fuck off."

"No sweat off my ass, Creep. Bottom line is, you eat canvas tonight, or else." The voice was calm and matter-of-fact, and Creep knew he meant it. And he didn't need to know what the "or else" was. But he asked anyway. It was his nature to piss people off.

"Or else what?"

"Do not fuck with me. You dive, or you're done. And I don't just mean this season. I mean your career as a fighter is over."

"I've heard that before. Hasn't stopped me from becoming your most popular meal ticket."

"All good things must end, you know that. You be a good boy, we'll see about the title next season."

"Yeah, sure we will. Like last season and the season before."

"You think about it, Maddock. If you know what's good for you."

Creep stared at the still outline of the man until his eyes formed an imprint from the lights. He stood slowly, scowling. "Right. Cheers, Jon. I'm hittin' the showers now. Talk to me tonight...after the match."

"You're asking for trouble, my furry friend."

"Yeah, well." Creep shrugged out of the straps of his Lycra suit, letting them fall down his hairy torso. Opening the metal gate at the far end of the pit, the furry gladiator headed for the locker room.

The Ace & Gryphon was *the* gathering place for anyone in the Sunset district awake during the day. And there were a few. An authentic 20th Century English pub, it occupied the northwest corner of 19th and Irving, sharing the block with such diverse merchants as 21st Century Computers, The Jade Garden Japanese restaurant, and Adonis Blue Bath house & Massage Parlor.

Sam ran the pub with the help of two Thai sisters and a Chinese cook named Kim, and she served the most notorious coffee in the district. She opened at nine for breakfast, and never seemed to be short of full capacity when it came to pre-noon patrons. The only other place to have a sit-down breakfast in the area was Chao's Donuts on the southeast corner of 18th and Irving, and both establishments had a fair split of the community. Sam didn't serve donuts, and Barney Chao didn't serve anything else.

And today, more than anything, Stilt wanted a big plate of British heart-attack and Tibetan tea. Not donuts.

At about eight thirty, Stilt and Cuda exited the storefront at 15th and Irving. The painted window proclaimed *SHIHO-DO SCHOOL OF MARTIAL ARTS* in big red letters, right at eye level. The words encircled a black and white *yīnyáng* symbol with compass points at the four directions. The two men turned and headed west on Irving, growling stomachs leading the charge.

The neighborhood was up: Ms. Richmond, clad in white sweats, walking her panda in Huey Newton Memorial Park; Burt, the resident space-cadet, stumbling confusedly into the sun from the 15th Street Shelter; Father Fisk tending the roses in front of Our Lady of Divine Tolerance Church; octogenarian Mrs. Collins leaving for work at the launderette on her antique Vespa.

The weather was mild, sunny, and the air was filled with the sound of smart cars and scooters whizzing by, and Melinda Eggels' Amazon parrot, who screamed profanity at passers-by from the open second-story window.

A boy of eight ran past the two men, backpack swinging with a load of heavy books. "Yo, *Sensei.*"

Cuda waved, grinning. "You're late, Murph. See you after school."

"I got it down. The *kata.*"

"Good. I'll see it after school. Now move your butt."

Stilt nodded as the boy dodged a messenger bike and disappeared down 16th. A year ago, he wouldn't have been able to wade through the slingers on the corner. "Murphy's a good kid."

Cuda laughed and they walked on. "Helluva kick too. He'll be splittin' boards in no time."

They passed the church and waved across the street to Father Fisk. The good-looking young Russo-Slavic man with chestnut hair pulled back in a ponytail looked up and returned the gesture. Stilt indicated via pantomime that his priest's collar had gotten smudged with gardening soil from the flower bed, and Fisk smiled, fanning them away with a sarcastic wave.

They passed the locksmith, and noticed a familiar Latina woman across the street opening up Citizen's Legal Center. The aroma from Chao's Donuts met their nostrils and Stilt was tempted to forgo his healthy breakfast, but his attention was snapped away by a noise from the Dragon Kung-Fu school on their right. Stilt adjusted the mirrored visor on his nose and peered in through the storefront window. Just old Carl Chen going through his warm-ups before morning class.

They continued, past the Korean barbecue restaurant, Awaken cafe and Li's Sporting Goods. At the corner of 19th, they could see the Ace & Gryphon with its majestic hanging sign and traditional British exterior. And there was Pezzoni, half a block south, outside The Stump. He stood astride his vintage Honda NM4, socializing with a couple of bikers—probably selling his services as Zen Master Lord High God Supreme Motorcycle Mechanic—which, in fact, he was.

They crossed at the light, and Van met them in front, hauling his bike back on its kickstand. The caustic odor of hair chemicals wafted out from Heather's Beauty Salon, but thankfully only lasted a few seconds before it was masked by the divine smell of fresh bread and sizzling eggs. Cuda led the way in, holding the door for his equally famished comrades.

Taking advantage of the windows, the interior was only dimly-lit. Several large panes, mounted in the walls above the booths and tables, invited the morning sunlight inside. The atmosphere was thick and pleasant, and the fragrant aromas from Kim's kitchen welcomed them with open arms.

The pub was an island of peace and culture in the sea of despair that was urban San Francisco. Rival gangsters, merchants, artists and professionals sat peacefully amongst one another, dragging from smokeless nic-sticks, sipping coffee or gulping down a host of items from the greasy spoon menu. There was no violence here, by Sam's decree, and everyone in the community respected that rule. Sure, there were active deterrents against it.

Maybe it was the fact that there were three martial arts schools within four blocks of the pub, whose owners were close friends of Sam's. Maybe it was the fact that Stilt, Van and Cuda walked a beat three or four times a week on a random schedule. Maybe it was the fact that Kim was three-hundred pounds of coiled muscle, and kept a loaded assault rifle behind the grill.

The bottom line was that everyone liked the pub, everyone liked Sam, and nobody was stupid enough to test the boundaries of a tightly-knit community's commitment to civility.

If Stilt was unpopular with the SFPD, one sure as hell wouldn't know it here. Folks of every ethnic group and creed saluted and smiled as the three walked in. They'd received the honorarium of *Yōgosha*—Japanese for "defenders"—due to their unflinching dedication to the welfare of the neighborhood. There was no guile to them, no ulterior motive to their service. They simply wanted a safe area to live and work in, and they were willing to do some heavy lifting to get it.

They approached the bar, and Sam popped her head up. She'd been shelving a five-pound bag of tiny bar pretzels, and a stray lock of brunette hair had come out of her ponytail, hanging sloppily down across her face. Hazel eyes sparkled under heavy lids, and the weight of twenty years in the restaurant business tugged at her naturally ruddy skin. She smirked and wiped her hands on an age-old bar apron that had been her father's. "What can I get you boys this morning?"

Stilt leaned against the bar and winked. "The usual, Sam. Thanks." Though the chrome shades masked the movement, she knew what it meant. Whenever his left cheek twitched like that, he was winking.

Sam saluted militarily and tapped out their order on the tablet on the bar, hitting the *SEND* button with her thumb. A moment later, a chime rang out from the kitchen. Kim's voice shouted the order back in Mandarin. Old habits died hard.

Cuda raised a finger. "And strain the coffee."

Stilt felt a tug at his jacket, and turned to see Van staring into another corner booth.

"Hey, there's Windy."

Sure enough, everyone's adopted little sister sat alone with her back to an interior wall, her face hidden by the shadows. The darkness posed no problem for Stilt, however, and his pupils dilated beneath the protective shade of the visor. Yep. Windy. Wearing her vintage Ray Bans, trying to be cool. "Good."

Van followed closely on his heels. "Go easy, man." Cuda knew he should be there too, if only to hold him back while Van wedged a ketchup bottle in his mouth to shut him up.

They arrived at the table, and Stilt pulled up a chair while the other two scooted into the booth on either side of Windy. She didn't speak, didn't acknowledge their presence, merely stared straight ahead with her face in the hazy shadow of the corner. A thin exhalation of gauzy vapor from her nic-stick spiraled delicately upward into the white glow of the hanging table lamp, where it dispersed into a fine mist.

Van reached out with a smile and a light touch. "Hey, Win —"

"Goddamnit, Windy," Stilt interrupted, his voice low and harsh, "I told you not to come out to the site."

Windy wrinkled her nose in a defiant scowl. "Fuck off, Stilt. I'm a big girl."

"Yeah, sure you are. Big enough to know that your presence jeopardized—"

Slowly, Windy reached up and removed her shades, folding them neatly on the table. Though Stilt could already gauge her condition, it was only when she leaned forward into the light that Van and Cuda were able to see.

She was a bloody mess.

Her nose was purple and her right cheek darkly bruised. The light revealed a deep gash in her lower lip, and her right eye was black and swollen shut.

They were silent for quite a few moments, then she spoke, flinging her razor-tipped words across the table at Stilt with deadly accuracy. "Pull your head out, Stilt. You are so fucking Timmy."

"Who did this?"

Windy took a long drag from her stick. "Who do you think?"

"Who!"

Windy leveled a withering look at Stilt. "*You* did, asshole."

"What do you mean?" The face beneath the chrome visor twitched. He clearly wasn't doing the math.

"Hello? You yell my name out to the whole world while you're beating up Bug and his crew. How stupid do you think the guy is?" There was a silent pause, and she took another drag on her electronic cig. "He came looking for me afterward, y'know. You don't want to hear what I had to do to get out alive."

Van clenched his jaw, trying desperately not to speak, as he knew it would simply be an incomprehensible white-knight tirade. His slim partner took care of the bravado for him.

Stilt leaned back and folded his arms, quietly fuming. "That psycho. I'm gonna fucking crucify him—"

Windy rolled her eyes. It was a painful gesture, but she managed to pull it off without wincing. "Stilt! Stop."

"Windy—"

"No." She flagged him to a halt with her right hand, and with her left snapped the disposable e-cig in two, flinging it to the center of the table. "Dude. Join us on *this* planet. You have to understand what's going on out there!"

Stilt was hurt. "You think I don't know?"

Windy leaned forward and reached for a well-used mug full of black coffee. "I think you know a little," she said, sipping quietly. "And a little, when you don't have the big picture, can get us all into a lot of trouble."

Van's eyes shot to Cuda, then to Stilt. His lips pressed anxiously together.

There was another pause, and Stilt reached out, caressing the side of Windy's swollen face. "I'm sorry. I just didn't want you to get hurt. Looks like that was a steaming pile of failure."

Windy smiled at his touch and sighed. "I know I shouldn't have gone. We were both colossally stupid."

"Colossally," Stilt repeated. He brought his hand away, noticing for the first time his comrades' uncomfortable silent expressions. Cracking a stubbly half-smile, he reached back out to nudge Windy's arm. "Buy you breakfast?"

Windy chuckled, blinking adorably. "Well, yeah. Least you could do, right?"

Cuda broke into a relieved smile, solid white teeth gleaming in the hanging light. He reached out over the table and with massive arms embraced both Windy and Stilt. "Now that's better! That's what I like to see."

Van shifted, letting an uncomfortable smirk disrupt the stoic lines of his face. He propped a fresh toothpick between his lips. An uneasy truce was better than no truce at all. *Yeah. Great.*

04

ove was almost a caricature of the corporate toady: short, bespectacled, the sharp point of a hawk nose almost matching the outward thrust of his knobby chin. His eyes were expensive Zeiss ColorShift 20s, and his hair wasn't really a particular color at all. Between the products forming a slicked-back helmet and the streaks of natural gray, it looked almost like translucent chrome. His taste was for pretty young men and prettier suits—all premium: double-breasted Armani or Dieter Meier, and only in black or charcoal-gray. Pinstripes may as well have been a capital offense. His ties and hankies were imported Chinese silk, his accessories platinum.

The door in the private express elevator chimed and slid open on floor 127, and Love stepped into The Office. It was cavernous, an executive palace with floor-to-ceiling ballistics-grade smart windows, soft acrylic carpet and just about every piece of custom bodymold furniture one could imagine. A jungle of engineered ferns lined the glass walls—one wall in particular served as a vertical surface for rivulets of water to play down in a feature that was half art installation, half Zen fountain. On the far side of The Office stood The Desk, and to the right of The Desk hung The Screen, a colossal, wall-sized, paper-thin 16K Sony monitor.

Tigress was on her earpiece, standing behind The Desk with her back toward Love, and he took the opportunity to look her over. Such instances were few and far between.

Her executive jacket and skirt were tastefully matched, as were her gold adornments. The pleasing orbital shape of a firm rear end showed through the wool skirt and grew even more pronounced as she shifted her weight. She was in good shape, and none of it was due to surgical sculpting. Her raven tresses were coiled into a bun on the back of her head.

Susan Kitayama was only thirty, yet she was worth tens of billions of any currency you cared to measure. Her corporate enemies claimed she knew nothing of business and had simply inherited Kitayamacorp from her father upon his assassination six years ago. Not many of those enemies were still around to claim it anymore. Susan was vicious, merciless, tireless—an intrepid corporate warrior who knew when to duck and when to duke it out.

She'd swallowed companies whole, orchestrated hostile takeovers and supply embargoes, broken unions, and all before her 8:30 breakfast appointments. The name Tigress was spoken with respect by her employees, and with fear and disgust by those at SelTec. Frank Selby just called her The Bitch.

He was probably jealous.

Love licked his dry lips and sighed, reaching for the plastic credit card remote on the giant meeting table. He turned his attention toward the television screen and caressed the power button with his thumb. As he reclined in a plush nylon chair, letting the memory foam mold to his bony rear end, The Screen blinked and a Coke ad came on, volume muted.

Susan heard the white sound of the monitor powering on and turned to face Love, earpiece still in place. She tapped her glasses on The Desk and nodded in response to the voice on the other end. "Yes. Perfect. Thank you. Goodbye," she said in English.

Love looked at her as she glanced at her micro-tablet screen and paged through some icons.

"Who was that?"

"Captain Cheryl Bonner of the SFPD. Do you know what happened here last night?"

Love turned back to the TV screen. "No, but I have the feeling you're going to show me." A Honda spot came on, and Love shifted his attention again as Susan thumbed an application open.

"Look at this." With a single touch of a slender, manicured finger, the media file opened and wirelessly cast to The Screen.

Suddenly Love found himself looking down into the alley between the twin spires of Kitayamacorp headquarters. A gray Acura coupe sat facing a black Lexus AV-50, and several disreputable-looking characters milled about, pointing and gesturing at one another.

Susan folded her arms and stepped back to get a better look. "Police confiscated some civilian surveillance from the south wing last night."

Love scowled. "Interesting vantage for civilian surveillance. What happened to our own security systems?"

"Someone hit that side of the building with a focused EM pulse, knocked out external security. Cameras, bots, everything."

Love raised an eyebrow. "Looks like some shady characters."

"Sure does. But who do they work for? Not me."

"Selby?"

Her silent glare was all the answer he needed. Shifting his appraisal back to the screen, Love squinted. "Who's the blond, muscular fellow? He's cute."

"Evidently, Special Agent Dennis Murray, SFPD Narcotics Division, working a joint DEA task force."

Love smiled, eyeing the screen carefully. "Ooh. Tough guy. He on the payroll?"

"No. He's straight."

"Too bad."

Susan started to respond, then thought better of it and returned her attention to the video.

They watched as an attractive woman in black leather got out of the Lexus and strode seductively to a short, dark-complected man in a trench coat.

"Now watch. This kitten starts mouthing off to Ace here…"

The image replayed his lashing out with a gloved fist, sending the woman sprawling. Love raised an eyebrow as he watched the man draw a pistol from his jacket and point it at her.

Susan gestured at the playback. "…and bam! These guys show up. Fall out of the damn sky."

Love watched Stilt and Cuda drop to the coupe, appearing from the left side of the screen. Cuda floored the Caribbean cop with a graceful areal kick, and Stilt leaped to the car hood, drawing the chrome rods and sending Dennis to the ground with one swipe as everyone else scattered. "Wow. Nice moves."

Susan fixed Love with a steely-eyed stare and pursed her lips. "Who *are* they?"

Love shrugged. "Starsky and Hutch? Riggs and Murtaugh?"

"Love, it was a rhetorical question."

"You check 'em out?"

Susan nodded. Her attitude condescended as if addressing a small child. "Yes, Love, I did. They're Kai Tokura and John Kapp. They run a martial arts school down in the Sunset. As a sideline, they walk neighborhoods, and make busts without contracts."

Love shook his head and gasped in exaggerated shock. "The villains."

Susan didn't smile. She often didn't, when she was lecturing her right-hand man. "Yes and no, Love. Why did I have to discover them on my own?"

"Susan, they're two *streeters* who run around with sticks. They're *nothing*." His scowl and vocal inflection made the common term "streeter" sound almost dirty, but Susan was not convinced.

"Anybody who gives the police department this much grief is not *nothing*." She tapped a long finger impatiently at the side hem of her skirt. "I don't understand, Love. Frank Selby has armies of *ronin*, but when two really extraordinary specimens walk right in under our noses, you miss them."

Love cast her a skeptical sidelong glance. "Susan. Hit squads? Really. I didn't think you were the type."

"Well it looks like I'm going to have to be the type. When this lunacy is taking place on my property, I don't see how it can be otherwise."

"What are you going to do? Give them a contract?"

"That's the idea."

Love shook his head. "I don't know, Susan."

Susan widened her eyes, and suddenly Love was three years old. Each word was deliberate and exaggerated. "Exactly, Love. You don't. I want you to keep your eyes open in the future. If someone is available, I want to know about it."

Love smiled sweetly, a mirror of her own sarcasm. Well. A hit squad she wanted, a hit squad she would have. And he knew she'd regret it. Especially when she already paid half the police department to play corporate security guard. This was sheer redundancy. Not good business. But Love liked being employed.

"As you wish, my dear."

The original Victorian apartments on the corner of 15th and Irving had been converted. The ground floor belonged to the Shihodo School *dojo*. Above the school were four large living units, all complete with baths and kitchens. Stilt and

Cuda occupied two of the four. The building was their lifetime investment, the school their passion. They were either wonderful landlords or terrible landlords, depending on one's point of view. They took care of all of the repairs and maintenance, but kept the rent so low that they barely made the mortgage. Fortunately, their tenants took pity on the woefully kind lords of the manor, often doing their own repairs and building maintenance.

Stilt emerged from the stairwell to the top floor, tying the sash on his gray workout *dogi*. He closed the door behind him and made his way down the hall, rubber *tabi* feet peeling and sticking, peeling and sticking, to the ancient parquet floor. He rounded the corner to the stairs and suddenly halted.

Jesse stood at the door to #3, arms laden with canvas grocery bags, fingers fumbling clumsily with her keys. She was fairly young: early to mid thirties, of Australian Aboriginal extraction, shoulder-length curly black hair tied back away from her face. She was also visibly pregnant, and wclearly struggling to unlock her door. Cursing, she shifted the weight of the bags to her other hip and tried again.

"Hey, Jess. Give you a hand?" Stilt approached offering his arms for her heavy bags.

"My hero." She gladly turned her burden over to the tall, slender martial arts teacher and unlocked the door. They entered, and were greeted by the grunt and guttural sniffing sound of a domestic wombat. The apartment was sparsely decorated, mostly with stained-glass antiques and old leather-bound books from her scholastic career. She led him through the living room into the newly remodeled kitchen, the small black creature sniffling along behind them.

Jesse mumbled something from the open refrigerator.

"Pardon?"

"I said, are you getting ready for class?"

Stilt handed her the canvas bags one at a time. "Yeah. I'm starting them on a new exercise today. I hope we won't bother you with the noise."

Jess set the bags gently on the tile counter and began to stow the produce in the fridge. "Are you kidding? This is the safest place to live in the whole city." Stilt watched the afternoon sunlight filter in through the kitchen window, shedding warmth and life on the tiny planters of sweet potatoes and alfalfa sprouts that sat in the sunbox behind the sink.

Stilt caught his focus drifting again and had to swerve back onto the road of cogent thought. Just one of those days, he reckoned. "I won't complain about a bunch of kids yelling and throwing each other on a mat," Jesse continued. "Now the guys upstairs…"

Stilt laughed. She referred to Mike and Étienne, the couple in #4, famous within the building for making their bed squeak. "They're young," he quipped. Again his attention shifted to the sunlit garden window, and he didn't notice Jess lean over to fill the wombat's feeding dish with kibble.

He *did* hear her scream.

"Jess! You okay?" Stilt dashed across the kitchen, grasping her by the shoulders as she doubled over, clutching her distended belly.

She straightened, rubbing her abdomen, a perturbed look on her face. "Yeah. Just bent the wrong way, and she kicked me."

"When are you due?"

"Not for six weeks."

Stilt caressed her arms, and she breathed deeply. "You sure you're okay?"

She nodded. "Yeah. Fine. Go on, you'll be late for class."

"You sure?"

"Yes. Go."

Stilt let go of her shoulders and smoothed a stray lock of hair from her face, peering at her from behind the chrome visor. He backed away slowly. "Well, you've got my mobile, just ping if you need anything."

Jesse smiled. "I know."

05

BUG PACED THE FLOOR of the armored warehouse near the new Embarcadero project he called The Fort. It was simply a corrugated metal cavern with space enough for the Lexus, a functional kitchenette, 8K wall screen and a well-used leather sofa. A sturdy black marble coffee table was littered with empty shell casings, beer bottles, and handguns in various states of repair. Open boxes of automatic rifles and ammunition lay scattered about the huge interior, and several short bar stools were placed randomly around the coffee table. Johann sat on one, the new guy Raoul on another.

Biggs stood menacingly in the corner, his primary vocational skill.

Bug shoved his hands into the front pockets of his designer Italian slacks. His trench coat was heaped over the back of the leather sofa, and a bright gold silk vest hung open on his chest, embroidered with ornate African designs. "You never seen 'em before?"

Biggs shook his head. "Nope."

"Then who the fuck are they?"

"They ain't cops."

Bug nodded. "No shit. But they know Windy."

Johann squinted and examined his manicured nails. "I think maybe she works for those guys."

Bug stared incredulously at the giant Norseman. "Selby surrounds me with brilliance."

"Don't mention it."

Bug turned his attention back to Biggs. "You think Ken Doll was with 'em?"

"Nah. You see how fast he got taken out? One shot. Guy's got a glass jaw. If anything, he's a cop."

Raoul shifted on the stool and scratched his short walnut hair. "No. I don't think so."

Bug was intrigued. Now they were brainstorming. This could actually be productive. "Why not, bruh?"

"Well, one: the bills ain't marked and the cards are clean. Two: the reason we ain't heard from him is 'cause the cops took him in. I figure he's gonna come whining for his money in about a week. He ain't no cop, man. Just a small-time white boy with a lotta *huevos*."

"So what about stick-man and homey Hercules? You think they're small-timers with a lotta *huevos*?"

Johann shrugged. "They ain't no gang. There's just two of 'em."

Biggs wagged a finger at his huge colleague. "We don't know that. They're too good to be small-time. They definitely work for someone."

Bug went back to pacing. "But who the fuck *for,* man? That's what kills me!"

Biggs scratched the back of his thick hand. "I dunno. Kitayama maybe. They're new."

"Well I don't want 'em hangin' around."

Raoul raised an eyebrow. "I bet Windy knows. You should've asked her."

Johann turned with a salacious smile. "He had other priorities." The commend garnered a look of disbelief from Bug.

"What," the hired muscle protested. "Punishment is a priority."

Bug stopped, warning Johann with a single index finger. "Raoul's right. We need Windy back."

Biggs cracked his knuckles and turned toward the warehouse door. "I'm on it."

Bug watched him leave, then turned to the other two. "Raoul, I want you to check with Selby's boys inside K-Corp. Find anything you can about the guy with the stick."

"No problem."

Quan entered, wiping down the bullpup with an oily rag. Bug watched him nod a greeting and cross to the limo. The young Thai fished a nic-stick from his pocket.

Bug turned back to Raoul and Johann as they stood to leave. "And keep it low. This is getting way too messy. Selby won't like it."

The painted sign in front of the garage read *PEZZONI & SONS AUTO SERVICE*. It was already a good fifty years old, battered, weather-worn, even shot in a few places. The facility itself took the entire northwest corner of 22nd and Judah, LED spots illuminating the sign and the garage below. Just above the open barn-doors sat the family flat, not quite last century, but probably only slightly newer.

The sun was dipping low on the horizon, already hidden by the neighborhood buildings, casting the usual radioactive red-orange glow over the city. Whoever named this place the Sunset knew what they were talking about.

Cuda and Stilt approached the open steel doors under the dim light of the billboard lamps outside. The walls were a soft lemon-yellow: the composite color of a million warehouse offices and automotive garages. Not a single tool was where it should have been. The pegboard was full of mismatched wrenches and socket sets, faint black outlines of other tools protesting behind them. A swimsuit centerfold from 2036 hung on the wall above an old land line, a testament to the Pezzoni men's enduring affection for fine literature and antiques. CO_2 lines dangled efficiently from their ceiling mounts, and at least four motorcycles stood about in different stages of cleanliness and repair. The metallic *tink* of metal on metal signaled the two visitors that Van was indeed present, slaving away on the antique Harley in the corner.

They decided to mess with him anyway.

Stilt put his hand over his visored eyes and pretended to search the interior. "Now where is that weenie?"

Cuda shrugged. "I can't see him, man. What a little turd."

Van stood, extending his middle finger. "Hilarious. Go ahead on up. I'll be there in a sec."

It was Tuesday evening, which meant Mama Pezzoni's spaghetti and homemade sauce. It meant a dozen simultaneous conversations, political discussions, and sports wagers. It meant whining children and gross-out contests. Most of all it meant family. Since neither Cuda nor Stilt had any other, it was fine by them.

They entered the upstairs apartment and stepped back in time: Papa on the sofa, SF Chronicle open on his tablet, glancing from the financial section to the corporate satellite news on the UHD wallscreen; Mama in the kitchen, flower print dress, gray hair in a bun, round body glistening over a steaming bowl of pasta; little Michael carefully placing the napkins around the old oak dining table; middle sister Veronica following him with the flatware; oldest sister Monica packing her school tablet and related gadgets up to her room; middle brother Alphonso, just short of his thirteenth birthday, washing up in the hallway half-bath.

The smell of freshly-chopped oregano, garlic and olives met them, and Cuda almost cried with sheer joy at the prospect of consuming this work of culinary art.

Mama Pezzoni caught the two visitors in her radar and turned, waving an acrylic pasta server in one hand. "Kai! Johnny! Welcome! Sit. Sit. You wash your hands?"

Stilt ducked his head and nodded politely. "Yes, Mrs. Pezzoni. Before we came."

"Good. That's good. Such nice boys. You see, children? You see how Kai and Johnny come to the table with their hands washed?"

Michael rolled his eyes and Veronica giggled.

Cuda pulled his hands from his pockets and ambled over the imaginary line that separated the dining room from the living room. "Evening, Mr. Pezzoni."

The middle-aged, balding man set his tablet aside and squinted over small reading glasses. "Evening, Johnny." He stood from the sofa, dropping the tablet on the threadbare cushion. "Fight's on tonight, if you boys want to stay. Heya, Stilt."

Stilt nodded. "That's nice of you, Mr. Pezzoni. Thanks."

Mama bellowed from the kitchen. "All right, everybody to the table! The sauce will be ice-cold!" There was a short blast of warm air, and Stilt caught the scent of fresh garlic bread with dried basil and Parmesan.

Cuda smiled at the dinner warning. "I've heard that before."

Papa sighed, smiling yellow teeth through thin lips. "Well, we'd better get to the table anyway. Makes her feel good. Like she's in charge."

Stilt chuckled. "Um, isn't she?"

"*Touché.*"

Van came in through the front door, and the large woman in the kitchen spun around to face him, armed with a potholder and an enormous serving ladle. It was like she could smell the grease on his hands, as if it interfered with the olfactory carnival of delights she'd worked so hard to prepare. "Giovanni Josepi Pezzoni!" There it was. All three names. He was in trouble now.

Van winced, holding his arms out almost in an open demonstration of his oil-covered, grease-smeared coveralls. "What!"

She waved the spoon like a Trojan sword. "What!? Look at you, that's what! You don't get supper coming like that to the table! No sir! You get right in that bathroom and wash your hands!"

"You know what, Ma?"

"Why can't you be like your friends Kai and Johnny?"

"I was just going in to wash."

"They're such *nice* boys. And already at the table with Papa!"

Stilt and Cuda grinned silently at each other and Van wandered off to the bathroom. "I love you, Ma."

Slowly, the children gathered at the table like a mass exodus to a great religious feast. The girls spoke in hushed tones. The conversation took perhaps twenty seconds and half of it was some kind of strange, adolescent female sign language. Stilt was intrigued. Alphonso relayed the tale of a schoolyard brawl he'd seen today, and Michael sat next to Cuda. "*Sensei.* I got the move."

"Oh yeah? Let me see."

Michael turned in his chair and threw a karate-style forward punch at Cuda's head. He knew he wasn't fast enough to actually make it through to his teacher. In fact, Cuda caught the whole of the child's 8-year-old fist in his great palm, holding it tight. "You're open." He reached down with his other hand and tickled the boy on the ribs.

Mama Pezzoni sat and addressed the giggling combatants. "No fighting at the table!"

Papa sighed, unfolding his napkin. "Mama, they were just playing."

"Well, I don't like it. People shouldn't fight."

Van came to the table minus his greasy coveralls, hands and face sparkling clean, though still unshaven. "That's right,

Ma. And they shouldn't kill, or steal or do drugs. But they do."

Cuda released Michael's hand and pivoted back to the table. "We just teach kids how to be safe around that stuff."

Mama shook her head. "I still don't like it."

Papa removed his readers and cocked his head professorially. "They are providing a service for the community, Mama. I feel better knowing our kids can protect themselves out there."

Mrs. Pezzoni began to reply, and Papa raised both hands in surrender. "Maybe just say the blessing."

Mama frowned and folded her doughy hands, and everyone else followed suit. Even Stilt closed his eyes beneath the visor. Though he'd been raised on Zen Buddhist philosophy and Japanese mysticism, he had a soft spot in his heart for the Roman Catholic religion when it was used by a faithful Italian family in honest prayer. It was beautiful like this. And he was nothing if not respectful.

Mama Pezzoni offered thanks for the food and the family gathered around the table, invoking divine protection for Stilt and Cuda. She finished in the name of the Holy Trinity, the children crossed themselves, and Cuda opened his eyes.

Papa unfolded his hands and reached for the bread. "Let's eat. Try the Caprese, boys. The tomatoes and basil are from our garden, and the balsamic is local."

Mama smiled and passed a huge bowl of spaghetti noodles to Stilt. "Dig in, Kai. You need some meat on your bones. You're too skinny."

Stilt took the bowl and nodded complacently. "Yes, Mrs. Pezzoni." He'd explained to her a hundred times that his strange metabolism was caused by his father's drug-altered DNA. It was impossible to keep "meat on his bones".

The entire family knew. He'd told them the whole story: his mother, a Japanese doctor with a UN medical unit in the North Korean conflict, who'd encountered an American super-soldier in her field hospital. Mariko Tokura managed to get a sample of the man's blood back to Japan, taking refuge in the corporate headquarters of a biotech firm in Kyoto. The company put her in charge of a reverse-engineering project, and in one undocumented phase, she'd coupled the DNA with one of her own frozen eggs.

When a corporate edict put an immediate end to her experiments, she panicked, enlisting the aid of a company surgeon, who implanted the lab-grown embryo. She'd saved her science project by smuggling it out inside her own body.

Eventually the lure of money became too tempting, and her surgeon ally turned her in. She was unceremoniously fired, blacklisted from the biotech industry on so-called "ethical grounds". Mariko fled north into the countryside, taking shelter with an elderly aunt and uncle.

After a difficult gestation, she delivered a boy with eyes like clear gelatin. From the moment of his birth, every medical professional or educator he came into contact with assumed he was blind.

He never found out what became of his father. His mother surrendered him before disappearing into the Tokyo sprawl. Mariko never told anyone how she'd become pregnant or the identity of the man who'd supplied half his DNA. Everything he knew of his origin had come from handwritten journals she left with the Buddhist monks at the orphanage in Imazu.

For most of his youth, he'd lived as a blind boy, honing his other senses and skills, mutated genetics pushing him to an amazing six-foot-one by his eleventh birthday, yet weighing an almost skeletal hundred pounds.

When Master Hisako found him, Stilt had no idea how permanently altered his life would become. The master was a former *ronin*, an enforcer-for-hire in the overlapping Venn diagram that encompassed the corporate world and the *Yakuza* —the Japanese face of organized crime. The term *ronin* was an archaic reference to masterless samurai who hired out their services in medieval Japan. Years of performance-enhancing drugs and exposure to various environmental toxins had left him with a rare bone cancer. He'd retired from the corporate life to spend more time in meditation and travel before the disease claimed him. To make an attempt at redemption.

The life expectancy for someone with his particular cancer was six to twelve months. Hisako had already survived for seven years when he found young Kai Tokura.

And until his death ten years later, he handed over to Stilt all the necessary elements to make his world a little better. The master gave him a crusade, the education to facilitate it, the drive to complete it, and the skills to perform it.

It was Hisako who'd discovered, on Stilt's thirteenth birthday, that the little boy from the orphanage in Imazu wasn't blind at all. Another side-effect of his altered DNA was that he'd been born with eyes so hypersensitive to visible spectra that a complex filtering device was needed just to see by starlight. Hisako called in some corporate favors and had the device created.

Without the visor Stilt could be blinded by the simple spark of a lighter in a dark room. With it he was immune to dazzle lights and flash units, and could see better than any sighted person could, especially in the dark.

Papa Pezzoni spoke, and it brought Stilt's mind back to the table. *Damn.* He was doing it again. Why couldn't he stay focused?

"So, Stilt. How'd it go down at the station last night?"

"Kinda rough, but Cheryl was cool about it. It went okay."

"Still no contract?"

"Still no contract."

Papa sighed. "That's too bad."

Stilt pondered the comment over a mouthful of heavy, starchy pasta and sauce. "Well, one of these days, they'll realize how helpful we are."

Michael leaned over and whispered in Cuda's ear, and Stilt thought they were probably gabbing about school. Suddenly, Cuda ducked backward and Michael flung a forkful of spaghetti in front of him. It hit Stilt squarely on the left side of his nose, a splatter of chunky red sauce dripping down his cheek.

His response was subdued, but not without humor, and he reached up to wipe it away with his napkin.

The rest of the children smiled but kept respectfully quiet. Michael giggled uncontrollably and Mama Pezzoni gasped as if she had never seen such behavior before.

"Michael Antonio Pezzoni!"

Yep. It was Tuesday night.

06

ove stood eyeing the video screen in the executive lift. He'd set it to VMAX for the opening pre-fight pabulum. The Arena was a big deal. As big as might be imagined, what with the sum of human history and the love of gladiatorial spectacle as precedent. It was the dominant American combat sport, and, considering the sheer violence one could encounter walking one city block in the Tenderloin, that was no insignificant demographic. *Everyone* watched, even the suits. It was a guilty pleasure. They'd deny they watched religiously, and then first thing Wednesday morning would be hassling those in the betting pool who had lost and were stupid enough to show up to work.

Susan Kitayama was about the only exception. Frank Selby owned most of the fighters and a sizable chunk of the Arena itself. Susan was neither impressed nor interested.

The doors slid open in the penthouse office, and Love stepped into the dim glow of variable LED track lights set on low. He sneaked one last look at the elevator screen before the doors closed. Nike spot. The fight wouldn't start for another five minutes—they were still doing the endorsements and locker room interviews.

He silently made his way into the office. Susan sat at The Desk, the screen of her Matsushita tablet sitting in its dock, her face awash in delicate flashes of color. Love watched her tapered fingers trip the projected sensors of the virtual keyboard with deft accuracy. *Tap tap tap. Enter.*

The small screen shifted colors, and Love could see white letters, sentences, paragraphs, scrolling in a reverse reflection across her designer glasses.

"Working late, my dear?"

"Yes, Love."

"The fights are on."

"Thanks, Love. But I'm kind of preoccupied."

"Luna, big screen on," he directed to the center of the room. The giant Sony wall monitor blinked to life. "Oh, but the power, the glamour. Two strong gladiators meet in the classic struggle. So romantic."

A promo for next week's new episode of the sitcom *Eat Me* interrupted the streamcast for ten seconds, then the feed returned to the locker room.

Susan pursed her lips, looking not at the giant screen, but the small one in front of her. "Yes, well I'm up to my ears with this buyout negotiation."

Love smiled. It wasn't really a smile, per se. More like a crack in old rubber after sitting in the sun for a year. "Well, you did say to keep my eyes open."

Susan paused. She glanced up at Love with emerald eyes that revealed a multitude of different emotions at once. Finally she sighed and touched the tablet screen with a graceful finger, putting it to sleep. "I guess this can wait 'til tomorrow."

Love nodded. Now he was the adult, and she the child. "That's a good dear," he smirked, turning to the Sony. "Watch the furry one. He's so cute."

Cheryl blinked, looked again. She brushed a loose braid of hair from her dark eyes in disbelief. That couldn't be right. Leaning back in her chair, she thumbed the filter on a fresh nic-stick. The monitor on her desk showed a priority requisition for a police contract. From Kitayamacorp. For a Mr. Kai Tokura, a Mr. John Kapp and a Mr. Van Pezzoni. Signed by Susan Kitayama herself.

What the hell?

Did she know what she was getting herself into?

Probably not.

And she easily made seven or eight figures more annually than Cheryl, which was why she could ask for fucking police contracts for a handful of Jet Li wannabes.

They had no clue.

Any of 'em.

Cheryl punched the code, hit return, and the order went through to the duty officer. She sighed, took another drag, exhaled. She grabbed the mobile phone in front of her and woke up the home screen, pulling up a name from her contacts.

"These guys better be worth it," she mumbled to herself, as she touched the green CALL button and put the phone to her ear.

The spongy, soft disk of garlic bread hit Cuda squarely on the nose, and the butter made it stick there. Michael slid from his chair, rolling in fits of laughter on the floor, and Alphonso winced when he realized the severity of his offense. Cuda reached up, plucked the piece of bread from his nose, disregarding the peals of laughter from the girls across the table. He silently loaded his fork with all that remained of his salad, all the while glaring viciously at Al as he prepared the missile. Alphonso ducked, but the ball of salad exploded, grenade-like, on the ladder-back chair, sending bits of carrot and cabbage and three kinds of lettuce down his shirt. His

hair suddenly smelled of oil and vinegar, and Stilt recom-
mended trying a new shampoo to get rid of those unsightly
croutons. Papa excused himself, and Mama retreated to the
kitchen, hurling threats of divine punishments for their sinful
abuse of her home-cooked food.

She must've forgotten.

It was Tuesday.

07

THE TABLE WAS CLEARED, the offenders made to scrape the food off the chairs and floor. Stilt, Van and Mama Pezzoni sat quietly at the oak table, discussing politics.

Papa waived to Cuda from the couch as a knock sounded at the front door. "Hey, Johnny. We're gonna miss the fight. Come on."

Cuda was already on his way. He hated the intellectual side of politics. To him it was an exercise in privilege. He'd much rather watch two gladiators in a cage, slugging it out for the West Coast title. It was simple and honest. Slumping down in Mama's overstuffed recliner, he focused on the screen. "Wouldn't miss it for the world. I got a C-note riding on this."

Al was the first to the door, and was not at all surprised to see Father Fisk standing before him, a fresh rose in one hand, bottle of wine in the other. Al smiled at the priest, and Fisk returned the gesture. There was a momentary pause, and then the weekly recitation began.

"I see I'm too late for supper, but perhaps your parents would accept these..."

Enter Mama, newly prepared plate of spaghetti in hand. "No no, Father. Please. Sit. I fixed you a plate."

"No, really. I couldn't think of imposing..."

"Nonsense. Eat. You need strength to lead your congregation and do all the things you do for the neighborhood..."

"Are you sure?"

"Am I sure?" Mama grinned and regarded Stilt across the table. "Kai, would you tell the kind Padre that I would like him to sit and eat my food, or I will be very upset?"

Stilt had only to glance casually at the young priest and the performance was over.

Fisk acquiesced with a warm smile and moved to the table. "Well, I don't want to upset one of my most loyal and active parishioners. I guess I could stay for a bit. But I do need to get down to the center tonight. Got a new batch of kids in today, and I haven't been over to see any of them."

Cuda looked over from the UHD screen and acknowledged Fisk. Papa fiddled with the remote, boosting the volume. "Hundred bucks, huh? Who you like?"

Cuda laughed and blinked at Mr. Pezzoni. "Who do I *like?* The Champ, of course."

Papa raised an eyebrow. "Really? I kinda' like the hairy guy."

Van's mobile buzzed in his pocket. He put it on the table and unlocked the screen to see a fresh text.

Windy: At ur place

Taking a deep breath, he thumbed a quick reply:

Van: BRT 10

Stilt turned a curious gaze toward his young companion.

"Gotta go," Van said, rising from the table.

Stilt nodded at him. "You be careful, little brother."

"Yeah," was the reply, and Van was gone, the front door swinging shut behind him.

Cuda wagged his head. "Doesn't stand a chance, man. This is *Cage* we're talking about."

Papa waved a dismissive hand. "*Cage shmage*. The Creep's fast—you seen him fight? Gonna be a real upset, I'm telling you."

Cuda scoffed. "You wanna put your money where your mouth is?"

Papa peered down over half glasses. "Sure. I'll put fifty on Creep to take it in five."

"Five rounds?" Cuda smiled and shook his hand. "It's a bet. Hate to take your money, Mr. Pezzoni."

It was a sellout crowd, of course. Twenty thousand screaming fans packed the coliseum. Not a single empty seat. Stage lights extended down from a vast ceiling grid, bathing the pit in a sickly pale yellow. The throng was enveloped in a cloak of nervous murmuring, punctuated by the odd cough or burst of laughter.

Jonathan Fox sat anxiously above the waiting mob in the executive boxes, a wireless commlink in his ear.

Enormous monitor screens flickered to life as the lights and lasers began to dance. The crowd stood in unison and raised a bellowing, fanatical roar. High-def cameras on glide mounts swiveled back and forth, capturing the fervor of the spectators and the roving spotlights.

Fox stood and straightened a tailored Meier suit, returning his earpiece to the inside breast pocket. He descended the concrete auditorium stairs to the edge of the pit as aggressive techno music and fanfare blared from the PA system.

From a secluded booth overlooking the house, an announcer's voice echoed out above the blaring score.

"Live, from Victory Mutual Coliseum in Los Angeles, California! Good evening, fight fans, and welcome to Arena: the West Coast Championship! Tonight's tournament is brought to you by Zeitaku: Because you deserve the best money can buy. And by 20/20 Vision: Introducing the new Nikon-Optica

line of electronic optical devices for home, office and recreation. And here's your host, Jonathan Fox!"

Fox ran a nervous hand through a blue-tinted goatee and adjusted a tropical pattern silk tie. With a deep breath, he stepped onto the elevator platform. The lights found him, and he saluted the audience. "Thank you, fight fans! This a very special bout, because the winner will be awarded the West Coast title, and be off to fight in the National Championship in Miami! So without further adieu, let's bring in tonight's combatants!"

Fox turned and retreated to the executive boxes, and the applause monitors blinked mercilessly, whipping the crowd into a violent frenzy.

The announcer returned to the PA: *"Our first competitor tonight is a native of the Los Angeles Area. He's big, bad and bald, and is undefeated the past two seasons! Weighing in at two-hundred-eighty-seven pounds, will you please welcome last season's West Coast Champion...Caaaaaage!"*

The Champ emerged from the darkened hallway through the steel gate, hands raised high, his massive alabaster body oiled down so that he glistened in the crimson stage lights. The crowd screamed and whistled with absolute delight. Deafening applause surged through the venue.

"Our challenger for the division title is originally from the United Kingdom. He's fast and furry-ous, fighting well outside his weight-class at a scant one-hundred-sixty-five pounds! Let's hear it for...Creeeeep!"

Everyone loves an underdog. David Maddock stepped from the shadows into the arena pit and the crowd knew it would be a good fight. His silky fur wafted in the breeze of the industrial fans that cooled the ring, and his brand new Lycra wrestling leotard was a reflective Mylar gold with black tiger stripes. It revealed an intricately muscled back and stomach, and hugged a firm butt. His fingernails had been filed to dangerous points. He wore his hair long, ratty and loose around his shoulders. In truth, he looked as though he'd walked out of a 1980s hair metal video.

Though most everyone had paid a steep admission to see Cage beat the living tar out of his challenger, Creep had his own cheering section—a small but vocal group of mostly teens and young women who found the hirsute gladiator incredibly sexy. The chanting began as the two combatants sought their corners.

"Creep. Creep. Creep."

Fox was back on the commlink. "Mason, put men at all exits, and give Sergei the go-ahead in case Maddock tries something…"

"Creep. Creep. Creep."

Fox stuck a finger in his other ear to hear the security chief on the other end before responding. "Of course. When I say 'go-ahead', I mean 'go-ahead'. Well, I pay you to make things look like accidents, don't I?" Switching the earpiece off again, he glanced at the north exit: two guards, Mac 10s, tasers. The Ingrams were little more than show. Fox couldn't very well have his security forces open fire in a capacity crowd on live streamcast. But hopefully they would be enough to deter Creep from doing something impulsive. He continued his visual sweep of the hazy auditorium. The other three exits were similarly guarded.

There was nothing else to be done. Fox slumped down at his VIP seat and watched the monitors.

A bright emerald laser beam erupted from a projection unit in the ceiling, igniting a pyrotechnic cartridge mounted in the center of the pit floor. The explosion was the signal to begin, and the crowd increased their already feverish volume. Fists raised. Hands waved. A twelve-year-old girl passed out from the thick atmosphere in the mezzanine. The fighters circled each other, creating the violent tension that was the hallmark of the show.

Cage sneered. He was supremely confident that size and brute strength would carry the day. Besides, the doc had just dosed him up with a medical-grade amphetamine. He couldn't possibly lose.

Creep backed up and dropped to a defensive position and Cage took the opening—and the bait, hook, line and sinker.

As his massive body careened forward in an attempted body slam, Creep adjusted his footing into an *aikido* dodge, giving Cage a friendly push as the huge warrior sailed past him to the padded canvas floor.

The audience roared. Creep's cheering section waved their banners:

WE ♥ CREEP

HAIRINESS IS NEXT TO SEXINESS

HAIL CREEPUS MAXIMUS

PUT YOUR BABY IN ME

Creep smiled, the corners of his mouth drawing back to reveal those sinister teeth. His eyes burned.

He wanted it.

Cage righted himself from the canvas. He turned, shaking his head like he was ridding himself of sweat, but he was really signaling Maddock to cut it the hell out. Creep read the signal, and promptly disregarded it. A spinning taekwondo aerial kick to the head sent Cage against the carbon fiber pit wall.

The crowd roared again, and Creep could hear a few more spectators turn to his side, adding to the chant.

"Creep. Creep. Creep."

Cage spun quickly, revealing an unexpected dexterity. Blood ran from a cut under his left eye. He snarled. Then he was in the air, a flying tackle that would have crushed an unsuspecting opponent.

But Creep was not an unsuspecting opponent.

A blazingly fast sidestep was all it took. Cage landed in a rib-crunching belly-flop on the mat.

Lights spun. The rest of the crowd joined the chant.

"Creep. Creep. Creep."

Cage rolled away, stumbling to an upright position just as Creep landed a crushing kick to his solar plexus. Again, he fell.

"Creep. Creep. Creep."

Cage groaned. "The fuck you doin'?!"

Creep scowled. "Winning. You mind?"

"Fuck you, Maddock."

Cage stood. The scoreboard counted down the remaining time in the two-minute round with large red LEDs.

0:52

He staggered forward, ready to launch into the air again, but he stopped himself and dropped back into a defensive stance.

Not a moment too soon. Creep vaulted into the air in a brilliant backward flip, coming down on Cage's broad shoulders. His legs locked, and Cage fell forward, choking. As the giant hit the floor for the fourth time, Creep unlocked his legs and sprang away from Cage into a handstand. The crowd surged with cries of anger and joy.

0:47

Cage raised himself off the floor, and Creep fell into a tuck and roll. Cage saw the opportunity to get Creep on the floor and he leaped into the air again, intent on crushing the hairy Brit under him.

Creep unrolled and Cage was frustrated to see a hairy, clawed foot snapping into his face. Again he found himself on the ground.

"Creep. Creep. Creep."

0:44

Cage rolled to his side and felt one of his ribs give way. The pain was excruciating, but he was resolved not to let this Limey punk take his belt. He was good enough to hold the title without some arbitrary executive decision from Jonathan Fox. There was a modicum of truth to the Arena. Wasn't there?

0:40

Cage staggered to his feet, clutching his right side involuntarily. His opponent leaped about in a wild dance, egging the crowd on in their bloodlust.

"Creep! Creep! Creep!"

0:36

Cage swung his right arm out, and Creep ducked instinctively. Cage felt the tendons in his steroidal shoulders rip and felt the sting of another rib crunching beneath a rear elbow jab.

0:33

The larger gladiator spun out of the grapple, barely maintaining his balance.

Creep dropped his smile. It was time to get serious.

"Creep! Creep!"

0:30

Cage felt a tingle of numbness seep slowly down his right arm. He knew his only chance was to get in close.

Creep spun again in an aerial kick, but this time Cage was ready. Creep knew he'd missed his intended target, and followed through to land. The next thing he felt was the crunch of cable-tight tree trunk arms around his shoulders, across his chest, locked. He couldn't wriggle free.

0:25

The crowd swelled. Someone else passed out. The chant broke for a moment as the audience gasped in surprise, then returned with fervent intensity. Jonathan Fox smiled. "Do it, Cage," he mumbled under his breath.

0:22

Creep swung out with his feet, but Cage remained balanced and in control. Creep gasped. He couldn't move, couldn't breathe. Then he felt the force of forward motion, and he realized in horror that Cage was going to ram his face into the pit wall.

"CREEP! CREEP! CREEP!"

"CAGE! CAGE! CAGE!"

0:18

Cage squeezed tightly, stumbling forward with all of his mass behind the plunge. Creep felt the *whoosh* of air through his fur, and saw the white fiberglass wall zooming in at him. Then he felt Cage lose his balance, and with it his iron grip.

Dropping quickly to his knees below the giant's midsection, he reached up and hauled down on Cage's arms, thrusting him forward.

Cage hit the wall face-first, blood spattered from his broken nose, and the giant gladiator slumped to an unconscious pile on the floor.

0:12

The crowd exploded in cheers and screams. Creep stood and backed away from Cage's huddled body. The timer counted down the final seconds.

Creep smiled inwardly. They had to concede the bout. In the Arena, there were no fouls to declare or rules to break. If Cage didn't get up, the title belonged to Creep.

The buzzer—signaling the end of the first round.

Cage didn't get up.

The audience roared. Spotlights whirled and spun. Fox frowned, stroking his beard with a troubled stare.

Not only was it an upset, but the smaller fighter had dethroned the Champ in less than a single round. Money would be exchanged, ordinary lives altered irreparably. Promises made, legs broken. Folks would talk of this fight for a long time.

The announcer came over the PA, his voice startled and confused. *"And...Creep wins it! What a...um, surprise victory for the hirsute Brit. A truly...historic result! And here's Jonathan Fox to present the title."*

Fox stood and made his way back down to the edge of the pit. Anger was only overshadowed by cruel disappointment. He'd thought Maddock smarter than that. In a perfect world, he'd grease the ungrateful fucker then and there. But he couldn't, not when the cameras were rolling. No, Creep would meet with a tidy little suicide or something afterward.

The elevator platform lowered into the pit, and Creep stepped forward triumphantly as medics scurried from the locker room to load the unconscious former champ onto a gurney.

With a mechanical lurch, the platform raised into the air again, and Creep stepped off onto the stage in front of the audience. He waved and saluted. The cheering section screamed.

Fox put on his best plastic smile and raised a wireless mic in one hand, a heavy bronze belt in the other. "Congratulations, Creep. You are now the West Coast Arena Champion, and will compete in the Arena National Championship in Miami. Your winnings tonight total more than five-hundred-thousand dollars!" The crowd applauded. Creep chuckled sarcastically. Yeah, like he would really let him have the damn winnings.

Fox lowered the mic and leaned in close. "You're finished, you little shit."

Creep accepted the belt, raising it over his head. He tried not to look like he was scanning the exits for guards. Fox held the microphone to Creep's mouth, and the new champion nodded at the mobs of fans. "Thank you! And cheers to the fans!"

The crowd surged forward, and Creep took the opportunity to make his break. Halfway between the pit and the south exit, a pack of reporters swarmed around a couple of baton-carrying riot officers.

Perfect. He headed for them.

The medias saw the champ approach and pushed through the guards, snapping pics and wielding digital field recorders.

"Hey, Champ! How does it feel—"

"After five years in the Arena league, what's it like to—"

"Mr. Maddock, my employers are prepared to offer you a substantial amount of money for an exclusive interview."

Creep blinked. Who the hell had said that? He dropped his gaze from the guards at the south exit to a slender brunette woman in dark gray business wear, with a large handbag slung over her left shoulder.

What bloody wonderful luck. "It's a deal. Where are you parked?"

The woman swallowed. "Huh?"

Another strobe went off in his face and he scowled. "I said it's a deal. Let's go."

"Uh, you mean it's a *yes*?"

"Yes. Come on." He turned the woman around and put her arm in his. She stared at the furry gladiator incredulously, and they headed for the exit.

They made the parking garage without issue. The doors slid open and they stepped out into a dank industrial cavern lined with vehicles of every make and model year dating back to the 2020s.

The woman pointed toward a long black Honda limousine parked next to some other luxury town cars. "I'm over there."

Creep grasped her arm and pulled her forward. She grunted, stumbled, and finally regained her balance. "Hey, Champ! What's the rush?"

They achieved the halfway mark when a pair of armed thugs stepped from behind a concrete support column in front of them. "Maddock!"

"Get down!" Creep whipped his arm, forcing the woman to the cold cement. There was a pop and a brief flash, and Creep felt his left shoulder explode. "Fucking 'ell!"

The woman glanced up in time to see a graceful trail of blood erupt from Creep's wounded arm. "Oh my God!"

He charged the thugs head-on, barking, "Get to the car!"

The woman brushed a wispy strand of dark hair from her face and sprinted as fast as she could in slacks and heels toward the limo, which immediately roared to life and squealed out of its stall.

She hit the door and flipped the mechanical handle release, tumbling into the back seat just as Creep made contact with the two hired guns. She watched intently through the tinted window as he floored them with two body strikes and an aerial combination kick to their heads. Guns fell. The men fell. Creep landed, rolled across the hood of the humming car and leaped into the back, slamming the door just as Jonathan Fox exited the second elevator with an armed guard and the commlink in his ear.

The vehicle revved and sped away.

"Sergei! Black limo! Don't let them out of the garage!"

The driver glanced up into the rear view mirror. He had an olive complexion and short black hair tucked under a traditional chauffeur's cap. The look in his olive eyes was one of complete terror. "Jesus Christ! What the hell was that?!"

Creep shifted in the seat as the car screeched around a tight curve, heading for the garage exit. "I'll tell ya later."

The driver breathed, struggling with the wheel. They fishtailed into a spiral turn, pulling some hard Gs. "Kel, why didn't you call me? I could've met you outside!"

The woman clutched the interior door handle as the motion of the limo bounced her to the ceiling. "Larry, don't ask, just get us the hell out of here!"

The limo swerved down the spiral ramp, careening toward the exit. As they rounded the last turn into the open exit driveway, three security guards dashed to the side. An enormous plate steel and cement barricade blocked their path, and several other officials were drawing guns.

Larry cursed under his breath and hauled over hard on the wheel, sending the huge car over the center island into the entrance lane. He winced as the first shots pelted the side of the limo. "Holy shit!"

The asphalt in front of the metal spikes read *WARNING! SEVERE TIRE DAMAGE.* A giant red sign on the inside wall proclaimed *WRONG WAY: DO NOT ENTER.* The gate arm was in the down position.

Larry inhaled. *Fuck it all.*

As the front suspension hit the striped speed bump at the bottom of the incline, Larry stomped on the accelerator, and the limo leaped into the air, soaring over the spikes, through the gate and onto the asphalt of the street outside. The broken gate clattered to the ground in several pieces, and the limo bottomed out with a metallic scrape and a shower of sparks. The road was sparsely populated with other cars and Larry easily guided the vehicle into traffic.

They were safe, for the moment.

Larry glanced in the mirror again. "All right, where to Kel?"

The woman combed back her dark hair with slender fingers. "My place—"

Creep turned back from the rear window. "101 North."

The woman stared uncomfortably. "What?!"

"Trust me."

She laughed, certain the furry athlete could tell she was terrified. "Ha. Sure."

David Maddock looked down at his shoulder. It was seeping blood. He shrugged and felt the steel projectile still lodged in the muscle. The pain was unbearable at best, but he wasn't about to let it bother him.

Aww, bloody hell. It *bothered* him.

"Please," he winced. "Just get me out of LA."

IF THE SUNSET was a safe district—any more safe, that is, than the rest of the city—it was due in large part to the social activism of about two-dozen people. A lot of them lived in the Irving Street neighborhood. And the major reason one could walk safely down Irving at midnight was because the community was overseen by itself, took care of itself. Those who could, walked: Stilt, Cuda, Father Fisk, Donald Kimm, Carl Chen, and the occasional advanced student of one of the martial arts schools in the area. There was no set schedule, just a haphazard word-of-mouth system of wireless, human communication. And much to everyone's pleasant surprise, it worked.

Many times, these "walks" were nothing more than impromptu street corner bull sessions. But it was enough. Of course, it often meant Kai Tokura would be out chatting with the local folk until the wee morning hours.

Given the other option—say, the Tenderloin after midnight —he didn't mind the lack of sleep one bit.

Stilt entered the dark apartment, shutting the ancient door softly behind him. He didn't bother with the lights. Not only could he see with perfect clarity by the light of the street lamps outside, he knew the place inside and out, where every piece of furniture and book and disc lay. The buzz from his jacket pocket told him he had a new voicemail. He padded quietly to the acrylic desk beside the genuine pine futon and pulled a small prepaid mobile from his jacket. Setting it on the desk, he spoke aloud, "Marci: play voicemail."

There was a pause and female voice from the shadows replied, "You have four new messages. First message, recorded today at 3:49 p.m."

"Hi, Stilt. This is Father Fisk. I've got a problem case down at the youth center. Definitely drugs, but I've never seen a kid act like this. Give me a call. I'll be down here from 8 to 5:30 tomorrow. Thanks. Bye."

Stilt frowned beneath his visor, slipping the jacket from his shoulders and draping it over the desk chair. "Delete," he ordered.

"Message deleted. Next message, recorded today at 7:04 p.m."

"Hi, Stilt, this is Mae Wong. I just wanted to say thank you for allowing Charlie's tuition to be late. You've done so much for him already. Thank you again. Peace be with you."

"Delete."

"Message deleted. Next message, recorded today at 7:16 p.m."

"Stilt. It's Captain Bonner with the SFPD. I don't know how you managed this one, but you got your contract. Just came down from our corporate liaison. Someone up there likes you. Give me a call at the station, or come down before 08:00. Ciao."

Stilt cocked his head. "Repeat."

"Stilt. It's Captain Bonner with the SFPD. I don't know how you managed this one, but you got your contract. Just came down from our corporate liaison. Someone up there likes you—"

"Pause. Save message."

"Message saved."

He plucked the mobile from the desk and put it to his ear. "Marci: Call Van Pezzoni."

There was a pause. He listened to the tones as the phone rang on the other end. Finally, "Hey, Van. Can you meet John and me downtown? Yeah. We got it. 'Bout an hour or so? Great."

He placed the phone softly onto the wireless charging pad, leaning forward over the desk.

He smiled, his guts almost bursting with joy, though in the dark, one would not have noticed. Clenching his left hand into a tight fist, he raised his visored eyes toward the ceiling. "Yesss!"

"Lights," Windy sighed. On her command, the room dimmed to barely a candle's illumination. The only other light came from the fiber-optic stars in her hair. They sparkled and danced, spinning in holographic, hallucinogenic color, and Van shifted under her as she straddled his waist.

The steady thrum of soft, bass-heavy dance music thumped at 93 BPM from a strategically-placed Bose system that used the internal geometry of the room as a reverberation chamber. The sonic vibrations through their bodies amplified the sensation of skin on skin.

Van gazed at the pale woman above him: the silhouette of her shoulders, the graceful, soft curve of her breasts, the fullness of her lips, the glint of playful passion in her eyes. She'd insisted on almost complete darkness to hide her bruises— even so, Windy couldn't make love without music, or without the glowing lights in her hair. It was a personal quirk, just one of those things, Van told himself. Everyone had their own hangup. With Windy, it was always like fucking on a dance floor.

It was the highest form of performance art.

She sighed again, and Van could feel himself strain beneath her. She clutched his shoulders, and his hips rose to meet her as she lowered onto him. The sound that escaped her lips was a sound he'd heard before, but Van knew it was genuine. She didn't have to sleep with him. She chose to, and she never charged him. He knew that she'd learned a great many of her techniques from her days in the glory holes and bath houses in Hustle City, knew that she could fake any emotion she liked. She was a consummate actress. But he knew this moment, above all else, was *real.*

She shifted her hips, and he moved to meet her thrusts. The sub-bass of the driving music pounded the air around their bodies, and they found themselves matching the rhythm.

Van growled. A bead of sweat formed on his brow.

Windy breathed, and the air she exhaled met his face with a welcome coolness.

Van raised up on his elbows, scooted back, leaning against the headboard.

Arching her back, Windy gasped and offered her breasts. Kick drum thumped, gentle melody loop circling above their heads in the fiber optic cosmos of light that played across the ceiling.

They were almost consumed now.

Van leaned forward, planting a soft line of kisses down her neck and onto her shoulders. Windy moaned as he moved down to her breasts and gently nibbled with just his lips.

The bass vibrated through the mattress, through her legs, her thighs, her mound. She moaned and gasped in cadence with her movements, pulling Van to her chest as she sped her pace.

They were a mass of hungry flesh, gyrating to the music from the air around them. Windy's lips parted and she gasped again. She could feel his crucifix earring dig into the soft skin below her neck as he continued to plant sensuous kisses up and down her throat.

Van shut his eyes. These nights were few and far between. Too few. He wanted to savor every moment of it.

She was close. He could feel her temperature spike as her chest flushed.

Windy threw her head back, and a few of the bright stars fell from her hair onto the bed, creating a brilliant erotic meteor shower.

Van reached around her waist with both hands, gently kneading her soft white haunches. His left hand ran up the small of her back, up her spine, to the nape of her neck, and they melted together in frenzied motion.

"Oh, honey," she whispered. "Yes."

She enveloped his head in her arms, smothering him in her soft cleavage. Her lips met his hair, and she cried out in climax.

Van inhaled, felt her tighten and spasm around him, and he exploded inside her, clamping his eyes shut as electricity shot through his body in waves.

His eyes finally opened, and he glanced dizzily upward. All he could see were the morphing multicolored shapes play across the ceiling, hear the bass pulse and drive through the nerves of his skin.

A delicate pale face lowered toward his, and the lights blurred. He closed his eyes again, lowering back down to the mattress, feeling the languid kiss of breath in his ear.

"How you feeling?" Van reached up and tenderly caressed Windy's swollen eye. She smiled. The lights were back up, the music gone. She sat, still astride him, naked and natural. No surgery here, no implants or cybernetics. Van let his eyes roam over her supple contours. She had a beautiful body. And she had absolutely no qualms about selling it for some cash and a place to sleep.

She wasn't trafficked, she had no pimp. This life of hers was by design. And it afforded her almost absolute autonomy in a world littered with the corpses of human chattel who never got to see the fruits of their labor.

On the one hand, she inspired him by her strength and independence. On the other, she often put herself in unnecessary danger, and he'd lost more friends to those situations than he could remember.

She touched his hand as it fell across the curve of her jaw. "Better. Thanks."

"Good. Good." He knew this was the worst time to start sermonizing. He really did. He didn't want to drive her away.

But he was Van, and she was Windy. The words came automatically. "You know, you really shouldn't—"

"Don't start, Van. Please." She pulled away and began to dress.

"Start what?"

"You don't get to preach to me about what I should and shouldn't do." She shrugged into a flimsy white chemise and lowered her legs to the floor.

He sat up and grabbed a clean pair of boxer briefs from the plastic crates stacked sideways against the wall. "Windy, I was just gonna say, if you keep hangin' out with Bug and his boys, you're gonna keep getting hurt. Or worse."

Windy paused, cast a glance over her shoulder, then leaned forward and found her miniskirt. "Thanks, *Dad*. But I can take care of myself."

Van laughed. It probably sounded a lot more vicious than he intended. "How's that workin' for ya?"

She frowned and stood, pulling up the skirt, tucking in the chemise with a practiced motion.

Van glanced down at the tangled bed sheets, littered with fiberoptic stars. "I'm sorry."

Windy sighed, sliding into her black ankle boots. "If you have to apologize..."

"I know. Don't say it in the first place."

She looked at him. He was gorgeous, if somewhat hairy and otherwise rough around the edges, but that was to be expected in a full-blooded Italian lad. Why didn't she just snag him and forget everyone else, the parties, the slumming, the hustling? "Look. I've been your friend for a long time. I've been your contact for a long time. You've got your way of fighting, I've got mine."

Van bent and stepped into his Levi's. "Bullshit."

She smiled. "Oh, now you're jealous. I should've known better."

He stared back, buttoning the top of his fly. "What."

She looked away, then back. "Van, we're such good friends. Don't ruin this by falling in love with me."

He shrugged. "Who says I'm falling in love with you?"

"I know that look, Van. You've done it to me before."

He moved forward, grasping her hands. "I care for you, Windy. A lot."

"Too much, Van. I'm a big girl. Let me go." She laughed sadly and met his eyes. Hers were red and beginning to sparkle with tears.

Van took a shot. "I want to see you again."

She looked away, searching for her bag and jacket. "You will."

"When?"

"Whenever."

The question left his mouth before he could stop them. "Where you going?"

"Out."

Van sighed. It was not to be—this time. Maybe someday, but not now. "Be careful."

Windy raised up and kissed him. "Thanks for a lovely evening and a great shag, honey. I'll see you." She ducked into her leather coat and grabbed her handbag. Turning briefly at the door, she winked and blew him a kiss.

Van waved back. "Bye."

Then she was gone. Van padded on bare feet to his giant lacquer dresser, noticing Windy had left her nic-sticks. Unconsciously, he flipped up the top of the pack and tapped one out. It was an inch from his mouth before he realized what he was doing.

Throwing a frustrated look at the small tube, he sighed. He broke it in two between his fingers, then dug into his pocket for a toothpick, cursing under his breath.

09

THE **DRONE** of the limo's engine hummed endlessly northward. Creep grunted and held one end of the makeshift bandage as the woman reached over and pulled the bar towel tight. The hirsute gladiator flinched and bit his lip, and she backed off the pressure, tying the two ends into a clumsy knot. She looked at him with plaintive brown eyes.

He nodded and winked back. "I'm sorry I had to drag you both into this."

The woman smiled nervously. "Me too. Why the hell were we being shot at?"

Creep paused. He might as well let them in on it—the hell with his NDA. He forced a smile. "I wasn't supposed to win."

The woman frowned. "What?"

"It may come as a shock to you, but the Arena's fixed."

Larry chuckled from the front seat. "I knew it! Always said those things were fake!"

"The fighting's real, but the outcome is predetermined." Creep glanced down at the bloody rag now tied around his left arm. He slowly leaned his head back on the seat. "Not to change the subject, but I'm a little short of cash at the moment, probably wont be able to access any of my winnings for awhile, if at all. How substantial is your employer's offer?"

The woman blinked and scratched her jaw with delicate fingers, now stained with the blood of her furry charge. Silver hoops dangled and reflected the oncoming headlights. "Well, uh, actually, I—"

"Lied," Creep finished for her. He nodded and sank deeper into the seat. The bluff made perfect sense. He should've known. "Well done."

Ah, well, at least he was out of the Arena. He sighed and braced himself for the explanation.

"Larry and I run our own magazine. It's pretty small, and we've had a hard time getting advertising. I was hoping I could talk you into an exclusive that I could show to our potential advertisers."

The Champ gave an ironic laugh. "Heh. Looks like we used each other."

She returned the smile, uneasy. "Looks like."

Larry glanced into the mirror, saw the dark spreading on the bar towel. "Kel, he's bleeding pretty bad. I'm gonna try to find a hospital."

Creep shook his head. "No."

The woman looked at Larry, then at Creep. "Come on, Champ. Larry's right. You look like shit."

"Thank you. The answer is still *no*. Keep going."

Larry returned his attention to the road. "Who the hell is after you?"

"No one you wanna fuck with, trust me. Just keep going, all right?"

The woman wagged her head and shrugged. "Keep going *where?*"

Creep didn't open his eyes. His voice was weak and he found himself unable to move. "San Francisco," he said.

"*San Francisco?!*" the other two exclaimed simultaneously.

Creep rolled his head. "I don't suppose you two have any money at all?"

The woman blinked. "A little, why?"

"We'll need a place to stay. Just for a couple of days. I'll go to a doctor up there."

"You promise?"

"Yeah. I don't wanna die any more than you want me to."

The woman leaned back. She ran a casual hand through her hair, oblivious to the blood on her skin. "What do you mean by that?"

"Your exclusive. An insider expose of the Arena. By the West Coast Champ. That ought to solve your advertising problems, eh?"

She paused, then smiled. The smell of sweat and blood hung thick in the air. She leaned forward to punch the button on the climate control. "Name's Kelly," she said.

"Kelly," he repeated, slumping tiredly into the corner of the back seat. "Pretty name."

Cheryl's office was just like they'd left it in the early hours of Monday morning. The green windows, the ancient wooden desk and vinyl chairs, the enormous trophy case where the file cabinet used to be. And, lord, the trophies! Champion marksmanship awards, academy instruction, undercover awards, community service plaques.

Cheryl leaned back in her chair, waiting for them, pretending not to look like she was waiting for them. Arrest warrants scrolled up her desk screen, and she followed them with glazed eyes.

Stilt and Cuda entered, followed by Van, who shut the office door behind them. Stilt waved. "Hey, Cheryl."

Cheryl looked away from the screen. "You got my message."

Stilt nodded stupidly, trying to put on his best-mannered front. "Yes. So, uh, here we are."

"Yeah, here you are. Now the first thing we're gonna stick you on is a corporate security bust."

Stilt blinked beneath the visor, stunned by the comment. "Wait a minute. Aren't we going after Bug?"

Cheryl blinked, an incredulous laugh caught in her throat. "Um, not only no, but *hell* no. It's gonna take some time to get back in the saddle with him."

Stilt began to fume, and the others could feel the tirade building within him. The tall vigilante held out his arms. "Time? He's selling poison to innocent people—to kids!"

Cheryl stood, leaning over the desk. It was a pose Stilt knew well. It meant she was having none of what he was peddling. He backed off the attitude and she glared at him from across the dimly lit office. "Look. If you're gonna contract with the SFPD, you're gonna learn how to follow orders, how to respect the law and the chain of command, *and* you're gonna realize we can't go after every little dealer that walks through a neighborhood. We've got bigger fish to fry."

Stilt flexed his fingers tensely at his side. What was this noise? They finally got a police contract, and the precinct captain was trying to cork them up. "Bug's no small time pusher, Cheryl—"

Cuda broke in, "—But we'll do as you say." He shot Stilt a familiar expression that said *are you fuckin' crazy or what?*

Cheryl nodded at Cuda. He was the most sensible of the three, but she already knew that. And she held no small amount of respect for his older brother, Oakland's chief of police. "Smart move," she said. "You'll live a lot longer."

She pressed a key on her computer panel and Stilt could hear a muffled buzzing sound out in the precinct office. Cheryl straightened and folded her arms in front of her. She was in big company, but big had never intimidated her. "First of all, contractors must operate under the supervision of a trained police officer."

The door opened and Dennis entered, a huge white bandage strapped over his recently broken nose, his eye sockets tinged with purple.

Cheryl indicated the three contractors to Dennis. "Special Agent Murray, meet your team for tomorrow night's activities."

Dennis stood agape, almost breaking out in tears. "Aww, you gotta be shitting me."

10

SOMEWHERE JUST OUTSIDE Climax, Colorado, the Genetech Biological Engineering (GBE) complex sprawled out against the mountains. The area was unmarked, completely fenced in, and absolutely enormous. Of course, not much showed above ground.

If, by some chance, one had possessed the correct top secret credentials and retinal prints, one might have seen a labyrinth of cement bunkers and steel-reinforced tunnels, high-security laboratories, doorways marked NO ENTRY, and the glare of LED lights on the polished laminate floor. One might have heard the electronic mumble of someone paging one of the many scientists engrossed in their genetic engineering experiments, or the soft repetitive *click* of footsteps down a dim hallway.

One might have even seen Dr. Thomas Ridley, a short, slender man in glasses and a pristine white lab coat, ambling alongside his rooster-crested Pawnee assistant.

Ridley squinted. "Are you sure?"

The young aborigine nodded. "You said recently scheduled. KML029 is the only one at this lab. Its orders are less than a day old."

"Alright. Looks like our best shot," Ridley sighed as they paused in front of lab 884. "Here we are."

They entered, Ridley stumbling in the dark. The space was suddenly bathed in red non-photo light, and the assistant pointed to the operating table in the center. It was a standard surgery suite, except that it had been altered to include a locking stasis capsule. The thing looked like a streamlined coffin—a black metal and plastic obelisk with a flashing read-out display.

"Watch the door." Ridley waved to his assistant. As the young technician exited, Ridley approached the stasis tube and wiped away the frozen condensation on the outside glass. The face it revealed made him jump. He took a breath and looked again: the nose was elongated like an alpaca or camel, fur-covered; the head was flat, its cranial lobe distended and square; its eyes were closed; a light mane of hair swept back, and two equine ears lay against its head; its thick neck tapered down to enormous broad shoulders and a vaguely humanoid chest.

One of Noah Jorgenson's desert soldiers. A bastard genetic crossbreed of animal and man. Thirty years ago it never would have gotten past the first phase. Now they could take one of these "manimals" all the way to phase four: simulated work environments. But none of them had gone into the field. Didn't look like this one was going to make it either.

Ridley reached down and touched the manual seal release. The light on the monitor below flashed a silent message: STASIS FIELD BROKEN. Hydraulics wheezed as the heavy lid raised, cold fog seeping from inside the casing.

The scientist reached into the large side pocket in his lab coat and produced a small computer deck. Flipping the unit open, he dug into his pocket again, this time pulling out a length of digital cable with a modified IV needle at one end. Probing with gloved fingers, he found the KML unit's input line, just behind the jugular vein, and inserted the cable. The other end was a simple digital interface, which he plugged into the back of the deck. Cradling the small box in his palm, he punched up a complex series of codes and formulae. He hit ENTER, and the chip drive indicator blinked a steady crimson for three seconds, almost a dull gray in the lab's red light.

And that was it. Gently removing the needle from the unit's neck, he dropped the digital cable back into his pocket. He ejected a small plastic storage card from the front of the deck and snapped it in two.

The assistant entered just as he was replacing the computer in his coat pocket. "Better hurry. New watch coming on."

Ridley met the young man's comment with an educated nod. "It's done. Selby's guys ought to be able to access the code immediately. All they've got do is kill it." He touched the hatch control, which closed the cover over the sleeping beast. "All right, let's ship it out."

Pausing at the door, he deposited the broken chip in the wall hazmat receptacle. He gave one last look at the KML unit, then shut off the lights and closed the door.

Dr. Ridley wandered away with his assistant, completely oblivious to the fact that he'd forgotten to lock and reset the stasis chamber.

The light on the monitor blinked its steady, silent message. Genetically-designed eyes blinked open.

The dawn sky was the usual conglomeration of salmon, pink and orange hues, with a subliminal hint of gunmetal blue—the color of night—behind it.

A road sign shot past: *San Francisco 44.*

Larry glanced in the rear view mirror. Creep was slumped over, his head in Kelly's lap. Both were sound asleep. Larry blinked and forced the fatigue from his tired eyes.

The limo's dashboard clock read 6:12 a.m. as the sun rose over the city. Larry yawned and negotiated the turn from Van

Ness onto California Street, making the final seven-block approach to the Comcast Fairmont Tower. Trends came and went, but the Fairmont was still the classiest hotel in town, and Larry knew the beds would be especially soft, and proportionately expensive. He yawned again, and the limo continued with a gentle hum, past the huddled shapes of winos passed out in doorways, past the panhandlers getting an early start, past the 24-hour cafés. The ornate stone masonry of the Fairmont greeted him like a sunburst in the center of a gray autumn storm.

He eased the limo into the renovated passenger loading area and came to a slow halt in front of the main doors. A red-suited doorman met them, lifting the rear door handle with white-gloved delicacy. He was not expecting what he saw. Maybe he should have, given the bullet holes in the frame and the sagging rear suspension.

Kelly was first, looking the kind of disheveled one would expect from a rock groupie at six in the morning. Her dark hair was tossed back, tied haphazardly at the shoulder-length base with a silk scarf. It had an interesting red blotch design that looked almost like spattered blood. Her lipstick was faded and smeared around the edges. Her eyes were hidden behind dark shades and she clutched a shoulder bag.

The doorman nearly fainted when he came face to face with the hair-covered apparition who stepped out next. Creep had donned Larry's black trench coat and sunglasses. His left arm hung limply at his side, hand submerged in the deep coat pocket. He was still barefoot from the fight. "Mornin'," he growled.

The doorman's eyes grew wide and he paused uncertainly. Then he broke into a nervous smile. "Champ?"

Creep nodded. Larry skirted the other side of the car and unlocked the trunk, unloading a single travel bag. He handed it to the doorman and headed back to the driver's side of the limo. Kelly hailed him as he sat. "Larry, park the car and then come right up."

The chauffeur saluted tiredly. "Yes, ma'am." He didn't care what the cover was. He was too exhausted not to play along. He was dressed like a driver, by God, he'd play the driver.

They entered the lavishly decorated lobby, and Kelly had to keep from staring open-mouthed at every decadent painting and crystal statue and marble column they passed. The front desk was enormous, marble-topped and shiny, and Creep found himself a nice big fern by one of the plush sofas to stand behind while Kelly did the honors.

She approached the desk, and a petite woman sporting a pink buzz-cut and round nose-specs looked up at her with a professional smile. "May I help you?"

"Yes, we need two adjoining rooms, please."

The clerk delivered a very convincing sympathetic look. "I'm sorry, we're all booked up this weekend."

Kelly bit her lower lip. "Are you sure?"

"I'm afraid so."

Kelly sighed. "You see, we've been driving all night, and the Champ specifically requested this hotel."

No sign of recognition flashed over the clerk's face. Evidently she wasn't a big Arena fan. "I'm sorry, ma'am. We don't have any—"

"Is there a problem here?"

Kelly sighed quietly in relief. The manager, a stocky Nigerian man in a gray designer three-piece suit, approached the desk from behind the clerk. Kelly forced herself to breathe steadily. "Maybe you can help. My name is Kelly Hines, I'm Creep's press agent."

The man flashed a smile over an aged face, his ebony eyes bright with admiration. "Creep?"

"Yes."

"Here?"

"Yes. We've been driving all night and—"

The manager held up a wide, wrinkled hand. "Say no more, Ms. Hines. Sally, bump Mr. Bartak and party from their Tower Suites. Tell them we're remodeling."

The clerk did a confused double-take. "Sir?"

The manager grabbed a couple of large plastic security cards from the box under the desk and ran them through the magnetic coding machine. He quickly shuffled around the front desk, clutching the key cards in an outstretched hand. "Ms. Hines, the Champ and his party are welcome...is that him?" He nodded at the potted fern with the trench coat and long hair behind it.

"Why, yes it is." Kelly smiled, accepting the key cards graciously.

"May I meet him?"

"Yes. Of course."

Creep peered out around the giant plant to check Kelly's progress. He saw the manager and ducked back, but he was too late. The wide man met him with a firm handshake and an enormous smile. At least the bullet wasn't in his right arm. "Welcome, Champ. I'm a big fan of yours. Great match last night. One round! Spectacular!"

"Thanks. But if you'll excuse me, I'm extremely tired after the match and the long drive—"

The manager nodded kindly and stepped back, waving them to the elevators. "Of course, of course, Champ. Uh, your manager has the keys. I hope everything will be satisfactory."

Creep managed a fatigued smile. "No doubt it will."

They exited onto the twelfth floor, and Kelly inserted a key card, unlocking the first security door: number 1218. It was metal and utilitarian, but lavishly cased in a wood frame, with a decorative handle of brass and crystal.

They entered the room and Kelly whimpered in disbelief. The motif was white, Neo-Colonial, with a bedroom beyond a set of French doors containing a king-size four-poster bed. A giant crystal vase full of freshly-clipped irises sat on an enormous sideboard along the inside wall. A large brick fireplace took up much of the west wall, furnished with antique brass-handled tools, despite the fact that it was gas.

They had southern exposure and a view of California Street, and the golden morning sun began to seep through a diffusion of gauzy white drapery. The door on the left connected to the adjoining king room; the door on the right opened into a spacious tile bathroom.

Creep glanced around the interior, nodding approval. "Yes. This will do nicely."

Kelly was speechless. She whimpered again, finally managing coherent words. "Nicely for what? There's absolutely no way we can afford this."

"Not yet," Creep admitted. "But soon."

"How soon? We don't have clothes, we don't have—"

Creep held up his good hand to halt her. Larry entered, stumbling like some zombie-esque George Romero creation to the adjacent suite. Creep regarded him, then returned his attention to Kelly. "Yeah, but we *do* have the West Coast Arena Champ, a very resourceful and clever negotiator, and one hell of a great driver. Get some sleep, Larry. You look terrible."

Larry waved back at him. "Way ahead of you, Champ."

Creep turned and undid the belt on the borrowed trench coat. "Kelly, get on the phone. Arrange a press conference." He padded softly to the main door, pulling it shut.

Kelly dropped into an antique armchair and folded her arms. "Wait a minute. You promised you'd see a doctor."

"I lied."

"But you've got a fucking bullet in your arm!"

"Keep it down," he warned, shedding the coat on the bed. The Lycra suit was stained with sweat and blood. "I'll need scissors, tweezers, a razor and some rubbing alcohol."

Kelly's eyes widened to the size of golf balls when she realized what he intended to do. "You're fucking crazy!"

Creep glanced down at his bloody shoulder. "Maybe."

11

ASANO SET his ceramic mug of hot tea on the rubberized coaster next to the sheet music on the Yamaha grand. He did not stop to stare out the living room window at the bay, or watch the AVs buzzing their way to their roosts atop the corporate towers. He sat, cracked his fingers, and opened the Sakamoto piece to page one.

His fingers came down, and the first scene hit him: A young, handsome, wealthy man, heir to the Tanaka tech fortune. An arranged marriage. Anger...doubt...rebellion.

Fingers caressed acrylic keys, urging the plaintive sounds from the strings inside. Sakamoto's *Solitude* was a longing piece, sad and forlorn. His hands moved instinctively. The music was second nature. It haunted him, stalked his dreams.

It was Lani's favorite neo-classical work.

He turned the page, and the second vision seized his consciousness: a beautiful young artist from the suburbs of Tokyo. Jade-green eyes, raven hair. Laughing, talking, making love. He could see himself, a young man, throwing centuries of tradition and custom out the window.

And honor.

He refused the arranged marriage. He wanted no other than Lani Kimura. He lashed out at his parents. Scared them. Why couldn't they see? Love should take precedent over money. The rest of the family despised Lani because her family was poor. A classic Japanese class struggle. If Asano hadn't been the sole Tanaka heir, they might have been happy.

He had made it to the fourth bar on page three when the next vision hit: driving along the darkened country road from their picnic near Mito. Going to make the announcement to Lani's parents that night. They loved Asano, already treated him as a son—and not because of his economic or social status.

Darkness...an explosion of halogen light.

Then, as his fingers came down on the mournful bass chord, he heard it: the screech of tires, the crash of glass and metal. The drunk jumped the center divide, hitting them head on. Asano's seatbelt snapped at the weld. He was hurled through the windshield, his face ripped apart like clay through monofilament wire. Lani, who had been driving, was decapitated by the steering column.

Asano flipped the piano lid shut and collapsed on his arms, sobbing like a child. That was the part that was so hard to accept. And the part that came afterward: when he'd awakened to the news that not only was his fiance dead, but the intoxicated driver and his passenger had been killed at the scene.

He wanted to die too.

The drunk driver had been his father. The passenger, his mother.

Asano blinked and sat upright. He forced himself to inhale, breathing deeply, steadily. He gingerly grasped the mug of warm tea and sipped. Three days to go. He wondered if it was worth the hell.

The steam from the brass shower head billowed and clouded through the bathroom. It clung to the giant mirror, collected on the door, circled and dispersed around the antique ceiling fan. A can of shaving gel sat open on the vanity counter next to the scissors and razor. Long strands of blond and auburn hair were coiled around the drain, punctuated by the occasional splatter of crimson. The stained Lycra leotard lay in a heap on the tile sink, and the bloodied bar towel pointed the way through the sliding glass door into the shower.

Creep had certainly looked better. His eyes were sunken and hollow, and his hair hung plastered down in wet clumps. He leaned against the expensively-tiled wall on his right arm, dazedly looking over the shaved portion of his left shoulder. This would not be easy.

Slowly, he raised the tweezers to the wound, right hand shaking with pain and exhaustion. He sighed, watched a little more blood trickle down his arm, drip from his fingers, and spiral its way down the drain. His right arm fell, and he groaned. Then, steeling himself, he raised the tweezers again.

There was a crack and a slight rattle as the glass door slid open and Kelly stepped naked into the shower. Creep knew it was her, but dared not turn around. He couldn't let her see him in this awful state. There was a slight pause, and David Maddock breathed a steady flow of hot steam. Finally, he felt soft hands on his waist, and Kelly slowly turned him to face her.

She knew what to expect. She didn't flinch, or gasp, or turn away. The entry wound was swollen and red, bleeding in small, broken trickles. The skin around it was white and puckered from the steam and hot water. She gently took the tweezers from his right hand. "Let me."

Creep closed his eyes, then blinked them open slowly. Kelly reached up and offered him a twisted washcloth. He immediately opened his mouth and she laid it between his teeth. He bit down, and she grasped the tweezers, holding his shoulder steady with her other hand. Creep shut his eyes tightly, telling himself the pain was non-existent. His teeth clamped down hard and a grunt escaped as the metal instrument entered his flesh. It took a brief moment of fishing around before she made contact. Creep winced and huffed hard through the twisted cloth, feeling every twinge and touch of metal on metal within his shoulder. A wave of agony washed over him, and he felt his knees wobble and give way.

When he opened his eyes, he was still standing, and Kelly was proudly holding the near-pristine .38 slug in the grip of the tweezers. Creep stared at her, breathing in and out through his nose. He raised his right arm, grasped her tightly by the shoulder, and nodded at the tiled shelf lined with bottles. The rubbing alcohol stood in front of the shampoo and other toiletries. Kelly took the plastic bottle and grabbed Creep's chin in her other hand, lifting his gaze to hers. She pointed at her eyes. "Look at me. Don't look away."

Creep blinked and stared helplessly into her dark eyes, taking a halted breath as she flushed the wound with the alcohol from the bottle. He shook violently, and she brushed back his hair to soothe him, as if such a gentle act could actually take this kind of pain away. His blood washed down the drain. She touched his lips softly, holding him close.

Numbness finally overcame him. David Maddock smiled dizzily and collapsed in her arms.

Class assembled for early weekday exercises at the Shihodo School of Martial Arts on Irving Street. The students ranged in age from twelve to sixteen, of every color and ethnic extraction. One common thread linked them all together: they were children of the urban labyrinth, forgotten by the corporations. No one was going to look out for them except themselves—and maybe a few of their community. Stilt always tried to time classes so that the students could be showered and gone before the morning school bells rang four blocks away.

Today was no different than any other. He was teaching them a combination *kenpo* stance and *Heian* karate block. A young Senegalese kid in the Shihodo School's gray workout *dogi* stood planted on the mat in front of Stilt.

"No, Jason." Stilt moved in and landed a soft slap on the boy's side. "You're still open on the right. Try it again."

"Yes, *Sensei*." Jason nodded, repositioning himself.

Stilt suddenly glanced out at the front window. "Cuda." He made a hand signal, and his class fell into ranks. The giant man entered through the old wooden door, fresh uniform from the laundry tucked under his arm. He saw the perfectly assembled students and smiled broadly.

On Jason's lead, the entire class bowed deeply, adding a devout, "CU-DA."

John Kapp laughed aloud, returning the gesture as he continued to the lockers. "Lookin' good, lookin' good, buddy. Gotta change, though. I got the adult class in ten."

Stilt watched his partner disappear, then turned toward the class and began to pace in front of them. "All right. Back to the work at hand. What do you say if a stranger offers you a ride?"

The class responded in sync. "NO!"

"What do you say if someone offers you drugs?"

"NO!"

"What do you say if someone touches you in a way you don't like?"

"NO!"

Stilt beckoned his lead student forward. "Jason, what do you do if someone tries to hurt you or take your money? Kevin, try to take Jason's money."

An adolescent Jason's age, but shorter and stockier, moved forward hesitantly. Stilt waved him on. Kevin approached, and Jason fell into the stance he'd just blown minutes earlier. This time, however, it was perfect.

Kevin moved forward in an aggressive choke attempt, and Jason easily blocked his hands, locked his fingers around

Kevin's wrists, and pulled him down with an additional *aikido* sweep to knock him off his feet.

Kevin landed in a huff on the plastic mat. He rolled over and glared up at Jason, then Stilt. His eyes were wild.

Stilt nodded at Jason. "Now what do you do?"

Jason stood threateningly over Kevin and bellowed, "Get out of my neighborhood, scumbag!"

Stilt nodded affirmatively. He continued pacing. "Good. But what's more important? What if there's lots of guys? What if they have guns?"

Jason looked back over his shoulder, casting a serious glance at his teacher. "Stay alive."

"How?"

"Run."

Stilt nodded again and turned to the class. "That's right. What do you call someone who's outnumbered and decides to run? Do you call him a coward?"

The class answered in perfect time. "NO!"

"What do you call him?"

"SMART!"

"Why is that, Jason?"

Jason blinked, calling the lesson to memory. "Because he knows the extent of his abilities and those of his enemies."

"Very good—"

There was a sudden whoosh of billowy fabric from the floor, and Kevin shot to his feet. A split-second later, he was in the air, a stupendous roundhouse kick sending Jason to the mat face-first.

Stilt was in the fray immediately. "Hey!"

Kevin's leg shot out again, sweeping Stilt's from beneath him. He righted himself with the speed of thought, grasping Kevin tightly around the arms in a tight bear hug. The young boy was not amused. "Fuck you! I'll take you all on, mother-fu—"

Cuda dashed from the office, *dogi* top untied and loose around his shoulders. "What the hell—?"

Stilt struggled as Kevin wriggled violently in his grasp. A kid his age and size shouldn't have been so strong. Cuda locked his huge arms around the student's legs.

Stilt was incredulous. "Jeez. I've never seen—"

Kevin continued to shake, purple mouth spouting foam. Cuda clutched his legs tighter and looked into his wide, bloodshot eyes. "Hey, hey! What are you on, boy?"

"Fuck you! I take you all, man!"

"What are you on!"

Kevin screeched, gurgling up more foamy saliva.

Stilt shot a quick glance toward a tall readheaded girl of 14 standing at the back of the wide-eyed ranks of students. "Elizabeth! Call 9-1-1." He looked toward the huddled form of his fallen student who was in the process of standing with the aid of two others. "Jason, you all right?"

The young boy cupped his bleeding nose. "Doe."

Kevin siezed, choking on the spit in his mouth. Cuda held tightly. "Take it easy, Kevin. We got somebody comin'."

"F—Fuh! Kyou!"

Cuda looked at his partner. "Man, I've never seen a kid act like this. Not Cat, not Indigo..."

Stilt shook his head. "Not Dust, either."

"That was my next suggestion."

An older Latino kid stepped forward. "*Sensei*, we'll hold him."

Stilt glared at the class. "No you won't! Everybody stay back. Wait 'til the medics get here. Nobody touches Kevin. Cuda and I have him."

Cuda nodded in agreement. "It's under control." He looked down at Kevin. The young boy's eyes rolled back in his head and he began to convulse. "It's under control," he repeated.

He didn't believe it for an instant.

No one else did either.

12

THE LOADING DOCK was unusually sparse. A single unmarked pharmaceutical delivery truck sat with its open rear to the dock, and a stocky Asian with a receding pinfeather buzz marked off parcels as they were loaded into the back. Workers wandered to and fro, running lifts and loaders, and two men in white lab coats escorted a large yellow forklift to the truck. The crate it carried was enormous.

Dr. Ridley patted the plastic exterior of the box as the lift's hydraulics lowered it to the open cargo area. "Okay, be careful. This one is very important."

The driver paused, raised an eyebrow. "What's in it?"

The young Pawnee aimed a small tablet at the driver's, and the work order blinked open on the receiving unit's screen. "Need to know only. Just deliver it to this address."

The driver looked it over. "San Francisco, huh?"

Ridley nodded, watching closely as two dock workers angled the huge container into a front corner of the truck. "That's right. You guard that crate with your life, and see that it gets there."

The driver casually marked off the work order, pinning it under the piles of paperwork on his clipboard. After ten years driving courier for GBE, he was used to pushy scientists and their James Bond wannabe attitudes. "You're the boss."

Ridley smiled. "That's right."

The assistant turned his head and gazed out over the stark gray Rocky Mountain foothills. A cloud of dust wafted into the air a few miles down the road, accompanied by the distant hum of a car. "Jorgenson's back."

Ridley looked, biting his lip. He turned to the driver and slapped him on the back. "Remember. Guard it with your life."

The driver gave them a tired look as Ridley and the lab assistant headed back to the complex.

Cuda sat hunched in front of the ancient flat screen monitor, tapping out commands with thick fingers on an equally old wireless keyboard. Stilt watched over his shoulder, every so often pacing the floor of the small office.

Reproductions of Japanese and Okinawan silk paintings hung from wooden scrolls and gold cords on the otherwise plain white walls. A single desk and chair sat against the wall, Cuda occupying the space. A pair of antique *sai* hung crossed on pegs above the workstation, and an old ID badge from a Japanese pharma corp displayed the photo of Mariko Tokura. It was the only memento of either one of his parents.

Stilt was just about to begin another round of pacing when Cuda grunted recognition. "Here we go. Kevin Cedric. Age 14. Last two months tuition were late, and a third was written off. You do that?"

Stilt peered at the screen over huge shoulders. "Yeah. Boy was I blind." They both let the unintentional joke pass.

Cuda paged down to the bio. "No father, mother's an alcoholic. Looks bad."

Stilt nodded, still scanning the words on the database. "He was paying for the class out of his weekend job money. I should've known something was up when he couldn't pay the first time."

"Think he's buyin' shit?"

"You know he is. Or someone's giving it to him and he's not going to work."

"But what is it?"

Stilt shook his head in frustration. "I don't know, man. Looks like there's some new rat poison on the street."

"You think we should ask Dennis?"

Stilt straightened, scratched his head. "Naw, he can't tell us squat. The case is still open."

Cuda turned in the chair. "What about Father Fisk?"

Stilt paused, smiled. "Now buddy, that's the best idea I've heard all day."

Susan Kitayama made her final edit to the Akai proposal just as Love burst from the executive lift, waving a tablet deck and shrieking wildly. "Susan!" he cried. "Susan! Turn on The Screen!"

Susan's face failed to mask her annoyance. "What? Why?"

Love grabbed the mini remote from The Desk and aimed it at the wall screen. "You won't believe our good fortune!" This was strange. Love, excited about something? She had never seen him so enthusiastic. That meant it could either be an issue of earth-shattering importance, or something completely inane and stupid. Was he serious, or was he mocking her?

Susan put her manicured hands on trim hips. "What?"

The Screen blinked to life, and staring back at them was an image of David Maddock—Creep—sitting at a desk full of compact microphones. The flash of camera strobe units momentarily saturated him in white. He wore a black trench coat, his furry face partially masked by a dark pair of shades. Next to him sat an attractive brunette with nose freckles and silver hoops in her ears.

Susan moved around in front of the desk to gain a better view. "Isn't that—"

"Creep. The West Coast Arena Champion." Love grinned wide, raising the glasses on his ears. "Used to belong to Selby. Now he's here."

"Here?"

"Here in San Francisco." Love was ecstatic. "Just gave an incredible expose of the Arena system. He wasn't supposed to win last night."

Susan didn't get it. "So?"

Love rolled his eyes and chuckled. The game actually seemed refreshing today. "So...he barely escaped with his life. Now he's here looking for endorsements. And probably some protection."

Susan cast a sidelong glance at the television screen before returning to The Desk. "Sounds very dramatic and awfully suspicious," she said as she popped the small computer monitor up from its panel. "Sign him."

Love's feet almost left the floor. "I knew you couldn't pass this up!" he chortled gleefully. This would be fun.

Susan glanced again at the image of Creep on The Screen. The predatory look of the woman known as Tigress pierced her green feline eyes. "If only to find out what's going on in Selby's back yard."

The air was filled with the odors of a million different ethnic foods: Gold Panda Korean; chow mein from Fortune House Chinese on 19th Avenue; the pungent smell of oregano and garlic from Cesaro's Pizza & Pasta; the sharp red peppers of Dragon Thai; and the heavy sesame smell of Nha Trang

Vietnamese Restaurant on the northeast corner of 15th and Irving, directly across from the Shihodo School. Above it all, the faint smell of bangers and mash, fish and chips, and venison pie wafted over from the Ace & Gryphon.

Cuda met Stilt on the front stairs of the 18th Avenue Youth Center with a couple of large cola Icees from the mini-mart. "You talk to Fisk?"

Stilt took one of the cups, and they wandered out onto Irving Street. "Yeah. The kid he had wigged out and ran off before he could do much. Looks like the same kind of thing."

Cuda sipped his drink through the obligatory red plastic straw. "Well this is pissing me off. We've got to find out what the shit is." They passed A Dead Mime Cafe, and Cuda winked at the woman waiting tables.

Stilt nodded at his companion's comment. "Yeah. I feel the urge to walk tonight."

Cuda clapped him on the back. "Can't. We got that security stakeout at Kitayamacorp with Murray. Or have you forgotten the contract we've been after for the past three years?"

Stilt sighed, taking too large a gulp of his frozen beverage. "I guess we can walk tomorrow..." Just as the cold seizure hit his chest and head, a gravelly voice rang out from behind them. Stilt coughed and tried to force blood to his sinuses, and Cuda turned to see a short, spindly man in a tattered olive-green overcoat and mismatched shoes stumble toward them down the sidewalk. He wore a hot pink fishing hat and a pair of duo-colored round hippie glasses. His nose was an enormous, pitted orb, and a walrus-sized mustache and beard covered most of his face. He gave the Vulcan salute from *Star Trek* as he approached.

"Zowie! It's the bad dudes from the space station!" Burt was as eccentric as they came, to state the obvious. Though clean and sober for a great many years, he'd sampled everything in his younger days, resulting in a consciousness unrestrained by the norms of society. He was known as a street prophet and neighborhood history guru, tolerated like a cute, stray puppy.

Stilt straightened, heat returning to his solar plexus. Why the hell did he continue drinking these things? He gave the community's resident deep space probe a nod of greeting. "Hey, Burt."

Cuda cocked his head in Burt's direction. *"¿Qué pasa?"*

Flashing the Hawaiian hang loose sign, Burt replied in a distinctly Californian drawl. "Nada, space-dudes!" Before Stilt or Cuda could fashion a question, he suddenly ducked and looked away down the street, as if tracking some invisible fighter jet strafing the city. "Hey! What was that?"

Stilt followed his gaze. "What was what?"

Burt held an index finger to his mouth and cocked his head at the sky. "Wait for it...incoming!" The vagrant dropped to a huddled crouch on the sidewalk.

Cuda rolled his eyes. "Ugh—"

The vagrant stood, wiping his brow with an exaggerated gesture. "Whew! That was close."

Stilt swished the contents of the paper cup absentmindedly. "Burt, you heard anything about some new juice?"

The tiny man tiptoed forward, gesturing for Stilt to bend down so he could whisper a secret. Stilt followed the instruction, recoiling instantly as Burt bellowed into his ear. "Spock, you half-breed! I'm a doctor, not a Venezuelan call girl!"

Cuda shook his head as his friend cupped his deafened ear. "Oh, man. Stilt, don't waste your time."

Burt grinned. "Phasers on stun. Really."

Crouching down again, Stilt presented a much less threatening figure. "Burt, you gotta help us out, man."

The Sunset Street Prophet nodded in serious understanding. "Three to beam up, Scotty." He looked back over his shoulder, then proceeded to break into song. "I'm a-leavin' on a jet plane..."

Cuda sighed and turned away to make sure no one was staring at them. Stilt cocked his head, raising a slender hand. "Wait, what was that?"

"Jet plane, jet plane, don't know when I'll be—"

Stilt rose, handing the small man his Icee. "Thanks, man."

"Zingo! I was glad to do it! Wanna hear some Yes?"

Cuda frowned. "What the hell was *that?*"

Stilt sighed, looked around casually. "Oh, just something in his spiel didn't sound normal."

"Does it ever?"

Stilt gave a two-finger salute as he and Cuda walked away. "You take it easy, Burt."

Burt sipped from the red straw and flashed a peace sign. "Groovy."

13

THE WALL DISPLAY SCREEN above the nightstand read 3:04 p.m. Wednesday. Creep reclined on the plush four-poster bed, thumbing through a Kelly and Larry's digital magazine. *Masque* was an interesting premise, certainly not oriented toward the corporate lowest common denominator. It exposed fashion, entertainment, sports, politics, anything that had an interesting or controversial angle. He was intrigued.

He shifted against the pillows at his back, wincing as the clean bandage caught a stray barb of the household adhesive holding his wound together. The stained arms of the leotard hung down around his waist, bedclothes pulled up to his chest. He returned his gaze to the magazine, swiping curiously through the pages as Kelly entered through the double doors, laden with a thick stack of papers.

"Well, your little theory worked. I've got no less than a dozen endorsement contracts here." She approached the foot of the bed, dropping the forms one by one at his feet. "Zephyr, Alphabet, HenselTech, PepsiCo, you name it."

Creep sat forward, tossing the tablet aside. He scanned over the contracts like a spoiled child with a gift card in a toy store. "Great. How soon would we see some cash?"

Kelly gestured at a couple of contracts with large corporate credit cards clipped to them. "Some of them brought front-money with them." She was glad to see him rested and, on the whole, doing better than this morning. The gleam was back in his crystal blue eyes, the pleasant Cockney patter back in his speech.

She hadn't understood what everyone else saw in the Arena, why everyone was so fanatical about it. Now she could see —at least as far as Creep was concerned—the attraction. He had a weird charisma, a savage, almost animal appeal, a distinct likability. She even found him sexy, in an odd, "forbidden" sort of way. Perhaps it had been their proximity in the limo, and then the naked bullet removal in the shower.

What the hell was she thinking?

He reached out and snagged a form at random, briefly perusing the fine print. "Great. You looked these over?"

"They all seem pretty standard. A couple of commercials, photo shoots..."

Creep looked up at her. "No public appearances."

She shook her head assuredly. "No retail grand openings, or that kind of thing."

"Who wants me the most?"

"Zephyr. They're offering a million for an exclusive contract. Twenty-five percent upfront."

Creep blinked happily. "Two-fifty large. Do it."

Kelly smiled, raising a provocative eyebrow. "You're the Champ."

Dr. Noah Jorgenson blinked, tempted to snap Ridley's neck then and there. "You did WHAT?!"

The burly black scientist was perhaps 65, tight fringe of white hair encircling his weathered head. He wore small rectangular specs on his nose, and clenched his hands into tight fists. His face was just inches away from Ridley's, the white mass of his beard almost touching the young doctor's nose.

The Pawnee lab assistant stood watching in the corner of the briefing room, leaning against a new Braun water cooler. There was a single table, littered with work order printouts, project reports, and military contracts. Dr. Blake, a silver-haired, hollow-cheeked woman in her late fifties, sat at the head of the table, quietly watching the conflict. Barb, Dr. Jorgenson's pale, Nordic lab assistant, stood in the opposite corner by the door, nervously wiping her round glasses on the hem of her lab coat.

Ridley shrugged his shoulders, protesting the very idea that he'd done something wrong. "It was scrapped, Dr. Jorgenson."

Noah was furious. "Who gave the order?!"

Blake slid back in her chair and held up an officious hand. "I did."

Noah turned his anger on the head of the complex. "For what reason?"

Blake cleared her throat, tapping her fingertips together on the table. "Your funding was cut."

Noah strode angrily toward Blake and slammed his hands down on the tabletop. A plastic cup of water jiggled and splashed. "Since when does the government cut funding in the middle of a military experiment?"

"Since your military experiment proved completely disastrous."

"Disastrous?!" Noah Jorgenson stood upright, offended by the very premise. "The Kensworth Military Logistics series is our greatest triumph!"

Blake shook her head. "Was."

Noah turned toward his assistant, and the door. "Cut the crap, Blake. Where is he now?"

Blake shrugged. "Ask Ridley."

Noah swung around to confront the smaller scientist, again just inches from his face.

Ridley swallowed. "Uh, well, we...I just wanted to help, so we terminated him. He's vaporized."

Noah frowned. "You're a worse liar than you are a bio-chemist, Ridley."

Hurt, Ridley turned to Blake. "Dr. Blake, I don't think that was necessary—"

Noah waved him away. "Oh, shut up, Ridley. I can smell the graft on you. Dr. Blake, it is extremely important that we find the KML unit."

Blake continued tapping her fingers softly against one another. "Why?"

Dr. Jorgenson sighed, leaning forward over the table. He swung his head around to check Barb's reaction. She was still, her thin face devoid of emotion. He turned back to confront Dr. Blake, his visage creased with lines of worry. "Because he's intelligent."

Blake closed her eyes, let out an incredulous sigh, telling Jorgenson silently in her mind to say it wasn't true. But she knew better than to question one of the most brilliant scientific minds of the century on such a subject.

If Jorgenson said the KML unit was intelligent, Jorgenson *meant* the KML unit was intelligent. It posed a whole new ethical dilemma for them. Sentient beings had certain rights and privileges under the law. The director paused, rubbing her eyes while Ridley and his assistant looked on anxiously. Finally she spoke. "Very well, Dr. Jorgenson, retrieve your unit. Dr. Ridley, Mr. Michaels, I'd like to see you in my office. Now."

Creep couldn't believe his ears. "Twenty million?"

Love smiled, waving a hard copy of the deal memo in a pale hand. "That's right, Mr. Maddock. Susan Kitayama authorized the offer herself. Ten million a year for two years. Exclusive."

Creep stood, pacing the main room while Kelly sat watching from the edge of the enormous bed. Creep appraised at the man in the silk suit, cinching the waist of his own white terrycloth robe. "What's the catch?"

Love cocked his head, wrinkling his thick glasses up on his nose. "Catch?"

"What's the rub? What've I got to do?"

Love raised penciled eyebrows. "Well, Mr. Maddock, I don't know if she's even thought it through. Truth is, we wanted you first. Probably no more than endorsements, underwear ads, that kind of thing."

Kelly giggled from the bed. "Sounds good."

Creep squinted at her. He took the preliminary contract from Love and briefly pored over the contents. "Alright, look, Mr. Love. If your boss is serious, tell her I don't do cheap public appearances—no mall openings, that kinda thing. And I don't do hits." He took the expensive fountain pen from Love's outstretched hand and signed the document.

Love craned his neck back, a shocked expression on his face. As if the head of Kitayamacorp wanted a celebrity of his stature to participate in common corporate skulduggery! The very idea! "Why...of course, Mr. Maddock."

Creep smiled, handing Love the signed memo. "And you can tell her she's got a deal."

Love returned the gesture, vigorously shaking Creep's hand. "Very good, Mr. Maddock. I'll have the finalized contract sent right over."

"Cheers, Mr. Love."

Love gathered his briefcase, snapped it shut, and turned to leave. He paused at the double doors. "Good afternoon, Miss Hines, Mr. Maddock."

Creep waved, shutting the door behind him as he exited into the hall.

Larry entered from the adjacent room, yawning. "Who was that?"

"While you've been asleep," Kelly answered with a raised eyebrow, "the Champ has been offered about fifty million in endorsement contracts."

Larry's jaw dropped. "Holy shit."

Creep shook a hairy finger at them. "Yeah, but with this exclusive Kitayama deal, we're gonna have to duck out of that Zephyr thing. Never signed anything anyway."

Larry blinked groggily. "What's so special about Kitayama-corp that you're doing an exclusive? That's bad business, Champ. All your eggs in one basket, etcetera."

Creep grinned his jagged grin. "A: None of these piddly sports merchandising or software companies can hold a bloody candle to the security Kitayamacorp offers. We're talkin' penthouse plush, me ol' tart. Armed guards every-where we go. Fox won't be able to touch us. B: K-Corp has a historic disinterest in the Arena. So they've got nothing to do with Fox and won't turn me over. When they say they want me, I know they're probably snatching me away from a rival. I also know they ain't interested in negotiating price, so their offer beats any top bid we would have been able to scam from another company, which is bloody fine by me. And C: Less work for more money has always been extremely appealing to me."

He walked to the buffet, picked up a silver teapot and filled a china cup with steamy brown Earl Grey. "I think it's bleedin' marvelous business, mate. And we still have seventy-two hours to reneg on the clothing ads."

Kelly blinked. "Oh, speaking of which...Larry, could you take me downtown? I'd like to get some clothes."

Larry scratched his head. "Oh yeah, we kinda ran off in a hurry, didn't we?"

Creep leaned against the buffet and sipped his tea. "Go for it. I'm gonna stay in a while longer. Find me some silk shirts, will ya? Men's long, low neck."

Larry saluted. "No problem."

Kelly grabbed her bag and jacket, and sauntered excitedly to the door. "I'll take care of it. Boy, am I gonna have fun."

14

SUNSET HUNG in successive layers of violet and crimson beneath the blue-gray rain clouds as the daily downpour ceased and retreated into the early evening sky. The glass towers and steel castles of corporate America were still dripping with the remnants of the deluge.

All over the city, the streets sprang back to life as a half-million denizens simultaneously stepped out onto the sidewalk, checked their phones and watches, testing the air. Rain was five minutes late today. Lasted eight minutes too long. Stupid Weather Bureau.

In the sparse warehouse area of Sacramento and Drumm, beneath the towering twin spires of Kitayamacorp world headquarters, a solitary black panel van sat quietly on the curb across from the locked service entrance. A hundred feet of rain-slicked asphalt separated the security door from the lone vehicle.

It was Dennis Murray's favorite stakeout spot.

Inside the van, three vigilantes squirmed and fidgeted into black suits of ballistics armor. Dennis adjusted Cuda's shoulder harness and sat back on a wheel well. He too was clad in the armored SFPD jumpsuit, and he'd changed his nose bandage to a black one. His badge gleamed in contrast from his left hip. The other three had identical deputy badges.

Dennis began the class. "All right. First of all, this here's your basic ceramic and Kevlar SWAT anti-ballistics body armor. It can stop a .44 slug point-blank, but the concussive force can still knock you on your ass, so you're not invincible in the stuff. And you'll bruise like a mofo."

Van punched a gloved fist into his hard breastplate. It made a dull thump. "Cool."

Dennis stared at him, shaking his head. "Babysitting. I'm babysitting." He reached to his left and hefted a cylinder the size of a small tile knife in his hand. "Okay, secondly, this is your standard issue SFPD taser."

Cuda looked at him sternly. "We don't use guns."

Dennis threw up his shoulders, tossing it to Van. "Hey, man. Whatever floats your boat. Use your old socks for all I care. But you are required to carry them."

Van checked the weapon over in his hands. "Cool.

Dennis disregarded him. "This is a security bust. Our sources tell us that there have been numerous attempts to access classified files on the Kitayama system. We think it's someone working for one of the other bosses."

"Good reasoning." Stilt flexed jaw sarcastically.

Dennis scowled, unamused. "Spare me, will ya? All we do is stake the place out. If they show, we go in. We hit fast, hard and get out, understand? Grab anything you can as evidence, and no deadly force unless they bring it first. And follow my lead. No heroics 'til I give the word."

Stilt bent his knee and strapped the Velcro down on his boots. He would've preferred his tabis, but regulations were regulations. "What if they aren't outsiders?"

Dennis frowned. "Huh?"

"What if they work for Kitayamacorp? It's gonna be tough to spot them forcibly entering a building they have card access to."

Dennis wagged his head in exasperation. "Very funny. Just watch me, okay?"

Creep reclined on the bed again, scanning the evening newspaper headlines on the tablet, wincing at his photo, when Kelly and Larry returned to the suite. Their arms were laden with shopping bags from every expensive boutique in the downtown shopping complex.

Kelly huffed beneath the enormous bundles. "We're back!"

Creep tossed the tablet aside and rose to meet them. "Whatcha get me?"

Larry dropped half his parcels on the bed and wandered off to his room, still shaken from his shopping combat duty with Kelly. He'd never seen her spend with such frenzied enthusiasm before. Neither of them had ever had such seemingly bottomless resources before. "I'll see you guys later. Gotta go eat."

Creep browsed the bags Larry had dropped. "Find any silk shirts?"

Kelly smiled, exhausted. "Sure did."

"And what about you?"

She winked and gathered her bags, skipping off to the bathroom. "Just a minute. I'll show you."

Creep rummaged through one of the larger bags, found half a dozen shirts folded neatly inside. "Armani? Nice."

Kelly's voice echoed from the tiled room. "Try them on. I'm pretty sure they're okay."

Creep shed the fluffy bathrobe and flung it into the corner chair. The Lycra leotard had gone out in the garbage with the afternoon maid service, and he figured as long as Kelly was in the bathroom, he was in no danger of being seen au naturale. Not that it would have been all that scandalous. They'd been naked in the shower together. After such an intensely vulnerable moment, anything else was positively pedestrian.

He pulled one of the soft bundles from the bag, unfolded and slid into it. The shirt was big and billowy and made him look like an eighteenth-century romantic poet. David Maddock as Lord Byron. It was the current height of fashion, and it flattered him. "I'm almost afraid to ask how much you spent."

Again, her charming voice drifted from the bathroom. "Don't worry. We've got accounts at almost every department store in the Union Square 'plex."

Creep laughed. "Really."

"Yeah. Under 'occupation' I just put 'manager of publicity —David Maddock'. Under 'gross income', I put 'five-hundred-thousand'."

Creep choked. "Half a mil? Who said I was going to pay you half a million dollars a year?"

Kelly emerged, and Creep's jaw hit the floor. She wore an elegant black evening gown, probably a Meier design, with a plunging neckline that showed a generous portion of cleavage. The sides were slit, the hemline low. Her nude legs ended in a pair of gleaming leather pumps. Her hair was down, hanging naturally around her bare shoulders. He was glad he'd put on the big shirt. It hid a growing problem.

Kelly's lips parted and she wrinkled her freckled nose sarcastically. "Are you saying I'm not worth it? I've got overhead, y'know."

Creep swallowed, putting his eyeballs back into his skull. "Looking like that, you ought to get a million."

"Can I quote you on that?"

Creep grinned. "You most certainly may not. My statement was out of passion."

Kelly gave a throaty laugh. "Passion? Now we're talking."

"We are? I thought this was just meaningless banter."

"Meaningless?" Kelly repeated, feigning emotional distress. "You mean you *don't* like the way I look?"

"Why, Miss Hines, are you trying to get me to say something I'll later regret?"

"Me?" she inquired innocently. "I just want to know what you think of the outfit."

Creep went to the mountain of bags on the bed to search for some trousers. "You look absolutely stunning. How's that?" He found some gray slacks with a pleated front.

"Fine," she answered, looking him over salaciously. "You're not so bad yourself. What do you say we go out for dinner and dancing at the St. Francis?"

Creep took another look at her and swallowed again. "What do you say we stay in and get room service."

Kelly reached over to the hearth tools and grabbed one. "What do you say I hit you over the head with this fire poker?"

"I'll get me coat."

Dr. Jorgenson assembled his retrieval team at the loading dock. Ridley joined them, strangely enough, at his own request. Noah had refused any further involvement on his part, but Dr. Blake had insisted. A variety of sensory gear and stasis equipment was stacked and ready to be loaded. The roar of trucks leaving the motor pool reverberated through the cavernous loading area as the team gathered around.

Arriving at their destination in a squadron of military AVs wouldn't maintain the desired level of secrecy. They would go by ground, like the original delivery van.

Jorgenson reached up and ran a hand over his smooth, brown head, studying the group of scientists before him. Barb stood behind him, checking records on a tablet.

The first truck backed into its loading stall, speaker emitting the high-pitched, repeating *beep* of a cargo vehicle in reverse.

Noah held up a battered data pad. "Now, the shipping log says that our most likely truck is headed to San Francisco,

California. It is important that we handle this with the utmost care and discretion. The KML series were designed under military standards for desert warfare." He glanced from face to face, adding, "Do not forget that the 029 unit is intelligent."

A scientist with genetically-engineered emerald hair raised her pen from her own clipboard. "What exactly do you mean by intelligent?"

Noah pursed his wide lips, grasped his hands behind his back. "He has the capacity for abstract logic, emotional reactions, mathematical calculations and communication."

The group erupted in surprised murmurs. One staff member blinked wide eyes. "A war construct with emotion?"

Noah looked at the cement floor, then back at the man. "The intelligence factor was a privately-funded experiment. It was completely separate."

The black panel van sat, dark and silent in the dim haze of street lamps and artificial moonlight, across the parking area from the service door. Dennis lounged comfortably in the front seat, indulging in the cop stereotype by munching on a donut, while Stilt peered over the passenger seat and out the windshield. Van and Cuda reclined in the back.

Stilt suddenly turned his head, listening. Dennis caught the motion and turned to the visored contractor. "What."

The blast of LED headlights preceded a car. It was a large, luxury model sedan, black. It pulled to a quick stop just feet in front of the security entrance, and three men in overcoats exited the car, moving toward the door. They weren't overtly suspicious—their mere presence in this location at this hour was enough of a red flag.

Stilt squinted through the filtering shades. First guy: white, five-ten, one-eighty-five, balding. Ten gauge pump-action shotgun on a strap under his coat. Second guy: Asian, five-seven, one-forty, corrective glasses. 9mm auto, left shoulder holster, heavy rectangular object in right coat pocket, possibly a deck. Third guy: white, six-one, two-hundred, infrared optic enhancement in right eye. Ten gauge shotgun. Two others remained in the front seat of the car.

Dennis leaned forward, just now registering the men at the door. "There. That's them."

Stilt pulled away from the passenger seat.

Dennis pointed, chuckling softly over a mouthful of donut. "There's our bozos. Mighty big access cards, eh, skinny?" He glanced back over his shoulder. The rear of the van was empty. "Hey!"

Joey Chinn thumbed his round glasses and produced a Kitayamacorp Security key card from his pocket. Brushing the long black hair from his almond eyes, he looked back at the other two men and smiled. Reaching forward, he held it up to the door's security scanner. A green LED blinked once, and the door clicked open. Joey moved quietly inside the hall, and the other two men followed. The bald one paused to shove a metal vaporizer in the crevasse between the hinge and the door jamb.

They were in.

Dennis leaped softly from the minivan and racked the slide on his .45. He stooped, peering around the side of the vehicle to the parking area. Pezzoni was crouched by the rear bumper of the mystery car. He flagged Dennis toward the entry door.

"Shit." Dennis took a breath, sprinting across the open asphalt parking area toward the building.

The driver glanced out the windshield at the blurred shape passing through the doorway and did a double-take. "Hey! Did you see that?"

The second thug looked up from his portable game pad. "See what?"

Without warning, an armor-clad body wearing a black beret popped up from the back seat and smiled a scarred face into the rear-view mirror. "See this!" he answered, hauling their heads together with a resounding *crack!*

Joey plugged the cable into the interface jack on the security computer deck. He powered up the portable and began punching menus. The two backup men stood close, nervously watching the darkened windows and halls. Joey cursed and tried again. The security deck blinked red, and a one-inch data chip ejected from the console's protective housing. Joey grabbed it, held it up, and smiled.

"Easy peasy," he said, unhooking the cable from the console.

The bald one nodded. "Let's go."

"Howdy, boys."

All three turned toward the hallway. Stilt grinned back at them, chrome visor flashing blue in the low LED-light.

Cuda stepped into the office cubicle from the other side. "Nice night, isn't it?"

The tall thug whirled toward the sound of Cuda's voice, whipping out the shotgun. "Huh?"

Stilt folded his arms and leaned against the cubicle wall. "You're under arrest."

The bald man's shot knocked Stilt to the ground and about two paces backward. He swiveled as the man tried to run past, grabbing his legs. The man tumbled and they rolled together into the tiled hallway.

Cuda saw the barrel of the other shotgun swing in his direction and he ducked in plenty of time, crouching behind a steel desk. He took the opportunity to produce a theatrical groan of pain.

Joey brandished his Glock and moved toward the hallway as the second gunman circled the desk to finish off the cop he'd wounded. As the thug skirted the corner, the blur of a rubberized foot came at him in the dark, clipping his jaw. He felt his inner ear pop and his equilibrium invert as he fell to the ground.

Dennis entered as the man crumpled beneath Cuda. "Freeze! Police!" Unfortunately, he hadn't seen the struggle in the hallway. Joey sailed through the air, the loud thump of a titanium staff still vibrating his ribs. He landed squarely on his face, sliding twenty feet down the slippery tile floor.

Stilt twirled the long staff, whipping it around to strike the bald thug he'd been grappling with before Joey'd had the misfortune of tripping over them in the dark. The round end followed through, but the target was no longer there. Stilt spun to face the darkness. No one was there. Frantically, he scanned the interior of the dark office: Cuda, inside the wide cubicle, cuffing the tall guy; Dennis, in the hall, bending over to cuff Joey.

There was a deafening explosion and Stilt whirled around to see the last spark of a shotgun blast. He ducked instinctively, although he was nowhere near the line of fire. There was an unholy scream as Dennis vaulted forward, knocked to his stomach, smoldering from his unarmored ass where he'd been shot.

Stilt rose to his feet and scrambled for the exit, but the gunman was already gone. "Holy Christ," Dennis cried, clutching his peppered behind.

Pezzoni saw the bald one come leaping out the door at high speed. The young Italian was ready. It was obvious the thug was not expecting the getaway car to leap forward, engine roaring.

The young Italian smiled. He was just chock full of surprises. The flash of the car's brights blinded the man and he dropped the rifle, backing against the building's outer wall and shielding his eyes.

The car barreled ahead, and Pezzoni slammed on the brakes. Tires squealed, leaving a black trail of rubber on the moist asphalt as the front bumper slammed into the man. He crumpled forward over the hood, bent grotesquely where his legs were crushed.

15

THE HOSPITAL ROOM was white. A flat, pale, dead white. Dennis wished to God he had a tablet or printed book or magazine or *something* to read, instead of staring at the goddamn wall wondering what the hell shade of white it actually was.

Was it eggshell? Antique white? Ecru? Or maybe vanilla? It was too light to be cream. Oh man. He really needed something else to look at. His bandaged rear end throbbed warmly and he hit the remote button for another quick dispensation of morphine.

He was just getting back to the wall color debate when Cheryl entered, smelling of expensive perfume and wielding a huge bouquet of roses. She wore a dark gray fedora and a matching wool overcoat, wet droplets beading on the shoulders from the unscheduled morning rain. She looked down at the department's number-one undercover man, splayed out on his stomach, his butt concealed under collagen packs. He looked like a fetish performance art installation. She stifled a laugh and moved to the head of the bed where he could see her. "How you doing, sport?"

Dennis smiled at her, relaxing as the morphine took effect. "Well, my ass will be okay in a matter of weeks, but my pride won't survive the lynching it's gonna get down at the precinct, or back at the task force office."

Cheryl nodded, her dark curls bobbing on wet shoulders. "Yeah, you'll probably be the butt of a few jokes."

Dennis winced. "Nurse! Call the police! I'm being indecently assaulted!"

Cheryl laughed and removed her hat, setting it on the counter next to the bed. "Sorry. Couldn't resist. Listen, I didn't come here to give you a bad time."

"You didn't? That's a first."

"Nah, the abuse comes standard anyway. I came to give you these." She glanced down at the glass vase on the night stand, removed the previous flowers, and inserted the fresh roses she carried. Next to the vase she set a card, addressed to Special Agent Dennis Murray in ornate gold foil stamp. The other flowers hit the bottom of the wastebasket with a wet *thunk*.

Dennis eyed the new roses suspiciously. "Thanks."

"Hey, don't get the wrong idea, Murray. They're not from me."

"They're not?"

"No way. It'd ruin my reputation as a cast iron bitch. They're from Susan Kitayama."

"Yeah? Tigress want me on the payroll?"

Cheryl raised her shoulders indifferently. "Who knows? The envelope is an invitation to the gala concert she's throwing this week. Asano Tanaka. I think maybe she wants to meet the best of the best, 'cause I got one too."

Dennis peered at her from under raised eyebrows. "Your modesty is astounding."

"I know!" Cheryl shoved her hands into the outside pockets of the overcoat. "I'll RSVP for you. Stilt and those guys probably got invited as well."

Dennis scowled. "Those idiots. This would've never—"

Cheryl sighed, frowning at him. "And all three suspects would've never been brought in." She turned and shuffled over to the window, looking out at the throng of people and motor traffic on the wet streets below. "Things have changed since we got into this biz, Murray. You should relax, do your job and stop worrying about Stilt's boys. Something tells me Kitayama will be doing a lot more with these guys."

Dennis turned his head to the other side, resigned to the truth she spoke. "It smells, Cheryl. It smells like pee."

Cheryl gave another sharp laugh, heading back to the bedside counter to retrieve her hat. "Maybe so. But without some real cops out there to look out for the wannabes, it'd be complete anarchy."

"As opposed to only moderate anarchy?"

Cheryl sighed again. She contemplated patting him on the ass, thought better of it, and gave him a friendly slap on the shoulder instead. "We've got our own job to do, bro-ham." She flipped the gray fedora onto her head and moved away toward the door. "Get better. Failure to do so will result in immediate disciplinary action." She winked and stepped out into the hall.

Dennis grunted after her, returning his attention to the wall color and, after a few more moments, decided that it was definitely ecru.

Definitely.

Stilt entered quietly though the ground-level door, shutting it behind him. A small canvas bag of fresh produce from Washington's Grocery hung at his side, the warm aroma of fresh bread from the Judah Street Bakery lingering alongside. While the corporate arcologies were supplied with food from factory farms and agrochem companies, there were still a few family-owned farms and co-ops in the north and east Bay that sold fresh produce to neighborhood markets.

He cleared the first four stairs in one jump, his long legs skipping two at a time by habit. As he ascended to the top landing, Jesse peeked her head out of her apartment door.

"Stilt?" It was a silly question. She knew it was him. No one else had the same pattern of climbing the entire staircase in four steps.

He heard the hail and strode over from his door. "Oh, hey, Jess. How are you?"

"Fine. Kicking a little more." Her belly protruded from the space between the door and frame, and her legs kept the wombat from escaping.

"I guess that's a good sign," he said.

"Yeah." There was a scratching noise from the kitchen, and Jess turned her head to look behind. "Wulfshall! Get down!" She turned back to Stilt. "Wombats. Uh, listen. A courier came by wile you were out, dropped these off for you. I had to sign for 'em." She held out two identical invitations, laser etched in gold foil. One was his, the other was addressed to Cuda via his legal name.

He stared, finally taking them from her. "What are these?"

"I don't know. Looks fancy."

Stilt continued to focus on the envelopes, shuffling them over and over in his hands. "Okay. Thanks, Jess." He turned away, then caught himself. "Let me know if you need a partner for birthing class this week."

"Oh, hey. Thanks, but Mike said he'd take me." There was a strange gurgling noise from the living room. She turned again. "Wulfshall! Spit that out!"

Stilt grinned, pointing toward the sounds. "You'd better go take care of your wombat."

"Yeah. Take it easy, Stilt." She closed the door, yelling at the top of her lungs. "Spit it out! Bad wombat!"

Ridley and Michaels were not having a good day. It was bad enough that they were even on this trip, but the midday desert heat had just spiked 110 degrees and the van's climate control hadn't been functioning at all for the past hundred miles. Ridley was sure Jorgenson had assigned them this vehicle on purpose, for just that reason.

Tightening his grip on the wheel with one hand, he swiped open the home screen on his phone and invoked the virtual assistant. "Carmen. Call Monoped."

A muffled electronic pulse told him it was ringing at the other end. Another pulse.

A man answered. "Monoped Systems."

"Give me Bartak."

There was a click, and an old digital recording of Joy Division filled his ear. Michaels looked sideways at him from the passenger seat, running suntanned fingers through his auburn-tinted rooster crest.

Ridley followed as the lead truck accelerated and signaled its way to the freeway interchange.

"Bartak here."

"Bartak. It's Ridley. We've got problems."

"That's not exactly good news, Ridley."

"Damn right. Listen, the KML unit will be at your place tonight. Do us all a favor. Kill it and retrieve the formula before we get there."

"That was the plan anyway."

"Yeah, well now we've got the added timetable."

"Don't sweat, *amigo*. We here at Monoped pride ourselves on efficiency and punctuality."

"I'm not kidding, Bartak."

"Neither am I, *amigo*."

"I hope not." Ridley frowned and killed the call, shoving the phone back in his coat pocket. He looked at Michaels. "Everything set for plan B?"

The Pawnee scientist scratched his forehead. "And C and D and E. I think we're even up to L by now."

"Fuck," Ridley spat, angrily thumping the inside of the door with a tight fist. "This better work. Even if we kill the thing, it'll take five minutes for the code to dissipate." He glanced at the dashboard clock. Thursday. 12:18 p.m. A sign whizzed by them on the right: *Welcome to Nevada*. "Fuck," he repeated.

16

Aꜱᴀɴᴏ ꜱʜɪꜰᴛᴇᴅ beneath the cloth armor, adjusting his head within the wire mesh of the *kendo* mask. He bowed. This time, his opponent was real. Grasping his *shinai* in the traditional sword grip, he raised the bamboo weapon and let loose a sharp *kiai*. His smaller opponent responded in kind, and the battle cry was just as loud, if somewhat higher in pitch.

Wood met wood, and the crack echoed off the paneled walls of the *dojo*. Another frenzied exchange followed, and the private exercise room reverberated with the sound of bamboo and screaming.

Sweat trickled down Asano's face and he backed into a defensive crossover position, angling the *shinai* downward. His masked opponent saw the opening and stepped in, *shinai* whipping down in a clearly-defined head shot. With a simple crouch and fluid movement, he dodged the blow, bringing his own weapon up into his target's hands. There was a painful gasp, and his opponent's sword flew against the far wall. Asano stood and bowed.

His opponent returned the formal gesture, using the same movement to peel the protective mask off and lower the canvas hood. Raven hair spilled out, most of it pinned in a haphazard bun. Asano's opponent raised up, emerald feline eyes smiling, though her arms throbbed in agony. "Good shot," Susan admitted.

Asano was stone-faced and formal. "Thank you. You are getting better, Susan. Just don't take any opening that comes your way. You'll tend to get trapped."

She laughed, and the sound was like wind chimes to him. "I guess it's just dad's leap-before-you-look approach to business that's rubbed off on me." She frowned and lowered her voice, imitating her father. "Can't wait. Opportunity knocks but once. If you don't lead, you get left behind."

Asano shrugged the hood down, prying the mask from his head. He regarded her with a serious look. "Do you really believe that?"

"Buddhist philosophy would suggest otherwise, I know."

"I ask you again..."

"I don't know." She padded silently to the corner bench, billowy uniform flaring out as she walked. "If my father hadn't, he probably wouldn't have built a multi-billion-dollar corporate empire singlehandedly."

Asano set the padded coif on the bench next to Susan. "Who's to say?" His black cropped hair was matted and sweaty. The longer bangs were parted in the middle and hung down in his scarred face. His brown eyes shone playfully through stoic features. "Everything that must transpire will do so in its own time."

Susan laughed, tugging the sash on her *keiko-gi* and *hakama.* The uniform pieces fell away, revealing a trim, athletic form clad in a gradient blue nylon body suit. "Yes, *Sensei.*" She turned and rested her hands on feminine hips, watching him as he disrobed. He too wore a body suit, but it was black, and wasn't of a material Susan recognized. "How's practice? You ready for tomorrow night?"

Asano fixed her with a thin smile. "Do you want me to correct your overhead attack, or not?"

Susan blushed, eyes downcast. "Sorry. Your *dojo*, your lesson." She gently massaged her aching forearms. "We can talk music over lunch, yes?"

Asano sighed, shaking his head in amusement. "Now about that overhead attack..."

"Alright," she chuckled, stepping back into the center of the exercise floor. "Alright. Tell me about this terrible travesty of *kendo* I have performed."

Asano shook his finger at her. "Tch, tch. Attitude, Susan. Informality between student and teacher. Whatever would we do with you back home?"

Susan stretched out a leg cramp, still smiling sweetly. "Probably ship me out to the States with the *gaijin*. Guess I saved them a big step by being eighth-generation American."

Asano frowned in mock seriousness. "Don't be smart with me, young lady."

"Smart young lady?" Susan marveled. "*Tanaka-san*, you know flattery will get you everywhere."

Asano sighed. Admittedly, he enjoyed the banter. And her beauty made him forget the past. A past he desperately wanted to leave behind, where it belonged. A past that he'd tried unsuccessfully for ten years to accept. He knew she had more in mind for him than just the recordings and concerts. He didn't mind the idea.

It flattered him, especially the concept that she could see the beautiful, passionate artist beneath his butchered exterior.

There was one fatal flaw in the romantic alternative—one aspect within the whole wonderful situation that made it impossible to let loose the past and be happy with the present, to be happy with Susan.

She reminded him of Lani. And he could not forget.

Susan's physical resemblance to his former love could not be discounted. His mind would not allow it. Susan would forever link him to the memory of the night, a decade ago, when he'd lost his fiancee in the course of a single drunken moment. His life and body had been ripped inside-out, his pain almost too much to bear. Certainly too much to expect Susan to bear.

"Hello," she waved. "Ground Control to Major Tom."

Asano shook his melancholy away, allowing himself a brief smile. "Sorry."

Susan laughed as he picked up her *shinai* and moved behind her to put her arms in the correct position. "Bahamas nice this time of year, are they?"

Asano huffed and ran a finger across her elbow tendon, making her drop the wooden sword to the floor. "Oops."

She whirled around, raising the arm that wasn't paralyzed in a threatened backhand. Asano didn't flinch. Her eyes still smiled and her attitude was playful. She growled a perfect James Cagney. "Why you dirty...I oughtta..."

He laughed aloud, turning her back around. "Yeah, ya pushy dame? Yous and what army?"

They continued the lesson. Susan didn't learn much.

The regularly scheduled evening sprinkle was delayed, due to the Giants game in progress—in essence, the rain was called on account of a baseball game. Those not at Zephyr Stadium watching the game could be found in the hood, going about their evening business with the usual fervor. The streetlights were bright, white-yellow beacons suspended on steel limbs fifteen feet above the sidewalk. It was warm, the humidity high from ionized particles of moisture, on hold until the end of the ninth inning.

The air smelled of urine and sweat.

It seemed as if everyone was on the streets tonight. The avenues were filled with tiny, three-wheeled electric city cars and leather-clad bikers astride powerful Hondas and antique combustion Harleys. Couples of every ethnicity and gender wandered the shops, hand in hand, sampling ethnic delicacies from all over the world. Even considering the relatively benign atmosphere at the moment, volatile elements were being brought together in a warm, wet environment. Something would happen tonight.

The southwest corner of 27th and Moraga in the Sunset was home to Mae Wong's place, a sort of all-night pan-Asian takeout, tea house, and sushi bar. Blinking neon spelled out the woman's name in faded pink bamboo letters. A service window opened to the street, and there was a faded brown resin picnic table in an old parking space in front, complete with an antique meter that had stopped working decades ago. Steam wafted from the holes in an iron sewer cover nearby.

Stilt ambled toward Mae's, hands swinging at the sides of his intercooled nylon jacket. Blue neon phosphorescence from the inside collar cast gloomy shadows over his unshaven jawline, reflecting off the silver rings in his ears. Thick gray cotton baggies and blue plastic-plated neoprene *tabi* shoes rounded out his uniform. The titanium staff was broken down into its two shorter components, strapped securely into the twin sheaths on his back.

Cuda strolled alongside, sufficiently clothed in a purple muscle shirt and neon blue fiber optic windbreaker. Nylon track pants and high tops covered his lower portion. Pezzoni wore his usual studded leather biker jacket, faded Levi's and huge Nike high tops. His black beret was cocked to the left, as usual, and a white Neopigs concert shirt hung untucked, the tail billowing from under his jacket. "So...you guys gonna go?"

They approached the window and paused. Mr. Chen waved from across the street. Stilt nodded at the elderly man and returned his attention to the service window. "I am."

Cuda laughed. "Hell, yeah. Chance to get down with the big fish in the little pond."

Mae Wong appeared in the window, silver-gray hair piled up and pinned in place. Her eyes were dark, and her friendly smile belied years of social and economic injustice. "Hallo, boys!"

Cuda leaned forward to the window. "Two coffees, Mae."

The woman made a soft clicking sound with her tongue. "Stilt? You want something?"

"Green tea. Thanks, Mae."

Van shuffled his feet on the grease-stained sidewalk. "I still think it's a little weird."

"I know what you mean." Cuda agreed. "It's all happened real fast."

Stilt sighed, shrugged unconvincingly. "Hey, it's simple. Somebody likes us." He snapped his knuckles under finger-less gloves.

Cuda gave a nervous chuckle. "...said the spider to the fly."

"No shit," Van snorted.

Stilt stared at them, the pink neon from Mae's sign creating rivers of light the color of cotton candy on his visor. "Would you two quit worrying? It'll be fine. This is what we've been waiting for."

Cuda pointed at him. "Yeah, but nothin' comes to you on a silver platter." Mae set the bio-plastic cups out for them, and shook her head when Stilt reached for his wallet. Cuda smiled and bowed courteously, heading for the picnic table.

Stilt leaned against the tabletop, while Van and Cuda each simply rested a leg on the bench. "Hey. If nothing else, it'll be some good classical music."

Van pointed down his throat. "Classical? Gack."

Stilt caught his younger friend's display of disgust and slapped him softly upside the head. "What do you think corporate bigwigs listen to, Viking death metal?"

"They'd be more fun to hang out with if they did," Van shrugged.

Their subdued laughter was interrupted by a familiar voice hailing them from the sidewalk. Burt approached, wearing a San Francisco Giants baseball cap, one lens missing from his glasses. A bright orange fish tie from a lost decade hung loosely around his neck. "Greetings, time travelers!"

Van cringed. "Oh no."

"Gentlemen," Burt declared, "that...*thing* outside is eating our ship!"

Stilt humored him. "Is it really?"

"Shhh!"

Cuda looked down at the funny little man. "What."

Burt cocked his head, listening to the air. "Wait for it..."

Van laughed incredulously, waving a thumb at the vagrant. "The hell is he—"

Burt suddenly ducked away from the table, throwing tattered, skinny arms over his head. "INCOMING!"

Stilt's gaze shot toward the night sky in sudden realization. "Jesus!"

"Stilt! What's up?" Cuda worried, reaching for his friend.

"He's right! Cops! Headed this way!"

Van's eyes flashed wide. "You're shittin' me—"

Cuda turned, glancing into the hazy night air. "Van, when Stilt hears cops, you better believe there's cops!"

The AV was over them only seconds after they heard the siren. It banked directly overhead, filling the street below with twisting air currents, sending dust and litter swirling around them. The sonic wave as it shot away down the street made Cuda spill his coffee. "Shit." He quickly wiped the front of his muscle shirt as Stilt vaulted from the table, sprinting after the flying car.

"This way!"

Van and Cuda followed, hot on his heels.

Burt raised a scrawny fist. "Use the Force, Luke!"

The patrol AV banked and turned several times, siren screaming, leading them deeper into the Sunset District. At the corner of 30th and Ortega, just three blocks from the old reservoir, the cop decelerated and fishtailed into a tenement alley. Three more blocks behind, Stilt scanned the air for dust clouds and ion trails only he could see. Cuda and Van pounded the pavement after him.

Stilt rounded the corner and skidded to a halt in front of the alley. The flashing red and blue strobes sent tall shadows of the vigilante into the street. There was no traffic here; all the avenues in a four block radius of the reservoir had been closed off for years, ever since the GEO movement blew up the powerhouse with about twenty pounds of C4.

Cuda clomped to a stop next to his tall partner. Van was close behind, breathing hard. Without a word, the three entered the alley, moving quickly into the vacant lot behind the tenements. This was truly a slum.

The lights from the squad car flashed brief glimpses of an old apartment building bordering a huge lot behind the two larger structures. Old timey clotheslines and makeshift network cabling stretched from building to building, from level to level, creating a miasma of spider web shadows. Wood and plaster pueblos for the working poor. Soft dirt under their feet: one small portion in a city of concrete foundations and asphalt streets.

A cement wall hinted at the former shell of a fourth tenement, probably burned out long ago in the fires that followed the bombing.

The AV was on the ground—its high powered forward searchlight had caught a large Hispanic male in its broad beam. He was stock still, backed against the single wall, a limp female form draped over his bulging arms. The man was a behemoth in baggy shorts, sandals, stained tank top torn and bloody. He stared into the light, hypnotized like a wild animal in the road.

The door to the small tenement on the left was open, swinging in the evening breeze. A moan echoed from the broken upstairs window.

Stilt ran to the driver's side of the squad car and flagged his young partner. "Van! Get inside! Check it out!"

Pezzoni ran. The officer glanced up from his seat, stepping out of the car altogether. "Hey! Hold it!"

Cuda passed him. "We're contractors! Kapp, Tokura and Pezzoni!"

"Uh, hold on a second." The cop turned toward his vehicle, tapping his headset.

Stilt moved forward, holding his hand open to the giant caught in the light. "Hey, *amigo*. Put her down."

The man's response was blunt. "Fuck you, pig!"

Stilt held up both hands, approaching slowly. "Not pigs. We live in this neighborhood. Come on, man. Just put her down. Let her go." This wasn't working. He stopped and glanced back at Cuda, who took several cautious steps toward the man.

"Come on, *amigo*. She don't look too good."

The man blinked red-rimmed eyes and looked down at the unconscious woman in his arms. Her flower print dress was ripped and hung off her emaciated body in shreds. She was covered in abrasions. The hulking giant sniffed and blinked again. "Oh, man. She don't look good, huh?"

Cuda approached, padding carefully past Stilt, stopping scant inches from the man. "No, no she don't. Why don't you just put her down, okay, bro? I'll help her. Nobody's gonna hurt you."

"Oh...okay. Uh-huh. Here."

Cuda gingerly took the unconscious body from the man's arms and backed away slowly. "She's gonna be okay, bro. It's all good."

Van's voice rang out form the upstairs tenement window. His timing couldn't have been worse. "Where the hell are the EMTs? We got a live one in here!"

The man shivered, snapping out of his docile state. "No! Oh shit! No! Give her back, *amigo*!"

Cuda continued to back away. "She's gonna be all right, bro." He cast a sidelong glance over his shoulder to the cop on the radio. "Can I get some help here?"

The man twitched again and reached a huge arm outward. "No! Fuck you! Rosita! I'm sorry! Give her back." He began to move across the lot toward the squad car and Cuda. The close up view of Stilt's titanium staff stopped him in his tracks.

"We're here to help you." Stilt looked him over carefully. The man's acne-scared face was dripping sweat and spattered with blood that clearly wasn't his own. His eyes were beyond bloodshot—they looked almost hemorrhaged. There was a single hypodermic track mark on his broad neck, near the carotid, the surrounding area discolored with shades of yellow and black. Stilt's pulse shot up when he saw the man's lips. They were thick and purple, as if all of the blood vessels in his body had expanded to twice their normal size.

Just like Kevin's had.

"Fuck you, *puta!*" A steel fist rocketed out and Stilt felt his ribs give way. How the hell had he done that so fast? Stilt landed, rolled and leaped back to his feet. He was instantly airborne, flying at the man, swinging the staff like an industrial sized baseball bat. The man raised his right arm automatically, and Stilt could hear the crack of bone snapping. The behemoth simply continued toward the car.

Stilt swung again, leaving a small dent in the man's forehead, but he trudged slowly forward, unfazed. His eyes were locked on Cuda's silhouette, kneeling over the unconscious woman in front of the police car, grunting as he counted off his CPR. Stilt swung again with full force, bringing the chrome staff squarely into the side of the man's head. It should've brought the guy to his knees. Hell, it would have decapitated any normal human.

The man launched out with his fist again, a supersonic open palm punch to Stilt's solar plexus which sent him flying. He landed ten feet away and rolled weakly to his knees, coughing. What the hell was going on? He shouldn't have been able to do that. Stilt should've been able to see it coming. Still the man marched forward.

Cuda's dark outline against the blinding light of the car was broken as the officer stepped out in front. He hefted the AR carbine and took aim. "Get on the ground!"

The man continued, blood leaking from his nose and scalp where Stilt's staff had hit.

"On the ground!" the officer repeated.

The man stepped forward.

The first slug hit his right shoulder and exploded in fragments of steel, bone and muscle. Blood painted the compact dirt, and he kept walking. The cop adjusted his aim and fired again. The shot tore open his abdomen, spewing blood and pieces of large intestine.

He continued.

The third shot ripped his left thigh to bloody shreds. The fourth and fifth hit dead on in the chest. His ribs shattered and blood bathed him from head to toe.

He still didn't drop.

The sixth and final shot took his right kneecap clean off, and the man sank to the ground, covered in gore and mumbling incoherently. The last words from his swollen lips were, "*Jesucristo perdóname.*" He slumped forward onto his face, less than two meters short of the car.

Van trudged over to the enormous blood-spattered corpse, eyes and mouth wide with horror. Six shots at close range from a police carbine. *Six.* "Man, what is this shit?"

Stilt came up behind him, staring down at the mass of mangled flesh. "Something we don't want to hit the big time." His ribs ached and he could feel a massive bruise beginning to form.

"Aww, fuckin' ay!" Cuda's anguished voice rang out from the front of the car.

Stilt turned. "What is it?"

Cuda jumped to his feet, throwing futile punches into the air. "She just died on me, man!"

Van put a hand on his lanky companion's shoulder. "Christ, Stilt. That's eight people here."

"Eight?"

"Eight. My live one crashed. There's five more in the hall and on the stairs. It's a fuckin' slaughterhouse, bro."

Cuda was furious. He leaped forward, grabbing the man's dead body by its bloody shoulders. "Motherfucker! You fucking son of a bitch! You killed 'em all, you fucking—"

Stilt dropped his staff, reaching out for his friend. "Easy, brother. Easy."

"I fucking hate that! Every damn time I see that happen!" Cuda began sobbing silently, and Stilt knew why. The situation was too damn close to his own history. He'd seen his wife and baby son go the same way, but consumed in flames instead of the mad rampage of a juiced-up predator.

Stilt turned his friend around and embraced him in a tight bear hug. That night long ago remained etched in his memory. He'd pulled all three of John's family from their burning home, had been the one trying to force life giving breath into the scorched dead lungs of his wife and little boy. He'd even been there when John wanted to eat the barrel of his cop revolver.

John dropped out of the police academy the following day, walking away from what had become the family trade.

It had taken Stilt three years to get him out of that state of depression. Nowadays, one would find nothing even resembling a firearm in Cuda's home, or on his person. But at times like these, Stilt felt as if the grieving process was set back years at a time. "I know. We all do."

The officer finished his audio report, turned down his headset radio and shut off the spotlight. "Looks like you boys check out. You wanna stick around? I could use some help with this mess."

Stilt ran a gloved hand back through his dark hair. "Pezzoni and I will. But we'd better send Cuda home."

Cuda looked up from the man's huddled corpse. "No. I'm staying."

Stilt moved toward him. "Look—"

"No! I'm staying!" He protested, gradually softening his tone. "I need to do this. I can handle it."

Stilt recognized the earnest need for Cuda to move beyond his own personal tragedy, finally clapping him on the shoulder. "All right. You're staying."

17

THE MAN WAS STOCKY, dark-haired, like a young, Slavic Raymond Burr. His pinstriped suit was Armani, his tie Chinese silk. He looked to be about forty, ruddy complexion stubbled with whiskers of salt-and-pepper gray. The light from the Archon workstation reflected against his artificial retinas, giving his brown Nikon orbs a devilish glow. The palatial glass office was dimly-lit—as he preferred it—and sparsely decorated with African masks and vintage hand weapons from the Middle East.

It was entirely appropriate and within character. Monoped Systems was in the business of weapons. Guns, missiles, personal armor and defense, deep sea and space technology. If it was propelled from point A to point B, Monoped could design it, test it, manufacture it. They were especially helpful if it exploded on contact with point B, or protected point B from the explosion.

The desk console chirped electronically. He shifted his hand from the Archon's touch screen and hit the comm button.

"Mr. Bartak, there's an unidentified delivery from GTB at the west gate."

The man squirmed in his artificial leather chair. "Thank you, Gordon. I'll be right there." Servos in his left leg whined almost musically as he stood. His limp was barely perceptible. The Hitachi cybernetic leg processed the nerve impulses from the flesh stump, matching the stride of his other leg with ninety-eight percent accuracy. Although many forms of cancer were now curable, such medical technology had not been available when a random sarcoma had claimed his leg at age 14. Thank goodness for micro-servos.

Bartak exited through the door of tinted bulletproof glass —Monoped Catalog Number PA9-220—ambled across the vomit-green industrial carpet to the elevators and punched the number for the ground floor.

The west exit bordered on 8th and Market, cement and steel rising from the foundation of an old Greyhound depot. The delivery area was open and well lit from above by long solar cable lights. The plain white pharmaceutical delivery truck was parked diagonally in the yellow zone, engine silent, lights dead. The stocky Asian driver leaned against the side of the vehicle, digital clipboard in hand. Two armed guards stood at the ready, Uzis slung at their sides.

Bartak strode through the outer doors of the west lobby, left leg whirring, servos buzzing as he approached. "I'll sign for it."

The driver noticed him and extended the tablet, scratching his balding head. "Thanks. Should I take it around back?" He watched Bartak press his thumb to a small light-emitting surface on the datapad and hand it back to him.

"That's all right." Bartak flagged the guards behind him. "Guys, come over here and give me a hand with—"

It sounded like a car bomb exploding.

Bartak instinctively drew a SIG P226 from a concealed holster and fell to the ground as the rear door of the truck was ripped apart by a flurry of savage pummeling from inside. The metal parted like dry cardboard, the driver hit concrete, and the guards followed suit.

Bartak looked up and saw the angular, almost equine muzzle, the low brow and wispy blond mane. It looked at him with sapphire eyes and vaulted forward through what remained of the sliding steel door. It landed silently—wide, two-toed feet absorbing the immense weight of its dense frame. It was short, maybe only four and a half feet tall, but its torso was that of a deformed linebacker, rippling alien muscle patterns beneath a taught, bristly hide. Its arms were long, almost apelike, with two fingers and an opposable thumb on each enormous hand. Thick, yellowish nails sprouted forth from the digits and toes, and its chest and the yoke of its back were covered with sprouts of longer, auburn hair. It leaped again, coming down in a defensive crouch several meters behind Bartak.

Bartak rolled to get up and found his guards already taking aim with their weapons. His mind raced. If the beast were killed here, right now, with no facilities ready, they would not be able to extract the code within the allotted five minute dissipation delay.

"No! Put them away! Get my car out here! And radio Dispatch and Retrieval! Move!"

The guards turned and sprinted inside, and the creature made a cautious circle of the shadowy front loading area. Its eyes never left Bartak, and vice versa.

The driver stood, staring wide-eyed. So that's what was in the crate. He moved behind Bartak, and the creature disappeared, ducking between shadows at the far end of the parking lot, vanishing out into a side alley near 8th and Mission.

"...the living fuck wassat?" the driver mumbled.

Bartak stared after it for quite a while.

Darkness posed no problem, once the pupils adjusted. The vehicle headlights were tough, however. Amber text scrolled through its heads up display.

AVOID MAIN STREETS.

Impulses shot through its brain, a biological reaction from electro-chemical DNA encoding. Responses were immediate, thoughts computer-accurate but at the same time organic in origin.

NARROW ALLEY. 1.95 METERS WIDE. OPTIMAL. LARGE PUDDLE. JUMP.

FELINE QUADRUPED, HOSTILE. RANGE: 6.8 METERS. AVOID.

CHAIN-LINK FENCE, HEIGHT: 2 METERS. CLIMB.

STEALTH LANDING. SCAN PERIMETER.

GPS LOCATE: SAN FRANCISCO, CALIFORNIA.

NARROW GPS LOCATE: 9TH AND HOWARD. DOWNTOWN.

SEARCH MEMORY: NOAH JORGENSON.

LOCATE.

NEGATIVE.

PRIORITY: SHELTER.

LOCATE.

SCAN PERIMETER.

ELLIPTICAL HORIZONTAL PORTAL. RANGE: 7.3 METERS. PROBABIL-ITY: SEWER SYSTEM.

BINGO.

SCAN LEFT: CLEAR. SCAN RIGHT: CLEAR. STEALTH.

PORTAL LOCKED. OPTIONS: LOCATE TOOL, CONTINUE.

SCAN PERIMETER. STEEL REBAR: INSUFFICIENT PHYSICAL IN-TEGRITY. FELINE QUADRUPED: INSUFFICIENT RIGIDITY.

PERIMETER ALERT. HUMANOID BIPED. HEIGHT: 1.7 METERS. RANGE: 10 METERS. ATTEMPTING ENTRY INTO STORAGE AREA. IRON BAR. LENGTH: 1 METER. SUFFICIENT RIGIDITY, SUFFICIENT PHYSICAL INTEGRITY.

ACQUIRE.

The Filipino kid turned a second before the bristly tank hit him square in the abdomen. He managed a startled, "Holy Christ—" before rocketing through the air, landing twenty feet away against a commercial dumpster.

Tilting his head groggily to one side, he watched in dream-like horror as the hunched monstrosity gathered his crowbar from the moist street, testing it on the asphalt with a couple whacks. Satisfied, it turned, flashed a toothsome smile at the youth and—was that a wave?—vanished down 9th Street. The kid heard a brief succession of metallic clangs and scrapes, and he cautiously rolled to an upright position, straining to see into the distance.

The hollow roll of a bent sewer cover vibrated in the distance, sundered steel rasping and wobbling to a stop next to the empty access way.

18

Vehicles and people littered the west entry. White trucks, white coats, sensory equipment scattered across the covered asphalt of the parking area. Noah Jorgenson stood imposingly over the shaken figure of the Asian delivery driver, Barb nervously tapping notes on a portable deck.

Bartak was gone, left for the evening, according to the night receptionist. Ridley stood well out of Jorgenson's way, listening anxiously to the testimony of the driver.

Noah folded his arms and glared at the frightened man as he sipped coffee from a bio-plastic mug. "How long ago?"

"About twenty minutes, I guess. Maybe a half-hour. Thing just broke outta the crate and ran off!"

Ridley inhaled, adrenaline pumping. "Michaels! Get the dogs! We've still got a chance!" He pulled open the back of his truck and hauled out an enormous sniper rifle.

Noah was furious. "What do you think you're doing?"

Ridley frowned innocently. "We are authorized to use tranquilizers, Doctor."

Noah turned to Barb and grumbled under his breath. "It's a damn lynch mob."

The bark of a hound echoed in the covered area, and Noah turned to see Michaels and another team member holding the leashed harnesses of a half dozen tracking hounds.

Ridley jogged over to them as the rest of the team pulled out the remaining equipment. Michaels tugged on one of the nylon leashes. "Looks like they have a scent."

"Great," said Ridley, "We'll track it on foot." Reaching into his pocket, he produced a small handful of 7.62-millimeter sniper rounds, slotted them, one by one, into the magazine. He glanced over his shoulder. Noah was securing his own equipment with Barb and hadn't seen. He leaned over to Michaels and smiled mischievously. "For self defense."

As the team dispersed, Noah turned to Barb, handing her a small electronic box, roughly the same size as a hand-held video game.

"What's this?"

"Tracker. He's got a subdermal GPS chip in the cervical area of the spine." Dr. Jorgenson hauled the van door shut.

Barb looked at him. "You mean, Ridley doesn't—"

Noah shook his head. "No one does. Except you and me. Keep it that way."

"Sure."

Noah scanned the shadowy area of the parking lot where the team had stared their search. He glanced at his own electronic tracker. They were a long way off, but on the right trail. "Shit. I hope we can find him before Ridley." He shook his head again and the two scientists followed the trail of the team. "That boy's done something to my construct. I'm gonna nail his ass to the wall."

TIME? UNKNOWN. ADJUST TO LOW LIGHT CONDITIONS. FOLLOW SEW-
ER LINE WEST. PROGRESSION OF MURIDAEAN QUADRUPEDS. SIZE: 24 TO
26 CENTIMETERS. NUMBER: APPROXIMATELY 50. THREAT: NONE.

CONTINUE.

How now, spirit! Whither wander you?

Over hill, over dale,

Thorough bush, thorough brier,

Over park, over pale,

Thorough flood, thorough fire,

I do wander everywhere,

Swifter than the moon's sphere...

HALT. SCAN PERIMETER. TURN RIGHT AT JUNCTION.

ACT TWO, SCENE THREE. CONTINUE.

O, I am out of breath in this fond chase!

the more my prayer the lesser is my grace.

Happy is Hermia, wheresoe'er she lies,

For she hath blessed and attractive eyes.

HALT. TURN LEFT. CONTINUE.

How came her eyes so bright? Not with salt tears:

If so, my eyes are oftener wash'd than hers.

No, no, I am as ugly as a bear;

For beasts that meet me run away for fear:

SCAN LEFT. SCAN RIGHT. HALT. MAIN FLOW HEADING WEST. KEEP
STRAIGHT.

ACT THREE, SCENE TWO. CONTINUE.

Up and down, up and down;

I will lead them up and down:

I am fear'd in field and town;

Goblin lead them up and down.

The creature grasped the iron rungs of the access ladder
with perfect dexterity. Upper and lower limbs climbed in sync,
enormous muscles rippling. It was at the manhole cover in
moments. It studied the mechanism for a brief second and

determined it was locked. Squatting down low on the iron rungs, it launched its upper body toward the steel barrier.

Arthur rolled over and blinked crusty eyes open. His long, unkempt gray beard hemmed a weather-beaten face.

What was that noise?

He reached out and jostled the man next to him: a skeletal black man in fatigues and a Navy watch cap. The skinny man groaned, sitting up slowly, painfully. A blanket of pink bubble wrap slid from his artificial legs and blew away down the street. "Aww, man. Look what you done."

"Shaddup man. Listen."

There it was again: the sound of slamming metal. It seemed to be coming from the street. "The fuck is that, man?"

"Dunno," replied the second man. "You check it out."

Arthur hauled himself upright, staggering to his feet. The avenue was empty—usually was, this time of night. He checked the traffic anyway, then trod carefully on spindly legs toward the column of escaping steam. There was another slam, and the rising vapor was momentarily interrupted.

Arthur stopped, noticing the large, raised dent in the manhole cover. He glanced behind, arctic army jacket buffeted by the advancing late-night wind. His friend had gone back to sleep.

"Yaah, chicken." He waved a dismissing hand, turned back toward the manhole and was immediately knocked on his back by the rocketing steel disc. The creature leaped from the opening and landed in a crouch, scanning its surroundings. Its eyes registered the unconscious vagrant on the pavement, and it reached out a large, pad-like finger. Suddenly its attention was drawn upward by the deafening roar of a police AV on low approach.

The officer blinked, looked again. "The hell was that?" He gestured at the street below.

His partner shrugged. "Hit it with the lights again."

The forward spot swept in a reverse arc, bathing the street in artificial light. A skinny homeless man lay unconscious next to an open manhole. The cover was nowhere in sight. "Stupid tweakers. You tell 'em the sewage gasses are toxic, an' they still go down there to keep warm."

"Want me to call it in?"

"Nah. Let him sleep it off."

The patrol car banked left and shot away into the city.

19

SUNLIGHT BROKE stark white over the Mission District like the flash of an atomic bomb. Today would be a hot one. Life-giving heat filtered down through the hazy gauze of low cloud cover, becoming trapped between the sky and the street, creating the sensation of a reservation sweat lodge.

The retrieval team gathered near the corner of 24th and Castro. Dr. Jorgenson and his assistant were nowhere among them. The electric hum of early city cars pierced the morning stillness.

Ridley signaled the rear, slinging his rifle. So far, the retrieval team hadn't attracted too much attention, despite the presence of tracking dogs, sniper rifles and a sea of white lab coats. Of course the city cops didn't usually patrol the streets without a specific mission. Still, it would only be a matter of time.

The party shuffled to a halt. Michaels crouched near the carcass of another hound. It was a mammoth beast, a huge, wiry haired, genetically designed Irish wolfhound. Its neck and spine had been snapped in eight places. Ridley approached, kneeling beside the Pawnee scientist. "Another one?"

Michaels squinted into the distance. "That makes four since 6:00 this morning."

"Fuck."

"You said it, chief."

Ridley turned to glance at the assembled group of suspicious-looking scientists behind him. "We've got to split up. Jorgenson's already gone off by himself. The locals aren't gonna be especially tolerant of a bunch of whitecoats toting around guns and shit."

Michaels rested his jaw on a clenched fist atop his knee. "Whatever. But it went this way." He nodded forward. "And if the local law enforcement turns onto it before we can, we're in some deep and stinky shit, *kemosabe*."

"I hear you." Ridley stood, marching back to the assemblage with grim certainty. "Where's McDowell?"

An auburn-haired youth, tall and spindly, turned and stepped from the crowd. "Yo."

Ridley approached and laid a solid hand on the young scientist's shoulder. "Get back to Monoped. Get your Carnivore unit and meet us at Portola and Clipper in twenty minutes."

McDowell stared in shocked surprise at his elder colleague. "You want to bring in the CRN04?"

"That's the one. And bring a truck with you."

"You got it." The scientist saluted and moved off to hail a cab. Ridley waved a couple of additional assistants after him. "You go too." He turned and proceeded down 24th toward Market Street, fished a pack of nic-sticks out of his pocket and cooked up. "C'mon, people. Let's catch us a beastie."

Stilt found Cuda in the *dojo*, kneeling center-mat in meditation. He was still, his breathing slow and measured.

Moving silently in his school *dogi* and *tabi* socks, the slender vigilante found a seat on the bench that stretched the length of the east wall. Despite his stealthy entry, Cuda could sense his presence in the room, stirring from his serene state.

"You ready?"

Stilt paused on the bench and breathed deeply. "Pezzoni coming? Said he wanted to practice today."

Cuda laughed, with volume. "Sleeping. The weenie." He rolled back, getting his feet beneath him, and stood to begin a well-practiced warm up routine.

Stilt chuckled. "Sure he's not gonna back out of the invite?"

"Awww, he'll be there. It's his uncle Vincenzo who's doing our tuxes for tonight. He'd be a prick if he didn't show. Speaking of which, we gotta go get measured."

Stilt shook with silent laughter. "I'll take a twelve, extra-long."

"You wish, buddy. I got the package delivery in *this* family." Cuda swung an arm across his chest, pinning it with the other to stretch his tricep.

Stilt rose from the bench and moved to the mat next to Cuda, joining him in the warm up. "I guess Windy stayed over at Van's place Tuesday night."

Cuda sighed. "It's none of our business, *amigo*. It's between them."

"Well," Stilt reasoned, grunting as he twisted at the waist, aggravating his bruised ribcage, "it's gonna be our business pretty darn quick if she keeps hanging with Bug and his boys. He could ID us though her. Then what would happen?"

"Okay," Cuda acknowledged. "I hear ya." His head rolled around the pivot point of his neck, and he felt the vertebrae crackle as it went. "Speaking of Bug," he added, "do you think we'll have enough to go after him anytime soon?"

"Dunno. We heard him on the mic Monday night. Said something about 'pure-strain Jet'. Then Kevin wigs on some new shit, and Burt sings a song about a jet plane. The poor hombre last night was shot up with the same stuff as Kevin was, I'm sure of it. Only had one hypo mark in his neck, no other tracks. Then there's Fisk's kid on Tuesday. Fuckin' un-real."

Cuda stepped into *Heiko dachi*, parallel stance, his bare feet gripping the mat. "So, we know that Bug's selling some-thing new. And all of a sudden, we got fuckin' superjacks rip-ping people up, taking six slugs from a police carbine to drop..."

Stilt rotated his shoulders and swiveled his neck. "And did you see the blood come outta that guy? His veins must've been twice normal size. His lips and eyes were bursting, man." He took up position beside Cuda, allocating enough distance for both to be able to go through their *katas*.

"So you think it's the same shit."

"I do."

They began their movements, synchronized in perfect time to one another.

"Some mean jack, brother."

Stilt exhaled. "I know, I know. That's why I'm hoping this Kitayama woman will put us on Bug's ass. I want the mother-fucker. I really want him. We can't have this Jet stuff in cir-culation. It's like..."

"What?"

"Well," Stilt mused, extending his left fist in a mock punch. "It's almost like I've seen that effect before."

Cuda frowned. "What. The eyes and lips and shit?"

"Dunno," Stilt puzzled. "Jet's supposed to be new, but how come I remember seeing images of those same symptoms?"

"Was it on the news or something?"

Stilt shrugged. "I don't think so. Would've been a long time ago, maybe back in Imazu."

The two men fell silent, pondering as they went through their forms. They said nothing else about the new drug or its creeping influence in their neighborhood.

"We canceling class today?" Cuda wondered, completing his *kata*.

"Nah. I'll call Elizabeth and Jason in. No need to cancel just because we have to get measured for formalwear." Stilt bowed at the framed photo of Master Hisako hanging above the *tokunoma* alcove in the main wall. Cuda followed suit.

"Bro, I cannot wait to see how ridiculous you look in a tux."

Stilt smirked, causing the visor to raise on his slender nose. "Meh. I'm not too worried about you and me." He turned to leave with a chuckle. "But Pezzoni shall be the lightning rod of ridicule for many moons."

20

BUG RAISED A SHOT of Irish whiskey to his lips and pounded it back, exhaling nigh-combustible fumes through flared nostrils. The sleeves of his new Armani silk shirt were rolled up to his elbows, and a Chinese necktie hung loosened around his collar. Feeling the warmth spread through his stomach, he set the heavy glass on the wet bar and poured another.

Four days, still no sign of Dennis. Eh, give him another couple to come whining, bitch about getting busted, bitch about the money, plead for another chance to sell the new shit.

Bug frowned. He didn't want to admit he needed the guy at the retail end of his operation.

The ridged metal doors slid open with a monstrous industrial scraping noise, and the Lexus rolled on thick wheels into the hazy, half-illuminated warehouse. The engine shut down, and Biggs stepped from the passenger door, followed by Quan from the driver's side.

The gargantuan bodyguard strode forward with a stern confidence.

Bug met him behind the leather sofa, nervously holding another shot in a bejeweled hand. "'Sup?"

Biggs didn't smile, though his face cracked like it. "We won't need the girl after all. I just checked with Pick. He says Susan Kitayama has an entire file devoted to these guys."

Bug gave a cognizant grunt. "Well, now. Ain't that nice? The Tigress has her own little corporate hit squad."

"I don't think it's a squad. It's just Kai Tokura, he's the stick-man."

Bug raised a skeptical eyebrow behind dark shades. "Tokura? Oh, man. Not another Pac."

Biggs affirmed the racial insult. "Yeah. Him an' John Kapp. And some guy named Van Pezzoni."

Bug slammed the shot, curling his lips away from his teeth. "A Pac, a wop and one brother outta the bunch. Jeezus." Quan disregarded the slur, went to the bar and pulled a large, silver can of lager from the tiny fridge.

Biggs moved to the couch, reclining with his feet on the cluttered coffee table. "Yeah. Tokura and Kapp run a karate school over on Irving. And...they just got a contract with the SFPD."

Bug paused and blinked hard, rage seeping across his upper chest with the heat of the alcohol. Finally he turned, inhaled. "Take 'em out."

Biggs sneered. Now they were talking. "What's the plan?"

Bug spun and smacked the back of the giant enforcer's head. "Plan? What's the plan? Take 'em out! That's the plan!"

"How?"

Bug rampaged, winging the glass at the side of the Lexus with a savage ferocity. "Find the building, blow it up. I want 'em out of the way, understand?"

Biggs sat forward, stood slowly and deliberately. He rubbed his eyes and spoke calmly. "There's other people that live there, Bug."

"Fuck!" Bug sprang into a furious whirlwind, kicked the side of the AV and hauled the couch over on its back, forcing Biggs to leap to his feet.

A candy wrapper spiraled silently to the dirt floor next to Bug's Italian shoes. He was instantly calm, breathing deeply, running fingers through black, curly hair. "Look, Biggs. You can't handle it, you get your big white ass off the bus and I'll give it to Quan or Raoul."

Biggs shrugged. "Hey. Who said it was a problem? I was just sayin'—"

Bug held up a hand, shaking his head impatiently. "I don't want to hear any more talking." He turned to Quan. "Huh? Okay? I want these boys dead." Throwing an accusatory index finger at Biggs, he added, "You can come talk to me all you want, after they been removed."

Biggs aimed a quiet glance at Quan. The young Thai shrugged and guzzled his beer. Biggs threw up his arms in resignation. "You're the boss."

Bug's jaw set sternly and angrily. He nodded. "Damn straight."

David Maddock sighed and leaned back in the enormous memory foam chair. The meeting table in Susan Kitayama's office was littered with printed documents, electroplated gold pens and white mugs of coffee. Kelly and Larry lounged on either side of Maddock, thumbing through papers and perusing fine print that may as well have been literally Greek to them.

Susan stood and leaned forward over the table, resting on her palms. Her suit was corporate black, her hair pulled back in a tight bun. Love reclined on the plush sofa, basking in the heady atmosphere of another potential acquisition.

Susan peered at Creep over tinted readers. "Well, Mr. Maddock?"

Creep looked at her, blue eyes dancing excitedly, though his outward appearance was solemn. "Let me see if I have it." He folded slender, furry hands, laid them on the table in front of him. "You're lookin' to do an image rehab for corporate law enforcement. Am I right?"

Susan pursed her lips, pushed away from the table. The sunlight from the tinted windows behind The Desk created a halo effect around her head and shoulders. "I guess you could say that, Mr. Maddock."

"I think I *did* say that."

"We just want to improve conditions in the inner city, bring the streeters back into the fold."

Larry leaned over to Kelly, whispering sarcastically, "What does that even mean?"

Creep bared his pointed, fang-like teeth. "Ms. Kitayama, I was a streeter myself. Shadwell, East London. Trust me. They don't want to come back into the fold. They've got their own economy, their own system o' justice. They're quite happy where they are. Havin' the filth pokin' 'round under the pretense of Justice For All only pisses 'em off. Everyone knows you can't trust the cops unless you're a suit."

Susan jutted a hip out to one side, and folded her arms defiantly. "That's exactly the attitude we want to change. We have a group, a squad made up completely of streeters from one of the local districts. They are going to return faith in law enforcement to the common people—"

Creep rolled his eyes. "Don't shit me, Ms. Kitayama. I know what you're doing. You want me to enhance their image by making appearances for the benefit of the press. It's to make you look good at Kitayamacorp, like you're doin' a community service."

Susan smiled. "Yes."

"Good. Now that we're being straight with each other, why don't you tell me what their real purpose is."

Susan huffed, chewed a nail and folded her arms again. "That is their purpose. I'm willing to take Larry here as your driver, and Ms. Hines may do as she sees fit. Perhaps she would consider Kitayama funding for her magazine."

Kelly's eyes brightened. She looked over at Larry, who was lost in paperwork.

"All we want from you, Mr. Maddock, is a few news appearances."

"I told you I don't do public—"

Susan scowled, leaned forward on the table. "They wouldn't be supermarket openings or conventions. Consider them endorsements for Kitayamacorp. We send our boys out to do the dirty work, Larry can drive you to the site, when the scene is secure, you jump out and arrest a couple of bad guys for the news cameras. Ms. Hines can have the locker room exclusives."

Creep mulled it over in his mind and took a sip of coffee. "So my presence would be as a celebrity *ronin*, and would lend credibility to this...operation."

Susan smirked, pushing away from the table. She liked him. He spoke his mind—a negotiator after her own heart. "That's right, Mr. Maddock. Your safety is guaranteed."

"So, I'm like a fake cop."

"Mr. Maddock," Susan smiled, resting her hands on slender hips. "You of all people should realize the media value of theatrics and deception. It's an art."

Creep swallowed a warm gulp of coffee and set the mug on the table. "Fair enough." He leaned back in the soft chair. "Alright, I'll do it."

Susan approached him with absolute glee, extending a hand. He stood, tucking in the loose portion of his shirttail. "Provided the concessions to Kelly and Larry remain in the contract."

"Of course, Mr. Maddock," she replied, shaking his shaggy hand with unbridled enthusiasm. She watched as he signed the large paper on the table. "I think this calls for a celebration. Will you three please be my guests at the Asano Tanaka concert tonight at the Opera House?"

Kelly shot to her feet and offered her hand. "We'd be pleased to."

Larry shrugged and stood, jamming his hands into the deep pockets of his black trench coat. "Sure. Thanks."

Creep handed Susan the contract. "Tonight, then."

Susan grinned. "Tonight. 8 p.m. Formal attire."

"See ya then." Creep shook her hand once more, and the three filed out of the office into the executive lift. Love stood and waved to them as the doors slid shut. Susan's smile dropped, and Love noticed.

"What's the matter, Susan dear?"

She turned to the computer console, flipping the monitor up from it's housing. The look of the Tigress returned to her eyes. "Bastard better be worth it."

Love blinked. His slicked-back hair was almost like transparent, ridged plastic in the softened sunlight. "Susan, relax."

She smiled at him, green eyes hard and predatory. "I'll be okay, Love. Just have to keep telling myself how ironic it'll be for Frank Selby to be neutered by his own pet."

Love wagged a finger. "Not his pet anymore. Yours."

Tigress leaned over the console and punched up a database. "That's right. And won't it be fun to watch?" Her fingers tapped out an executive cadence on the keypad, colors flashing, text exploding on her eyes and face, reflecting in psychedelic patterns across her glasses.

Love planted his feet, watching intently. He grinned. "Susan, you naughty girl."

21

NOAH JORGENSON glanced down at the sensor and frowned. "Damn interference." He swore silently at the electric Honda three-wheeled bubblecar as it buzzed past.

Barb shuffled to the curb in front of him, scanning the crowd of pedestrians at Haight and Market. The panhandlers were out in force, begging legless in military camos, veterans of a thousand forgotten wars of the past decade. Unconcerned suits strolled casually by, either unseeing or unconcerned. She turned back to her mentor. "When we had the lock, it was pointing back downtown."

Noah squinted through his rectangular specs. "Right. He's doubling back, leading us in a corkscrew." They had ditched their rather conspicuous lab coats in a scrap metal dumpster four blocks back. Noah rolled up the sleeves of his plaid Oxford shirt, loosening a navy blue knit tie. His oversize khaki trousers snapped and billowed about his stocky legs, revealing bare brown skin, leather deck shoes and no socks.

Barb was clad in a simple yellow t-shirt and blue jeans, with a khaki photographer's vest. Her short, curly bob ruffled in a warm breeze. "Where do you think he'll go next?"

A police AV made a high pass overhead.

Noah scratched his bald, brown head, wrinkled his nose. "The pattern would indicate a westward progression. We may want to head further in that direction and cut him off when he returns to course."

Barb nodded, extending a slender arm to approaching traffic. "Taxi!"

The plain white truck came to a squeaky halt where Clipper Street intersected Diamond Heights Boulevard, two wheels up on the sidewalk, hazard lights flashing. McDowell hopped to the pavement. "Dr. Ridley! Where do you want it?"

Ridley turned, waving the young scientist and his team to the position they had taken a block away, near the Market Street offramp.

The two assistants yanked open the heavy back doors, and one man jumped onto the bumper, lowering the hydraulic lift to the sidewalk. The crate was immense, two meters tall by three meters long, a rolling steel/titanium cage with a gunmetal fiberglass shell. Small holes in the bulky, oblong box hissed and sucked, as air was pumped in and out by powerful lungs. The assistants popped spring-loaded handles from the side of the crate and began to guide it forward.

"So this is the Carnivor," Ridley admired as the group approached. "You think it can do better than the dogs?"

McDowell *harumphed* at the comment, patting the top of the box. A low snarl escaped through the oxygen holes. "If you've got a scent, this baby'll pick it up, follow it, hunt down your KML and kill it. No sweat. This prototype tested with positive results in the Chimera Search-and-Destroy Simulations."

Ridley rolled his eyes. "Yeah, spare me the infomercial, will you? We're gonna lose the trace here."

McDowell saluted, and the two assistants swiveled the front of the crate toward the residential area above the Market Street overpass. "Ready when you are, Dr. Ridley."

Ridley secured his rifle, tightening his grip on the shoulder strap. He glanced up at the structure, teeming with transport. "It won't have problems with the traffic, will it?"

McDowell shook his head. "It's trained to follow the scent in a roundabout way if necessary, adjusting for traffic conditions and population."

"Very well then," Ridley smiled, "If you please, Dr. McDowell."

McDowell slapped the top of the crate. "Release the unit."

There was a metallic click as the front door released, and a scaly claw reached out into the light. The retrieval team backed away behind the huge box as the CRN04 unit stalked cautiously forward onto the city street. Crouched over on all fours, the thing was a hideous amalgam of canine, reptile and primate.

Its head was long and flat, a huge reptilian mouth overflowing with jagged teeth and dagger-like incisors. Tufts of shaggy, steel-black spines thrust backward from its stocky neck in a frightening punk hairstyle. The musculature of its shoulders and upper torso was like that of a gorilla, long arms tapering almost gracefully to scaled talons, and its lower portions resembled that of a bear or badger. A tail was conspicuously absent from the tip of its bony spine, which looked as if mutant armadillo armor plates had been welded there.

Ridley whistled through his teeth. "Most impressive, Dr. McDowell."

The young scientist smiled proudly, folding his arms. "Just watch it work."

The team followed slowly as the beast lumbered down the sidewalk, sniffing air currents and testing the ion trails on the white concrete. Suddenly, its head snapped up, and it was off. The team scuffled excitedly after it, and Ridley smiled to himself. Now they were getting somewhere. He'd like to see that little KML unit try to snap this thing's spine like it had done to the hounds.

The group came to the corner and watched as the killing construct deftly scaled the supports of the offramp. Ridley squinted and the smile dropped from his face. The piercing bellow of a 10-ton electric Peterbilt blasted from the curve, and the thing shrieked a split-second before impact.

The creature opened like a spring bloom, organs exploding onto the grill and bumper, muscular limbs crushed under tons of speeding force.

The truck honked again and sped away down Diamond Heights Boulevard, the driver convinced he'd hit a sick dog.

Ridley stared blankly at the dark smear on the warm pavement, crimson tracks leading away in the semblance of tire treads, the chunks of wet flesh and tufts of mangled fur as they began to bake in the sun.

McDowell blinked and began to sob.

KML029 leaped softly from the chain-link fence to the pavement below. Its left arm was ripped and bleeding through a strip of torn muslin. Two sets of bite marks oozed from its neck and right shoulder. Flared nostrils tested the air, instinct prodding him forward onto the green carpet of nature in the midst of this chaotic techno-jungle. It scanned the grassy plaza through deep-set eyes, shifting beneath the shadow of a medium-sized elm. Two South African businessmen in matching silk suits shuffled casually past, swinging chrome briefcases in their arms and mumbling confidentially. The creature rolled silently under a vacant park bench, scanning the structure across the street: City Hall.

The men passed. It squeezed out from under the wooden bench, turned away from the plaza and dashed down a column of cement stairs, into the darkness of the underground parking garage.

Stilt twisted, examining the black tuxedo jacket in the un-flattering yellow-orange light of the tailor shop. He glanced up at the floor-length mirror, cocking his head. A tux on Stilt was like motor oil on mashed potatoes: It may look like the real thing, but just wasn't right.

He turned around again to check on his companions. Cuda looked even more out of place, with a mismatched paisley cummerbund and tie, his white athletic socks shining in high contrast to the formal black trousers. Stilt smiled, chuckling to himself. Van stood with arms outstretched, looking quite the Christ figure as Vincenzo Pezzoni measured him efficiently, yellow tape a blur of motion as the old man shouted numbers into the air. It was for his own benefit, more than anything else. He liked yelling, liked waving his aged hands in the air.

"Okay, Giovanni! That's all for you! Go sit and I'll make the alterations right now!"

Van shrugged and shoved nervous hands into the pockets of the tuxedo trousers, wandering aimlessly toward the chairs lined up next to the mirror. "Thanks, Uncle Vinny."

"Giovanni! The trousers, boy!"

Van blinked, then realized he needed to give the pants up. He sighed, dropping them there on the spot. Stilt and Cuda applauded, and Uncle Vincenzo threw up his hands in resignation. "What is it, Lord?" he asked, peering up at the ceiling. "What did I do to deserve this nephew and his friends? I try to be good. Why can I not have a normal family, Lord?" The old man bent to retrieve the crumpled trousers, and Van stared after him as he hobbled to the sewing room.

Cuda nodded at Van's choice of undergarments, neon purple boxer-briefs with a random pattern of yellow stars. "Nice. Windy give you those?" He stifled a laugh.

Van simply flipped Cuda a middle finger and flopped down sullenly in one of the enormous chairs. "I'll be glad when this whole thing is over, man."

Stilt checked his reflection again, held his long hair back and decided he'd better ponytail it for tonight. "You thinkin' you want out, Van?"

The young man shot him a confused look. "No. I'm just saying I don't like getting all dressed up for some suit who just wants us for PR."

"You don't know that."

"Aww, come on, Stilt. What, you think she wants to do the community a service?"

"Maybe she does."

"Bullshit."

Stilt turned to face him. He was getting used to the confining space of the formal attire. "I repeat: we don't know that. We should at least give her the benefit of the doubt. I'm sure she doesn't want the kind of PR like Monday night's bust on her property."

Cuda folded his arms. "Both o' you gotta chill, man. Go in open-minded, y'know what I'm sayin'? Just think positive. We're already dressed for success, and...well Van here, he's dressed for some kinda *major* success." He gestured at the purple briefs, shaking his head. "Whoo! Them's some serious love clothes, boy."

Van scowled, spreading his legs wide in the chair. "Drink it in, Becky."

The two tall men looked at each other, throwing their hands up in a perfect imitation of Uncle Vincenzo. "Why me, Lord?" they asked the ceiling in perfect harmony.

Asano adjusted his black silk bow tie, jutting a scarred jaw at his reflection in the bedroom mirror. The concert line-up was surging through his brain like a runaway locomotive: Begin with the Litolff scherzo, get the audience on his side. Then, a segment featuring pieces by George Winston and Akiko Yano.

He'd sneak in an original composition next, the one he hated least. Then the Sakamoto, as a tribute to Lani. Once finished, it would close a painful chapter in his memory, forever. And the finale, And the finale, the 3rd movement of Rachmaninov's *Piano Concerto No 2*. It would be a fitting close, a dynamic, difficult piece that would wow the suits and make them talk of the event for years to come.

He finished his tie and peered at his image in the glass. The mangled face of a dead man stared back at him, and he closed his eyes.

Japan. The hospital. The news.

The anger.

He'd limped out of the hospital in his bloody slacks and a loose gown, his face still swathed in bandages, his veins still full of morphine.

The endless wandering.

Wandering without aim or purpose. Out of the city, into the green countryside. And then, finally, at wit's end and half delirious with pain and morphine withdrawal, he'd stumbled into the wooded retreat of a bizarre, monastic collection of cowled priests. He'd thought maybe they were hallucinations.

They weren't.

They were real.

Solid. Flesh, bone, blood.

They were mostly Japanese. Ex-soldiers with a venerable Korean master, an unusual structure in Japan's rigid social order. They healed him, brought him out of the morphine dependency, accepted him as society's outcast.

They taught him their way, to return to the old values of harmony with nature, taught him the art of mystic *hwarang-do*—the healing techniques, the extra-sensory perception, the fighting forms. They tried to get him to accept his past and work toward improving his future.

He learned how to transfer energy from one source to another destination, how to move on the wind, unseen and unheard. He learned the silent, priestly art of serenity, but was never able to apply it to himself.

Five years later, he was still angry, unable to let the memory of Lani's death go. He was unwilling and unproductive, they said. If he was incapable of letting go of his own hate and fear and depression, then he was unworthy of their attempt to do so for him, unfit to walk the path of the *hwarang* priest.

He was asked to leave, again an outcast in a world that seemed all too eager to swallow him back up. He had seen only one possible alternative before him: America, Susan Kitayama and his Yamaha grand.

This concert would do one of two things, and then he'd know for sure: It would cleanse his mind and soul, free his spirit from the nightmares, the waking dreams, the ghosts of his former life. It would allow him to experience life again with the same passion as when he was a young man. Or it would reawaken all of the demons from within, sending him back down into the grim psychic abyss.

And that simply meant that he would die.

It was up to the music to decide.

22

ITHIN THE NEWLY renovated walls of the Louise M.
Davies Symphony Hall, a small army of stage hands
and multimedia techs ran through the cues for the imminent
show. The stage was dark, a single black grand piano illuminated by a soft purple spot from above. Beneath the giant instrument, several techs made last-minute adjustments to the
orchestra pit that would hold the fourteen-piece chamber ensemble.

The cavernous auditorium was vacant, save for a couple of
ushers, making the rounds with carpet sweepers.

Outside the hall, the setting sun cast its orange cloak over
the city. Something moved in the shadows of the alley behind
the health center across the street.

Strained blue eyes peered nervously left and right. A drop
of coagulated blood dropped to the dusty street. The eyes

blinked, searched the area again, then the shadow backed away.

At 7:30, they began to appear: the tuxedo-clad, smiling corporate executives and their surgically-perfect spouses and partners, the local sports celebrities, ranking law enforcement, political figures. All expensively bedecked, the sparkle of designer jewelry glimmering from every wrist, neck and earlobe. The silk was real, the expensive leather vat-grown and shiny.

To witness Kai Tokura and John Kapp getting out of a two-seat Honda city car was to witness the reverse of a perplexing theoretical impossibility: how the hell had they gotten *in?* It looked like a hundred clowns climbing out of a Volkswagen, only the clowns were sitting atop one another's shoulders and dressed like a single concert-goer in black formal wear. Van revved his bike into the underground parking slot next to Cuda's electric city car, rolled to a halt and shut down.

"Well," he remarked, locking his helmet in place and stripping the gloves from his hands, "here goes nothing."

The trio marched across the grassy plaza, Stilt waving at the occasional streeter. Every single one of them did a double-take when they saw the Irving Street *Yōgosha* clad in formal attire.

"Stilt?" someone asked, passing by.

Kai turned to face an elderly black woman wearing a threadbare army blanket and scorched Keds wrapped in silver duct tape. "Yeah, Mol. It's us."

The woman cracked a wrinkled, toothless smile. "Holy Moses. I never thought I'd see the Shihodo boys become suits."

Stilt smiled, dug into his pocket for some cash. "Well, don't give up on us yet. It's just for tonight." He handed her two fives. "Now, Mol, I want you to go down to the Goodwill and get yourself some shoes, okay?"

The ancient woman smiled endearingly. "You bet. God bless the three o' ya." She nodded at Cuda and Van, and hobbled away down McAllister Street.

They crossed silently in front of City Hall, almost reaching the Symphony stairs before Cuda broke the quiet. "That was cool, bro. But you won't have nothin' left over if you keep up that shit."

Stilt ascended the concrete steps, not looking back at his partner. "I'm in it, man. I can't help it. What do you want?"

"Just think about yourself once in awhile, that's what." Cuda sighed, jamming his hands into the front pockets of his tux trousers.

They entered through the wide series of open doors and flashed their invitations at the security forces, clearing the scanners without a hitch.

Van looked like a completely lost kindergartner on his first day in a new school, staring at the array of sculptured beauties and glittering bejeweled outfits.

Stilt managed to locate one beacon of familiarity in the milling sea of corporate fish, and he headed straight for her. Cheryl was dressed in a very fashionable Goddard evening gown, draped with a fiber-optic feather boa. Her spike heels were a deep gunmetal blue, like the dress, and her tightly braided hair was pinned up in the ever-popular Japanese style.

Cuda's jaw dropped. She looked amazing.

As the trio approached, they noticed she was locked in a friendly conversation with a slender Asian woman wearing a black satin Dieter Meier sleeveless gown with long gloves and a similar hairstyle to Cheryl's.

Cheryl turned tough brown eyes toward the approaching men and smiled politely. Susan gave a tentative bow, and the three men returned the greeting.

"So these are the gentlemen responsible for saving our company secrets two nights ago," she observed.

Cheryl gestured at Stilt, a mild note of cynicism in her voice. "Susan Kitayama, this is Kai Tokura…"

"Stilt," he corrected, shaking her hand graciously. "Nice to meet you."

She looked at him quizzically, a smiling glint in her eyes. "Stilt?"

"Yes. Cuda, er, John gave it to me—"

Cuda pushed Stilt aside and offered his hand. "Forgive him. Rented lips. John Kapp. Pleased to meet you." He pointed a thumb at the uncomfortable young man next to him. "This is Van Pezzoni."

Van nodded, shaking Susan's hand. "Pleasure's mine, ma'am."

Susan flashed brilliant white teeth, the grin of the Tigress returning. "No indeed, the pleasure is mine." She turned back to Stilt. Her Tigress look melted, and she folded her arms, sipping a glass of champagne to mask her internal confusion. "So, you run a *dojo*, I hear. What style?"

"It's a hybrid style," Stilt explained. "We call it *shihodo* ."

Susan nodded, getting the meaning immediately. "The way of the four directions. Very poetic. How long have you had the school?"

Stilt pursed his lips, and Susan blinked, glancing away briefly. What the hell was going on? The bubbles from her glass tickled her nose, and her stomach grew warm.

"John and I just bought the school about two years ago," Stilt answered, scratching his recently clean-shaven jaw. "But I've been teaching about ten years."

Susan feigned interest, cocking her head provocatively at the tall gentleman. "And how long have you been aiding the police?"

Cheryl huffed, raising her glass to her lips. "Longer than I care to mention."

Stilt glanced at Cheryl, then back at Susan. "It's pretty rough in the neighborhoods. Kids can't walk to school without getting mugged or abducted or sold to."

Van sighed and looked away casually. "Here he goes."

Stilt continued, oblivious. He had Susan's attention, and as long as he had it, he might as well give her the pitch. "John and I teach kids not only to defend themselves, but to take back their neighborhoods."

Susan smiled, took another sip from her glass. She wondered what his eyes looked like under the chrome visor. "Interesting. In essence, you're vigilantes."

"Well, the cops don't do much in the neighborhoods—" Cheryl cleared her throat and Stilt balked. "Present company excepted, of course."

Love suddenly descended upon the group but focused solely on Susan, ignoring everyone else. "Has Maddock showed?"

In the Fairmont suite, the thick polyfill comforter had become a makeshift tent, and the giggles of hotel bedroom games leaked out from underneath.

The structure shifted, and there was a surprised feminine gasp. "Oh, my. You shaved there just for me?"

Love sighed. "Ah, well. We'd better get moving. It's almost time."

Susan handed her half-empty glass to Love and bowed to her guests. "If you will excuse me, duty calls. I've got to go emcee this little event. Love, will you take everyone to my private box? I'll be up shortly." She ducked away through the gathering lobby crowd and the house lights flashed twice.

Love guzzled the remainder of the champagne in Susan's glass and set it on the bar. He paused momentarily and frowned as the dry carbonation swelled in his throat. It was an act that, performed by any lesser man, would have been considered a burp. "If you will?" he beckoned, pointing the way up the side stairs to the balcony.

The auditorium filled from wall to wall, a sea of excited faces and bored stares, a flat field of corporate humanity packed efficiently into a prime specimen of late 20th century modern architecture.

Stilt, Van and Cuda found seats in the private box near the balcony railing, and Cheryl took a seat next to Love. Echoed mumbling soon gave way to applause as the spotlight found Susan Kitayama center-stage, in front of the piano. She wore a small wireless mic earpiece, and the bright follow spot illuminated a few of the ensemble musicians, sitting patiently in the pit, already tuned. The rest of the stage was bathed in the soft purple of LED spots suspended from the overhead grid.

Susan held until the applause died, then gazed out at the darkened hall. Four personal security guards flanked her, out of sight of the public: One offstage on either side; One on each end of the front row in the audience, near the fire exits. A major corporate player could never be too careful. Some of these business folk probably weren't too thrilled with Susan. Some had been executives in companies that'd sunk in the voracious K-Corp "acquire" phase two years ago.

She smiled sweetly at the assembled crowd. "Thank you very much. Thank you for coming. I'll try to keep this short, as I know you're all waiting anxiously for the same thing: The triumphant return performance of the maestro, Asano Tanaka!"

The auditorium erupted in a spatter of applause and polite theater whistles. Asano, gaunt and regal in his black tux and tie, strode purposefully onto the stage. He wore a paisley vest of swirling gold and purple designs. The severity of his scars seemed diffused in the harsh light of the follow spot.

Susan met him halfway, leaving him with a friendly kiss on the left cheek. He bowed graciously at the audience, then turned and faced the giant Yamaha grand, settling onto a padded bench in front of the acrylic keys.

Silence fell quickly, a blanket of anxiety in the midst of the celebration, and Asano cracked his fingers to stop them shaking.

This was it.

The falling circle of light from the towering street lamp was shattered by the fall of an oversized shadow. Once again, bioengineered eyes pierced the dark, scanning back and forth down the street. A few tired leaps across Mason Avenue, and the unit found itself treading upon soft grass.

The "Panhandle" of Golden Gate Park.

Equine ears flipped up from their stealth position and twitched in the evening breeze. The thing crouched, scampering once again into the shadows as the bark of a dog echoed two blocks away.

Asano's fingers clutched the keys like talons, striking each and every note in dexterous, rapid succession. The opening piece moved, and the chamber ensemble was good. It warranted exactly the applause it received.

He gave a brief nod of thanks and went immediately into the selections from George Winston's *Autumn,* and continuing the theme with *Autumn Song* by Akiko Yano. They were equally popular with the crowd, and he forced himself to breathe steadily, anticipating the Sakamoto. But that was a way off yet. He still had to get through to the intermission.

The construct stopped, peering out from behind Strybing Arboretum. It scanned left, locating the source of the smell: Two humanoid bipeds, armed with rifles. A third, armed with a single sidearm, hobbling forward on a cyberleg. It could hear the dogs on MLK Drive, the scientists closing fast.

LOCATE DR. NOAH JORGENSON.

LOCATION UNKNOWN. CONTINUE WEST.

It leaped into the street, rolling to a running start. There was a sharp crack of gunfire, and it heard the dogs howl as they were let loose.

The steady cadence of tribal rhythms was unexpected, and produced a shocked murmur throughout the crowd. Two Senegalese musicians with drums slung in front of them strolled onto the stage, hammering out a steady, moderate beat.

Asano actually smiled as the woodwinds picked up the atonal opening of composer Stella Chen's *Ritual*. It was certainly upbeat—and it was short, Asano merely plucking out the adorning chords with sleepy, relaxed hands.

He knew it would get a standing ovation, and it did. Suits like to think they're intellectual, and even something shoved into the performance as an eclectic joke is often treated as high art.

He stood, took a low bow, and strolled from the stage. The lights came up for intermission.

KML029 rolled and found itself in the middle of Lincoln and 17th. An Asian couple making out on the bench at an old bus stop looked up and screamed, dashing away into the night.

The creature bared its teeth, more out of fear than aggression, and continued its run to the shadows. Another shot rang out, and this time its left shoulder blade shattered. Thick crimson spattered the ground, and it scrambled desperately for the darkness across the street. The savage barks of dogs just meters behind it spurred the engineered creature onward, and when it looked up, it saw the glow from a stained-glass window.

The lights dimmed again, Asano taking his seat as the applause and fanfare drifted away. This was Sakamoto's *Solitude*. His farewell kiss to Lani Kimura. Fingers fell lightly, as if such a feathery touch could wring from the keys the absolute emotion that its composer had meant him to. The orchestra sat still and silent, allowing the notes from the solo piano to fill the space, and the lights slowly shifted overhead.

Avant garde holograms and projections played across the stage, the black piano and the cyclotron against the upstage wall, forming an amorphous visual texture to the music Asano urged from the strings in the giant box.

He sighed. Closing his eyes, he shifted on the bench and surrendered to the bass tones, the melody, the plaintive cry of the notes plucked by his right hand in sheer muscle memory. As the piece drew to a close, he felt a certain happiness enter his chest—he felt Lani's spirit move through him.

He let her go.

And the piano fell silent.

There was a long pause, while the audience collected their wits. There wasn't a dry eye in the auditorium. The applause was slow and gradual, building up to thunderous whistles and roars, echoing through Asano's head. He didn't need to wait for the end of the performance. He was cleansed. He knew he would let himself live.

Stilt glanced at Cheryl, watching the police captain delicately dabbing away her tears with a cotton hanky. Cuda sniffled and wiped his sleeve along under his nose, while Van cleared his throat in an effort to stow the emotion somewhere. Stilt smiled. It was a good thing he was wearing his visor.

The concert revved to a spectacular climax, Asano deftly plinking out the notes in *Nohemi,* his own composition, and moving straight into the 3rd movement of Rachmaninov's *Piano Concerto No 2 in C minor,* an impressive show of skill and dexterity. He finished to a standing ovation, leading the ensemble in their bows, then taking a few more for himself. He let himself bask in the attention, the adulation, feeling clean and free and actually happy for for the first time in years.

Flowers from Susan. More bows.

Curtain.

The VIP room backstage was packed with corporate schmoozers, eager producers and sleazy managerial types. Stilt, Cuda, Van and Cheryl stood in a frozen tableau near the bar, scanning the laughing group like deer at a sport hunting convention.

Susan entered on Asano's arm, and they stopped briefly in the doorway for a photo op. When they'd been rendered blind by the warm LED panels on the news cameras, Susan waved them away and made for the buffet table with haste.

Cuda reached out a massive hand. "Brilliant performance, Mr. Tanaka."

Asano shook it, and Cuda was impressed by the focused strength of the man.

"Thank you," he said, unsmiling. The scars on his face were quite visible now, but no one bothered with the burning question.

Susan blinked a sudden realization. "Where are my manners? *Tanaka-san*, this is John Kapp, Van Pezzoni, Captain Cheryl Bonner, and Kai—um, Stilt."

Asano bowed to each one, and the gesture was returned when he came to face the tall, visored man. His eyes scanned the chrome filter, the angular jaw—broken twice—and the slender features, maligned by some hidden suffering, an unseen inner turmoil. "You've seen much pain." The words spilled out before he could stop them.

Stilt tilted his visored head, looking curiously at the pensive artist, and it was his turn to be flabbergasted. Who was this man? He exuded a serenity and peace that was almost tangible. "It was a magnificent performance, *Tanaka-san*. You practice *kendo*?"

Cheryl and Susan glanced at each other in surprise. Van and Cuda did the same.

"Aah," smiled Asano. "Just from walking out on the stage...very observant. Yes. I do."

"If you ever need a sparring partner, just come on down to the school. I'd be happy to—"

"School? That wouldn't happen to be the Shihodo School? The one in the news?"

Stilt frowned. "News?"

Asano scratched his chin. "You had a problem with a student on drugs?"

Stilt sighed with recognition. "Oh yes. It was most unfortunate. We didn't see it until it was too late."

Asano grinned, and everyone relaxed visibly. "Your eyes are observant, but your heart wishes not to see."

Stilt chuckled in mild amusement. He was dead on. "Yeah, I guess that's it."

"I would like to see this school."

Stilt nodded. "Anytime. And Ms. Kitayama, you're invited too. See what we do down there."

Susan flashed a defensive smile, bowed her head. "Most gracious of you, Mr. Stilt."

"Just Stilt."

"Boy, only on the payroll for three days and already I'm on a first name basis with the guy." Everyone laughed politely, and Susan glanced around for her toady. "Where is that Love?" She shook her head. "Oh well. How about coming up to the office for a celebratory drink?"

Cuda was just about to nod emphatically when Stilt shook his head. "Sorry. Don't drink."

Asano glanced at him. Had they just said the same thing, simultaneously? A quick look at Cheryl and Susan told him they had. Asano raised a tilted black eyebrow, creating a series of flesh mosaics in his forehead.

Stilt slapped a hand on Cuda's shoulder. "We should be getting back. John and I have early classes in the morning."

Cuda blinked, nodded. "That's right." Then he added pointedly, "But we really should get together soon."

Susan displayed another plastic grin. "Well, it just so happens I'm throwing a celebratory dinner Sunday night. I'd like you to come, that is, if your schedules permit."

Cuda nodded emphatically, completely bypassing Stilt. "Schedules permit. That would be lovely."

Susan bowed, the green eyes of the Tigress returning to their former glory. "Wonderful. We'll see you at eight sharp. At the Marina building. I'll leave the floor and room number with lobby security for you."

Cuda bowed in return. "Thank you. We'll be there."

They said their goodbyes, the three neighborhood toughs exiting into the unseasonably crisp night air. They found their way across the plaza and strode solemnly to the parking garage, watching the homeless slug it out for the last of the cardboard shipping boxes. Finally, Stilt spoke. "Cuda..."

Cuda held up a large hand in protest. "Don't say it, brother. Somebody has to look out for us. You were about to blow it, big time."

Van nodded, uncabling his helmet from the back of the bike. "He's right. You were knocked flat on your ass by that Kitayama chick."

Stilt pressed his mouth in a tight line. It was probably true.

Cuda smiled and held his right thumb to the sensor lock on the car. An electronic chirp echoed from the dim yellow light of the garage. "I don't believe this. Van saying I'm right? Can I get that in writing?"

Van gave him a sarcastic smirk as he straddled the Harley. "I got something for ya. It's in my pocket."

"That's okay," Cuda chuckled, opening the driver's side door. "I know where that pocket's been."

The hotel room was a mass of twisted sheets, strewn across the giant bed and onto the floor where the comforter had changed its basic shape, but not its function. There was a surprised gasp, and the huge blanket began to move.

"Oh shit, Kel. We're gonna miss the concert!" The comforter surged and twisted, and Creep's furry, disheveled head poked out, blue eyes blinking in the soft light of the bedside lamp which now lay on the floor.

"What time is it," asked a fatigued feminine voice.

Creep glanced at the bedside table and noticed his new phone had been knocked off. He dug through the sheets, and finally found the tiny rectangle. A few swipes on the screen displayed the time with glowing white numbers.

"12:22 a.m." he said.

Kelly sighed. "The concert's over. We missed it." Suddenly two slender, pink arms appeared around Creep's chest, hauling him back under the blanket. It surged and rolled, then surged some more, and Creep's hapless voice cried, "Again?!"

23

Saturday morning was quiet, at least on Irving Street. The garbage dumpster behind Our Lady of Divine Tolerance Church rattled and scooted on its heavy casters, and the plastic lid lifted a scant few inches.

Reflective blue eyes, like those of a giant raccoon or predatory alley cat, peered out of the darkness of refuse and recycled paper. The alley was silent and still in the morning light. The lid closed. Inside, the construct ran an automatic bio-diagnostic. Left shoulder was damaged, not much use of the limb. Several infected cuts, scrapes and gouges. Torn ligaments in right knee joint. Nutrients low but not yet critical.

THE TEMPEST. ACT IV, SCENE I.

Monster, I do smell all horse-piss; at which my nose is in great indignation.

It was true. KML029 stank. The only way to throw off the scent had been to leap into the dumpster and roll in the garbage and animal waste at the bottom. He was covered in the stuff: a mixture of musty rainwater, cat urine and rat feces, old milk and rotten food. It certainly didn't smell like a genetic military construct anymore.

The plastic lid flipped up completely, and the creature dropped to the ground, scanning the area carefully.

AUDIO ALERT: 6 METERS, RIGHT. INSIDE STRUCTURE.

The pleasant whistling drew it closer to the outer brick wall of the church, and it pressed its head delicately to the masonry. The tune was familiar. One it had heard before, in the lab.

MEMORY SEARCH: INTERNAL MUSIC.

Ave Maria.

Dr. Jorgenson always whistled it. It had only heard the tune when Jorgenson whistled it, and because it had never heard the hymn whistled by anyone else, it could only assume Dr. Jorgenson was the only person capable of whistling that particular song. Therefore, Dr. Jorgenson must be inside.

Father Fisk waved the worn green feather-duster over the silver candlesticks on the modest altar. These were the only valuables he'd allowed into his church. They had been a gift from a prominent neighborhood businesswoman, the last of his parish gunned down by a Neo-Nazi street gang during the riots of '57. They were placed on the altar in her memory, and as a reminder to his flock: Forgiveness is the way.

Fisk was a Neo-Franciscan, a believer in the poverty of the Church, but not quite content wearing burlap robes and open sandals. He was a modern man, living in modern times, and truly believed those in the priesthood should keep up with the societal changes that had posed a constant problem for the Church throughout its history. He was only as traditional in his dress as to wear a black shirt, white collar and silver crucifix on his rosary. The rest of his garb was dictated by fashion and functionality, as were any other normal man's.

After all, one could not very well run down vandals and drug-crazed purse-snatchers in sandals, or even dress shoes.

Converse Rockets were much more useful, and also improved his basketball game.

He flung his long, black hair back over his shoulder, grudgingly accepting of the early gray streaks that had appeared at his temples. Resuming his whistled song, he picked a piece of lint from his vat-grown leather jacket, ran a finger across the stone surface of the simple altar and peered up at the wooden statue of the crucified savior. The rainbow effect from the early morning light through the stained glass Gothic windows was dazzling.

His whistling stopped in mid-note, nose wrinkling in disgust. *What was that smell?*

The sound of a large, naked body crumpling to the concrete floor made him turn, every sense on high alert. The creature lay sprawled in the aisle, near the rear pews, trying desperately to right itself. The heavy doors swung closed behind it.

Father Fisk dropped his jaw and quickly made the sign of the cross, eyes wide with uncertainty. What in God's name was this creature? He'd never seen anything like it. What was he to do? It looked terribly wounded, but was it safe to approach? And did any of his fear or worry negate his duty to serve any and all of God's creatures as best he could?

Fisk stepped forward down the carpeted cement steps, anxiously gathering what wits he could muster. The muscular construct writhed in agony, its mouth open, jaw distended. It looked as if it were trying to speak, or at least cry, but all that came out was a steady hiss of air.

"Holy Mary, Mother of God," whispered the priest as he knelt down a foot away from the creature's head. It stared up with plaintive, desperate crystal blue eyes, its fur matted, stained with crimson and reeking of garbage and feces. Some of its blood had pooled on the floor next to its wounded shoulder. Shakily, it dipped the index pad of its right hand into the mess and began to scrawl on the ground.

Fisk swallowed as the childish scrawl became letters before his eyes. He read the word and swallowed again.

Father

The creature looked up at Fisk's unshaven face and sighed, its heavy brow raised in hapless exhaustion.

Stilt raised the sparring glove, and the young Scottish girl leaped into the air, a graceful foot striking the target with a resounding *slap*. She landed, whirled around in a new combination defensive stance, preparing for her next strike.

"Very good, Elizabeth. You get an A for the day." Stilt looked around the assembled students, scanning their faces. With even breaths, he surveyed the room. The walls adorned with practice weapons and Asian artwork, the large storefront window that read *Shihodo School* backward from inside, the empty visitors' bench against the inside wall. "Alright, so you see the importance of immediate return from a strike. Even if your kick was successful, you never want to relax until you are completely and safely away from the situation. Elizabeth has volunteered to be the new tutor, in Jason's absence. You can talk to her if you need extra help." He glanced up, pausing suddenly.

Asano sat quietly against the wall on the visitors' bench, expensively tailored shirt billowing out from pleated black slacks. A black raincoat was neatly folded beside him. Stilt frowned, and felt a shiver down his neck.

"Um, so that's all. Check with *Sensei* Cuda if you want to use the *dojo* for private practice, and Van should be available for evening workouts, so check the schedule." He waved the young students away with a strong hand. "Okay, *vámonos*."

The dispersing pupils wandered away toward the front door, and Stilt made his way toward the bench. *"Konichi wa."*

Asano stood politely, gathering his coat under his left arm. *"Konichi wa."*

Stilt offered a formal hand. "Good to see you, *Tanaka-san*. I have to be honest with you, I wasn't expecting you to show up so soon."

Asano shook his hand and smiled, his face cracking into a million shards of broken flesh. "Didn't think a celebrity would take your offer seriously, yes?" He shoved graceful hands into the front pockets of his slacks. "I thought it would be better to see your *dojo* as it really is. I prefer things without the pretense."

Stilt nodded thoughtfully, the chrome surface of the visor reflecting Asano's smile, warping the image into the likeness of a terrible fun house mirror. "Well you certainly came in quietly. I didn't even hear the bells on the front door."

"I didn't wish to disturb your class. Doorbells are distracting."

"Yes. I guess they are." Stilt reached up, scratching his chest through the cotton canvas of his workout *dogi*. "Listen, I need to shower and change. If you don't mind waiting here, I can just run up and be ready in fifteen minutes."

"Please. Do your thing. I will be quite content to wait down here. I was just admiring the prints on the wall."

Stilt shrugged. "They're the cheap ones. We don't like to keep the originals out here in the *dojo*."

"What do you fear?"

Stilt paused. "Nothing. We just don't ask for trouble, and nobody comes looking for it from us." He paused again, then headed for the entry hall stairs. "Be down shortly. Make yourself at home."

The tall *sensei* disappeared up the wooden stairs, and Asano counted four leaps. He turned, letting his dark eyes roam over the mounted *bokken* and *sai* in neat rows along the wall.

They left twenty minutes later, the musician with fluttering overcoat, the vigilante stopping to lock the front door with a quick press of the keypad. They headed west along Irving, Stilt acting as neighborhood tour guide.

Deep in conversation and heading in the opposite direction, they didn't see the Lexus roll forward from 15th Avenue. It paused at the corner. Large Viking eyes squinted through dark sunglasses, Biggs' heavy forehead glistening with nervous sweat. Quan's gloved fists gripped the wheel, and the two sat quietly, watching the men as they disappeared down the street.

Stilt and Asano walked all day. Asano asked questions, and Stilt was only too happy to answer them. He was relieved that someone outside of the community actually cared enough to ask pertinent questions. After awhile, however, Stilt turned the tables on his new companion and grilled *him*.

Asano told him of the accident, of his fiance's death, and shared the element of cleansing he'd felt through the music the previous night. He'd released himself from a prison of his own making.

They stopped for sushi at Mae Wong's. As they sat, sipping tea and chewing *kappa maki* rolls at the plastic picnic table, the conversation turned to the spiritual. Asano pointedly asked Stilt what his quest was, and for five solid minutes, the two ate quietly while Stilt mulled the question over in his mind. Finally, he answered, and Asano was not expecting what he heard.

"I've seen a lot of horror. Most of it has had to do with man playing god with technology they have no command of." Stilt paused, finishing his bite. "There's been no guidance. We're like children with a lighter in one hand, and a stick of dynamite in the other. And we've just learned how to work the lighter."

"An interesting metaphor," Asano commented, "because I sense your quest is for children."

"I guess so, on one level. Children are probably the most oppressed in the human pecking order. They've always had to put up with being the prey. No one has taught them how to stand up and fight for their rights as people."

"Is that your quest? To teach children to fight for their own security?"

"Some of it. The biggest single factor has been drugs. It's the most insidious thing in the neighborhoods. And kids are always the catalyst for their introduction. Now it looks like there's a new one. Makes people nuts, beyond anything we've ever seen before."

"That was your student?"

"Kevin. Yeah. But then, two days later, we went on a call and had to take down this guy, totally jacked out of his mind. It practically took blowing him to pieces with a police rifle to make him drop. I'll bet he was dead fifteen seconds before he fell."

"And you think it's the same drug." Asano sipped his tea as an electric city car whizzed by.

Stilt rubbed his jaw. "Sure do." He paused, lost in silent thought. "I guess, to answer your question, I feel a need to right the wrongs of the past. I'm a product of military drugs. According to the monks in Imazu, my father was an American soldier during the North Korea conflict." He stopped, mouth half open with his next sentence.

He blinked.

That was it! He remembered where he'd seen those clinical photos. Back in Japan. Hisako's medical texts. "Holy shit."

Asano raised a suspicious eyebrow. "What?"

"Holy shit, that's what it is."

"What *what* is?"

"Jet. The drug." Stilt rose, turning slowly toward the street. "It's a variant of the military superdrug."

Asano watched him carefully. "Superdrugs were outlawed immediately after the war. All formulas were supposed to have been destroyed."

Stilt waved a cynical hand. "Eh, since when does the US government listen to the United Nations? I tell you, that's what this is."

Asano finished the last of his tea. "So have you told me what your quest is?"

Stilt laughed uncomfortably. "Whatever I told you, strike it." He shuffled to the sidewalk, still staring down the street. "This shit has got to be removed. Now."

Asano smiled at him. "I think that's what you have been saying all along."

No rain scheduled tonight.

They walked back to the school with the afternoon sun low on their backs, stopping every so often to chat with a local shopkeeper or resident. Asano was well received. Any friend of Stilt's was a friend of the community. They took a detour for some produce at the grocery, and finally made it to the school shortly before six p.m.

"You gonna be at the dinner tomorrow night?" Stilt asked as he balanced the bags in preparation to input the key code at the door.

"I have little choice," Asano mused, taking one of the canvas totes from Stilt. "Susan keeps me on a short leash these days. She's worried about my depression. I need to let her know I'm okay now."

The first digit of the security code had just been entered when a voice hailed them urgently from across the street. "Stilt!" They turned to see Father Fisk waving them desperately toward the church. "Please! It's important!"

Stilt glanced at Asano, and the two men rushed across the warm pavement. They found the priest in the front garden, his hair tied back in a long ponytail, his jacket gone, bare arms smeared with blood. His face was pale, his gaze sunken and hollow.

"What's the problem, Father?"

Fisk licked his dry lips, glancing around the street. "I need to tell someone, but I'm afraid to go to the police."

Stilt frowned, reaching out to grab Fisk by his quivering shoulders. "Father. What."

Fisk regarded Asano. "He safe?"

Stilt nodded.

"This way." Fisk led them out of the front garden, around the side of the church, toward the basement utility shed.

The room was tiny, four stained cement walls illuminated by a single battery-powered camp light on an antique wooden school desk. An old metal hospital bed stood in the corner.

Fisk often hid political refugees and Nulls down here, granting sanctuary to anyone who asked for it. He'd never harbored an escaped zoo animal before, however. And Stilt had to do a double-take to realize that it wasn't a zoo animal at all.

"—the hell?" Stilt breathed, adding, "Sorry, Father."

The creature was sitting on the bed, upright against the corner, huddled under a moth-eaten Army blanket. Its eyes were ice-blue orbs of reflected light in the darkened room. There was a bloodstained cotton bandage around his chest and shoulder, and even more gauze around portions of both muscular arms. The really creepy thing was how it was smiling, kind of baring its teeth in an odd grimace. Its brow was furrowed in a saddened look, and it made no move to escape, if indeed it could manage the strength.

"It came to me this morning, into the sanctuary upstairs."

"What do you think it is?"

"Well," Fisk sighed, "first of all, *it* is a *he*. And I believe he's intelligent."

Asano approached the creature, which made no reciprocal move except to follow the musician with its eyes. "Has he communicated?"

Fisk wiped a bloody hand across his brow. "You could say that. He can write. But he hasn't spoken. There weren't any head or throat injuries, so I don't think the capability exists."

Asano moved closer, and the thing looked up at him.

Stilt leaned against a broom handle standing upright near the wall. "This kind of genetic engineering's pretty rare, if that's what he is. You think he escaped from somewhere?"

Fisk nodded, watching as Asano lay a cool hand on the construct's broad forehead. "When I was dressing his wounds, I saw a serial number tattooed under his left arm: K-M-L-0-2-9. He could be military."

"Could be anything, Father."

The creature sighed, moving his mouth in silent discussion with the tall Asian who soothed his brow. Asano knelt beside the bed, as if listening to the mute monologue. He pulled a ripe tomato from the canvas shopping bag and gave it to the construct, and it was wolfed down whole, the gooey seeds dripping from the corners of grinding teeth.

Fisk scratched his head. "I don't know what to do with him." He reached into his pocket and produced a thin, warped metal slug. "Found this in his shoulder. Looks like a rifle round."

Stilt looked at the bullet. "Someone didn't want him running loose. You did the right thing, not calling the police. I'll see what I can do with my our connections."

"Yes, thank you, Father."

All eyes turned toward the stairway. The broom was instantly in Stilt's hand, and he moved toward the large black man on the bottom step. A slender woman with glasses and curly, bobbed hair stepped from behind the man, brandishing an enormous Glock G55. The red laser from the sight hit Stilt between the eyes and he froze.

"Don't move," she said sternly.

Fisk held out bloody arms. "What in God's name—?"

The elderly scientist moved cautiously into the dark room, his body casting gargantuan shadows on the stairs and wall. Stilt's finger twitched on the broom handle. "What do you want?"

The woman stepped forward confidently, both hands holding the huge pistol steady. "I said, don't move."

Stilt eyed her carefully. "I'll take you both out before you can pull that trigger."

The woman flashed an angry sneer. "Wanna try?"

Suddenly the scientist looked down at his left arm. The creature's muscular hand was wrapped gently around his wrist, and big, reflective eyes gazed at him lovingly. It stepped forward and embraced him around the waist. Noah signaled Barb to lower the gun. "Put it away. I don't think these people mean him any harm."

Stilt followed the woman's hands as the weapon was slowly lowered and holstered carefully under her left arm.

"Who are you?" he asked, leaning the broom against the wall once more.

"If you don't mind, we haven't much time." The rotund man led his creation to the hospital bed and gestured for him to sit. The creature did as told. The doctor spoke, and his voice was at once sad and tired. "My name is Noah Jorgenson. I am—or was—a genetic engineer at GBE. This unit is the KML series twenty-nine. He began as a military prototype for hostile desert regions, and I've gone and played God with the poor thing."

Fisk shifted his feet, watching as the doctor produced a strange-looking hypo from his pants pocket. "What do you mean by that?"

Noah glanced at him, bowing his head. "I tried to push the experiment further with genetically-designed artificial intelligence. Electrochemical stimulus. DNA receptive to computer input. It worked, or has so far."

Asano moved to the far corner, clasped his hands behind his back. "He's sentient."

Noah nodded. "That's right."

Stilt cocked his head and folded sinewy arms across his chest. "Who the hell was shooting at him, then?"

"The hierarchy at GBE has become more corrupt over the past several years. My thought is that the KML is carrying something stored in his genome. Kind of a live courier." He inserted the needle into the back of the creature's neck, forcing a yellowish, clear liquid into the skin. "The scientists responsible for this mess want him terminated to save their positions." As the liquid collected under the fur-covered flesh, a small, rectangular shape gradually rose to the surface, and the doctor reached into his pocket again, this time drawing out a metallic clipping device. "Look out for a scientist named Ridley, and his assistant. Michaels. Native guy. Tinted rooster crest."

Stilt blinked, and the visor twitched on his face. "What do you mean, look out for them?"

Noah held the clippers delicately against the raised portion of the creature's skin. "You're going to have to watch him for awhile." There was a snapping sound, and the creature winced a little. A trickle of thick red blood seeped out of the hole. Noah dug into his pockets and found some cotton wipes and gently held one over the wound.

Stilt was incredulous. "Watch him for awhile? The fuck is that supposed to mean? Sorry, father."

Noah turned to Barb, held out his hand. "Barb, give me the growth hormone." The woman fished a small bottle from her photography vest, handing it to Noah.

"I asked you a question!"

Jorgenson regarded Stilt tiredly. "Look, I don't have time to tell you the whole thing. But there's something going on here beyond Ridley wanting him dead. We've got some investigating to do, and we'd be a target if we took him with us."

Stilt swallowed hard. "What are we supposed to do with him?"

Noah inserted the tube into the bottom of the hypo, and there was a burst of air as the instrument forced fluid into the injection mechanism "Just protect him. I don't care how. Try to find out what he's carrying. It'll be encoded in his DNA. Could be a formula for just about anything. Chemical weapon, drug, new genetic process. Use the information to your benefit. Bring Ridley and the lab down."

Stilt couldn't believe what he was hearing. He watched as Noah injected the liquid hormone into the side of the creature's throat. "How are we supposed to do that?"

Noah pulled the needle from the construct and gave Stilt a serious look. "It may never happen. You may not be able extract it while he's alive. The most important thing is that he's kept safe. And I have no choice but to depend on you to take care of that." He stood, turned to Barb and handed her the chip he'd extracted from the unit's neck. "His speech capability should develop normally from here on out. You should start hearing coherent words in a few days, maybe sooner."

Stilt, Fisk and Asano stood dumbfounded as the scientist and his partner turned to leave. Noah paused at the second step. "It's important, you know. He's the first successful biological AI. He can learn." Jorgenson turned briefly, and his bespectacled eyes met their reflection in Stilt's visor. "Good luck, friends."

Stilt inhaled slowly and shrugged his shoulders as he watched them leave. "Yeah, great." He crouched near the construct and met its gaze. The thing's giant eyes roved from face to face. It managed another haphazard grin.

Asano bent next to Stilt and mumbled softly. "Do you think I could have a few moments alone with the creature?"

Stilt stood, perplexed. "Um...sure, I guess. Father, you wanna take a walk with me?"

Fisk nodded stupidly. "Yeah. We gotta figure out what to do with this thing."

The two men climbed the cement steps and exited out into the dazzling hues of the setting sun. As they strolled to the front of the church, Fisk rolled his sleeves down to hide the blood on his skin. "I have no idea," he confessed.

Stilt paused and shuffled his feet on the cement. His hands found the front pockets of his nylon jacket, and he stared thoughtfully at the church sign a few meters away. "Look, Father, this shouldn't be your problem."

"But he is."

"Yeah, but that's what I'm saying. The boys and I are going to dinner with Susan Kitayama tonight. I think I can talk her into helping out."

Fisk looked skeptical. "You sure?"

"Not *absolutely* sure, but I can try. Just keep him here for a few hours. Don't let him go anywhere."

Fisk shrugged. "Yeah, okay."

Asano was two feet away before they saw him. Stilt noticed blood on his right palm. The fingers on his left hand were white with cement dust.

"What were you up to?"

Asano breathed steadily. His eyes were wide and his pupils dilated. "Haven't done it for awhile," he mumbled. "But he'll be alright."

Before Stilt could question him further, someone called out from the sidewalk in front of the school. He turned and saw his tenant Etienne at the door. The young Franco-Asian man wore jeans and a simple T-shirt, hailing across the street. "Jesse just went into labor this morning! Mike's with her at UC Med!"

Stilt waved. "Thanks!" Why was everything happening today? *Well, buddy,* Stilt heard Cuda say in his mind, *that's life for ya. Sometimes we all gotta duck when the shit hits the fan.*

Steve pecked out the door code on the security pad, and the storefront exploded.

The young man's body was ripped apart by the deafening fireball from a half-kilo block of ignited EPX and a canister of steel ball bearings. Glass shattered on every floor, sprinkling Irving Street like a hard, frozen rain. Intricate stone masonry became a million hurling projectiles. Stilt hit the ground to find Asano already flat, covering his head. Father Fisk was clipped on the side of the face by a spinning piece of hot metal and fell writhing to the pavement.

Stilt glanced up as the fireball gave way to a thundering column of smoke and flames, licking the ruined structure in a hungered frenzy.

Barney Chao sprinted from the donut shop, eyes wide with terror. Everyone from the cafe stood and collected in the street. Sheila Nan dashed out from the doors of Nha Trang, aghast at the wreckage. Her restaurant was just across Fifteenth Avenue from the school, and she nervously watched the sky for renegade embers.

As Stilt hoisted himself from the pavement, Asano scurried to Father Fisk. He was gushing blood from a wide neck wound, and his eyes showed a rapid descent into shock. Stilt scanned the area, but could find no trace of a strange car or suspicious perpetrator. The work must have been done earlier in the day, when everyone was out. He glanced back at Asano and Fisk.

The thin pianist gently hoisted the priest's head into his lap, cradling it in his right hand. His fingers clutched the bleeding wound, and he reached out with his left hand, exhaling audibly as he brought it slowly down to the white concrete. His eyes were closed, and his chest rose and fell in heavy, controlled breaths.

Suddenly, Asano snapped his head back, bellowing a deafening *kiai*, the powerful shriek echoing several blocks down the street. There was a muffled crack as the cement split beneath his flattened hand, and Fisk blinked. Asano let out a sigh and helped the young priest to his feet as the crowd began to gather around 16th Avenue.

Fisk reached up to feel his neck. The wound had sealed completely. He marveled at the scarred musician. "Mother of God."

Asano patted him weakly on the shoulder. "Something like that."

Stilt glanced at the roaring fire, then at Asano, the split concrete, Fisk, then Asano again. "There something you wanna tell me, *amigo*?"

Ridley glanced up at the rising column of dark smoke four blocks away. Michaels stood, clutching the discarded tracking device. "Looks like they found it, chief. What now?"

Ridley scowled, grabbed the tracker from his assistant's hand and switched it on. "They meet with a sudden traffic accident. Blake's orders were very specific." He looked down at the blinking green LED display. "Looks like they're heading south on Highway 1, toward 280."

He signaled the rest of the retrieval team, waving them to the parked truck. Handing the scanner back to the Pawnee scientist, he added, "Michaels, you follow them and make sure this thing is flatlined. I'll head back to Monoped to see what the hell happened to Bartak." The group dispersed, but Ridley wasn't finished. "We've gotta split clean, *amigos*. Cops will be crawling all over the area pretty soon now. Call me when you run 'em down. And do it somewhere quiet."

24

IT WAS A GIRL. But everyone already knew it would be. A small brown blob of waxy flesh and puffed-up eyes, and tiny round hands that wiggled in silent protest whenever Jess shifted in the bed. It was also the most precious thing the guys had seen in a long time.

"They blew up the whole building?" Jess was beside herself and in tears.

Van and Asano took turns pacing the tile floor.

Cuda sat with Mike in the hall, comforting the red-haired man on the loss of his husband. They'd been together for ten years, since high school graduation. Mike reckoned it was lucky they'd left with Jess when they did. The only other casualty had been Jesse's wombat. The two men sat and cried for a long time. Cuda could literally feel his pain.

Stilt reached down a gentle hand to caress the new infant's face. She wriggled some more, and pushed his fingers away with surprisingly strong arms. "Looks like this little one saved a lot of people today. I hope it comes back to her in her lifetime."

"My God, Stilt. What are we going to do? Mike can't afford to live anywhere else, neither can I. You've been so good to all of us..." she trailed off, breaking into a fresh round of tears. Stilt handed her the box of tissues from the bedside table. "You let me worry about that. We'll take care of everything."

Van came up behind Stilt and put on a stern face. "We'll get whoever did it, too. We'll get 'em back."

Stilt bowed his head. "This smells like Bug. Or whoever owns his operation."

Jesse blew her nose, and the baby yawned. "We're behind you guys," Jess offered, grasping Stilt's hand.

"Thanks."

Asano approached, motioning at the wall clock. "We should go to the police now, or we'll never get to talk to Susan tonight."

Stilt nodded and gave the baby a tiny high-five. "Hang tough, mi amiga."

"Fucking hell, Cheryl, you know damn well who did it!" Stilt protested, slamming a wide fist down on her desk. The Green Room, as they now referred to Cheryl's office, was becoming much too familiar a location to Stilt. Cuda and Van were beginning to agree. Asano had never been there before, but found it had a particularly depressing atmosphere. He hoped they wouldn't be there for long.

Cheryl folded her arms and leaned on the desk with her usual side-eye. "You think it was Bug."

Stilt slammed his fist down again, then took a deep breath. "Cheryl, I *know* it was Bug. I don't know how he traced us. Windy, maybe."

Van stepped forward, angrily shaking his head. "No way, *amigo*. She wouldn't give us up, man."

"You know that for a fact, Pezzoni?" Stilt straightened, took another breath. Van frowned. Stilt only called him by his last name when he was *really* pissed off.

"Yeah, as a matter of fact—"

"Aww, knock it off." Cuda pushed away from the water cooler, thrusting out his hands, martyr-like. "We ain't goin' nowhere, you keep that shit up. What we gotta figure out is how to prove it."

Cheryl raised a thin eyebrow, ran a hand through her thick, tightly braided tresses. "Easier said than done, John. If it was Bug, he's not stupid enough to leave any calling cards."

Cuda clenched his fists tightly at his side. "Calling cards, shit. I ain't talking about no calling cards. I'm talking about tracing it like he got us. Go through the pipeline, backwards. I say we go get the motherfucker."

Stilt nodded. "Damn straight." They exchanged a low hand slap.

Cheryl laughed. "Well that's good to see the homeys hanging tough together, but you still haven't come up with a plan that I'm ready to back. And until you do, all I can do is oversee a normal investigation."

Asano moved forward, hands in pockets. "Stilt, maybe you should consider disappearing for awhile. Bug will be waiting for an immediate reaction. If you wait him out, let him lower his guard..."

"That's good," Stilt acknowledged, "except you gotta know he was after a complete flatline. The news has already said that Steve was the only one killed. When Bug hears all his boys did was blow up an empty building and one innocent bystander, he's gonna be pissed, maybe even can 'em. We could use his disorganization against him."

Cheryl shook her head. "Hey. This is not some private little gang war, amigos. You go after Bug only when we have proof positive. I don't want to blow it. Once we've got him in here, I don't want to be the one apologizing while I unlock the cuffs and send him on his way 'cause of a microscopic loophole, like a contractor ripped his suit with undue force or no one asked him if he understood his rights."

Stilt looked surprised. "Well...yeah. Of course we don't wanna let him walk. But we don't wanna let him get away with blowing up private property and killing people."

"There, now." Cheryl stood. "We're all on the home screen. You boys do your legwork." She looked at each of them, speaking plainly. "Come to me if you have anything to go on. I promise you'll be in on the takedown."

Stilt pursed his lips. There was still ash on his face from the explosion. "Promise?"

"I said I promise, didn't I?"

"Alright. Deal." Stilt shook her hand. He turned to the other three. "Let's jam."

"Oh, Stilt?" Cheryl pulled up an encrypted message on her workstation, pressing the screen once. "This came in a few minutes before you did. Susan Kitayama. Offering a place to stay and any other assistance you might need."

Stilt's phone buzzed. He pulled it from his pocket, swiped to unlock the screen and read the message, staring at it in bewilderment.

Cheryl sat again on the corner of the desk. "Frankly, I don't know what she sees in you guys. You got plenty o' balls, but they're all in your head where your brains should be."

Stilt smiled, and the group filed out.

Cuda waved a thumb at his tall companion. "Yeah. You should see him when he has a headache. His eyebrows get an erection."

Cheryl nodded knowingly, pointing at the door. "Uh-huh. Out."

The truck was marked *SoftBrite Linen Service*, and was flanked by two pizza delivery AVs mounting 50-caliber machine guns under the front grille. No one asked Fisk to explain what an obviously corporate courier team had been doing at the church. He couldn't lie, and no one wanted him to endanger themselves or the community any further by divulging unnecessary information. They were content to stand around, watching as a dozen uniformed delivery workers transferred a particularly heavy bundle of "linen" from the church basement to the back of the large truck—watch as the neighborhood volunteer fire department worked into the night, trying to squelch the flames in the blasted-out corner building.

Fisk stood on the sidewalk and squinted at the dancing flames as the three vehicles dashed away toward the corporate sector downtown. When they were gone, he wandered back to the church and began to pick up some of the debris from the trim green lawn.

He was reprimanded by Barney Chao, who told him to get his ass home and in bed. Fisk blessed him and staggered into the sanctuary, collapsing exhausted in a front pew. "Merciful Lord," he said aloud, quoting Brother Domingo de Santa Clara, the radical Los Angeles prophet. "What troubled times do we live in, when such marvelous and terrible things are possible?" He shifted uncomfortably, caressing his neck where Asano had touched him. "And how do we answer for them?"

Bug stared blankly at the wall screen. One citizen and an exotic pet dead, one entire city block destroyed. Kai Tokura, John Kapp, Michael McCann and Jesse Hawkins all safe, due to a miraculously early labor on Jesse's part.

He sat absolutely still, quietly watching the sculpted blond centerfold deliver the details with gleaming white acrylic teeth and pouty collagen lips.

"Police are investigating the crime, the whereabouts of Kapp and Tokura unknown, but they are assumed to be somewhere in the city."

Bug calmly removed his shades, rubbed bloodshot eyes. Then he sighed, drew his pistol and shot the television screen. It exploded in the usual shower of plastic, sparks and silicon. It was far from the first wall screen dispatched in this manner.

Biggs frowned, slumping back on the couch. "Win some, lose some."

Bug stood, stone-faced, took aim and pulled the trigger.

Biggs' knee erupted in shards of bone and a cascade of warm red blood. He crumpled to the floor, clutching his wounded leg in bewildered shock. Quan and Johann stood cautiously from their stools and backed away, joining Raoul in the kitchenette.

Biggs let out an agonized grunt. "Fuck, man! You shot my fuckin' leg!" Blood continued to gush from his shattered kneecap.

"Win some, lose some," Bug repeated calmly.

Quan was hysterical, eyes bulging, sweat collecting on his brow. "Hey, man, what the fuck?! Why'd you shoot him?!"

Bug turned to the young Thai and all three of the remaining thugs flinched.

"Don't sweat, Quan. If I didn't shoot one of you every now and then, you'd forget who I was."

Quan blinked, eyes still wide. "I-I won't forget, man. I told him to wait."

Bug shook his head, casually waving the pistol around the room. "What did I say about talking? Huh? No talking 'til the deed is done. Now, do I have to call Selby and ask him for some better boys, or what?"

Biggs grunted again, trying to roll over without crunching the blasted knee under his considerable weight. Bug pulled out a nic-stick and cooked up, pistol still dangling from the trigger-guard around his finger. "Tell you what. Quan, you take him to St. Francis, get him patched up. Have 'em bill Selby. He can even go tech if he wants. How 'bout that, Big Guy? No hard feelings?"

Quan and Raoul rushed to his side, hoisting the large thug upright.

Biggs winced and spat onto the dusty concrete. "Yeah. Sure." He glared at Bug with eyes like high-intensity lasers. "No hard feelings."

They helped him to the back of the Lexus, and Quan paused momentarily to throw a bewildered glance Bug's way. He ducked into the driver's seat, the engine revved, and the Lexus rolled out through the open warehouse doors.

25

SUNDAY MORNING light glowed softly through the diffusion of tinted armorglass in the hotel suite. The air smelled of fresh coffee and flowers, thick with steam and the fragrance of aloe bodywash from the recent shower.

Kelly stuffed a bundle of shirts into the new vat-leather luggage, slapped the cover closed and zipped it. Her hair was tied back in a wavy brunette ponytail, and her leather jacket was open, revealing a DJ Mind Fuck concert shirt, collar purposefully torn away so that the thin cotton edges curled outward. Her faded jeans were tight, the cuffs tucked neatly into flat-heeled boots.

Creep paced the floor, glancing nervously at the silent wall monitor. "Bloody cowards."

Kelly finished packing and dropped the bags to the floor. "What?"

Creep continued to stare at the screen. The BayNews morning anchors ran the footage and sound bytes recycled from the previous night's late broadcast. Creep scowled as the shot cut to a wide view of the raging fire. "Fucking slingers who pulled that stunt. Blew up a whole fucking building with a *dojo* and apartments. Makes me fucking ill."

Kelly moved behind him, wrapped her arms around his chest. His baggy poet's shirt puffed out from a gold brocade vest. His feet were ever bare and his fur smelled of Venom cologne. "It's not our problem, you know." She felt him bristle at the comment and redirected. "I'm gonna be glad to get out-ta here and into some permanent lodging. Kinda cool of Ms. Kitayama to give us a penthouse with the deal."

Creep turned and embraced her. "—she said, changing the subject. What are you gonna write for the first cover story, by the way?"

Kelly raised up on her toes and nuzzled his fur-covered cheek. "I dunno, lots of locker room underwear shots, though."

"Remember, I don't do underwear shots."

"Aww, but—"

"No buts, Missy. An' no butts, either."

Larry entered, grumbled something about how they should "get a room". Creep broke the embrace and glared sar-castically at him. "Sorry, what wassat?"

Larry smiled, grabbing two of the travel bags from the floor. "I said, the limo's ready outside. They sent one of the new BMW stretches, and a driver."

Kelly laughed and swatted his butt as he bent for the oth-er bags. "Well, finally you get to ride with the celebs."

Larry paused as he asked himself why he was always tot-ing the bags. "I'm just glad I don't have to drive anymore. I was thinking, Kel, if you wouldn't mind going back to the old setup, that I could just hang out with a camera and snap the shots." He hefted the heavy luggage in broad arms. "Kitaya-ma's gonna have us set up with drivers anyway."

Kelly shrugged, leather jacket squeaking. "Sure. I don't care. You're a damn good photographer, so whatever. Do what you want. It is *our* magazine, after all."

"Yeah, but I thought I should ask," Larry joked, heading quickly for the door. "You want me to help squeeze you through the door? What with your big swollen head and all..."

Creep burst into loud guffaws, and Kelly swung a booted foot at Larry's retreating rear end. "Eat me, you ape!"

Kelly threw one of the pillows angrily from the bed as both men continued to giggle in the doorway. "You guys are both in deep shit!" Then she dashed past them into the hall, taunting, "Last one to the car buys the first round tonight!"

The ride from the Fairmont down California Street was quick and uncongested. The first couple of blocks, anyway. Once they entered Chinatown, however, the atmosphere changed dramatically. The police roadblock looked official enough: A patrol AV, one riot cop and a couple of undercover guys, and meters of yellow tape reading *CRIME SCENE - DO NOT CROSS.*

They pulled to a stop at the intersection of Grant and Clay, and Larry mentioned something about everything being fine. But when the Kitayama driver powered down his window to find out what the hell was going on, he found himself looking down the barrel of a 10-gauge shotgun. Kelly gasped in horror as the driver's skull opened away from the blast, completely covering the partition window with blood and brain. Creep punched the lock open on the rear door and leaped from the car.

"Larry! Drive!"

Larry scrambled forward, powering down the gore-spattered partition window. "Kel! Get down and stay down!"

Creep rolled and untucked into a rocketing handstand, and the first gunman dropped, his jaw shattered by a powerful, hairy foot. The cop spun, pumping a second round into the chamber.

Larry launched himself through the partition, coming down headfirst into the bloody lap of the headless driver. His hand was immediately on the window button, bulletproof glass whirring quickly upward to a tight seal. Still flailing halfway through the small window, he punched the glove box release with his right hand, and was gratified to find a .38 holdout revolver neatly slung in a plastic sleeve. He pulled it out and tossed it back through the window. "Kel! Here!"

The bewildered woman caught the small piece of hardware, and leaned toward the left door where Creep had exited.

The cop snarled, and Creep knew he recognized the man. They'd trained together for the Arena circuit in LA five years ago. He was no cop. He was still acting out a show. Before the man could pull the trigger, Creep was below him, thrusting five hairy knuckles up into the man's groin. The shot went off into the air, and the man sank to his knees. A spinning roundhouse to the head finished him and he sprawled unconscious.

A third gunman stepped behind him and took aim with a high-caliber assault carbine. Creep turned just as four loud shots rang out. He glanced down at his chest, then at the assassin. The man collapsed to the ground and revealed Kelly in the back of the limo, tensely gripping the revolver.

Creep dashed in through the open door, diving across her lap. As the false cop began to shake the stars from his head, Larry punched the accelerator with his hand and, with a single head-butt to the steering column, knocked the transmission into gear. The limo squealed on spinning tires, bursting away in a low electric whine.

Larry sucked in his gut and wriggled the rest of the way through the partition, shoving the dead driver aside as he swerved to avoid an elderly pedestrian. "Everyone okay?"

Creep checked out the rear window. "Yeah. Fine. You?"

"Good."

Creep shot Kelly a worried look. "How 'bout you, princess?"

Kelly blinked twice, realized she was still clutching the gun with both hands. Shrugging, she lowered the weapon and nodded emphatically. "Yeah. Great. Fun times."

Creep sighed, slumping back in the seat. "Good."

They drove in silence for a few blocks, and then Larry peered into the rear-view mirror, the image of his dark eyes glossed over with splattered blood. "Kel?"

"Hmmm?"

"You think I can drive *and* take pictures?"

26

STILT LET OUT a relived sigh and terminated the call, and the phone's screen went dark.

Clouds began to roll in off the Bay, and the light through Susan Kitayama's office windows painted the interior with tints of of mercury and gunmetal blue.

Susan stood quietly near The Screen, and Van nervously tapped a pen against his seat at the meeting table. Asano gazed out the fern windows in the outer lobby. Cuda approached Stilt, noting his new growth of beard and the haggard look under his eyes. His cheeks were pale and drawn, and he hadn't showered in two days. "Wha'd he say, *amigo*?"

Stilt folded his arms and let his eyes roam about the office. "He said everything went well, no one has asked any questions, he doesn't expect any more trouble."

Cuda's mouth fell into a deep frown. "Until we come back. You saw the news, man. Bug's not gonna stop until we go or he goes, an' then someone else will just waltz on into his place, and we start again."

"Chill, brother. Not gonna happen." Stilt shuffled across the carpet to where Van sat. "You two should head back to the school and check out the site. See what you can find.

Cuda, call your brother in Oakland, see what he can swing over there."

Cuda flashed a pensive look, then nodded agreement. "Yeah, alright. Van, let's go, *amigo*."

Van rose, clapping Stilt on the shoulder. "We'll find out, buddy. Don't sweat."

"Thanks, *amigo*."

"Ain't nothin' but a thang, brother."

The two left, and Susan broke her silence. "I think we should talk."

Stilt nodded, looking blankly into the distance. He slumped down into a bodymold conference chair and cracked his fingers one by one. Asano looked at him briefly, then turned back to his view of the darkening sky.

Susan scratched her neck, straightened her suit jacket and walked slowly to the table. "You say the man responsible for the destruction of your school was a slinger known as Bug. The same man you tried to bust last Monday night."

"Uh-huh."

"You know he doesn't work for me."

"Okay."

"And I don't particularly like drug deals going down on company property. *My* company's property. I'd like to see him gone too."

"Great," Stilt mused, scratching his temple beneath the chrome eyepiece. "At least we're all in agreement."

Susan tried to find his gaze, a task made impossible by mere presence of the visor. "Stilt, I know how much this means to you. I want to help. I'd like to rebuild your school."

Stilt's eyebrows raised over the visor in surprise, creating the effect of an animated car bumper. "Are you shitting me?"

Susan smiled and slid gracefully into the adjacent office chair. "I never shit people when it's in my best interest to play straight."

"You'll have to excuse me, Ms. Kitayama," Stilt said formally, trying to find the right words to convey his meaning without directly insulting her. "I'm not in the habit of trusting suits in matters of the neighborhood. Especially since we haven't actually done anything yet."

"You stopped the break-in Wednesday night."

"That was squat," he replied a little too quickly. "No offense, but we didn't think getting a contract was gonna get us childcare duty."

Susan knew he referred to the stakeout with Murray, and shrugged it off. "None taken." She stared into the chrome, saw her green eyes reflected back. It made her uncomfortable, and she looked away. "Up until now, you have been contracting with the SFPD, and that's fine. But if you really want to go after Bug, I want to invite you to work for me."

Stilt wasn't really shocked by the revelation, though he looked it. "What's the deal?"

"You work for me. You, Kapp and Pezzoni. I give you bleeding-edge gear, comms, transportation. I rebuild the school, and you hire teachers to run it. You'd get a higher profile, and you'd be going after much bigger prey than mid-level slingers."

Stilt rolled his tongue around in his mouth, shifting nervously in the chair. "You giving me Bug?"

Susan winked seductively, and for the first time Stilt realized how absolutely stunning she was. "Today, Bug. Tomorrow, who knows? There's a lot of big game out there, Stilt. And you and your boys are too good to be hanging out on the street. You can do your community a much greater service by going after important quarry. Why screw around with slingers when you can have the satisfaction of taking down a supplier? Or even a boss?"

Stilt found himself mesmerized. "You think so?"

"I know so." Susan pursed her lips. The gesture was so subtle that someone else might not have noticed.

But Stilt was good at noticing things. His stomach began to feel warm, and he let himself smile. "Okay." He offered his hand across the corner of the conference table, and Susan grasped it firmly.

The elevator door beeped open in the lobby, and Van stepped out. "I wanna check with Windy, see what she knows."

Cuda followed, holding the door open for three bustling people who had just dashed in through the clear lobby doors. The furry one with the dark round glasses nodded at them as he and an attractive woman in jeans skipped across the threshold into the elevator. "'Scuse me, blokes."

A tall, olive-complected man in a black overcoat followed, and Cuda let the door close behind them.

The two friends walked a couple of paces, then froze in the same stunned realization, crying out simultaneously: "That was the Champ!"

Stilt entered the lab and was immediately disgusted. Love held out his hand and gestured proudly at the setup: a clear Plexi box, about nine by nine, with nickel-sized holes for air-flow. A plastic plate full of half-eaten fresh fruit lay on the floor near the bolted hatch. The KML unit sat depressed in the far corner, picking its fur with soft pads, stopping every now and then to look at his cracked yellow nails. It noticed Stilt and the short executive, and slid to his feet. The techs hadn't even bothered to dress him; his genitalia, though retracted and covered by a thick flap of skin, was visibly wet, and smelly from recent urination.

"Get him the hell out of there," Stilt ordered plainly. "And give him some clothes."

Love dropped his proud smile. "Why, Mr. Tokura, surely you can't be serious. It's a military construct. We don't know what it is capable of."

Stilt strode forward, bypassing several astonished lab techs in white coats. He knelt by the security pad, and the construct scuffled toward him, reaching a three-toed hand toward him. It flattened against the hard plastic, and the construct cocked his head inquisitively.

Stilt glanced at Love, punching up the prompt on the screen. "What's the code?"

"Mr. Tokura, please. Let's not be hasty."

"The code, Mr. Love."

"Don't you think you're being a little rash...?"

Stilt sighed, leaned his forehead against the plastic wall. "The only little rash around here is you, Mr. Love. Give me the code. Or shall I tell your boss, Ms. Kitayama, that you decided to lock a sentient, intelligent being in a plastic cage without benefit of clothing or waste facilities?"

Love squirmed, frowning beneath thick glasses. His armpit began to itch. "C-4-M-E-L-B-0-Y."

"What?"

"The code."

Stilt shook his head incredulously. "*Camel Boy?* Holy shit." He punched up the pattern on the small keypad, and the tungsten bolt retracted. He stood, swung the door open, and extended a hand.

The construct reached up and grasped it, and together they strolled from the lab.

"Oh, Mr. Love," Stilt added, pausing in the doorway. "He will be staying with us in our suite, and taking regular meals with us as long as we are here."

Love grimaced with sour lips as he watched the creature waddle away like a child clutching a father's hand. Shivering with disgust, he realized he was beginning not to like that man.

27

RESIDUAL CLOUDS from the morning rain still hung low in the sky, leaking a depressing but merciful drizzle on the soaked wreckage of the Shihodo School of Martial Arts. The fire had been long extinguished, local volunteers aided in their efforts by the downpour Saturday night. Half the block had been blown away. The storefront of the school was nonexistent, a single concrete support rising behind the demolished staircase, a few sundry pipes and broken pieces of furniture poking up out of the rubble.

Cuda trudged through the saturated plaster, wood and stone. The heavy mist from above beaded and collected on his nylon jacket in tiny wet pinpoints. A couple of arson experts from Cheryl's precinct poked about as promised, watched by a handful of fire officials who had cordoned off the surrounding area. The resident population on Irving was sparse at the moment, due to Fisk holding mass across the street.

Cuda scanned the wreckage for several minutes, then suddenly looked up from the ground. The large, impressive form of Kim, legendary cook at the Ace & Gryphon pub, appeared on the sidewalk, outside the police line. He was only five-nine or so, but weighed three-hundred easily, all of it solid muscle. He wore a grease-stained apron with the Ace &

Gryphon logo on a front kangaroo pocket, and his thick, hairless arms were bare. Salt-and-pepper hair circled the back of his head like a wire fringe, and a few long remaining strands were slicked back against his pale scalp. His features were pleasingly round and jolly, like a Buddha statue. Cuda smiled when he noticed the wriggling form in the cook's arms. Jesse's wombat, completely undamaged and, so it looked, completely well-fed. Leave it to Kim.

"Cuda. Look who showed up yesterday afternoon."

"How the hell did you get a hold of Wulfshall?" Cuda strode amused toward the yellow tape, reaching out a large hand to scritch the pudgy marsupial between the ears.

Kim flashed a gap-toothed grin. "The little bastard showed up yesterday afternoon. Must've got out the window when Mike took Jess to the hospital. Found him poking 'round the garbage out back, so I took him in to feed him. I know Jess doesn't like it, but I can't help myself, y'know? Probably a good thing, too."

Van appeared at the corner of 15th, and ambled up to the two men. Cuda turned to greet him, reminded of the purpose at hand. *"¿Qué pasa?"*

Van saw the wombat and his eyes brightened. "Talked to Windy. She didn't give us up."

Kim frowned. "Windy in trouble? She's a good girl. Drinks a little much, but a good girl..."

"Wha'd she say?" Cuda interrupted.

"She saw Pick yesterday. He said a couple of Bug's boys came asking questions. Real nasty. They made him bust Kitayama's network to get our information. Must've been a bitch and a half, too, cause they broke four of his fingers before he said yes."

Cuda scowled in contempt, but continued to pet the wombat automatically. "Ain't never heard o' Pick."

Van shrugged, jamming a nervous hand into the front pocket while positioning a fresh toothpick with the other. "Yeah, he's a small-time Null hacker in the Mission, real close to Hustle City. But he's apparently got some primo custom software. Lotta people want him to freelance, but so far, the suits haven't noticed him."

"Windy work with him a lot?"

"Sometimes. She knows him alright, I guess. Enough to trust him."

"You get names?"

"Yeah," Van nodded, as Kim's eyes shot back and forth, hypnotized by the intrigue. Van pulled a scrap of yellow paper from his pocket. "There was a Thai, long hair, name's Quan. Kinda itchy, spastic. There was a big guy, too."

"Name?"

"Biggs."

"No shit?"

"No shit." Van crumpled the paper and shoved it back into his pocket. Cuda removed his hand from the wombat's head, and it let out a frustrated whine.

"Can we get him to testify?"

Van frowned. "Testify? Shit, everyone I've talked to wants Bug six-feet-under. They've all faced the fact that it's the only way to get rid of the sombitch. But it ain't too likely with the corporate protection he keeps around."

Kim nodded vehemently. "'Bout time the streeters stood up against the suits. We gotta show everybody the damn corporations can't turn fight their fucking wars in the hood."

Van reached up and adjusted his beret. "Windy's gonna get him to do a check on Bug, see who he's tied to."

Kim raised an eyebrow. "You guys going after Bug?"

Cuda sighed apprehensively. "Kim, you gotta help us out, *amigo*."

"Sure, man. Anything. You know that."

"I want you to spread the word. Me and Stilt and Van, we gotta duck out for awhile. We got ourselves some resources, and it's gonna be a full-time job. You tell the other *dojos* they're gonna have to watch the Sunset while we're gone, 'cause the Shihodo boys are radio-silent 'til further notice."

Kim agreed. "That's kosher. 'Bout time we paid you guys back for everything."

Cuda blushed, stepping away. "Don't sweat, *amigo*. Just let everybody know we won't be able to watch their backs for awhile. They'll have to do it themselves."

Kim nodded, waving as he ambled away with the squirming wombat. "You got it, amigos. Stay alive."

Van saluted with an index finger. "Later, Kim. Peace."

Cuda slapped a hand on his young companion's shoulder. "Alright. We know Kim will spread the word."

Van sniffed, wiggled the toothpick around with his tongue. "Did you talk to your brother?"

"Yeah. He says he'll back us up as much as he can, but he can't take any officers off the beat."

"That's cool. We may not even need 'em."

Cuda smiled sadly. "Oh ho, don't fool yourself, little brother. When we dive into this, we're going deep. And we ain't coming up 'til Bug is drowned."

Either the retreating storm clouds had completely blocked out the sun on their way out to sea, or Susan Kitayama had turned the window tinting all the way up. Or both.

Susan impatiently tapped at the virtual keyboard beneath the blue computer screen. She cradled her head in her right palm, while her left index finger poked at the projected letters and numbers. The nearly silent hum of the computer's auto-save met her ears, and her green eyes glowed aqua with the light from the portable screen. She sighed, drumming her fingers against her graceful jaw. Her pinky found its way to her mouth, and she bit down on the sculpted white nail.

"Susan, darling, I really must complain..."

"Hello, Love." She sighed again, staring blankly at the field of blue in the pixels of the UHD monitor.

Love huffed into the office, pulling a chair from the conference table. The remainder of the office was vacant and dark, except for the monitor's sapphire light. "Susan, this Stilt person is behaving most rudely."

"What did he do?" she asked without emotion.

"He stormed into the lab and demanded we release that monstrosity from its container."

She continued to stare into the blue abyss of the screen. "He was right."

Love snarled. "Susan! I'm surprised at you! You've worked very hard to get where you are today. I find it impossible to conceive that you would just step aside to a bunch of foul-mouthed, bad-mannered cretins from the hood."

Her eyes darted away from the screen and found his. He clamped his mouth shut immediately.

"Love, these are my guests," she explained in a tired, maternal tone which set him on edge. "They have just had their homes and livelihood destroyed. They need patience and understanding and our full support right now."

Love swiveled in the chair opposite his boss, grimacing sarcastically. "Oh, come now. Don't play the humanitarian. We both know why you're being so nice to these poor sods. You're *buying* them, Susan."

She continued to stare at him. "You have a problem with that?"

"Not by a long shot. I just want you to be honest with me. With yourself." He ran a pale hand over his plasticized hair. "How long do you think it'll take before they realize you're using them for your own anti-Selby campaign? This Stilt won't be very happy, knowing he and his friends were promised glory and retribution and got used for nothing more than corporate espionage. Something they know nothing about, and are completely unqualified for, I might add."

Susan stood, glaring at him with furious eyes, and he shut up again.

"They don't *need* to know about corporate espionage. All they *need* to know is how to take down, kill and extract. I'll give them the appropriate targets. And what I don't need right now is a sniveling turd telling me how to run my business!" She turned and threw one of the gleaming metal pens at the window. It clacked sharply against the acrylic transparency and fell silently to the carpeted floor. She blinked slowly, re-centering herself. "I'm sorry."

Love stood and pushed in his chair. "No apology necessary, Susan. It's quite obvious you know what you're doing. I'm behind you one-hundred percent." His tone was completely unconvincing, but Susan decided to let it go. This was not the time to let loose the Tigress. If she ever needed the loyalty of the little man, it was now.

"Has Maddock and his party arrived?"

Love nodded, turning toward the executive lift. "Affirmative. They said the suite will be most satisfactory."

Susan sighed, running a slender index finger along the smooth finish of The Desk. "Will dinner be served on schedule?"

"On schedule," Love replied, heading for the elevator. "See you then."

Susan breathed deeply, shaking the melancholy from her head. What the hell was wrong with her? What was the problem? This project was absolutely no different from any other.

Why wasn't she convinced of that?

28

RIDLEY STEPPED from the fourth floor elevator and strode purposefully through the corridor of Monoped Systems headquarters. The receptionist waved a desperate hand. "Dr. Ridley, you can't—"

"Fuck off," he answered curtly, bypassing her desk completely and pushing through the huge doors of tinted glass. Bartak sat behind his enormous black desk console, fingertips pressed together expectantly. The dim red fallout light from the mounted LED lamps cast foreboding shadows around the darkened office. Some of the light caught the arms dealer's brown Nikons, giving them an eerie, predatory glow.

Ridley was not about to be intimidated. "Where the hell have you been, Bartak? We've been out there trying to track down the KML unit, and you've been nowhere. Do you know how many times I came by the office yesterday? What the hell have you been doing for the past forty-eight hours?" He continued pacing the floor, thin face beginning to turn red. "I thought you said you could handle it!"

Bartak leaned forward slowly, folding his hands on the desk. "Dr. Ridley, as it so happens, I have been in satellite conferences with Frank Selby. After my retrieval team tried and failed, I went directly to the top, fully expecting you to fail as well."

Ridley clamped his eyes shut, blinking stupidly. "But my team is following Jorgenson's chip. They may have already—"

"Your team," Bartak explained, rising calmly, "will find exactly what *we* found *yesterday*. An abandoned GBS van and a homing chip under the front seat. The truck's just south of Bakersfield on the shoulder of I-5. Jorgenson and his assistant are onto you. They flew the coop, Doctor."

Ridley stared at him uncomfortably. "That's impossible. We know he has the construct."

Bartak smiled bright acrylic teeth. "If he does, we now no longer have any way of locating them."

"Well?" Ridley spat.

"Well what?"

"What the fuck are we going to do?"

"*We,*" Bartak answered softly, "are doing nothing. The cover has been blown, the professionals have been called in. And I am tired of taking Selby's heat on your behalf. Whatever brilliant formula you discovered for the new generation of Jet has been completely negated by your incompetence in the delivery."

Ridley scowled. "I don't have to take this from you."

As he turned, he caught the brief buzz of a servo motor in the hall, and suddenly the soldier was behind him.

He was slender, with tight, sickly-green/white skin, pale to the point of looking dead, shaved head stocked with monitors and LED readouts. A streamlined Minolta multi-optic eyepiece covered the left side of his face almost completely. A fiber-optic cable ran from the interface socket in his right temple down his armored shoulder to another socket on a computer console strapped to his forearm. His right fist was steel and chrome, and he wore the drab gray uniform of a Baltic soldier. There was a patch over his left arm—three simple initials, probably referencing the force he'd served with:

I-R-K.

A tight harness hissed and contracted, intravenous chem-gates opening, internal computer delivering a boost of artificial adrenal compound.

Ridley panicked. "What the hell...?!"

Before he could move, the soldier had him by the arm and was pulling him out of the office toward the elevator.

Bartak stood, following as far as his office door. As he watched silently, the pale specialist dragged Ridley, thrashing and screaming, down the hall. The receptionist smiled politely as Ridley was drawn through the open doors into the lift. His glasses hung to one side from his ear and his eyes were bursting with absolute fear.

The soldier held his arm, patiently waiting for the doors to close. As they did, there was a high-pitched scream and a series of mechanical ripping sounds. Several seconds later, the elevator beeped open, and Ridley lay in a disemboweled heap of razored flesh. Blood coated the walls. The soldier was gone.

Bartak unfolded his arms and pushed away from the frame of his office door. "Sara, call down to maintenance. Get a clean-up crew and file an accidental death report with Genetech Bio."

The young woman smiled and winked. "Right away, Mr. Bartak."

They gathered at the table in the executive dining suite, artificial candlelight setting them aglow in fiber-optic colors. The windows were set on low tint, and the stars were beginning to peek out from the thinning gray clouds. The Bay Bridge was visible, illuminated by the steady flash of AV strobes and color-shifting E-light tubes.

The table was set lavishly with platinum candlesticks holding the LED candles. Place settings included both western flatware and a pair of beautiful lacquered maple chopsticks. The dishes were vintage Mikasa, and the meal consisted of the finest West Coast Asian-inspired cuisine Stilt had ever tasted.

The visored teacher wore a stylish tunic and trousers, purchased for him by the company to replace his immolated wardrobe. Cuda sat next to him, picking at his rice, clad in a similar outfit. Van kept to his usual uniform of denim and leather, but had shucked out of the biker jacket to hang it from the back of the chair. He kept his beret cocked to one side as he ravenously slurped up the noodles.

Asano occupied the end chair, dressed in a formal white shirt and black sport coat. Larry was next, then Kelly, having changed into another lavish outfit. Creep leaned back in his chair, casually sipping the twenty-year-old wine from a Murano crystal goblet. Love nervously poked at his fish, touching nary a bite.

Susan occupied the hostess position at the head of the table, and the KML construct sat politely next to Stilt to her right. He was a most inquisitive creature, watching everyone else closely before eating his own food. He would sit for minutes on end, observing the manners and habits of the dinner guests, processing the data into a practical application. Susan actually found the thing amusing, not foul or disgusting as she'd been led to believe.

They ate in silence, each locked in their own private world of thought. Occasionally, Kelly would stop to ask Susan or Love a question, then, once answered, go back to her food. Finally, Cuda broke the ice, addressing Creep. "You know, I lost a hundred-fifty bucks on you."

Creep beamed, a bit inebriated. "Sorry 'bout that, mate. Kelly, can you punch the guy a cred?"

Cuda laughed. "No, it's alright. I can swing it."

Creep protested, waving a furry hand, Armani shirt puffing and billowing loosely around his arms. "Really. I lost a lot o' people money."

Cuda shook his head. "No, man. It's alright."

"You sure?"

"Yeah, bro. We got us a corporate gig. The school's going back up. For once, everything looks pretty okay."

Creep swallowed another sip, reached forward for the old bottle, and refilled his glass. "What school is this?"

Stilt took a bite of salmon and grunted. "Our *dojo* down on Irving got blown up yesterday. One of our friends was killed in the blast."

Creep froze. "What, the one on the news?"

Stilt nodded, and KML029 duplicated the motion. It opened a wide, toothsome mouth and let out a strangled bleating sound.

Everyone looked at the construct as he stared back at them with deep-set eyes, full of wonder at the interest he had just caused by exercising his developing vocal chords. He smiled, and Creep returned to the subject.

"Bloody shame, mates. I saw that. Fucking cowards."

Kelly leaned to her right and quietly suggested Creep take it easy on the alcohol. It was his sixth glass at dinner, and he'd already had two beers upon their arrival at the suite. He looked at her, melted and put down his glass. "Alright, punkin. Jus' fer you."

Stilt glared across the table at the hirsute gladiator. He clearly wasn't wild about the idea of a drunkard fighting in the ranks of the team, but Susan had insisted upon it as a provision of the contract. Still, what the hell kind of use was a television wrestler in a street fight, or a bust? The answer, of course, was absolutely *no* use, that it was a completely manufactured public relations scheme. Stilt recalled having complained just hours ago to Van and Cuda about being used this way.

Cuda had put on the well-worn hat of friend and counselor, explaining the big picture: They had to make certain concessions in order to succeed at the goals they'd set for themselves. Explaining the big picture to Stilt was something Cuda just had to do from time to time, to keep the slender guy's thoughts and priorities in order. Hell, *someone* had to keep the train on the tracks.

Susan leaned forward, green eyes glinting in the soft light. "So, Stilt. I've arranged practice facilities here at the building. You can start whenever you're ready. We should have uniforms and equipment in a week or so."

Stilt bowed his head graciously. "Thanks. I'd like to begin training as soon as possible. Tomorrow, maybe. We have to go over official police procedures. John's brother has agreed to lend us some expertise in that area."

Cuda paused thoughtfully. He was happy to hear the *sensei* in Stilt returning to the surface. He had truckloads of leadership quality when he had a target, a goal, a motivation. When confronted by bureaucracy or cynicism, however, he tended to lapse into the depressed lethargy Cuda and Van had seen so many times.

Stilt was a doer. And without the means to do, he tended to let priorities fall by the wayside. Cuda swore silently to keep Stilt's mind active, keep the quest alive for him. With an impassioned Kai Tokura leading them against Bug—or anyone else for that matter—and with a coherent and well-trained team, they would be a force to be reckoned with.

Asano set his chopsticks aside and glanced up the table at Stilt. "Would you mind if I sat in on some of the workouts?"

Before Stilt could answer, Susan glared down at the musician. "*Tanaka-san*, don't you have a recording session to think about?"

Stilt shrugged. "You're still welcome, anytime you want to stop in."

Asano offered him a nod, then quietly went back to his food. Susan caught herself too late. What had she done? She didn't have to protect Asano. Or did she? And if she did, what did that say about the fate of this new project of hers?

The construct bared his teeth and let out a surprised belch. He'd never done that before, and found it a bizarre but satisfying sensation. The diners looked at him with raised eyebrows, and he held a thick hand over his mouth, managing a guttural, "Pardon."

For some reason, the gravelly comment struck a funny chord with Van and Creep. Both men lapsed into loud spasms of laughter.

Love scowled at the unmannerly thugs, but Susan took the lighthearted moment to raise her glass. "A former teacher of mine once said 'the straight and true point, when properly directed, has no other course but to the inner circle'. She was referring to archery, but I've always found a deeper meaning in her words. That those people who are given the proper chance have no alternative but success at anything they put their minds to."

Her eyes met Stilt's and an electric moment passed between them. The right side of her mouth crept up into a seductive half-smile. "To the *Sakuru*. Like its very shape, may it be without end."

Stilt mimicked her smile, lost in thought. *Sakuru. The Circle. Okay.* As long as she was footing the bill, Stilt figured she could call them anything she damn well pleased. He reckoned The Circle wasn't the worst of names. "Hear, hear." He matched her toast, raising his goblet with the rest of the assembled group, who added their own well-wishes.

"Cheers."

"*Mazel tov.*"

"What he said."

The construct hoisted his glass in an awkward-looking but dexterous hand, offering an animal grunt.

29

IT SEEMED LIKE the plot to a cheap spaghetti western: Three angry vigilantes get deputized, team up with an Indian guide and a talking mule, and ride out into the desert on the trail of the evil cattle rustlers.

From any other point of view, at any other time, such a gathering might have spawned media ridicule and public laughter. For some reason, however, the public was too busy fighting the looters, vandals and gang bangers who now ran uninhibited in the streets of the Sunset. Stilt and his school were gone, that's all anybody knew. And when he'd be back, if at all, was anybody's guess. So grab a tire iron or a gun, and live it up while the cat's away.

The cops had always avoided the neighborhoods, venturing into the slums only upon the rarest occasion. Now the citizens' main link to the SFPD was in the wind, and whatever progress the Irving Street *Yōgosha* had made over the past few years toward neighborhood peace was quickly swept away with the resulting anarchy. The fact that two gang treaties were broken within a week of one another didn't help matters.

The underground arms market did swift business with neighborhood property owners once again. They continuously sold through stocks of ammunition and high-caliber automatic pistols within the first three days. The new lightweight plastic armor jackets sold especially well.

Donald Kimm from Kimm's Han Mu Do and some of the boys from Dragon Kung Fu really did make an effort to keep the peace. They organized evening patrols and ran armed escorts for the kids on school days. But after only two weeks, Donald was shot in the head with a .44 automag at close range while on his evening beat.

Community depression set in quickly.

Heather's Beauty Supply was firebombed twice during the month. 21st Century Home Appliance on 19th resorted to contracting local gangs for security as the streeters from the Mission District filtered down into the Sunset.

Local chapters of Guardian Angels sprang up overnight, generally improving some conditions on the street, but still unable to bring the random mega-violence to a stop. Bouncers at The Stump confiscated an average of thirty weapons per night, and stopped at least eighteen homicides from taking place on the premises during the month.

After a bloody gang conflict in the Ace & Gryphon which included two fatal stabbings and a drowning in the toilet, Sam radically reduced her business hours, and Kim spent long nights atop the pub with a loaded assault rifle. The cafés closed completely. Customers at the outdoor tables were too much of a target for the daily drive-bys.

Kevin Cedric was found face down in a rain puddle behind the Ace & Gryphon dumpster sometime during the second week of mayhem. His eyes had ruptured, and the major blood vessels in his head had burst. An empty tube with a one-shot hypo lay next to his foot.

A string of deaths by overdose followed like no other in the history of the plagued hoods. After awhile, undercover cops began to turn up, asking questions, taking blood samples. It was obviously a problem that surpassed the negligible importance of the community. Prominent people in the neighborhood began to fall victim to the thick red liquid in the disposable hypo.

Bug's outlook brightened significantly. Even without Dennis Murray's alleged distribution chain, his demand skyrocketed. The public was eating the shit up, and revenue was breaking records. Bug's operation alone reported a monthly gross of ten million dollars to the shell company Selby used to launder income from the illicit pharma trade.

The mood in the Sunset was dark, dimming to the level of the other districts, and seemed to grow darker with each passing day until the video showed up.

It was a standard thumb drive, unlabeled, left somewhere on the bar in the Ace & Gryphon. Copies began to surface soon after, and before long everyone had a duplicate of the eyewitness footage. BayTV's evening news ran it every day for a week.

No one knew who shot it, but if it was anything, it was explicit. The total footage ran about eight minutes, and focused on a six-year-old black kid from the moment his older sister shot him up with the single-use hypo. It was a generic alley exterior, and the single shot centered on a graffiti-covered brick wall. It looked as if the videographer had been shooting from an upstairs tenement window opposite the alley. There were about half a dozen older bystanders, laughingly content to watch as the poor child quickly lost his mind, screaming and slamming headfirst repeatedly into the graffiti wall. It wasn't a particularly long time, but it seemed like excruciating hours to those who saw it. Somebody in the video counted off twenty slams before the child collapsed twitching to the wet ground, his skull beaten and crushed grotesquely by the self-inflicted trauma.

No one so much as raised a finger to stop it.

No protest at all.

Then a militant gay street gang made a radical turn from their usual skinhead prey and began to concentrate on the new plague of the Sunset—the Jet slingers. Leather was the chosen style, an automatic pistol the weapon of choice. The Diamond Dogs were flamboyant, tough and highly visible. Led by the one-eyed Halloween Jack, they resolved to strike fear back into the hearts of the underworld. Or something like that.

Unfortunately, Halloween Jack and his boys were occupied in a three-way skirmish with two other gangs the night a little subset of the Golden Gate Trolls decided to shoot Barney Chao and loot the donut shop.

Barney lay on the floor, bleeding from a massive chest wound. The half-dozen armed streeters watched him closely for a moment, making sure he wasn't going to get up and shoot back. The gang was an ethnic mix. One dude jumped the counter for the cash register while two others ran to the back for the inventory. The remaining three stood watch—two at the front door, one over Barney's sprawled body.

They didn't see any police lights, didn't hear any vehicles. A common state of affairs nowadays.

They'd only looked toward the counter for a second to check progress, and were understandably surprised to see three men standing inside the broken door when they turned back around. The strangers were clad in black uniforms, with a shell of ballistic armor pads molded strategically over the exterior. There was some kind of weird animal-thing with them, and it peered angrily out of luminescent, sunken blue eyes. It wore a matching uniform, and seemed to have some kind of slingshot apparatus strapped onto the back of its left arm.

The tallest of the four had a slender frame and loose black hair, and wore a shiny chrome visor over his eyes. He held two lengths of steel in his gloved hands.

The huge, dark-bronze man next to him sported a shaved head and thin beard, and the short, scarred Italian wore a black beret cocked to one side. His jaw flexed as her gnawed on a toothpick.

All four were geared with wireless earpiece mics, probably linked with a mastoid implant.

One of the thugs, a short Asian with a green rooster crest and gleaming .45 was the first to speak. "—the fuck are you?"

"Gun," ordered the tall, visored one.

"Gotcha," replied the animal-thing.

There was a brief whistle of air, and the astonished criminal's gun was pelted away across the shop.

The tall one folded his arms, twin lengths of metal sticking up from his hands like strange antennae. "You boys wanna put everything down and come along nicely?"

The dude at the cash register broke into an amused smile. "No," he said, raising a sawed-off 12-gauge at the standing group.

"Didn't think so," was the knowing reply.

The arrest was completed in less than a minute: KML029 pinpointed the guy with the shotgun, letting fly a second steel shot that hit the kid squarely between the eyes. Stilt convinced the crested thug with a simple *escrima* whirl of titanium, and sent the youth unconscious to the floor. Van and Cuda floored the other thugs on the way to the back.

They were expected, and Van got the wind knocked out of him with a shotgun blast against the wall as he entered the kitchen. Cuda more than covered the disparity, grabbing the muzzle and whipping the stock back into the gunman's face. He freed the rifle, completely shoving the kid to the floor and pumping another round into the chamber as Van managed a convoluted and inelegant brawling maneuver, smashing the criminal's face into the garbage receptacles by the back door.

Stilt burst in, sweating profusely. He glanced down at the kid Cuda held at rifle point. "Let that one go."

"What?"

"You heard me."

Cuda backed away, allowing the kid to stand. Stilt approached and grabbed him by his ripped army jacket. "You get to do us a favor."

The stocky thug nodded emphatically, eyes wide. "Y-yeah, *amigo*. Anything."

Stilt's eyes drilled into the youth from behind their chrome mask. His hands were firm, his jaw set like granite. "I'm not your *amigo*, jackhead. You and your friends been partyin' a bit while we've been away, haven't you?"

The punk kept nodding. "Y-yeah, I guess."

Stilt gathered his jacket lapels even tighter around his fists and raised the kid into the air, their faces only inches away. "You're gonna go back out there and you're gonna let everyone know that The Circle is here, right?"

"R-r-right, s-sure. The Circle."

Van huffed forward, clutching his bruised abdomen. "If you forget, just tell 'em Stilt's back and he's pissed."

They let him go, and as he sailed out the back door to land in the gravel of the rear lot, Stilt repeated, "The Circle."

When they exited the kitchen, the press was already there, including their own contingent. Larry snapped pictures while Kelly covered the scene with a UHD lasercam, and Creep posed with an unconscious thug. As he cuffed the punk behind his back, the furry celebrity fed the news cameras a creative but totally fabricated story about following the trail of a notorious gang.

KML029 hobbled over to Stilt and Cuda, assisting Van through the swinging door. Barney Chao had been moved already. The only trace that he'd been there was a smeared pool of crimson behind the counter.

Cuda scowled at Creep and the medias. "Look at that, man. Fucker didn't do nothin'."

Stilt shrugged. "He's doing his job, we're doing ours, bro. I don't care, as long as he shows up to practice."

The medias *oohed* and *aahed* as Creep slung the youth over his shoulder and exited to the police van outside. More news cameras awaited on the sidewalk outside the cracked storefront. Pezzoni coughed, wincing as his ribs contracted. "Son of a bitch."

Stilt patted him on the shoulder, and the remaining four trudged slowly toward the bright halos of the media lights outside.

The day was almost retaliatory in its brightness. The soft, white hum of television voices babbled into the midst of the penthouse suite at the giant Kitayamacorp arcology. Van and the KML construct reclined on the plush sofa, beers in hand, sleepily watching the morning news. The debut digital copy of the new and improved *Masque* lay looking up from a tablet on the marble coffee table, Creep's hairy mug smiling viciously out from the cover.

Cuda busied himself in the kitchenette with an enormous construction project he called a sandwich.

Van belched, pointing toward the television monitor. "Hey, Stilt. Look. You're on, bro."

Stilt exited the expensively-appointed bedroom, still buffing his wet hair with a thick cotton towel. "What."

Van gestured at the enormous wall screen. Stilt's image had just appeared behind a wall of microphones and television lights.

"Jesus, I look terrible on camera."

KML029 squinted at the portion of the screen that included the top of his flattened forehead. He grunted in his usual tone. "Me too." His speech capability had evolved much as Jorgenson had predicted, vocabulary increasing by leaps and bounds. Still, he was hesitant to utter anything more than short, gravelly commentary.

Stilt watched the image for a moment, slinging the damp towel around his bare shoulders. A black pair of Lycra workout shorts molded perfectly to his lower half. Finally disgusted with the pretentiousness of the whole media thing, he turned back toward the bedroom and was abruptly halted by a familiar female form in his way.

Stilt smiled, and Kelly matched his expression. "Hey, handsome. Care to dance?"

"I was just going to change."

"Oh, but Stilt, we love you just the way you are."

Stilt laughed quietly, then turned back toward the television screen and pointed at the beers in Van's and the construct's hands. "Gotta get dressed. Meeting in half an hour."

Kelly giggled at the boys' reaction to having to give up their beers. She followed Stilt with her eyes as he retreated toward his quarters. "Business, business, business."

Cuda nodded, a plate full of towering sandwich in one hand, a can of soda in the other. "Yeah, that's Stilt alright. Honestly I'm glad to see him so intent on something."

Van snarled, rolling from the couch to his stocking feet. "I kinda wish he'd chill. We're not goin' out tonight. I don't see what the big deal is..."

Cuda shook his head. "You don't know we're not goin' out tonight."

"But the contract says we only gotta go out twice a week —"

"—on company business," Cuda finished. "The rest of the time we can do what we want. Stilt worked hard to get us that provision, *amigo*. You may wanna see if your armor's repaired an' ready to go."

Van dropped his head angrily. "Aww, shit, man. This is gettin' old."

"I seem to remember little Van Pezzoni in the back of a police truck, playing with a taser and sayin' '*cool*'. You want out, you can talk to Stilt."

"No way, *amigo*." Van smiled. "I have too much fun complaining." He pulled on his Velcro high tops and dashed from the suite.

The construct stood and muttered, "Screen off." The television went dark, and he ambled slowly to his own room off the common area.

Cuda sat back on the sofa, and Kelly reclined next to him. "Speaking of complaining, that's what I came to talk to you guys about."

Cuda took an impressive bite of the sandwich and looked at her, mumbling through his food. "Wha'd we do now?"

Kelly shook her head and smiled beautifully, brushing her dark mop of wavy hair back with both hands. "Nothing. Actually, I wanted to talk to you about Creep."

Stilt entered the living area with a fresh pair of cotton baggies and a blue cotton *dogi* top slung over his bare shoulder. "What about him? He want more air time?"

Kelly turned, her face wrinkled in a mask of hurt and pity. "No, no, Stilt. That's just the problem."

"What, then?"

She stood, and Cuda followed visually, nervously chewing another bite. He hoped Stilt wouldn't pull the self-righteous shit that tended to alienate so many potential allies. He liked Kelly, and Larry was a Golden State Warriors fan, which made the man instantly compatible with Cuda. When Kelly spoke, he was impressed by her patience and understanding.

"He wants more action."

"Action?"

"Yes. We were just talking about it this morning. He feels like the cute little puppy in the pet store window, like he's being idolized and treated like a celebrity but no one will let him do anything."

"Has he tried talking to Susan?"

"No use. She put certain stipulations in his contract to quote-unquote 'protect' him. He's only allowed into the scene after you guys have it secure. Quite frankly it bugs the shit out of him, not being able to help out. He likes you guys. And the fact that Susan will let an intelligent military construct duke it out with the boys, but won't let *him* do squat...it really ly pisses him off."

Stilt folded his arms, not entirely convinced. "Why didn't he come personally?"

Cuda set his plate on the coffee table and stood tiredly. "Come on, man! She's trying to help us out here! What the fuck are you trying to prove, *amigo*?"

Kelly put up her hands, rapidly becoming both peacekeeper and negotiator. "Guys, come on. He didn't come because he was afraid you'd snub him. He thinks you have this elitist attitude or something. Like you're too good for him. He feels like you treat him differently."

Stilt produced a sarcastic half-smirk. "*We* treat him differently? Who the hell does he think set him up for that?"

Cuda shook his head. "It's true, man. You do. We all do."

Kelly bowed her head. "He just wants to help. Really help. Not just pose. That's all he ever wanted out of the Arena—to really win, without the glamour and artifice. Now that's all he wants out of The Circle."

Stilt shrugged into the robe, leaving it to hang open on his muscled chest and emaciated washboard stomach. "What do you want us to do, Kelly? He signed a contract."

She approached him, hands thrust into the tight pockets of her jeans. "Just, maybe...talk to Susan. She listens to you. I think maybe more than listens. Maybe she'd relax her grip a little if you hit it right."

Stilt paused, rolling the idea around in his head. He knew Maddock was good in the *dojo*. He was a belt in *aikido*, adept in many styles of *tai chi* and *taekwondo*. Years of grappling and learning how to fall, combined with a natural agility and fearlessness of heights, made him a potentially brilliant enforcer. But a contract was a contract, and if Creep had signed up to cuff some bad guys and smile for the cameras, that was his problem.

Stilt let out a frustrated sigh. More than anything, he hated to see talent, especially such raw, unbridled talent like Creep's, go to waste. "I'll see what I can do."

Kelly smiled and stood on her toes to kiss him on the cheek. "Thanks, big guy. I knew you wouldn't let me down."

Stilt blushed. "Well don't count your blessings yet." He was really going to have to get used to women kissing him like that. It had happened a dozen times in the past twenty-four hours, and he knew that as long as he was going to be a public figure, he had no choice but to expect those displays of affection.

Kelly gave Cuda a quick hug and peck on the cheek, then bid them farewell and skipped out of the apartment.

Stilt and Cuda looked at each other. Cuda shrugged. "I hope you can work something out. I'd like to see the Champ get in there and kick some ass with the rest of us."

Stilt laughed softly, running a hand through his recently-trimmed hair. He hated it this short, but knew it'd grow back quickly. "I'll let you know when hell freezes over."

30

PICK WAS NOT what he appeared to be. He was probably the most brilliant freelancer in the city, an expert at security networks and deadly Intruder Countermeasures Electronics, author of many a killer virus, defiler of many a so-called "secure" system. What he looked like was something entirely different. Of average height, he was round with bulldog features, unkempt gray hair sprouting in a shock from his pale head, matching wiry chin-beard, and the wardrobe of a touring roadie.

The apartment was a nondescript top-floor unit near Church Street. It was small, lovingly decorated in early Chuck E. Cheese and Godzilla, littered with broken action figures and alien-looking sex toys. Apparently Pick had an active social life, despite appearances.

An entire wall was dedicated to the storage of various flash media and digital storage cards, and a small table sat in the center of the living area where the "leetest haxxor" did his magic, mouth full of pizza, left pinky still in a splint.

The deck was a portable Sony UHD unit with onboard stealth WiFi, VPN and an automatic neural kill switch (which had already saved his brain on more than one occasion). An expensive toy, certainly, but not out of reach for someone with enough street contacts to acquire an antique Rolls Royce with a clean VIN on twenty-four-hour notice.

Pick was the poster child for the "Nulls" of the urban working class who were forgotten or ignored by society. Whether due to a bureaucratic mistake or to their own clever subterfuge, Nulls had no way of being traced through normal government channels. There were no birth records, tax records which he didn't pay, or utility bills which he also didn't pay. As soon as a debt was run up, it was erased by a simple excursion into the net, a few taps of the keyboard, a vocal command, maybe a small anti-ICE subroutine. Simple as that.

He never had to pay for anything except for what he bought for cash on the street—and most of that was financed through freelance work, or phony payroll credits from one of the larger corporations too fat and lazy to forensically audit their internal divisions.

He simply had no traceable identity, but also no rights and no legal recourse. He tended to stay indoors a lot because of that. It was the only drawback to being who he was, doing what he did, but it was a major consideration nonetheless.

Windy pulled up a chair and straddled it backwards. Her fishnets were torn at the left thigh, and her leather jacket was coated with a fine layer of dust. She hadn't been home since it'd been blown up by Bug's men, only two weeks after they'd done the Shihodo School. Her hair had gotten longer, rattier, wilder. Dark roots now spread from the crown of her head. Most of her fiber-optic stars had disappeared, and she'd been too busy hiding and running errands for The Circle to bother to replace them. The bangles and earrings still glowed, however not with their former intensity. She hadn't been out in the light for the past couple of days while Pick had been on what he affectionately called The Bug Hunt.

Now he was close, and it had certainly been an interesting journey. The Lexus AV-50 was owned outright by Monoped Systems, a splinter company of Harquebus Technologies, which in turn was a subsidiary of SelTech. Selby had some tough-ass security software, and Pick's deck was forced to punch out automatically on no less than seven occasions. The viral security guards tended to fry fifty terabytes of memory in about two nanoseconds—really nasty shit. Pick had no choice but to allow auto cut-out in those situations. It was either start back from the beginning, or lose everything he'd learned, downloaded, and/or saved from the Selby net. It took a long time to break in, but once there, he was like a child with an unlimited ride ticket in an amusement park, and no waiting in line.

Since the AV belonged to Monoped Systems, Bug could now be associated with them. Through Monoped and Harquebus, Bug could be traced back to Selby, though there were no official records stating anything of the kind. SelTech, through another couple holding companies, also owned a significant share of stock in Genetech Biological Engineering in Colorado, and paid the salary of one Jonathan Fox, creator and host of the Arena Combat League in Los Angeles—but it was not exactly a well-kept secret that Selby enjoyed the fights.

It got even more interesting with each passing day, every subsequent data run.

He discovered that SelTech had an entire directory dedicated to Kitayama's *"Sakuru"*, with complete bios and all sorts of very personal information.

This morning, he'd decided it was time to see where all of this intriguing information had come from. And to do it right, he had to go virtual. Manual input on a touch screen or keyboard was no match for the subtlety of mental commands at the speed of thought.

Windy helped him into the cybersuit. He zipped up the plastic jacket, powered up the cells, ducked into the optical helmet, and donned the tight sensory gloves. The contacts connected to a web of fiber-optic veins that encased his upper body, glowing in cycled colors with each new thought or nerve impulse.

Windy thought he looked like one of those time-lapse photographs of the freeway, with the red and yellow-white smears of psychedelic color streaking over his body in a beautiful, complex pattern. Pick flexed his left hand into a fist, wincing at the pain in his immobilized pinky. He sat again, plugged a cable into the back of the Sony, and jacked the other end into the helmet port. Leaning back, he shut his eyes and left reality behind.

"Mole. Run."

Windy descended back to her chair and watched the monitor as the aging hacker weaseled his way past the Selby security system. He was now inside virtual space—his senses were, anyway. The small UHD screen displayed his view of the digital environment, including his traveling avatar: A polygonal cartoon mole that tunneled through the red clay of the primary firewall, under the feet of the Patrol program ahead. The cop avatar stood there scanning the distance with mirrored eyes, oblivious.

Suddenly the clay ended and the mole scurried out into the light of a neon sign labeled MENU. The tiny avatar reared on its hind legs, and Windy could see Pick turning his head slightly, reading the word intently. Was it a fake menu? He'd been forced out of the Selby network under similar circumstances. Sometimes, to punish hackers and pirates, a system designer might hide false menu prompts or home pages in a data bank. When accessed, they had a tendency to transform into hideous flying maggots that bored into an icon faster than it could run away. Sometimes they would just explode, leaving the intruding unit's memory severely damaged. Thank God for the Hatasaka Cut-Out.

"Dome," ordered Pick, and the tiny mole became instantly encased in a hovering transparent bubble. "Gun." The mole reached into a fuzzy pocket, drawing out what looked like a Dirty Harry .44 magnum revolver. Windy followed his hand movements as he pantomimed them next to her in his chair.

There was a loud shot, and a blinding flash of light from the barrel of the gun. An enormous hole opened in the data wall behind the sign and the bubble-covered mole rocketed forward, leaving little mole droppings along the ground behind it. The menu sign flashed and became a platoon of Uzi-toting clowns, descending upon the false trail of defecation. The mole penetrated the bullet hole, leaving the security clowns to slip and slide in the trail of shit.

Once through the wall, Pick swiveled in his chair and mimed throwing something behind him. "Plaster," he muttered. Windy watched the display, and saw a fresh coat of cement over the hole he'd just shot in the wall. Within seconds, it was as if no damage had been done.

The electronic sound of rushing water caught Pick's attention, and he turned back to the interior of the directory he'd entered. "Sherlock," he ordered, and his avatar transformed into a floating magnifying glass. Pick scanned back and forth, taking in the dark interior of the directory. Suddenly, Windy saw an eruption of neon blue in the warped image of the glass. Flying digital droplets of water whizzed through the virtual space, and Pick smiled. "Groovy."

"What is it?"

"Datastream. Hidden. Only a few specific people would even know it's here."

"How do you know? It wasn't guarded."

"It wasn't guarded, named or labeled at all. None of this stuff is. That's why it's so dark in here."

"What's in the datastream?"

Pick wrinkled his nose and scanned around under his VR headset. "Well, this is the Circle subdirectory. I assume it has something to do with your boys, maybe even Kitayama. Sample." A small plastic beach bucket appeared in front of the hovering glass and dipped down into the rushing neon river.

The bucket disappeared, and Windy watched the flash drive in the Sony light up green. "Now," said Pick, wiggling his unbroken fingers within the wired gloves, "let's find out where it goes."

Windy was mesmerized by the images she witnessed on the Sony's tablet screen. Pick swiveled again and smiled. "Surf's Up." The magnifying glass transformed, becoming an amorphous silicone blob, and within moments it was an elegant silver surfer, complete with a sleek, chrome board.

"Cowabunga," he said, and the surfer leaped into the air, swinging his board down beneath him. Upon contact with the datastream, the water surged to life, erupting in azure neon color beneath the swiveling surfboard. The desk speakers suddenly blasted *Pipeline,* and the silver icon let out a shrill war cry as the first wave hit him and began to carry him forward.

The stream ran through a hundred different subsystems, all interconnected, all owned by Selby. Huge, sprawling metropolitan virtual realities opened out before him, whizzing by at rates impossible to comprehend visually. Windy was suddenly overcome with dizziness and had to look away. She took a deep breath and swallowed, and the motion sickness eventually subsided. She wasn't sure if she should admire Pick for being used to the speed and virtual motion, or not.

The pipeline ran from Los Angeles to San Francisco, a great, spreading mass of silicon-based grids and virtual arcologies of towering crystal. And Windy gasped when she saw the approaching complex on the screen.

Kitayamacorp.

Suddenly, the river dropped down beneath Pick's surfing icon, and the chrome man toppled with the cascading water. The surrounding environment looked like a rabbit hole, and it gave Pick an idea. "Alice," he said, and the surfer became a small animated girl, identical to the illustrations in the original Lewis Carroll book, tumbling head over heels through the tunnel. A moment before impact, she spun upright and her dress and petticoats opened out like a parachute. As soon as she touched down, the water surged again, pushing her forward uncontrollably.

"Shit," Pick mumbled. "Trout." And Alice was a fish.

Pick turned his head and the screen moved as he followed the datastream into the Kitayamacorp metroplex. "Looks like Kitayama's got herself a mole." Suddenly the water dropped again, this time flowing down through a heavy steel grate, slits too small to fit through. The giant, silvery trout wriggled and flopped over the thick mesh. "Hmm. Have to try it from the other side. I wonder who wrote this." As if in direct response to the question, the surrounding floor suddenly blinked in a rainbow of neon scrawl. *Joey Chin. Joey Chin. Joey Chin.* His name was literally written all over it. Pick laughed. "I don't believe it."

Windy frowned. "I don't get it. Who's Joey Chin?"

Pick had his fish cough up a small glowing marker to keep his place, then he jacked out, powered down and removed his helmet. "No, I mean I really *don't* believe it. That's gotta be the biggest load of crap I've ever seen on a program." He stood and pulled the gloves off one at a time.

"You mean he didn't write it?"

"Oh, he could have." Pick unzipped the cybersuit and folded the jacket over the back of his chair. "But it's too obvious. It's a total Timmy move. My money's on someone else using our pal Joey Chin as a misdirect."

Windy nodded, finally grasping this inside knowledge of the hacker world. "So now what?" she asked.

Pick found an open pack of nic-sticks on the toy shelf and cooked up a fresh one. "Now we gotta find out who *is* on the other side of that grate."

"We're doing what?" Cuda paced the hardwood floor of the enormous *dojo*, his feet sticking and un-sticking as he went. "Bug?! Are you crazy?"

Stilt leaned casually against his staff, the gleam from its polished finish casting stationary sun-pixies throughout the cavernous exercise room. A vast array of both modern and ancient martial arts weapons were suspended in hanging racks on the military gray walls. An array of variable-tint windows angled out in a neat bank facing east. The KML construct stood at attention, listening intently. Van lounged on a mat in the corner, chewing a toothpick and cracking his toes. Asano leaned silently against the entry wall, high-fashion clothes in direct contrast to the cotton workout garb of the others.

Stilt licked his lips and nodded. "Maybe. But we're gonna tear him down."

"What the fuck are you on, *amigo*?!"

Stilt frowned. "Not funny, John."

"Sorry. I just seem to remember a very irate Cheryl Bonner threatening us with certain emasculation if we tried to go after Bug again—"

Stilt waved his hand tiredly. "—without her authority." He paused, raised an eyebrow. "We've got it."

"How?"

"Just talked to Susan this morning. Cheryl's giving us the go ahead, now that we're hot shit. We all passed the exam," Stilt said, invoking the Federal Law Enforcement Civil Service Examination. "We're all authorized to make arrests in the corporate sector."

Cuda laughed awkwardly, eyes full of sadness. "The hell are we gonna do? Wait 'til he comes back to the alley downstairs to make another deal with Dennis?"

"Yep." Stilt grinned and leaned more weight against the staff. "Dennis has been contacted. Bug wants him back in the distribution network. He got worried when Dennis didn't show right after the bad bust last month, so he went looking for him, found him in the hospital with his ass in a sling. Evidently, our favorite cannon-fodder fed him some bullshit about trying to escape and being shot in the butt. Bug ate it up, and they set a date to renegotiate the distribution."

Van looked up. "You're kidding."

"No. It's tonight. Only the site isn't here. It's out at the warehouses by the Embarcadero project. But it's still corporate territory. Frank Selby's."

Cuda blinked. "No shit?"

Stilt shook his head. "No shit. The deal's set for 1 a.m. I say we should be out of there by 12:15 or so."

There was a long pause, then KML029 nodded knowingly. "Oooohhh."

Cuda blinked again. "No way. No way, man. We're not just gonna walk right into Bug's fucking living room without the cops."

"What are you afraid of, brother?" Stilt's heart was behind his words, even if his brain wasn't. "You're hot-n-spicy now. Corporate Hercules in black armor, man. If we can't take Bug now, what made us think we could take him a month ago, with no armor, and no intel?"

Cuda listened to his breathing for a moment, employing all of the Buddhist serenity he could muster, then swallowed hard. "Okay, I'll let you spill, but if it's tweaked, I'm out."

Stilt brought up his grin again. He knew Cuda couldn't stay away. This was what he was. "Alright. I say we make it a surprise visit."

Van hopped to his feet. "Like what? Dress up like Jehova's Witnesses?"

Stilt laughed. "I like that. Remind me to use it sometime." He brought his weight away from the staff and began to pace, twirling and hefting the titanium rod. "We scope out the right warehouse, then have Larry drive us through the damn wall."

Cuda stared blankly at him. "Then what?"

Stilt halted in mid-stride, expecting the brazen plan to have seized their imaginations. "What do you mean, 'then what'?" he replied.

"Do we just jump out the car an' start kickin' butt?"

Stilt's blank look was evident to everyone in the room. "Well...yeah."

"It's tweaked," Cuda offered matter-of-factly.

"It's *not* tweaked."

"It's *tweaked*." Cuda folded his arms, rocking his head back and forth emphatically. "The plan is *tweaked*. It is a *tweaked* plan, and I don't want no part of no *tweaked*-ass plan."

"You got a better idea?"

"Yeah."

"What?"

"Wait for the cops," Cuda insisted, mere inches from Stilt's face.

Stilt sighed, throwing his arms out in disgust. "Don't you see, man? If we go in with the cops, it's back to being the small guy, bowing and taking orders. I say we do the cops a favor and have him pressed and folded when they get there."

"You wanna kill him?"

"I don't wanna kill anyone. But I don't want him killing any more kids, either. And if he makes it difficult, I sure wouldn't hate myself in the morning. Know what I'm saying?"

Cuda bowed his head and whistled out through his teeth. "Yeah. Yeah, I hear ya."

"You down with us, John?"

"Yeah, I'm down with you. Just one thing, *amigo*."

Stilt glanced sidelong at him and visor met eyes. "What."

"If we get our asses handed to us, we don't do anything else toward Bug without the cops, man. Scares the shit outta me, now we know he works for Selby. If it don't work, we're gonna have some serious professionals on our ass."

Stilt beamed. "You got it. Now, we drive into the warehouse—"

Cuda cringed. "Aww, man. Not that tweaked-ass plan again." He shook his head, laughed and turned away, and no one noticed that Asano had left. But that was normal.

31

11:56 P.M. WEDNESDAY. The fog was in—thick, gray and smelling of dead fish and chemical waste. Of course, some of the stench was due to the geographical location. The new Embarcadero project, still under construction, ran parallel to the waterfront, and the wind from the Bay swept most of the stink west into the industrial zones.

The armored limo came to a silent halt behind the abandoned Caterpillar crane. Larry had killed the headlights a kilometer back. The interior of the spacious vehicle was silent until Stilt leaned forward, nodding toward the greater of three warehouses across the empty lot. "Look. Lights. Somebody's home."

Cuda shifted uncomfortably in the leather seat across from him. "Are you sure this is such a good idea?"

Stilt was unsmiling. "No. But we may not get another chance." He scanned the limo's dark interior. "Well, Creep, here's your chance to party with the big boys. You down?"

Creep showed sinister teeth, wagging his furry mane over the invisible blackness of his armor. "Wouldn't miss it, mates."

Van sniffed and ran a finger under his nose. "We better do this right, amigos. They pack heat, y'know."

KML029 bared equine teeth and raised his right arm, displaying the compact ballista device. "Me too."

Van shook his head. "No. Those are *ball bearings*. Bug packs *serious* heat. We're not talking holdouts here." He turned toward the tinted window. "Just wish we had something a little bit bigger."

"We do," Stilt reminded. "We have surprise."

Van rolled his eyes. "Whoop-de-doo. If we wanted to surprise 'em, we could've just got a stripper and a cake."

Kelly shot him a shaming look, wagging her finger. "Van. Strippers don't wear armor and arrest drug slingers."

Stilt continued to stare out the back seat window. "Everybody ready?"

Kel hefted the lasercam in her right palm. "Ready when you are, amigos."

Stilt made one more visual scan of the car. Even in the almost pitch-darkness, he could see their faces with perfect clarity. His eyes moved from person to person, then finally up to the rear-view mirror. Larry's gaze was fixed on the warehouse. "You ready, man?"

Larry's eyes shifted into the mirror, and he shrugged. "I'm not gonna get any readier sitting here."

"Alright, boys and girls, let's kick it."

Bug pivoted on his heel and decided to pace in a different direction. His Italian shoes left a straight rut in the soft dirt of the warehouse floor. He glanced down at his Rolex and paced some more.

Quan sat in the open driver's side of the AV, amusing himself with a videogame. Raoul lounged on the single catwalk, dangling his legs over the side of the steel frame. A fully-loaded Ingram rested in his lap, and the butt of a shiny new .45 auto stuck out from a plastic shoulder holster.

Johann and Biggs occupied the minutes with hands of poker, wagering M&Ms and tiny bar pretzels., their weapons holstered and secure. Biggs had evidently decided not to go with a full cybernetic replacement. It had been an easy decision to make—his leg was repairable, and you don't just throw out a perfectly good steak to grab fast food instead. The joint replacement was a biomechanical wonder, simulating all the actions and sensations of a real knee. The rest of his leg, however, was still meat, and he intended to keep it that way.

Bug paused, listening to the air, his dark shades making him look very much like a blind man waiting to cross a busy intersection. The 9-millimeter Glock hung loosely in his palm. He glanced back at the miniature army of Selby thugs he'd been sent. Most of them were Thai and Cambodian refugees shooting guns for profit instead of for their farms and families. There were about twenty of them, sitting or milling around. One of the younger guys was reading the latest issue of *Masque* on a tablet.

Somebody coughed, spitting an unwanted hunk of nic-stick filter onto the ground.

Bug turned back to the giant steel door.

The crash was tremendous, vibrating through the vast structure with all the intensity of a mortar shell. Corrugated metal burst aside like a flower at the end of bloom.

The smiling chrome grill of an armored limousine met the occupants of the warehouse with a angry growl, and bright LED eyes flashed bright in their faces. The Circle was like a collection of black-armored rats evacuating a ship.

Leaping through the sunroof, the construct launched pellet after steel pellet. Stilt and Cuda rolled from either side onto the dirt floor and came up in stance. Pezzoni followed, sprinting directly into the scattering crowd of Thai soldiers. Creep vaulted from the left side into a cartwheel, then a tuck-and-roll, then sprang into the air, screeching and howling like a wild creature.

Van vibrated with the impact of several nine-millimeter slugs in the torso, the shock sending him sprawling to the ground. He righted himself, bruised ribs still smarting from the previous night. Bringing his arms up in front of his head, he let out a tremendous *kiai* and charged. His armored limbs shook and stung with the impact of a dozen high-caliber rounds, but he knew the specially layered pieces on his forearms, designed to stop even ceramic and monomolecular blades, could absorb the kinetic punishment.

He leaped, aggressively striking out with his foot. A sharp pain swept through his jaw as he was clubbed in midair by the stock of a shotgun.

Stilt whipped the staff, which gleamed almost ethereally in the yellow warehouse light. One thug panicked immediately, dropping to the floor. Stilt stepped over the man, spun the staff in his armored palm and swung the long weapon in a low, backhand attack. His target stumbled backward with a broken jaw.

Cuda found himself face to face with Biggs and Johann. Their pistols appeared from concealed holsters and they managed four shots apiece before Cuda lay flat on his back. Johann strode forward, aiming the barrel at the vigilante's head, but felt the sharp, electric explosion of Cuda's muscular foot launching up into his crotch. In less than a second, their positions were reversed; Johann lay unconscious with his face embedded in the dirt, and Cuda hefted the stray Walther into a large hand, pointed at Biggs.

The giant pink golem fired first, and Cuda felt another bruise form on his left thigh—thank God for the reinforced codpiece. It was a moment of truth for John Kapp. The last time he'd held a gun was the last time Stilt had stopped him from pulling the trigger in his own mouth. And yet the hardware felt natural, comfortable to him. He held it upright, like a pro—none of this sideways gangster business.

He felt a wave of nausea wash over him because he hadn't thrown it away. Guns had taken three of his family, fire had taken two. A million thoughts invaded his brain simultaneously, all drowned out by the single question: If you do this, can you live with yourself?

He fired.

Biggs stumbled backward, canvas and nylon feathering from the hole in his clothing. He regained his balance three steps later, then raised his gun and fired again. It took Cuda another shot to realize that his target was armored too.

"They're armored!" he cried, flinging the pistol across the room and stepping into an aggressive tiger stance.

Creep had already found that out. He'd also found that a sharp piece of metal from the ripped warehouse door did significantly more damage to ballistics armor than the blunt impact of a bullet. Two men fell, their bowels ripped and strewn about the floor under the furry gladiator's feet. He wasn't prepared for the onslaught of automatic gunfire from behind. The combined impact shocked him forward and he fell to the ground.

KML029 had launched only four of his steel missiles before he was knocked from the limo roof by Raoul's sputtering Ingram. Kelly continued recording the scene, pressing her lasercam to the dusty glass of the backseat window. *Shit,* she thought, *they're getting their asses kicked in there.*

"Shit!" Cuda bellowed over the staccato cadence of automatic gunfire, "we're getting our asses kicked in here!"

Stilt winced as a bullet grazed his ear, clipping away a chunk of skin from the side of his head. "No shit!"

Suddenly there was a loud *thump* from the roof outside, and all the interior lights went out. The stream of ghostly white from the limo's high beams was the only illumination in the dusty warehouse. There was another *thump*, and the gunfire stopped. All eyes craned to the ceiling.

Creep stood, black armor frizzy and torn from the dozens of rounds he'd taken.

Stilt scanned the crowd of combatants: Van had been bludgeoned about the face and head, and was slumped unconscious over the hood of the Lexus; Cuda was locked in a grapple-hold with the giant Biggs; KML029 was in the process of climbing back onto the roof of the limo, his ballista shattered and broken; Larry stood behind the armored driver's-side door of the limo, covering the construct with the holdout .38.

There were still roughly ten thugs standing, Bug at the point, aiming double-fisted with a couple Berettas.

The occupants froze in tableau. Time slowed. Raoul glanced nervously skyward.

The ceiling buckled and ripped open, and the figure that descended was the angel of death. It was of slender but definitely male build, clad in a form-fitting black bodysuit and a cape and cowl of charcoal gray. The enormous cloak billowed out, parachute-like, covering Raoul as the specter landed atop the steel catwalk. There was a strangled cry, and Raoul's lifeless corpse tumbled to the limo trunk, sinking into the armored metal like a foot into wet sand. The figure turned, and all eyes followed.

Stilt blinked, shook his head. What was that? Did he just hear a voice in his head? *Leave. Leave now.* What the hell was going on here? Hearing a voice in his head was strange enough, but hearing Asano Tanaka's voice was just a bit specific and freaky. He scanned the warehouse for the rest of the team, found everyone running for the limo. Bug's gang opened fire again, and the mysterious figure leaped from the catwalk into the air.

Bug fired incredulously into the dark. "The fuck is *this* shit?!"

Creep scrambled over the top of the AV, scooping Van into his arms, flipping the unconscious enforcer over his frayed back in a slapdash fireman's carry. Stilt heard a sound behind him, like a pistol being cocked. He flung the round tip of the staff to the rear, satisfied with the shocked *whuff* and exhausted crash of a large body falling backward over the couch onto the marble coffee table. He dashed for the limo's open rear door.

The figure came to a near-silent landing atop the limo roof, waving the enforcers into the car. Larry ducked into the driver's seat, engaging the electric motor with passion. The

KML unit slithered headfirst into the sunroof, and Creep tumbled into the opposite door with Van, a tangled mess of arms and legs. Cuda followed them, shoving their battered bodies into the car like a Tokyo subway packer.

Stilt made Kelly's side of the back seat, diving in as Larry flipped the car in reverse and spun backward into the dark night. The gyrating wheels threw a cloudy wall of dirt and dust into the faces of Bug and his men, and Stilt looked up from the pile of writhing warriors in the backseat just in time to see the flutter of a gray cloak disappear in the headlights and the blast of soil.

The frazzled passengers righted themselves and arranged into a coherent order in the seats, grunts, groans and profanity akimbo.

Larry spun the limo in an efficient donut, fishtailing out of the vacant warehouse lot. Cuda wiped his lower lip, licking the fresh blood from his finger. "What the hell, man. What was that?"

Stilt slid the two halves of his staff back into their holsters. "Would you believe me if I told you I knew?"

"Maybe. Who?"

"Asano."

"Get the fuck outta here."

Stilt shrugged. "It's him, man. I swear to God." He leaned forward and caught Larry's gaze as they made the turn onto Columbus. "Larry, take us straight to the Kitayama Marina building."

"What?!"

"You heard me. Step on it."

Kelly continued to let the camera run. "Why the Marina building?"

Stilt held up his hand, and Kelly shut the camera down. "It's where Asano lives. I have a feeling we'll find our answers there."

Cuda stared at him, wide-eyed and sweating. "You're fucking kidding. Asano? Mr. Concert Pianist? Running around with a cape and hood like some ninja superhero?"

"Stranger things have happened."

The KML construct nodded emphatically, gently rubbing his swollen jaw. "Yup."

Cuda looked at the construct, then sighed and laid his head back against the seat. "You gotta be kiddin' me."

32

PICK FLINCHED as the Kayak flipped and bobbed in the rushing neon water. He could see the glowing marker up ahead. "Nautilus," he muttered. The Kayak instantly became a submarine.

Windy was impressed.

Pick breathed evenly as the submerging craft hurled forward toward the steel grate. "Atomize." The sub promptly exploded into tiny pixels of virtual data, riding the surge like so many fine particles of sand. He was through the grate. "Reconfig."

The submarine reintegrated, dropping down a steep spiral into a brightly-lit room. Windy marveled at the complexity of the environment: The convoluted series of miniature roads and street signs; the security forces roaming at random along the computer-animated sidewalks; the helicopters, planes and AVs soaring overhead. The datastream plunged down into what looked like a bathtub drain set into a small green hillock next to the main street—an environmental directory, maybe?

The stream continued in its downward spiral, finally slowing to a crawl as it entered a thick aquamarine pool of waiting data. Windy almost found herself gasping for breath as the submarine icon blew its tanks and surfaced.

The neon billboard said *MONOPED SYSTEMS*. A lone figure hovered silently in a single beam of light, just over the glittering pool. It looked like a medieval knight, armored in bright silver and red chrome, casting brilliant reflections from its radiant shell. The rest of the surrounding area was completely dark and unlabeled.

"Whoa," Pick worried, diving his icon below the surface of the glowing water. "Periscope up."

Windy watched, dumbfounded, as the suspended knight reappeared in the crosshairs of the submarine scope. "What is it?"

Pick tilted his head, shifting the virtuality helmet from side to side. "We're in Monoped. Somehow we got into Monoped. I can't believe this."

Windy frowned, bit at a jagged fingernail. "I thought you said it was a mole in Kitayamacorp."

"I thought it was. But if so, what the hell are we doing in Monoped?" He pursed his lips and sighed. "If Kitayama has a mole, he's sure not taking any chances."

"Could it be that guy Joey?"

"Nah. He just wrote and installed the filter program. What we got here is someone within Monoped, hacking data with the established leak, processing it within the Monoped system, and then shipping it back to Selby." He leaned forward, rubbed his jaw thoughtfully. "Pro job," he admitted. "Real pro job. If Kitayama ever found the filter in the datastream, they'd spend their time on an internal investigation."

Suddenly the knight shifted, staring directly into the periscope.

"Oh shit." Pick raised his gloved hands and straightened. The knight descended, bright sword cocked back to strike. "Down periscope!" Before the words could form in his mouth, the screen went blue with the color of the neon water. "Bombs away! Bombs away!"

There was a blinding flash, followed immediately by another, and the scorched remains of the armored guard plopped down into the bright, murky data pool, sinking slowly in front of them.

Pick took a deep breath, then leaned forward and jacked out of the deck. "Good thing I always arm my programs."

Windy sat back, her mind numb with the information she'd been exposed to over the past several days. "So, this Joey Chin writes a filter program. Installs it in the Kitayama system. How come there's no record of him having worked there?"

Pick pulled the helmet from his head. "Because he didn't. Remember the police record I said I found? He was arrested by your friends last month on a break-in."

"So that's when he installed it?"

"That'd be my guess."

Windy blinked and rubbed her eyes. It was getting late. Not late by way of her usual hours, but she'd been forced into a really weird schedule recently, due to Pick's info search. "Alright. Let me get it straight. Monoped harvests the data, launders it, sends the good stuff back to Selby in "

"That's pretty much it, yeah."

"Shit, man, Stilt's boys are gonna have some heavy hitters coming after them pretty soon."

"I'd say so. GBE already put a contract out on their construct, and that scientist Jorgenson. Plus you've got Fox and the Arena trying to shut the furry guy up. And if they're hitting Bug now, you can bet Selby's gonna be real pissed real soon." Pick unzipped the jacket and swiveled in his chair to face her. "Frank Selby has contacts with the previous presidential administration, Win. If he starts sending the old Agency folks after your boys, the Circle's gonna be hamburger in a short matter of time."

Windy grimaced, turned away and bit another nail. This whole situation was rapidly growing scarier and scarier. She thought about skipping town, seriously considered changing her face and her name, leaving the country. But they could trace surgery. They could trace travel. They could pay off foreign officials. They could make her disappear. It was kind of funny, in a morbid sense, because that was all she wanted to do in the first place.

No, she decided, it would do absolutely no good to run. It wouldn't help her and it wouldn't help the only people in the world she actually cared about. Rising, she pulled her leather jacket from the back of the chair. "I gotta go."

"Sure," Pick nodded, smiling sadly at her. He knew what their chances were, and he didn't try to fool himself into believing any outcome was possible, other than the complete annihilation of The Circle by Francis Selby. "No charge this time, eh? Paid 'em for my fingers."

"You sure you can't do more?"

"Windy, I gotta be real careful. I'll see what I can do for ya, I really will. But if things get serious, you know I gotta duck out. You understand, don't you?"

Windy smiled. "Yeah." She blew him a kiss from the door. "C-Y-A, Pick. Stay alive."

"Stay alive, Windy."

Windy exited into the humid Tenderloin night air. It was thick as always, and smelled of cheap cologne and cheaper prostitution. Windy turned the corner and headed north. A taxi approached, and she flagged it down. Kitayamacorp headquarters was about three miles across town. She dug into the pocket of her jacket, pulled out her credit-card-sized daytimer. A series of tiny red marquee lights ran the time across the display screen: 12:16 a.m.

She hoped she could catch them before the bust.

They found Asano in his apartment, reading Descartes on the sofa with a seltzer water in his hand. Stilt entered, and the musician stood formally. "Good evening, Stilt. I wasn't expecting you—"

"Cut the crap, Asano. You were there." Stilt began to scan the interior of the spacious abode. Cuda staggered in behind him, saw the elegantly dressed man and shook his head.

"I told you, man. It wasn't Asano."

"Shut up, Cuda. I want to hear it from him." Stilt padded forward on rubber soles, searching the corners and shadows with discerning eyes. His visor flashed purple in the faint glow from the *dojo*. He turned his gaze, watching Asano's reaction. It was as he thought.

The scarred pianist flashed an instantaneous look of distress toward the practice gym. "What was it you wanted to know?"

Jaw set grimly, Stilt bypassed the living room, heading directly through the archway into the expensively-paneled workout room. "You always leave the *dojo* light on, *amigo*?"

"Sometimes." Asano furrowed his brow, following curiously. Cuda and Creep found their way through the sunken living room to the target of Stilt's interest. The construct hobbled after them, toes grasping the plush carpet.

The *dojo* was pristine, immaculately cleaned and in order, except for the ancient wooden box beneath the bench. It was well-hidden from the normal eyes in the room, but Stilt could see what they could not—a small tail of dark gray fabric poking out from the lid. Asano followed closely, but made no move to stop him.

Stilt strode with purpose across the hardwood floor. The room echoed with the familiar ripping sound of rubberized *tabi* boots. Kneeling in front of the bench, he reached underneath, produced a rectangular plumwood box and turned toward the others.

Creep was impressed. "'Allo? Wotsis?"

Stilt looked up tiredly at Asano, carefully opening the lid in front of them. It looked very much like a cloak and cowl.

Asano shrugged. "What is this about?"

Stilt shut the box and handed it over to him. "Come on, Asano. Don't shit me. You were there, man."

"What if I was?"

"Were you?"

"What if I was?"

Cuda scowled, large, frayed armored arms entwining across his chest. "Come on, Stilt. How could he have gotten back so fast?"

Asano turned to give Cuda a serious look. "Many things are possible with the right knowledge."

Stilt patted him on the shoulder. "Well maybe you can tell us about it on the way back to Susan's office."

The Tigress found herself in a state of utter fury like no other she had ever previously experienced. "You tried to bust Bug *before* the cops?! What the *fuck* were you thinking?!"

Stilt paced the floor nervously. "Susan, we don't have time to argue. We've got about thirty minutes before Dennis shows up down there, and we've still got to get re-armored."

Kelly entered from the executive lift, supporting Van as he limped forward. The construct stood near the window in the midst of the ferns, mushing his nose against the cool Plexi. Creep crouched on an office chair, his clawed toes making a deep imprint in the memory foam. Cuda and Asano stood side by side next to the Sony wall screen, arms folded identically. Susan eyed them all with extreme disdain.

"What makes you think I'm letting you back out there? You're *all* in breach of contract."

Creep frowned. "So dock me."

"Believe me, Mr. Maddock, that is an option. As are some real pain-in-the-ass lawsuits."

Stilt shook his head. "We had the authorization of the SFPD and the CEO of Kitayamacorp. We're no longer required to act in the company of a police officer on corporate property."

"Not *my* property."

"No," Stilt admitted. "Selby's. But our contract does not distinguish such a difference."

Susan moved forward and glared up into Stilt's eyes, through the gloss of his chrome visor. "You son of a bitch, Tokura! What the hell do you think you're up to?!"

"No good. And it's working."

"Working, my ass! Look at you!"

"Like I said, we have to get re-armored."

Asano stepped forward boldly. "Susan, if we don't go back tonight, we might as well make funeral arrangements for Dennis Murray and his undercover team. Bug will be onto them now."

"Straight facts," Cuda grunted in affirmation.

Susan cast a look at him, squinting through feline slits. She turned toward the lift and saw Kelly and Van standing perfectly still. Van held his ribs with his right hand. His left was slung across Kelly's shoulder.

Susan took a deep breath and turned back to the group inside the office. "Alright," she hissed. Stilt dropped his shoulders, and the Tigress pounced. "Don't fucking relax! I'm not finished. You do it my way, or you don't go. Understand? You stick to the bust. You stick to the contract. Creep goes in *after* the area is secure. Asano stays *home*." She threw the musician a vicious look, and his jaw surged forward like an angry gargoyle.

"How dare you!" He strode forward, and in two steps he towered over her. "I have signed no contract forbidding me to fight. I am a free agent in this matter. And if I see fit to aid a friend in an important action, you cannot prevent me from doing so!"

Susan balked. She'd never seen him so outraged. He was usually more reserved, and she wasn't expecting that sort of verbal thrashing. "Fine," she allowed. "Do whatever the hell you please, my friend. Get yourself killed."

He glared at her with piercing dark eyes and spoke to her in Japanese. *"And what are you asking them to do? Don't their lives matter at all?"*

"Look, I said you could go! So go! Just don't fucking complain when Bug's little army is ready and waiting. It was your own stupid fault."

Stilt bowed his head, and Susan saw in her reflection exactly how savage she looked. Ugly. Brutal. Full of fear and jealousy. She swallowed some of the anger. "Go on. Get out of here. Do it, and come back in one piece, alright?"

Stilt agreed. "Alright, amigos. Let's kick it."

The team filed toward the elevator, and Asano remained. "I'll be right down." He leaned against The Desk, slapping a fist softly into his palm, watching as the elevator doors slid shut. Susan remained planted next to the conference table, staring blankly at the floor. He examined the curvature of her neck, remembered how Lani used to pin her hair up, the stray strands curling around her nape. He sighed, letting his mind flow back to the concert, trying desperately to recall the feeling of liberation he'd felt as the Sakamoto piece drew to a close. The feeling warmed him. He pledged not to lose it. Susan was now Susan, not someone who bore an uncanny resemblance to his late fiance. He wouldn't forget again. "I know you're not okay with this."

She didn't look at him. "That's an understatement." Her eyes welled up with tears, and she cursed the Tigress for abandoning her. "I was only protecting you."

Asano began a half-smile, then dropped it altogether. "You should know well enough that I don't need protection. Nor do I desire it." He slid from The Desk and wandered toward one of the large, potted ferns on the carpeted causeway. "Stilt has become a friend. He has a crusade that he is willing to fight for."

"And die for?"

"Yes, perhaps. I think so. But it's more than just fighting and dying. For me it is a release of all my anger. I was never able to before, because I was consumed with self. Everything was me, and my own internal dramas. No room for anyone else. The man you just dressed down has shown me who else is out there, and it isn't necessarily our kind, Susan. There are others who are less fortunate, and although it may sound cliché, history would judge us quite remiss if we turned our backs on them."

"Asano, no one is telling you otherwise. I won't try to protect you anymore. Go and be some mysterious superhero with a conscience. See how far it gets you."

Asano smiled sadly, heading for the elevator. "It has already taken me miles within my heart. And that is more important to me than concerts and contracts and recordings...and money."

The doors slid open, and Asano Tanaka exited into the shiny mirrored box.

Susan turned and reached out. "Thanks for keeping an eye on them."

He managed an actual smile before the lift doors shut.

The Circle had gathered in the mammoth *dojo* on the 100th floor. Creep shrugged into a new suit of black armor, while Cuda adjusted the Velcro straps on his *tabi* boots. KM-L029 flexed his left hand within the constraints of the reinforced half-glove. A nylon strap kept his fingers and thumb exposed, while protecting the palm with a carbon fiber mesh, ideal for grabbing sword blades. Van sat atop the corner massage table, his entire torso wrapped tightly in bandages, his black beret still cocked to the left as Kelly worked on his bruised shoulders.

Stilt locked down the front of his suit and shoved the titanium rods into their holsters. He glanced up at Van, frowning unevenly. "You don't have to go, *amigo*."

Van grimaced, rolling his toothpick on his swollen lip. "Fuck you."

"That's fuck you, *Sensei*."

"Sorry. Fuck you, *Sensei*."

Cuda scowled. "I think Stilt's right for once, Pezzoni. You should sit this one out."

Van winced as Kelly finished wrapping his right shoulder. "Fuck you too. I'm going."

Asano entered, clad in his black robes and carrying the cloak and cowl under his arm. Stilt turned and examined the outfit. "Hey, *amigo*. You better get yourself some armor."

Asano shrugged. "Slows me down. I prefer to travel light."

"You sure?"

"Sure."

"Your ass." Stilt rotated his shoulders, then turned to Cuda. He'd seen Asano in action and didn't doubt the man's methods for a moment. "Now what were you saying about blades?"

Cuda pursed his lips. The Shihodo yin-yang symbol with the compass points showed like a glowing disc above his left breast panel. He folded his arms, plastic and Kevlar plates covering him like the exoskeleton of a crab. "I was thinkin', this is pretty stupid, us trying to take these boys down with our bare hands, while they're blowin' us to shit, right?"

Stilt nodded. "Yeah. Follow you so far."

"And they're armored too, so if we used guns, we'd still be stuck there shootin' the piss outta each other. Then I saw Creep using the piece of metal on one of 'em, and I think, 'whoa there'. Ballistics armor is meant to stop the kinetic impact of a bullet. It's not meant to be cut. We could do a lot more damage with, say, the monomolecular knives and swords they got in the armory."

Van shook his head. "*Duh.* I knew it was stupid to just drive in and try to beat 'em up with our fists."

Stilt twitched. Holy cow. How had that very simple physics lesson missed him? Of course! If Bug's men could outgun them, surely six combat-hardened martial artists could out-*cut* them. Right?

"Alright, John. Secure the blades."

Van chuckled painfully. "I can't believe you didn't think of that before, Stilt."

Stilt threw up his hands. "Hey! I'm making it up as I go!"

"One more thing, bro," Cuda added. "I know you don't like to do the gun thing, and that's cool, but this is the big time. We're in the shit now, and we can't balk if it comes to taking a life."

"Fuckin' ay," Van nodded.

Creep slammed a furry fist on the conference table by his chair. "'At's right. Law of the fucking jungle, me lads."

"Agreed," Still muttered from a face so granite-still that it silenced the room and drew all attention to the tall vigilante.

Clearly the others expected more of a debate, but Stilt knew the horses were already out of the barn. "Obviously, try to arrest some of the high-value targets," he explained, "but we're K-corp enforcers now." He turned to the darkened window, watching the reflection of Cuda as he left for the armory.

When it came to small-time criminals, Stilt had always preferred to stick to non-lethal methods, but now they were going after the big game. Career criminals and murderers who wouldn't be there if they were innocent. As Cuda said, they were in the shit, and didn't have the luxury of principles.

Asano padded over to the massage table. Kelly helped Van to the floor and secured the front of the armor suit. Asano put a soft hand on the Italian's shoulder. "How are the ribs?"

Pezzoni actively tried not to wince. "Like shit, why?"

"Come with me, Van."

"Where?"

"Just a short walk, down the hall."

"Why?"

"It will make you feel better."

"Really?"

"Trust me."

33

BUG STOOD CALMLY on the damp concrete, silhouetted by a thin aura of white halogen light from the AV. The underground Embarcadero was still incomplete, had been for years, continually stalled by a thick haze of bureaucracy and special interest lobbying. If it were ever finished, it would be a marvelous specimen of early 21st century design. Too bad it was already more than halfway toward the 22nd.

The waterfront pier section was about a mile long, six lanes wide, long LED strips running parallel to one another, still without power. It was blocked off at either end, and its relative seclusion and security made it Bug's most favorite meeting place on his turf. His small army—minus Raoul and the two men Creep had disemboweled—gathered behind him, cuts bandaged, bruises purple and swollen. They looked as if they'd just seen action in a Central American bush war.

A shuffle of footsteps echoed down the tunnel, and Dennis appeared in the distance, flanked by Ricardo and LeGrande, and two other undercover officers. Bug stood planted on the spot, the Browning loose in his hand.

Dennis approached cautiously, hailing Bug. "Yo, 'sup, *amigo*?"

Bug grunted only the slightest acknowledgment.

Dennis held up a hand to shield his eyes against the headlamps of the Lexus. "Whassup, man? We're on time."

"That's right."

"So what is it, man? You wanna talk distribution, or not?" Dennis frowned, watching as Bug raised the pistol and suddenly every gun in the area was trained on them.

"Reach. Down on your knees." His comment was punctuated by the staccato echo of eighteen guns being cocked behind him.

Dennis swallowed. The whole thing had been a trap. He slowly raised his hands, lacing his fingers on top of his head. It was suddenly very hot in the tunnel. He sank to his knees, and his partners did the same.

Bug pursed his lips, and Biggs and Johann stepped forward from the lights. Bug gestured toward the kneeling cops. In less than ten seconds, they collected five sidearms and kicked them over against the west wall. Bug crouched down a few meters in front of Dennis. "You had me going for a while, Special Agent Murray."

Dennis closed his eyes. "Shit."

"Yeah, but your *kung fu* buddies let me in on the surprise, see? And I don't like surprises. Neither does Frank Selby."

Dennis bit his lower lip, frowning. "I don't doubt it."

Bug stood. "You a smart boy, Denny. But you blew it. You were *sooo* close. You know how close you were?" Bug held his gloved hand out so Dennis could see. His thumb and index finger were only a few millimeters apart. "That close. But *no cigarillo, mi amigo*." He waved Quan forward, and the young Thai moved toward Dennis, flashlight in hand.

Bug rose, twirling his gun on his finger, gunslinger style. "I wanna show y'all somethin'."

Quan aimed the light at the cement floor in front of Dennis. The bright circle roamed across the ground, illuminating several crimson stains. Next to each stain was a name scrawled in black spray paint, with a cross. Dennis recognized many of the names—cops he'd worked with, some on the payroll to Selby, some working undercover to expose Selby's operation. Stillman. Elias. Roeder. Lee. Msangi. Kushnir. All reported missing over the past five years. There were more, some of them he recognized: Forbeck, the reporter. Belyaev, the freelance hacker. Heinrich, the promising young photojournalist. And Joey Chin, the whiz-kid arrested on the Kitayama break-in.

"Selby doesn't take any chances, does he?"

Bug stared at Dennis, smiling his wide, toothy smile. "Truth. Once you been taken in, you become a security risk. Adios, amigos."

Dennis smiled back. "Then it won't come as a surprise when he nails *your* ass."

Bug uttered an unstable laugh. "Selby and me, we're tight, *amigo*. You see how long I stay at County. *If* your homeys ever nail my ass. I'm too important to him."

"You seem pretty damn sure, Buggo."

"It don't mean nothin' anyway, Murray, cause your white ass is dead. You got it, *amigo*? Now, you tell Quan what you want on your epitaph."

Dennis sneered. "Fuck off."

"You got it. Quan, he wants '*fuck off*' on his epitaph."

Quan smiled, reached into his jacket and pulled out a small can of spray paint. Bug stepped forward and put the barrel of the Glock to Dennis' head. "Been real, Murray."

Dennis laughed sadly. "Yeah. See you in LA, *puta*."

The explosion was like the Fourth of July in a coffee can. A huge wall of sulfuric smoke, wafting in phosphorescent pinks and greens toward the bright headlights. Spinning colors, dazzling white sparks, ear-piercing whistles. A grand display of explosive psychedelia, impossible to ignore. Several silhouettes approached through the white smoke, back-lit by a pulsing strobe.

Dennis rolled to the ground, bracing as Bug pulled the trigger. He heard the bullet come down next to his ear and felt his right shoulder burst open. "Aww, shit!"

The army of gunmen surged forward, most of them blinded by the high-intensity strobe and the dazzle of spinning fireworks. Before they could fire, half were cut down silently in their tracks by Asano and Cuda. The other half dashed into the smoke for the far opening.

Van stood majestically at the front entrance, bathed in the snapping light of the portable strobe. Bruises gone, he occasionally stooped to toss another smoke bomb or dazzler into the tunnel. The smoke blew forward at the urging of a medium-sized wind machine next to the limo.

Larry smiled, tapping his fingers on the steering wheel, doors open, wireless PA broadcasting aggressive techno music. Kelly peered out of the sunroof through the lasercam, keeping a wide angle on the tunnel. An occasional thug staggered out at full speed, coughing from the smoke, and Van efficiently took him down with a leg sweep and backhand to the neck.

Creep cuffed the criminals, while Windy danced her stress away from atop the limo trunk.

Quan fell to his knees in the tunnel as he tried to scramble toward an access way fifty meters back. LeGrande was on him immediately, shoving him to the cement with her sidearm at the back of his head. "You ain't goin' nowhere, *mon frere*."

Quan cursed in Thai as the cuffs snapped behind his back.

Dennis scurried across the bloody concrete to the west wall, grabbing his pistol in his left hand, kicking the others to his backup men.

Turning, Johann immediately bolted for the opposite exit. The wail of sirens drifted out of the distance with blue and red bursts of light. He slowed, color and hope draining from his face as he watched two police AVs skim the road, flanked by motorcycle cops and a SWAT team.

The AVs came to a quick landing, repulsors booming, airjets whipping dust and debris into the air. Johann squinted against the storm, and Captain Cheryl Bonner stepped out of the first AV, sidearm aimed over the armored door.

"Eat cement, dude! NOW!"

Johann closed his eyes and stretched out on the warm, wet floor, hoping to awaken in his bed any second.

Biggs fired, and Cuda huffed as he felt the impact in his chest. His breath hissed through the nasal air filter in the new ballistics cowl. "You just don't learn, do you?" He raised a translucent *katana*, and Biggs threw his gun aside, smiling innocently. His huge trench coat flapped and billowed in the smoky breeze.

"Come on, *amigo*. Why don't you drop the sword and we'll settle this like men."

Cuda paused only momentarily. Was Biggs insinuating that he was less of a man for wielding a sword? "Nah. I'm kind of on a schedule." The *katana* cocked back and Biggs raised his hands.

"Alright! Alright! I'll go peacefully. Take me in."

Cuda smiled, though Biggs couldn't see through the wheezing filter. He lowered the sword, and Biggs turned around with his hands on his head.

Bug saw the cops enter from the rear of the tunnel and decided to make a break for the front. He was halted by a heavy two-toed foot in his groin, followed by the whistle of air from a titanium staff. KML029 rolled away, and Stilt followed through, snapping Bug's head to the side with a subdued blow from the weapon. It was enough to stun him.

The construct caught the dazed man and laid him out on the ground. Dennis approached, bleeding profusely from his shattered shoulder. "Good work, amigos. Looks like I owe you an apology."

Stilt pulled his cowl down around his neck and grinned. "Ain't nothin' but a thang, Dennis. You don't owe us shit. Just stick this bastard away in a hole somewhere."

Dennis laughed. "I'll do my damnedest." He waved one of the undercover cops over, signaled him to cuff Bug. Cheryl found her way through the smoke and vapor, clad from head to toe in riot armor. It was a duty she missed, and this had been a good excuse to get out of the office.

"Well well well. If it isn't Bug." She glanced down at the writhing drug dealer as he snarled in a daze. She sighed. "If I wasn't such an intellectual, I'd probably use some sort of sophomoric squashed-like-a-bug joke right about now."

Bug turned his head on the ground. "Fuck you, bitch."

Cheryl batted her brown eyes and smiled sweetly. "I think I'm a bit pricey for you, dear." She glanced at Dennis, noting the sinister shoulder wound. "You better get yourself to the meat wagon." She thumbed him back toward the assembled police vehicles, then turned to beckon another cop over to Bug. "Enrico, read this jackhead his rights, and put him in my car. I'm looking forward to the conversation."

Dennis wandered off, and an armored cop crouched to haul Bug away.

Stilt pulled down his cowl as Cuda and Asano approached from the east wall. "Cheryl, if you need any of the data from our files on Bug and Selby, let me know. We just got some new stuff today."

Cheryl laughed incredulously. "Hey, Tokura. One thing at a time, okay? Yes, I wanna see your data. But we may not be able to pin anything on Selby. That's gonna boil down to Federal."

Stilt raised a finger. "But—"

"Look. Stilt. You're clearly effective, and your heart is in the right place. And I'm glad to see you got some more hands." She glanced down at the genetic construct. "Strange collection, to be sure, but they're ace. My advice to you is to keep up the good work for Kitayama. Work hard, work clean, and eventually things will fall into place. Didn't you learn that in Buddhist Sunday school?" She slapped him on the shoulder. "Good work tonight, Stilt. I look forward to having the pleasure again sometime." She waved at Asano and Cuda as she walked away. "I'm glad you're on our side, boys."

Cuda watched her disappear into the smoke, then turned to Stilt and smiled. "Fuckin' ay, man! Rock and roll! We kicked some ass tonight, hombres. Did you see Asano, man? Nasty with the blades. I only got three of 'em. He got all the rest." He turned to Asano. "Never think o' you as a piano player anymore, man. You the straight-up *Daisho*. And what you did to Pezzoni...hoo-boy!"

The construct grinned his wide smile, and Stilt slowly trudged away. The other three followed him, curious. Cuda hugged him around the shoulder. "What the fuck, man? We kicked butt. What the hell we gotta do to make you smile?"

Stilt raised his head and obliged. It was a sad, sort of depressed smirk, but a smile nonetheless. "Nothing like a conversation with Cheryl Bonner to take the air out of your balloon."

Cuda let out a loud guffaw that echoed down the tunnel walls. "Amen, brother. Amen."

34

"*IN A MANEUVER that shocked the city, the San Fran-cisco Police Narcotics Division, in partnership with the DEA, apprehended a man they contend was the biggest sup-plier of Indigo Ice on the peninsula. Gerald Bowles, known to police and his associates as 'Bug', was arrested at the Pier 15 section of the incomplete Embarcadero project, along with eighteen hired guns.*"

The team watched from their corporate common area as the news ran shots of Bug being cuffed by...Creep.

Stilt grimaced from the sofa, and Creep shifted nervously next to him. "The news guys wanted a good shot, so they had me reenact it."

"But you didn't even—"

Kelly frowned, holding a finger to her lips. "Shhh."

"*Assisting the police was 'Sakuru', The Circle, a corporate enforcement unit sponsored by Kitayamacorp and headed by ex-martial arts instructor, Kai 'Stilt' Tokura.*"

The video cut to a shot of Stilt, flanked by Cuda and Van, with the top of the KML construct's head making its usual sterling appearance. "*Bug's operation has hurt a lot of inno-cent people. It's about time it got taken down. And to which-*

ever corporate interests were backing it, we're comin' after you."

Cuda, Windy and Van cheered from the floor, and Kelly whacked the backs of their heads. "Down in front."

Larry laughed, and Susan smiled from her seat next to Stilt.

"The arresting officers reported significant armed resistance, and yet no deaths occurred. Those wounded in the ensuing fight were rushed to San Francisco General and treated in the trauma center. Several members of the Bowles gang, including eleven Thai refugees, are now in stable condition."

Cut to a shot of Dennis, bloodied arm in a sling, directing the removal of the wounded thugs by the police medical team.

Van glanced over his shoulder at Asano, who stood stiffly against the wall, arms folded. "Too bad you couldn't do your shit on Dennis, man."

"It's not something I want to broadcast to the general public. I'd never get any work done."

Kelly rolled her eyes. "Would you two please shut up?!"

"A spokesperson for Kitayamacorp competitor SelTech issued a prepared statement critical of the action, calling The Circle, quote, 'Nothing more than a corporate hit squad run by a jealous rival,' unquote. Meanwhile, Gerald Bowles was released early this morning on two million dollars bail.

Cut to a shot of Bug blowing kisses at the crowd of reporters as he climbed into a car.

Creep scowled. "Bloody 'ell. I would've paid that to keep him in."

Stilt ran a worried hand over his mouth, glancing around at the depressed faces in the room. "Too good to be true, huh guys?"

"Luna, screen off," Cuda addressed the room, and the screen went dark. "Makes my blood boil, man."

Susan rose, pressing out her jacket. Her hair was down, hanging soft and loose around her shoulders. "You guys hereby have the day off. Stay in the complex, though, just to keep yourselves safe."

The tired occupants of the room stood and began to filter out toward various bedrooms and sleep. Creep put his arm around Kelly's waist, shot a look over his shoulder as they headed toward the front door. "Practice tonight, Stilt?"

Before he could answer, Susan shook her head no. "You are required to do absolutely nothing but relax for at least the next twenty-four hours, and that's an executive mandate."

Creep looked at Stilt, they shrugged simultaneously. Then the room was empty, and Stilt found himself alone with the Tigress. She stared into his visor, obviously getting used to her distorted reflection. It still made him nervous. Her green eyes seared into his mind like no one else had ever done before, and he was suddenly very self-conscious. "What," he wondered softly.

She tilted her head and her lips pursed in an alluring half-smile. "Nothing. You did good work."

"Bug's still out there. He wasn't even in jail twenty-four hours."

Susan paused, folding her arms casually. "Can't win 'em all, Stilt. You know that. But you did good. Selby's been on my ass for years. His *ronin* killed my father six years ago. Until now, I never really had any teeth to bite back with."

"Is that what it's about? Biting and biting back? Killing and killing back?"

"Of course not. It's about keeping society from crumbling. That's the big picture."

Stilt laughed. "Come on, Susan. That may have been the big picture thirty years ago, but you missed it. That *is* society now." He padded to the bank of windows and gestured out at the city. "It's already crumbled. For me, and Cuda, and Van, and even Asano, it's about rebuilding it. From the ground up. Without foundation, there can be no skyscraper culture, no shining glass arcologies. Creep's even coming around, Susan. He's from the street. He knows what it's about." Stilt let the words hang in the air a moment, cracking his knuckles to punctuate. "I have no problem leading your own private hit squad, as long as I'm not harming innocent people, and as long as you keep your end of the deal. I want my school back."

Susan licked her lips. He was certainly a challenge. "Dinner?"

"Huh?"

"I'm inviting you to dinner."

"Why?"

Susan gave a soft laugh, amused at his hesitation. "I want to discuss the school. I want to discuss The Circle. I want to discuss Selby." She strode forward, hands on hips, emerald eyes probing him mercilessly. It killed her that she couldn't meet his gaze—eye contact was usually her greatest advantage. "I want to talk business."

"I thought you said we were required to have fun tonight."

Susan let the jab slide in favor of pressing the attack. "I gave you the night off. That means you're free. And don't worry. I'll make sure you have fun." She winked at him, and he was in the middle of determining whether it had been a come-on when she turned to the door. "You choose the place. The car will be ready at eight."

Stilt wasn't about to let her get away with such blatant manipulation without a fight. "I've chosen," he said, smiling sternly. "And I'll pick you up at seven thirty. Dress casual."

"Sure." She uttered a defiant laugh and stepped out into the hall, shutting the door behind her. Stilt inhaled slowly, the wheels of his mind madly spinning away. His stomach felt queasy and he turned to the window.

Oh, God. He really didn't want to fall in love. Not now. Not with her.

"You sure you like Vietnamese? It can get a little spicy." Stilt pulled Cuda's city car to an electric halt in front of Nha Trang at 15th and Irving. Susan wasn't particularly thrilled about taking this little foray into the Sunset, what with security in its present condition. But she was resolved not to show fear. It wasn't even fear, really. It was more a serious misgiving, a slightly morbid anticipation.

She could have deployed a security detail to watch them, but not doing so showed a level of trust in Stilt to keep her safe—not that she was deficient in her own self defense skill.

"*Tokura-san,*" she smiled, lashes fluttering, "I'm not afraid of a little spice in my life."

Stilt laughed under his breath and released the door latch. The small dome swung upward with a tired hydraulic whine, and Stilt helped Susan onto the street. She wore a simple ensemble of white silk top and black vat-leather pants with chrome heels, and matching earrings that resembled triangular silver shards. He wore his nylon jacket over a gray Italian shirt, black chinos and creepers. It was the first time he'd actually worn shoes since Asano's concert.

The street was full of people, and the smells of the many local eateries met her nose. The burned-out lot across the street had been cleared of scorched debris, and she caught Stilt looking wistfully at the site of the old school. They turned toward the large Vietnamese restaurant, and Susan noticed a pair of Guardian Angels on almost every corner—and a group of six on the sidewalk next to Newton Park—huddled in discussion. Things had certainly gotten better since Stilt had reappeared in the neighborhood.

As they crossed the sidewalk, Stilt felt himself grabbed by the collar of his huge jacket. He spun, grasping the target by the arm, cocking back into a body strike. Susan gasped. The pale, thin gangster just smiled.

"Stilt man! Good to see you! Didn't recognize you without the hair." Halloween Jack had gone through an awful lot of trouble to look like the David Bowie character of the early 1970s. Facial surgery, hair implants, skin bleaching. The shaggy mop on his head was a bright, flame-red. His left eye was obscured by a black patch, and a shiny gold cross dangled from his right ear. He was clad in leather, leather, and more leather, covered in buckles and studs and zippers from neck to toe. The back of his jacket read *DIAMOND DOGS* in gleaming rhinestones. Two other gang members flanked him.

"Hey, Jack. Looks like you and your boys have been doing some cleaning up around here."

Jack grinned, stained and crooked teeth flashing yellow in the light from the restaurant sign. "We do what we can."

A shorter version of Jack, without the eye patch, stepped forward and knocked fists with Stilt. His left lapel read *ZIG-GY*. "You guys kicked some serious butt last night, *amigo*."

Stilt shrugged. "For all the good it did."

Ziggy waved a pale hand in dismissal. "Hey, makes our job a lot easier, brutha-man."

The third Dog folded his arms and looked suspiciously at Stilt. His face was airbrushed in artificial shadows of gray and black, and the name stenciled on his lapel was *SCREAM-ING LORD BYRON*. "So when you comin' back to the 'hood, bro?"

Jack slapped the thug upside the head and smiled again. "What Byron's trying to say is that we miss you out here and it'd be nice to see the *Yōgosha* back on the beat."

Stilt laughed. "Times have changed, Jack. We're *Sakuru* now. The Circle." Suddenly, he remembered Susan. "Oh, Jack, this is Susan Kitayama. Susan, Halloween Jack with the Diamond Dogs."

Susan nodded politely. "Pleased to meet you."

"Charmed," replied Jack, elegantly bending to kiss her hand. He winked his good eye in Stilt's direction. "Pretty girl. If you're into that sort of thing."

Susan's face flushed and her jaw dropped. She had never been reduced to simply a Pretty Girl before. She was used to being the center of attention and not arm candy for someone else. The whole interaction messed with her head.

"We want you back, buddy." Jack waved, and Ziggy followed suit.

"Say hey to the boys, eh? Stay alive."

"Will do. Stay alive." Stilt saluted and opened the door for Susan. She stalked into the restaurant, still shaking off the confusion.

Sheila Nan met them at the front and screamed ecstatically when she saw Stilt. "There he is! The handsome devil. So good to see you, big boy! Who is the pretty lady, eh? Is your girlfriend?"

Susan blushed. "Business associate."

Stilt nodded. "Can we get a table, Sheila?"

"Oh, no problem!" Beckoning them to follow, Sheila sat them at a table next to the front window. Stilt's favorite spot. He remembered the long dinners he ate alone, or shared with Cuda or Van, staring out the clear glass at the people on the street. He found himself suddenly swimming in nostalgia, and a wave of melancholy washed over him.

Susan flicked her phone to life and pulled up the Nha Trang menu, pretending to read the selections. "Who were those guys?"

Stilt blinked beneath the visor, not needing to consult the culinary options. "Who? The Diamond Dogs? They're a gang. Usually out punishing Nazis, but they lost a couple of guys when the Jet came big time, so Jack decided to turn the gang's attentions elsewhere." He leaned back in his seat. "They're good guys."

Susan accepted the explanation and redirected. "So, about the school..."

"What about it?"

"You tell me."

"What do you mean?"

They paused as Sheila brought two water glasses to the table and filled them both from a carafe.

Susan set her phone down as Sheila retreated to the kitchen. "It means you tell me what you want. I'll have it built to your specifications. Right here on the old site, if you want. It's the least I can do."

Stilt cupped his hands, leaning forward on the table. "Why are you doing this?"

"I told you why."

"You told me what I want to hear, but not what you're actually up to. I may have been pretty ignorant a month ago, but I sure as hell know a mind fuck when I see one."

"Stilt, I swear it's not a mind fuck—"

"Alright, an *ego* fuck then. If there is something I have learned working both sides of the corporate coin, it's that suits do not give a shit about anyone but themselves. The only reason you let us go after Bug is because it would damage Selby. You wouldn't have done it otherwise."

"I wouldn't?" Susan feigned shock, curious as to where this was heading.

"Come on, Susan. You know you wouldn't. Selby's breathing down your neck and so you got yourself some streeters to play *ronin* for you. I never wanted to be a part of a corporate war. I just wanted Jet off the streets. That's all."

Susan swirled the ice in her glass around with a slender finger. "And how do you expect to do it? You take Bug down, another Bug pops up in his place. You don't just cut down a diseased tree—you grind the stump and kill the root." She sat back, regarding him across the table, watching the play of light across the chrome visor. "You could really be a great figure, Stilt. The potential is there. But your focus is narrow. If you really want to stop the Jet, you find out where it came from, who's making it, who's shipping it, who's selling it. You take them down, buy them out, turn their industry around to something else."

Stilt glared at her. "Is that all it is to you? Take 'em down, buy 'em out, turn 'em around? Doesn't it matter to you that kids are being destroyed for profit?"

Susan glanced out the window, watching the scrawny figure of Burt stumble blankly down the sidewalk. "Of course it matters. Just take a look at the big picture."

"There's the big picture again. Did it ever occur to you that *my* picture is only as big as protecting my neighborhood?"

Susan shook her head. "I don't think so, Stilt. You're greater than where you came from."

"I'm proud of where I came from."

"You're still greater than it. You always will be. I think you know you'd be wasting your talent and the talent of your team if you spent your days pummeling thugs in the street."

Stilt leaned back and folded his arms. "What are you telling me?"

Susan sipped her water. "I'm telling you things change. You have a much more important role to play in the world. The neighborhoods have the Angels and the Diamond Dogs to protect them."

"They still need us."

"No, Stilt. The hood survived before you came, it will survive after you're gone. There will always be somebody with Stilt's crusade, fighting crime and drugs and oppression at the street level. But you are going to have to realize that you've graduated. You aren't a gang anymore. You aren't a teacher anymore. You're a *ronin*, and a damn good one. I wouldn't replace you with anyone else."

Stilt looked quickly out the window at the vacant corner where the school and apartments once stood. He hadn't spoken to Mike or Jesse since they'd been relocated. And he hated Susan's insinuation that he was no longer a teacher. That was all he ever wanted to be. "I want to put the school back where it was."

"Fine," Susan replied quietly.

Stilt mused, adding, "I want to choose the teaching staff."

"Done."

"And I don't want to talk about it anymore tonight."

She cocked her head suspiciously as he raised his glass and offered a toast.

"To the Shihodo School."

She smiled and clinked her own glass with his. "To the Shihodo School."

They drank, and Nan came and took their orders. As they waited for the food, Stilt gazed out across the street, watching a small congregation leave evening mass at Our Lady of Divine Tolerance, saw Fisk wander out onto the grass and look up into the sky. Stilt hoped the man was praying for them.

He looked at Susan, looked away. It seemed every time he glanced at her, she was staring back with those graceful emerald eyes. She became more and more beautiful as the night wore on. They completely stuffed their faces full of *Phở,* jellyfish salad and crispy pancakes. They began to laugh, and smile, and actually loosen up.

Susan became real, more than a corporate employer. Stilt became more than a strategic asset.

Each became human to the other.

They walked the neighborhood for hours after dinner, and everywhere they went, Stilt was saluted, or fist-bumped, or slapped on the back by a friendly hand.

Susan got to meet Sam in front of the Ace & Gryphon, and Kim told Stilt that Barney Chao was going to be alright. His condition was upgraded to stable and he'd been removed from the ICU.

Stilt found Elizabeth and Jason among a group of Guardian Angels patrolling 19th. He told them he was proud to see them using their skill and talent for the community. They smiled and nodded, *yeah yeah, bullshit bullshit, how are Cuda and Van, and when the hell are you gonna be back?*

Susan was impressed. She found herself wondering what it must be like to live on the streets all of one's life, without the benefit of corporate expense accounts and health insurance, and a seven-figure salary. Whatever empathy and genuine compassion she kept locked away in her heart for special occasions was hauled out of the crate tonight.

She began to feel an unfamiliar warmth in her chest whenever she looked at Stilt, saw him interact with the locals, how they embraced him wherever he went. She kept finding herself distracted by the imposing presence, his chiseled half-Asian features and wild, dark hair. But it might have been the Kim Son wine.

She decided to seduce him, regardless.

They made it back to the arcology shortly after 1 a.m. Behind Susan's securely-locked penthouse door, a trail of clothing led from the living room through the kitchen, across the tiled hallway floor, to the chrome and tinted glass of her bedroom door.

35

FRANK SELBY HAD the best body money could buy. His expensively-tailored silk Meier suit bulged with grafted muscle. His skin carried a custom tan, a product of extensive melanin manipulation. His hair was permanently dishwater blond, and the matching Van Dyke beard surrounding his thin, cruel lips was sculpted and trimmed daily.

His eyes were covered most of the time with trendy mood contacts, shifting in color from purple to green to blue to brown—red when he was angry.

The pain of a hundred surgeries didn't seem to register— he was quite happy with the product he'd paid for, especially the penile implant and auditory boost. The better to hear the squeals and gasps of the expensive prostitutes he frequently rented.

His office was a wonder of antiques collection and early twentieth-century design. A solid oak desk worth half a million dollars occupied the corner by the tinted window, accented by a high-backed genuine leather recliner.

A commissioned portrait hung from the wall, next to Van Gogh's *Sunflowers.* He was not a casual art collector, evident in his extensive display of Greek busts in the soft light of the oak bookcase. He'd purchased the marble head of Alexander the Great from the New York Metropolitan Art Museum for an estimated ten million. His Renoirs were all originals. For a sixty-year-old man held together by pharmaceuticals and repeated bodysculpting, he placed an ironic emphasis on the genuine article.

He wasn't pleased with the turn things had taken over the past month. One of his biggest Arena crowd magnets had defected, that scientist Jorgenson had disappeared, leaving an experimental military construct in the care of his most hated nemesis, and his primary distributor in San Francisco had just been arrested. One of his goons had promised to talk. It had taken millions of dollars and the mobilization of all of his moles within the justice system to retrieve Bug. Something had to be done. He didn't like being on the defensive like this.

Turning, he glared sternly at the image on the wall screen. "What is the next move? Maybe you should tell me."

Bug's bruised face squirmed uncomfortably in closeup. "I dunno, Mr. Selby. These boys are fuckin' ridiculous. They just pop outta nowhere. We can't have Biggs spillin' his guts to Cheryl Bonner, either. She hates me."

Selby pouted theatrically at Bug's image on the screen. "Aww. The big bad police captain doesn't like you. So unfortunate. You know, that's the least of your problems, Bug."

"I just need some better guys, boss. Somebody I can count on."

"Bug," Selby lectured, raising an electronic target rifle to a receptor screen above the brick fireplace opposite the desk, "I have learned over the past forty years in this business that one can only count on oneself. So far, no one has proved me wrong. Pull."

A soaring holographic clay pigeon hurled from the laser projector in the ceiling. Selby aimed his weapon and fired. The image shattered into tiny flaming pixels, scattering to the projected grassy field where they disappeared. A sultry, feminine voice said, "Score: one-hundred-twenty. Good shooting, Frank."

He turned back toward the hi-def screen filled with Bug's face. "And you least of all. Don't I pay you enough?"

"Yeah, Mr. Selby. The pay's fine. I just...need you to call out the big guys. I can't handle the situation by myself. You understand what I'm sayin'?"

Selby smiled, father-like. "Certainly. In fact, it restores my faith in Man's integrity, to hear an employee admit a project is too big for them. I appreciate your honesty, Bug. Rest assured, The Circle will be taken care of."

Bug shuddered, and the effect was almost like losing the satellite. "So what do I do in the mean time?"

"Action items as follows: Wait for the lawyers to contact you. See if you can work on the Jet production in Daly City. Try to motivate Bartak to borrow the construct and secure the new formula. And this is your last chance, Bug. I'll be honest with you. Don't fuck up again. End call."

Bug scowled, and the screen went black.

Selby raised his voice and addressed the room. "Get me Dexter. Audio only."

The same female voice replied, "Dialing," followed by three seconds of silence before an answer came.

"Dexter. Kuvalda here."

"Kuvalda, it's Selby. How soon can you be available?"

"Any minute now. Just finishing a gig."

"Good. I've got one hell of a cleanup for you. End call." Selby raised the rifle again. "Pull." The target spun into the projected crystal-blue sky. Selby fired. The image exploded, as before.

The computer voice cooed. "Score: one-hundred-forty. Good shooting, Frank."

The woman was the perfect magazine beauty: long, thick hair the color of honey, cascading in a soft fall around her bare shoulders; smiling blue eyes—the expensive Nikons; full, pouty red lips; a sleek, sculptured body accentuated by capacious hips and firm, cantilevered breasts. Her legs were long, slender, muscular. The tattoo of a small scorpion glowed in luminescent red from her inner left thigh. Senator Means was happy with the agency's choice.

The aging politician smiled and gently poured champagne into two crystal glasses. He ran a hand through his slightly disheveled gray hair and winked at the beautiful professional girl.

She parted her lips and accepted the drink, raising the glass in a delicate hand. Her red-sequined dress shifted, revealing a generous portion of cleavage. The tight hem rode up on her thighs. "To the election, Senator."

"You did say *election,* didn't you?" Means chuckled, leaning back on the velvet sofa. A white tux shirt hung open across his hairy chest. His eyes dashed briefly around a typical posh D.C. hotel suite. His gaze returned to the woman, and he raised his glass. "To tonight, my dear."

She sipped delicately from the champagne flute, setting the glass on the coffee table and scooting forward. He saw the move and responded in kind. She was on him in an instant, sucking his lips and wrestling his tongue with professional fervor he'd never experienced. He reached for the back of her dress, drawing down the zipper with a shaky hand.

She murmured a husky groan of affection in his ear, and her right hand came up to caress his neck. His eyes grew suddenly wide as the hypo extended from under her acrylic fingernail into his carotid artery.

Paralysis was instant.

She broke away, smiling at his look of astonishment. "To tonight," she laughed, sipping his glass of champagne as he stared helplessly, slouched back against the throw pillows. "What you've just been injected with is a highly concentrated paralytic compound. It affects the central nervous system, rendering motor controls and vocalization impossible. But you already knew that."

She laughed again, setting his glass down next to hers. "Don't look so surprised, Senator. I'm just doing my job." She grabbed his belt and, with a strength that belied her delicate frame, hefted him into the bedroom. He flopped like a doll onto the king-size bed, and she proceeded to undress him.

"Once the compound is introduced into the system, it begins to mutate, attacking the heart wall, causing failure within the hour. The effect is much the same as a natural rupture, and the drug decays ten minutes later."

She left him naked on the bed and winked cruelly. "Pleasure doing business with you, Senator."

A knock sounded from the door, and the woman smiled. "There's part two, now. Sleep tight." She left the politician, terrified and dying, and went to recline on the sofa. Picking up her drink, she sipped casually.

A second knock rang out.

"Come in."

There was a soft click, and the door swung open. The gigolo was tall, handsome, long brown hair brushed down about his shoulders. He wore the clothing of a hustler who did very well for himself.

"Hi," he said. "I'm Dick."

The woman grinned viciously, her back to him. "Of course you are."

Kuvalda was huge. A mammoth Russian with a dark crew cut fade, rippling Mr. Universe muscles and one hell of a surly attitude. He wore black fatigues and a red vat-leather jacket. His Nikons were a light chestnut brown.

Thumbing the release on the Tesla's passenger door, he watched the woman slip into the passenger seat. She pulled the door shut, and the big Russian engaged the motor, pulling into traffic.

"How'd it go?"

The woman looked at him and gave a proud, professional smile. "Senator Means will flatline in about ten minutes. The whore died in his sleep from a heroin overdose."

Kuvalda shook his head. "Sad, really. The senator's wife will be so distraught."

The woman smiled. "Do you think there's something terribly wrong with liking your job?"

"Nah. You have a solid work ethic. 'Course it probably helps, being a complete harlot."

"That's my name, don't wear it out."

Kuvalda negotiated a turn onto the freeway ramp. "You'll need to change your hair. Selby just called."

"What's up?"

"Clean-up. Have a feeling there's gonna be some wetwork. But you should be ready, in case we need data retrieval."

"My dear Kuvalda. I am a professional. I can hold my own just as well with a flamer as I can in an evening gown."

Kuvalda smiled. "I know. But you're treading on sacred ground there, Harlot. We have an agreement, do we not?"

"Yes, my dear," Harlot sighed. "You can blow up your buildings and shoot your big guns. I certainly won't get in your way." She reached up to wipe a small clump of mascara from her eyelash. "How much?"

"What?"

"The job."

"One-point-two-five. And I doubled our retainer. He said it might be a challenge."

Harlot perked up both at the number and the c-word. "A challenge? Sounds dangerous."

"Right. And I like to have something to work for. Keeps me hungry." Kuvalda licked his lips, glancing into the rearview mirror before changing lanes.

Harlot leaned against the armrest and gently massaged her scalp. "Well, could you front me for the hair job? I'm dry."

Kuvalda nodded. "No sweat. Go see the Warper tomorrow, get a makeover too. I'll cover you 'til payday."

Harlot smiled sweetly. "You're a dear, Kuvalda."

The large Russian reached down and squeezed her knee. "Anything for a friend and comrade, baby."

36

THEY HEARD ABOUT the explosion on the police-band radio. Irving Street. Between 16th and 17th. Our Lady of Divine Tolerance Church, completely destroyed. Localized damage only, clean blast, obviously professional.

The blue strobe of code-2 police lights flashed endlessly against the charred pile of stones and plaster. It looked like the meteor crash scene from *War of the Worlds*, small beams of splintered wood still aglow with tiny tongues of fire, sending thin columns of wispy gray smoke into the morning sky. Cheryl had the area cordoned off, and it took several units of riot cops to keep the swelling crowd from bursting through.

Stilt was in uniform. He'd decreed that when The Circle went on call, armor was mandatory. No one challenged him on the matter. They were all there, casting LED beams from the portable flashlights that were now standard field equipment. Cuda was the first to find the body, and Stilt fdropped to his knees when he saw.

The wooden statue of the martyred Christ had been removed from its giant cross. Father Fisk was nailed there in its place.

There was very little skin left on the charred corpse, but it was enough for Stilt, Cuda and Asano to identify as the priest. Stilt stood and wandered aimlessly from the rubble. He wept, saltwater tears streaming from transparent eyes past the confines of the alloy visor. Cuda and Van each put arms around him, walking in silent mourning onto the scorched lawn. They could hear voices, crying accusingly over the din of police radio. *Where were you?! Where were you?!*

What did they expect? Stilt looked up, saw a woman he didn't recognize, who obviously knew who he was. Her mouth moved in harsh expletives, and he lost control.

"What the fuck do you want from us?!" He pounded his armored chest, as if emulating the impact of a gunshot. "I gave my life to this neighborhood! How dare you ask me where I was! I bust my ass for you people!"

There.

He'd said it.

You people.

He'd become different, separate from the other streeters. And in one hasty sentence, he'd admitted that he was no longer one of them.

In an attempt at damage control, he tried to draw himself back into the context of the ruined neighborhood. "I never saw you walk a beat, lady. I never saw you going after jack-heads and slingers on a day-to-day basis. So get the fuck off my back."

His tirade worked to some extent. She shut up. But he sure didn't feel any better.

Cuda patted him softly on the shoulder. "Come on, brother. Let's get back. We don't want to draw any more fire here."

Stilt breathed, felt his stomach twitch and growl. He felt sick, dizzy with anger and hate, vengeance and fear. He looked back at the scene, watching as the forensics team pulled Fisk from the charred cross and covered him with a metallic polyester sheet.

KML029 stood close, silently observing the procedure, confused by the saline liquid that leaked from his giant blue eyes.

Asano scowled beneath the gray hood and mask. "Stilt. This has gone far enough."

Van nodded. "Shit yeah. I say we get the motherfuckers who did this."

Stilt spun angrily to face his young comrade. "Get who? Huh?"

Van frowned, worried that his leader had developed amnesia. "Bug. This is so obvious."

Stilt sighed. "Pull your head out, Pezzoni. Bug's isolated now. He can't do shit like this by himself. And how did he suddenly get better than his grunts?" Perplexed, he gestured at the destruction around them. "This was done by somebody who knew what they were doing, who left a calling card with the way Fisk was dispatched. The only obvious thing to me is that Selby's brought in heavy hitters, just like Pick said he would. There's at least one new kid on the block, and he wants us to know he's here." He turned and stormed off to the limo. "So before you go plotting revenge on every small-time thug, think it through, boys."

He wondered what had made him say that. Since the beginning, that was all he'd wanted. To take Bug down. What the hell had changed his mind?

He knew damn well. Susan. The Tigress was becoming an influence on him. He was actually starting to see the big picture, and it frightened him. He'd fought for so long to keep his tunnel vision, keep a low profile and his integrity as a member of his community. A community he clearly no longer belonged to. He though of Susan and marveled at how intimacy with someone could make you completely shift your worldview. After awhile, he decided that maybe it wasn't such a bad thing. Maybe they'd get to the bottom of it, follow the trail back to the source and cut out the cancer before it spread anymore.

He frowned. Starting to refer to crime as a cancer—now there was some original police elocution. He hoped it wouldn't become a habit. After all, he *hated* cops.

Susan blinked and tried again. Damn touchscreen was frozen and the virtual keyboard wouldn't register. She tried to access the power cycle control, but the same message came up:

1865 OCEANSIDE DR. DALY CITY. J-FAC.

YOU DIDNT HEAR IT FROM ME.

LOVE, P.

She grabbed a pen from The Desk, scribbling down the information. The message flashed once more in a ten-second lockout, then disappeared.

She tapped a couple of keys—functional again. She shrugged and glanced down at the paper on which she'd scrawled the clandestine message. "J-fac?"

The electronic beep from the executive lift pierced the office. Susan snapped her head up and shoved the loose page into her top drawer.

Love entered, sullen expression on his weasel face, a common look for him recently. Now that she was spending all of her spare time with that Stilt person, they never got to hang out anymore.

Sigh. No time for Love. How sad. He missed her attention, the debates, the arguments... the games. God, how he missed the games.

"What are you up to today, Susan?" His tone was bored and patronizing. "More hits against Selby?"

Susan glared at him. "Fuck off, Love."

"*Tch tch*, Susan. Spending all of your time with those Circle boys has made you a bit rough around the edges, don't you think? It might be time to scrap the whole idea and start fresh."

"I repeat, Love—"

"Fine, fine. I thought it was worth a shot." He adjusted his cuffs, flashing a knowing smile. "Actually, I came to check on the Akai deal. Have you finished the contract revisions?"

Susan lowered heavy eyelids. "No. I've been very busy with all of the—"

"I see." Love clasped his hands behind his back. "Well, don't let me tell you how to run things. If it were important to the company, I'm sure you'd do it. After all, you are the President and CEO." He turned to leave, and Susan hailed him.

"Love, please understand. A lot is going on right now. If I ever needed you, I need you now."

Love smiled, his back to her. "Would you like me to finish the Akai revisions?"

Susan bowed her head. "Would you?"

"It would be my pleasure, darling." He continued to the lift, and the doors opened before him. "You should really get more sleep. You look exhausted, like you were up all night."

Susan blushed and closed her eyes. The lift doors slid closed and she took the paper from her desk.

"J-fac," she mused again. "What's that?"

"Jet factory." Stilt examined Susan's shorthand scrawl. "Probably."

They'd gathered in Stilt's suite, Cuda reading intently over his tall partner's shoulder. KML029 sulked in the recliner, curled into a pseudo-fetal position. Asano crouched next to him on the floor, stroking the construct's fur with a gentle hand. Father Fisk had been the first kind soul he'd encountered in the world outside Jorgenson and the lab.

Van paced the kitchen floor, absentmindedly opening the refrigerator door. He scanned the shelves blankly, shut the door, then repeated the entire process again.

Creep and Kelly were still off in their suite, probably sleeping. Larry had gone to the arcology auto garage to tune up the limo.

Susan grimaced, hands on hips, her eyes full of consternation. "It didn't come through on the email server. I checked the rest of my executive staff. No one else got a message. Why did it come to me?"

Stilt shrugged. "I'd guess this was Pick's doing. Signed P. If I were sending a time-sensitive top secret message to a single terminal in Kitayamacorp, I'd try someone who's in on the cause, someone with some amount of power, someone who's sure to be at a workstation at 11:30 in the morning."

"I don't know if I should be honored or scared out of my wits."

Stilt chuckled. "Susan, your network is not the most secure entity around. I told you about Pick and Windy finding the data siphon in our directory."

Cuda nodded. "Maybe you should hire Pick. He's kinda impressive with this shit."

Stilt mused. "1856 Oceanside. Daly City. That's out of the SFPD's jurisdiction. We'd be on our own."

Van paused, glaring at them from the kitchen. "What about the Daly City PD? What about the Feds?"

Stilt shook his head in a definite negative. "DCPD doesn't know us, and we don't know them. For all we know, half their department could be on Selby's payroll."

Cuda sighed. "Yeah, and Cheryl just told me this morning that she found three moles in SFPD narco last night, all Selby's."

Susan swallowed. "Selby's got some tight contacts with the Feds. I'd rather not risk it."

Stilt handed the page to Cuda, began to pace, the mutegray overcast sky reflecting sickly on the visor. "But we've gotta go. If this is legit, we can't drop the ball."

Van held up a hand, as if to point at an invisible light bulb that had just appeared over his head. "I got it. Go back to the neighborhood, get help from the ones we can trust. The Dogs, maybe the Angels. They'd go for it."

Cuda widened excited eyes, glancing up at Stilt. "Yeah. Yeah. Jack's boys would go for it, sure. And Van could talk the Angels into it. He used to be one."

Stilt paused silently, lost in thought. Finally, he looked to Susan for approval. Her eyes were soft and warm, comforting. "Well, Susan. It's up to you. We can hit 'em tonight if you want."

Susan blinked, staring back at him. Her world was crumbling away under her feet, and he was asking her to make a decision. She wasn't sure where she was, *who* she was, what she believed in anymore. She had seen warmth and love and unconditional acceptance of the unusual, and she liked it much better than the cold handshake of the glass office—the only home and family she'd known her entire life.

Being in control was not a familiar sensation anymore.

She wanted to hide away somewhere, get her thoughts together. Her emotions were completely unbalanced around this Kai Tokura. He truly saw her. He respected her. He challenged her. And possibly even loved her.

She'd had her share of sexual encounters, but Stilt had made *love* to her.

She had never been part of a community. Since she could remember, it had been personal tutors and *dojos*, private jets and limos, security guards, legal contracts, and plenty of money. Dim computer light, chrome furniture, and bullet-proof glass.

Stilt had accepted her into his family, without question, without judgment, based solely on her own conscience and merit. She wondered if she loved him. And if she did, could she send him out to face such a deadly force as Selby?

"Tell me what you need," she said finally.

Stilt set his jaw, and Susan could tell the gesture was meant as a determined smile. "Alright. I want to take an AV, if you can spare one. Cuda, ask Larry if he can fly an AV."

Cuda smiled and saluted. "You got it, *amigo*." He ducked out through the door.

Van leaned against the open kitchen archway, growling a guttural gangster tone. "You want I should get the gangs together, boss?"

Stilt found himself laughing, felt the adrenaline begin to pump. "You do that. And Susan, I want vests for the streeters. As many as you can manage."

Susan hugged him, and Van did a shocked double-take. Was something going on here that he wasn't aware of? She broke the embrace, went to the door and opened it.

Windy was crying, covered in blood.

Susan gasped, and Windy ran sobbing to Van. He caught her in his arms.

"What's wrong, babe? Are you hurt?" He held her at arm's length to take stock of her physical condition. She didn't seem to be wounded—the blood smeared on her face, arms and torn shirt was dry. Asano stood, approaching the two on silent feet.

"Oh, God," she cried. "Pick's dead."

Stilt startled, his body suddenly rigid. "When?"

Van held her close again. "How'd it happen, Win?"

Her words came in halted sobs. "I went to see if he'd found anything else on Selby. Just a little while ago. My God, Van, they'd slaughtered him. He looked like he'd been put in a blender. He was still jacked into his deck, and it was still warm. And the screen was shot out." She broke from Van and scurried to the kitchen sink to throw up. He followed, turning on the faucet for her.

Stilt felt wound like a spring. "Well. We'll just have to assume they know we're coming."

Asano turned from the archway to Stilt. "It could have been someone else. It's not the same MO as the church."

"Like I say, we'll just have to assume they know we're coming. We have no way of knowing if the message was planted or real. We have no way of knowing who murdered Pick and why. We'll just have to be especially careful."

Susan gulped, standing petrified in the doorway. "Are...are you sure you still want to go? You don't have to."

Stilt looked at her, smiling sadly. "You sound like you don't want us to."

"I don't."

Stilt bowed his head, breathing slowly. If he wasn't sure of her feelings before, he was now. "Thanks. Get the AV. I want to leave at dusk."

37

THEY ASSEMBLED at the top of the hill just off the Skyline Freeway, in city-cars, AVs and motorcycles. There were about forty of them: Streeters of all shapes, sizes, cultures. There were ten Diamond Dogs, including Halloween Jack, Ziggy, Weird, Gilly, and the Thin White Duke. Half a dozen Chrome Sisters had arrived by Harley, looking quite the lesbian biker militia. There were five Zulus from the Free Africa tenement in the Richmond, and ten Guardian Angels had rallied together for the event. It reminded them of the good old days, when criminals would give themselves up rather than face the Angels' wrath. All except them were equipped with a gun or a cudgel, and everybody had an armor vest that read *CONTRACTOR*.

The Circle made up the rest of their number. Larry landed the AV near a dead oak and the group piled out one by one.

Halloween Jack hailed Stilt and flashed a broad smile. "So this is it, eh, *amigo*?"

Stilt clasped the man's hand. "Be careful. Let us do the grunt work, okay? Just hang and catch the ones that filter out of the house. Probably a lot of small-time thugs and pharmajocks." His armor was dark, almost invisible in the starless night sky. The Shihodo symbol gleamed on his breast like a highway reflector.

Ziggy cocked his Sig Sauer P320, shoving it into his belt. "They ain't gonna wanna go quietly, I'll betcha."

Cuda nodded. "You'd be right on that one, Zig. Don't be afraid to use what you got."

"But remember," Stilt added, nervously rotating the titanium rods in his leg holsters, "you can't shoot if they surrender. Just make 'em lay on the ground with their hands on their head, frisk 'em, cuff 'em."

Larry exited the AV and began to pass out handfuls of plastic zip-ties.

Creep adjusted his arm guard and shook out his mane of dirty-blond hair. "Oi, Stilt. Kelly wants to shoot the bust with us when we go in."

"No way, man." Stilt shook his head with finality. "Too dangerous."

"She says she'll never speak to you again unless you let her go too."

Stilt sighed. "Fuck. Tell her to put on a vest."

"Roit. Cheers."

KML029 slapped his palms together, stalking among the crowd, mumbling, "kick butt, kick butt, kick butt." Asano monitored his comrades in The Circle, checking straps and armor, adjusting scabbards. A red-tint *monokatana* stuck samurai-like from his black sash.

Stilt asked him again if he was sure he didn't want to wear a vest. He smiled, offering a handshake instead. "Good luck."

Having spent half his life in the States, Stilt had become used to the more affectionate western greetings employed by his friends. It was a stark difference between New World and Old World Japanese culture. Even so, he respected Asano, and shook his hand. "Good luck yourself."

Cuda paced through the dry summer grass, watching the flashing lights of the air traffic above. Stilt trudged up behind him, putting an armored hand on his shoulder. "We're ready, bro. You good?"

"Yeah."

"Whatcha thinking about?"

"Just hoping."

"Hoping what?"

"Hoping we come back."

Stilt laughed almost silently. "We will."

"You guarantee?" Cuda smiled, raising an eyebrow. "I want my money back if I die."

"You're not gonna die, John."

Cuda sighed, glancing up at the sudden flash of a meteor shower, like a burst of lightning behind the clouds. "Lotta garbage coming down tonight."

Stilt looked skyward. "Yeah."

Cuda paused. "You know what you're doing?"

"What, here?"

"With Susan."

"No." Stilt scratched his head. "But it feels right, man. Why?"

"Just wondering. I care for you, bro. You always been there for me. I just wanna be there for you."

Stilt clapped him on the back. "You are, brother. Now I wanna take advantage of this adrenaline rush, if you don't mind."

Cuda smiled. "Right on."

They slapped hands and bumped fists in an age-old sequence. Cuda bared his teeth, felt the strength rush up from within him. "Set to kill, brother."

Stilt matched his hands. "Set to kill."

Cuda nodded. "Let's get it."

The door ripped to pieces in a quick series of sparks and flame. Bug reached into his jacket and whipped out the Beretta. Bartak pumped the first round into a shotgun and took position behind an overturned table.

Six Vietnamese pharmajocks quickly stuffed the remainder of the manufacturing equipment into large cloth sacks and tossed them into the corner. The pale soldier lowered his left arm and shot an arc of fire from the nozzle at his wrist. The flame landed on the pile of white canvas, setting the bags ablaze.

Stilt was the first one through. "Pezzoni! The bags!"

Van jumped into the entry hall, scattering a handful of dazzlers into the fray. He dived for the flaming bundles as Cuda stepped inside, *katana* poised at the ready.

Creep and the construct scampered into the living room, leaping into the air as previously hidden gunmen opened fire from the upstairs balcony. The pharmajocks cried out with pistols drawn, and found themselves facing a cowled phantom with a monoblade in hand. A brief whip of air sent all sidearms clattering to the floor, and the men panicked and scattered.

Creep saw the sofa and it gave him an idea. He vaulted into the air, coming down hard on the springs, using the boost to throw himself up to the balcony. He felt the repeating sting of the automatic rounds as they punched at his armor with increasing fury—then he was on the banister, grabbing two thugs by the shoulders and flinging them headfirst toward the tile floor below.

The KML unit rolled, coming up between the legs of the pale soldier. The man flew backwards, crashing through a plate glass window into the sculptured backyard.

Bartak turned and fired at the short, rotund figure in black. The shotgun blast hit, and as the impact knocked the construct to the floor, he recognized the equine head and deep-set blue eyes. "Sonnovabitch. There you are!"

The construct raised himself and Bartak fired again. The shot missed completely, and before he could pump the next round, the thing vaulted forward, propelling him back against the wall. Bartak felt his ribs give way and he grunted in agony.

Kelly ducked inside the still-flaming door, breathing steadily through the air filter that covered her nose and mouth. The lasercam blinked silently, capturing the mayhem as she scanned the interior desperately for a glimpse of Creep. Suddenly Van was in front of her, clutching a fiery canvas sack. He fell, long shard of a flechette spike protruding grotesquely from his back.

"Oh fuck," he muttered as his eyes rolled back and he fell forward on the tile, spitting blood at Kelly's feet.

The pale soldier lowered his arm and was instantly bulldozed by Cuda, back into the yard.

Kelly gasped, and Asano descended over Van's fallen body. There was an ear-splitting cry, and the cloaked figure was gone, as was the spike. Through the smoke and haze of the flashing dazzlers, she could barely see the outline of a large man on the opposite balcony, aiming an extremely large rifle in her direction. Panic set in, and she scrambled out the front door, Van and the fsmoldering bag in tow. A split second later, the floor in the entry hall burst and exploded into sizzling atoms.

"Oh shit oh shit oh shit." She could hear the chaos from the surrounding streets, as the gathered contractors tried valiantly to subdue an army of pharmas, slingers and hired guns. She kicked open the bag, grabbed a small packet of red liquid from the burning mass and made a dash for the AV on the hill. She made it to the middle of the street when a female figure in red and black stepped out of the shadows and lowered a high-caliber pistol at her head. There was a sound like the seal breaking on a can of soda.

Kelly fell.

"Nice party, stick boy?" Bug smiled, tossing his gun aside. Stilt saw the man's wrist snap out, and he barely had time to duck before the stiletto made contact. Stilt's left arm went up instinctively, and he winced as the blade sunk through the armor, deep into his flesh. He set his jaw forward, clenching his teeth. He wasn't about to give in to something as trivial as pain. Not yet, at least. "Thanks," he managed, and launched the end of the staff straight forward in a titanium punch. Bug's shades burst into pieces, along with the bridge of his nose.

Grasping the staff with his right hand, Stilt spun the weapon around in a pinwheel snap to the side of Bug's head. Bug toppled sideways, and Stilt whirled around completely in a reverse circle, holding his wounded arm close to his body, shrieking a focused *kiai*. The staff caught Bug on the other side of the head and his skull collapsed under the force of impact. The man dropped to the ground, head open and leaking into a crimson pool.

Bartak managed a strike to the construct's eye with the rifle stock. KML029 winced and rolled away into the living room. Bartak dived through the south window, glass exploding in a spider web of clear shards.

There was another explosion from the west balcony upstairs, and half of the east balcony collapsed into the living room. Smoke and dust rose to the vaulted ceiling with the cries of wounded gunmen. Creep scampered away from the jagged edge of the demolished mezzanine and brought his head up into his next target's solar plexus.

As the gunman toppled backward down the stairs, Creep glanced up through the haze and saw the big gun being aimed in his direction again. He ducked instinctively, but the explosive projectile hit the beam support dead on. The floor ruptured beneath him, and Creep felt every nerve in his body cry out in agony.

Cuda scowled and summoned all of his strength into the mono-molecular blade in his hands. His filter wheezed. The pale soldier only stared with vacant electronic eyes. Cuda struck, and the soldier brought up a chrome fist to block the attack. There was a slight click as the soldier's right hand twitched, and his fingers became razor-edged talons of steel. The soldier sliced at the air, and Cuda ducked away, bringing a foot into his opponent's side. The soldier grunted slightly, then swung a dexterous roundhouse kick to Cuda's head. Cuda rolled with the impact, spinning completely around, fluid in motion. The *katana* came out again, and the result was another block.

"Fuckin' ay," Cuda gasped, and was suddenly blinded by the headlights of an oncoming AV. The soldier gave him one last swipe with the razors, then he was gone, and Cuda crumpled to the grass, holding his cheek with a bloody hand.

Halloween Jack had not been having any luck. Nobody wanted to surrender. They all seemed to know what would eventually happen to them if they were arrested, and were even more inspired to fight to the death. Weird and Gilly fell within the first two minutes, 45-caliber slugs through their heads. The Chrome Sisters did remarkably well. Not one of their group emerged scathed to a major degree. The Angels lost four, and all of those fell because they'd removed their vests to increase agility. The Zulus lost only one.

Stilt found the support beneath the big guy and severed it with a single *monokatana* strike. The beam split, the blade lodged in the steel frame at the end of the balcony, and the floor collapsed above him as he ducked out from under it. The large Russian fell, and Stilt took advantage of the moment. The air whistled by Stilt's hands as he pummeled the man with lightning strikes, the slap of titanium on flesh resounding from the dusty pile of rubble. Suddenly, Stilt's view was of the ceiling, as he rocketed back through the air. Who the hell *was* this?!? He grunted as his shoulders hit the broken tile of the entry hall. He rolled backwards, leaping to his feet, half-staves at the ready.

The man was gone.

"Pretty damn good," Stilt muttered, "I wanna party with you again, cowboy."

Another AV banked over the luxurious house and shot away into the clouded night sky.

The remaining enforcers assembled on the enormous front lawn. Van and Cuda carried Asano from the smoldering house. He was unconscious, and Cuda explained he'd overextended himself healing Van and the others. KML followed, right eye swollen.

Creep limped from the doorway, leaving bloody footprints on the warm cement. He scanned the group anxiously, heading slowly toward the street.

Then he saw her, slumped like a marionette without strings beneath the white umbrella of a single streetlight. The Arena Champion trudged forward and sank helplessly to his knees. Gently reaching down, he lifted Kelly's head into his lap. The tears were formidable, and continuous. Stilt and Cuda silently approached, followed by Van.

Larry pulled up in the new AV and stepped out through the door. He saw Creep kneeling over Kelly's spattered body and immediately turned away. "Aww hell..." Van went to him, putting an arm around his shoulder. He shrugged away, knocking Van in the chest. "Just leave me the fuck alone." Van watched as he stalked away, trench coat whipping out behind him in the night breeze.

Stilt knelt down, leaning on his staff. "Creep..."

"Fuck off," he moaned. "That son of a bitch. Son of a bitch Selby." He gazed down at hazel eyes that stared blankly out into space. Her hair was wet and matted where the bullet had passed through. Blood clotted around the ruptured exit point just forward of her left temple. Her lips were blue and cold. He gently caressed her pale cheek, sweaty auburn fur leaving a damp trail across her cold skin.

His breathing suddenly accelerated, and he snapped. Leaping to his feet, he bellowed in a voice that was grief personified. "Fucking hell! I want that bastard! I want Selby now!"

Stilt rose in surprise. He and Cuda tried to hold back the furry gladiator as he jumped and swore, thrashing about like an unrestrained child having a tantrum. "I want him now! I want him now! I want him now..." He slumped forward onto Stilt's shoulder, sobbing pitifully. "I want him now..."

Stilt could only stroke his long hair and hold him while he cried.

The construct approached and went to the other side of the body. He knelt, staring down at Kelly's lifeless face for a long time. Then, reaching out, he gently pushed her eyelids closed. He stood again and sighed.

"Sorry."

38

"**WHAT IS IT?**" Selby frowned tiredly, peering at Kuvalda's angular mug on the screen. "Good news, I hope."

The chiseled face on the monitor blinked, and for the first time Selby noticed the bruises.

"Not exactly, Mr. Selby. Several of your chemboys got taken. I'm afraid there's going to be more dirt when they spill."

Selby leaned back in the contoured chair, leather upholstery squeaking plaintively. He ran a calm finger through his bushy mustache, tracing the line down to the bottom of his chin where the goatee ended. "Next you'll ask me for hazard pay because you're getting beat up."

"Not at all, Mr. Selby." Kuvalda smiled painfully. "You said these guys were a challenge, and you were right. Our contract says C-O-D. We'll deliver, or we don't get paid."

Selby sneered. "Aww, that's most gracious of you. I'd hate to think you would try to cheat me out of another four mil."

Kuvalda dropped his smile. "It's a matter of pride, Mr. Selby. You can pay us when we deliver Stilt and his boys."

Selby fidgeted, nervously twisting a gold pinky ring around his finger. "I want you to lie low for a few days, see what happens. Don't do anything further until I give the word."

Kuvalda paused, pursing his swollen lips, and finally nodded compliance. "Whatever you say, Mr. Selby."

Selby raised an eyebrow and leaned forward in the chair. His hands folded gracefully on the authentic leather desk blotter. There was something mildly, sadistically satisfying in the knowledge that a real animal had died to make something that sat on his desk all day. "You know, Kuvalda, it's really a shame more people don't share your opinion. I am where I am today because I make good decisions. And yet I find myself having to pay more and more money to people to follow my suggestions."

Kuvalda shifted. "Strange world, Mr. Selby."

"Indeed. Give my regards to Harlot, will you?"

"Sure thing, Mr. Selby. Good night."

Asano entered the *Sakuru dojo*. The only light was from the city outside. He strode to the window, peering out at the night. The lights on the Transamerica building made the old skyscraper look like a metal Christmas tree. Air traffic was heavy, even at this hour. Lights swarmed and banked against the black velvet backdrop of sky. He bowed his head, shrugged out of the cowl and cape. His black bodysuit was torn and burned in several places, but he hadn't been hit. He wondered if his luck would last. He wondered if any of the others would last.

Sighing, he turned his eyes to the hardwood floor. Stepping silently a few paces away from the window, he turned and knelt before the harsh city lights. His head bowed in prayer, and he set the short *wakizashi* blade in front of his knees, next to the red *katana*.

He should have been able to heal all of them. He should have been able to save Kelly. He should have been able to see the drunk driver coming, all those years ago. He should have been able to do a lot of things. Grief played across his patchwork face, transforming it into a topographical map of sorrow.

Susan opened the door to her suite to find Stilt standing in front of her.

"Good. You're up."

She smiled, directing him in. "Of course I'm up. You think I could sleep tonight?" She'd hastily wrapped a white silk kimono around her naked body. The skin under her eyes was dark and puffy, like she'd been crying. "You want some tea?" She was in the kitchenette before he could answer.

Stilt shrugged, plopped down exhausted on the plush sofa.

From the small kitchen space, Susan could see he'd come directly from the field, and hadn't cleaned up or changed. The air filter was pulled down around his neck. His armor was covered in a fine layer of white plaster-dust, ripped in several places and bristling with ragged bullet holes. His left arm guard had been replaced with a stained bandage. The arm was still bleeding where Bug's knife had entered.

Susan held a ceramic pot, dropping in a couple nylon bags of an expensive ginger green tea blend, filling it with instant hot water from the tap. "How'd it go?"

Stilt squeezed the release mechanism on the front of the armor, shrugging out of the top portion of the suit. The breastplate came away with the shredding sound of velcro. "Kelly's dead."

Susan felt like she'd been hit with a wrecking ball. "No."

"Yes." Stilt leaned forward, slender, naked chest concave and bruised with multiple bullet impacts. He lay his head on his right hand and rubbed his eyes under the visor. "One of

Selby's hired guns. Kelly was trying to get away with some of the evidence so we'd have a case, 'cause it looked like they were prepared to go down with the ship. She didn't make it across the street."

Susan covered the pot and went to the sofa with a tray laden with tea, cups, and rice cakes. "How are the rest of the guys? Where's Creep now?"

"They're okay, at least physically. Asano overdid it and the construct's got a shiner. Van was close to being a human towel rack there for a moment. Creep got a bit singed. They're hanging together tonight, getting drunk. They need that right now. Need each other."

"What about you?" Her instinct was to pour the tea, to give her something to focus on. But it hadn't steeped enough.

Stilt didn't care about the tea. "I'm a party pooper. They'd rather talk about all the havoc they're gonna wreak on Frank Selby. None of 'em want to hear depressing speeches and appeals for reason."

Susan looked sadly at him, her green eyes radiating love and concern. "Appeals for reason? Boy have you changed."

His lips tightened into a thin smile. "It's your fault."

"I know." Gently reaching forward, she grasped his left hand, worried at the crimson stain on the bandage. "We should take a look at this."

Stilt withdrew. "It's fine."

She fawned. "Sure?"

"Sure. I didn't come to get my bandage changed." He turned his head and found her gaze.

She wanted to look away, but forced herself to stay put. "Why did you?"

"To talk."

"Alright then," she replied formally, "talk." She decided the tea had brewed sufficiently, delicately filling two cups from the steaming pot.

Stilt leaned back, accepting the drink and sipping gently. "The Dogs lost two of their boys tonight. Angels lost four. One of the Zulus, too."

"I'm sorry."

"I know." He slouched forward, setting down his cup. She began to refill it, but he held out a hand. "No thank you."

She glanced over his bruised chest, his rippling shoulders, the tarnished chrome finish of his visor.

He continued. "We came away with three of Selby's chem-boys who are willing to talk for reduced sentences."

"That's great."

"I haven't decided whether we're gonna bargain or not. We have most of the lab equipment and some samples. I guess we hit 'em just in the nick of time. They were packing up real quick, and someone knew we were coming."

"Like you said earlier today."

"Yeah." Stilt sighed, ran his hand through a sweaty crop of dark hair. He was in rough shape. Hell, they all were.

Susan watched him silently for a long time. Then, finally: "Is the talking over?"

Stilt sighed. "I guess so."

"What else did you come for?"

"You." He sat up, rubbed a sore muscle in his left bicep. "That wasn't too obvious, was it?"

She smiled, eyes welling with tears. She could feel his simple human need for connection. Just to have someone to hold onto. It radiated off him. And yet, she sensed his fear. He'd just seen a good friend lose his lover on a dark street corner. He didn't want to lose Susan.

"You won't."

"Won't what?"

She slid forward, caressing his cheek with a soft hand. "Lose me."

He swallowed, and suddenly she was kissing him. Her lips pressed softly against his and for a split second he was tempted to just run away. Back to the neighborhood, back to relative obscurity, where he wouldn't have corporate assassins killing his friends. This woman had power and resources beyond anything he could imagine. And yet, she had empathy, humility, and a colossal target on her back. For all these reasons and more, she scared the shit out of him, but he couldn't tear himself away from her.

He felt her tongue search gently for his, and he knew he could never go back. They clearly shared a mutual desire beyond the sexual, although neither of them had ever been so attracted to another person.

She pulled away, and he suddenly found he was on his back, naked, the soft plush upholstery of the sofa beneath him. She mumbled something toward the window, and the thick armorglass darkened to a pitch black. "Lights off," she ordered, and the dim E-light tubes blinked to darkness.

"What are you doing?"

She steadied herself above him, let her kimono fall gracefully away. Her raven hair cascaded softly to her shoulders. "I want you to see me." She reached forward and touched the visor, running slender fingers over the smooth chrome.

"No. You shouldn't." His hands went up and encircled her wrists.

"Please. I want to see you. There's no harsh light in here."

They froze in a stasis of willpower and desire, and finally Stilt let go. The visor came away from his eyes and he blinked, letting the visual impressions flood in. She was beautiful in the saturated light of this darkness. He blinked again, let his unencumbered eyes roam over the soft contours of her slender body, her elegant neck, round shoulders, pale skin. He ran his right hand softly up the back of her left arm, down her throat, caressed the small firmness of her breasts.

She smiled down at his almost transparent eyes, shivering as they looked into and through her. Her hands roamed the bruised tightness of his chest. A week's growth of beard bristled on his jaw. There was a small round welt of raised skin on the left side of his neck. He winced when she touched it. She lowered her face toward his, and they kissed again.

Somewhere in his mind, Stilt thought he heard Hisako's wind chimes. He wondered if it were his mentor's way of showing his approval. Stilt smiled, kissing her passionately. His arms entwined around her, and she melted against him. A slight shifting of hips, and he entered her.

The room slowly began to turn, and Stilt could hear the subwoofers of the old neighborhood, pulsing in time to their movements. Their thrusts were of desperation, a frenetic drumming of flesh and panic, spurred by the thought that they might not make love again. It was almost like Selby was there, standing in the corner with a stopwatch and a gun, counting off the seconds until he would lower the barrel and shoot them both.

"Susan, I—"

"Shhh, Stilt...I know. Me too."

The sofa rocked in tiny, frantic jumps on the laminate floor. She slumped forward on his bruised torso, nuzzling his ears, his neck, kissing his chin, his shoulders. Her throat filled with guttural moans and she began to sweat, tenderly nipping his face and neck with tiny bites, steering clear of the wounded areas. He held her tightly, forcing her hips down against his. The noise she uttered as she came was a vulnerability he'd never seen from her, and it urged his own climax. They held each other afterward for a long time.

Stilt breathed, blinked his eyes open. The room was still once more. Susan's soft form was collapsed against his chest, velvet cheek pressed into the crook of his shoulder. He wrapped his slender, muscular arms around her back and kissed her head. They slept, still entwined on the sofa.

39

THE FOLLOWING WEEK was eerily quiet. Now Susan found herself gazing up into a flat blue eternity.

The AV came down on the concrete rooftop, repulsors whipping dust into the bright morning sky. Susan stood alone in front of the glass doors into the roof lobby, shielding her eyes from the hot silver sun. The wind whipped her skirt around her legs, sending tiny pieces of litter and nic-stick batteries from the tech shack through the arch of her black heels. She anxiously scanned the AV. It was a Mazda, sleek and red, sporty airfoil erupting from the trunk. The motor whined down to a stop, and she could hear the blowers kick in, cooling the thrusters.

The passenger door flipped up from a hydraulic hinge in the front. She saw his feet before anything else. Black wingtips—genuine leather. Gray chinos. He stood slowly, gazing across the wide rooftop, eyes hidden behind dark shades. He had a tan Asian complexion and stood about five-nine. A chrome briefcase dangled from a gloved hand. He wore a black Meier overcoat and a white formal shirt buttoned to the top, split with a skinny black tie. His raven hair hung long and loose around his shoulders, and he smiled when he saw her.

"Ishido!" She ran forward, mincing her stride in her business attire.

He took a step toward her, dropped his case and embraced her. It wasn't the affectionate western greeting she was used to, but even this perfunctory gesture was something reserved for family. "*Konichi wa, Kitayama-san.*"

She held him at arm's length. "You look terrific! My God, how are you?!" She hugged him a second time.

He sighed. "It's good to see you, cuz'." His English was flawless, and had a coastal Californian accent.

She let him go, and he picked up the shiny case from the rooftop. They walked back toward the glass office.

Ishido suddenly wasn't smiling anymore. "Dad's worried the Akai contract won't go through on time. He sent me out to check on it, although I think he really just wanted me out of his hair for awhile."

Susan grinned. "Well I'm glad he sent you. You'll be able to report the Akai deal will go through as promised. Love's working on the contract changes."

"Oh. I guess I should be getting back then." He jokingly turned back toward the AV.

Susan grabbed him by the arm. "Oh no. You're hanging with us for a while. West Coast style...bruh." She elbowed him as she uttered the colloquial term for "brother". It was so out of character and beneath her social station that he had to laugh.

He turned toward her, this time smiling broadly. "Bruh..." he mimicked.

He wasn't ashamed of the acrylic implants. Lots of folks had them. Most of the time, you couldn't even tell, but Susan remembered the motorcycle accident in Oakland when they were fifteen. He'd given her his helmet. The car had run a red light and swerved left in front of them. Ishido had been vaulted over its hood—he'd literally eaten asphalt.

They continued down the concrete steps into the sunken glass hollow that was the roof lobby. A blue-blazered security man saluted, and Ishido laid his hand on the ID scanner next to the control console. A soft feminine voice said, "Identification registered and logged."

The guard nodded. "Thank you very much, Mr. Takashi."

Ishido offered a small bow of acknowledgment, and Susan escorted him into the executive lift. The doors closed, and Susan punched the number for her office suite.

Ishido removed his glasses, shoving them into his breast pocket. "How you been, Suzuki? There's been a lot of gossip back in Tokyo. Dad's starting to think you're losing your edge."

Susan blushed. "Oh? Why is that?"

"Four multinationals went under during the past month, and Kitayamacorp didn't make a single bid. Dad says the Tigress is hibernating."

"Well, you can tell my uncle the Tigress is doing no such thing. Selby's been on my ass, that's all."

Ishido nodded thoughtfully. "Ohhh. That's what it is. How you been coping?"

The doors slid open, and Susan exited. Ishido followed her into the plush, fern-covered glass environment.

Susan went to The Desk and sat on the corner, folding her arms. "We're doing alright. Got a team of *ronin*. Ex-streeters."

Ishido pulled up a chair. "*Sakuru*. The Circle. It's been big news. Ever since the Champ joined up. What's the *jonin's* name? Tokura?"

"Stilt. Yes."

Ishido shot her a knowing glance, saw her blush again. "You've been spending a great deal of time with him, haven't you?"

"Me?"

"Come on, Suzuki. We grew up together. I haven't forgotten how to read your mind."

"I'd appreciate it," she corrected, "if you'd stop calling me by that nickname. And yes, we have been."

Ishido raised a single eyebrow. "Wanna tell me about it?"

"No. Yes." She blinked, bit her lip. "He's...quite a...visionary."

Ishido grinned. "I didn't know you fell for visionaries."

"Neither did I. Never happened before."

"Are you happy?"

Susan unfolded her arms and braced them on The Desk, leaning forward girlishly. "I guess. Took me awhile to get over the feeling that I was dating a security guard."

"Uh oh," Ishido warned. "He's still working?"

"Well, yes. It's what he does."

"A bit dangerous, isn't it?"

"Yes." Susan slid her feet to the carpeted floor. "But we're really close to taking Selby down."

Ishido cocked his head inquisitively. "We? You sound like you're out doing the dirty work with them."

Susan watched him with wistful, telling eyes. "I really wish I was." She fell silent, shuffled her feet. "Anyway, how are things in Tokyo?"

Ishido let it go at that. If she didn't want to elaborate, she didn't have to. "Oh, you know. Same old stuff. Dad wants me to go take over the family business, but I'm not wild about the increasing number of *Yakuza* playing at the table."

The elevator door beeped and Love strolled excitedly into the office. The way he was waving his hand was reminiscent of a heart attack, and Susan frowned curiously.

"What is it, Love?"

"We've done it, Susan!" He saw Ishido and brightened even more. "*Takashi-san!* It's been too long! How are you?"

Susan rolled her eyes. "Love. What is it?"

He held out his hand. Nervously cradled within it was a small, square vinyl package. The clear sleeve held a two-inch square memory card. "The lab found a way to extract the chemical code in the KML unit's DNA."

Susan was stunned. "What?! I thought he had to be dead."

Love grinned with a satisfaction usually reserved for intimate encounters. "Turns out your lab boys are top, Susan. They found a way to extract it without doing the poor beast in. And it's right here." He glanced back and forth from Ishido to Susan. "You want to take Selby down," he breathed, filled with an almost sexual excitement, "you tell him you have this. He'll come personally."

Susan's eyes grew wide, and she burst into a smile. "Oh, Love! That's wonderful!" She leaned over and hugged the ecstatic suit.

Ishido laughed to himself, masking his mouth with a gloved hand. "Maybe I should stick around for this."

Love showed the card again. "I'm going to put this in the vault. There are no copies, because we didn't want any of the data hanging around in an empty sector somewhere where Selby's hackers could get at it."

Susan frowned. "Well, have you even looked at the formula?"

Love nodded, bespectacled eyes stark blue and wide open. "Oh yes. And trust me. It's all up here." He tapped the side of his head confidently.

Ishido continued his stifled chuckle. Love always amused him.

The corporate toady ambled happily away, and the doors to the exec lift closed behind him.

Susan looked at Ishido and her eyes smiled. "Hot shit," she mused. "For the past six years, I've been trying to figure out how to get payback on Selby for my dad's murder. Finally that dirty fuck is going down."

Ishido had to do a double-take. Was he in the right building? Was this his cousin? What had this alien done with Susan? He shook his head, bewildered. "You've changed, Suze. I'll give you that."

She winked at him. "Is that bad?"

"Maybe. Maybe not. We'll see."

"Does that mean you're staying for a while?"

Ishido crossed his feet under the chair. The carpet was soft. "I guess so. If only to meet this Stilt guy. Must be some kind of special to loosen you up like this."

She blushed, turning away from her cousin in an uncharacteristic show of coyness.

"Mr. Selby, it has just come to my attention that Kitayama's lab personnel have extracted the Jet formula from the escaped KML unit." Bartak squinted his dark Nikons out of the giant screen as Selby worked his way through a turkey sandwich, smacking his lips delicately. "...You may want to check into it."

"And how did you come by this information?" Selby inquired, taking another bite.

"Our mole inside K-corp. Could be a deliberate leak, but I don't see why they'd risk it."

Strong implants chewed the bread and meat with a powerful grinding action. Selby swallowed and sipped from a can of Sapporo. "Alright. Go ahead and call Dexter in on it. Acquire the data. Use Irk, if you have to."

Bartak's head turned in a fish-eye close-up. "Oh, he'll be more than happy. Has unfinished business with John Kapp, he says."

Selby licked a couple of fingers clean. "Very well. Keep me posted."

"Yes, Mr. Selby. Good afternoon."

"End call." Sinewy hands swept bread crumbs onto the floor. "You're good, Susan. The Bitch has gotten an education. We'll just see how far your brilliant tricks take you versus vast experience." He raised the Sapporo into the air. "May the biggest balls win."

40

Harlot smiled, approaching the lower level security desk. Her hair was now black and wavy, sporting silver streaks and highlights. Her eyes were hazel-brown, and she swiveled full hips beneath the tight beige skirtsuit. Her skin was a full shade darker. She pursed her thick lips and winked at the uniformed man on duty. "Excuse me, but I have an appointment with Mr. Tokura."

The guard stood, professionally composed and trying not to stare at the gorgeous piece of molded flesh before him. Her generous breasts were pushed together into a soft vortex which he kept having to peel his gaze away from. "Mr. Tokura isn't seeing anyone right now, I'm sorry."

She feigned disappointment, reaching into her bag. "Oh damn. Can I leave my contact data?"

The guard paused, finally allowing himself a look at the woman's long legs. The military taser was in his armpit before he knew what hit him. A silent pulse surged through his body and the guard slumped dead into his chair, gray smoke rising from the singed hole above the armor vest.

Harlot dropped the large black cylinder behind the desk, the weapon now drained and useless. She turned toward the glass entrance, waving her partner in.

Kuvalda entered, shedding the enormous navy blue duffel bag from the Milkor 40-millimeter grenade launcher. It was like a portable artillery piece with a double drum full of explosive projectiles, with another full drum duct-taped to the shoulder stock. Kuvalda wore his usual black tactical pants and a tight black muscle shirt beneath a heavy gray armor vest. Intricate tribal designs and gang affiliations in Cyrillic script advertised from tree trunk arms.

Harlot pulled the guard's sidearm and tossed it to Kuvalda, and he stuffed it into his belt. She grabbed the dead man's wrist, pulling him forward. The body slumped to the floor, but she gripped his arm, pressing his palm against the exec lift authorization panel. The door beeped open.

The two off-duty guards only had time enough to raise surprised eyebrows before they were pumped through the head by Harlot's suppressed Brigadier pistol. Team Dexter entered the elevator, and the door shut.

The voice from the speaker was thin and urgent. "Security alert on levels one through eight."

Stilt checked the video monitors on the Circle office console. "Damn."

He turned to the assembled group. Cuda slapped the Velcro gauntlet over his wrist. KML029 brayed and smacked a fist into his palm. Van adjusted his belt and probed his lower lip with his tongue, searching for a toothpick that wasn't there. Asano stared vacantly through his gray cowl, while Creep bared savage teeth in a violent sneer.

Stilt breathed, checking the monitors again. "Let's get it, boys." The titanium rods were in his hands instantly.

Harlot relaxed against the elevator wall. "What level's it on?"

"Eight. In the vault." Kuvalda wiped a smudge from the shiny gunmetal. The doors opened, and the waiting guards were pulverized in a barrage of explosive gunfire. Five shells later, the room fell silent. As the smoke began to curly away, Harlot wiggled a finger in her ear. "Shit, baby. That thing's loud."

He held a muscular hand to his ear. "What?"

"Oh, you're a laugh riot today, aren't you?"

She exited the lift and stepped cautiously over sundered bodies into the hall that led to the armored vault. "C'mon. This way."

"Mind if I tag along?"

Stilt halted in mid-stride, and the team stopped behind him. In the hallway ahead stood a long-haired Japanese gentleman clad head-to-toe in black Shihodo armor. He smiled pearlescent white implants, fingers gripping a sheathed monomolecular blade.

"Who the fuck are you?" Stilt watched him carefully, gloves tightening as he clutched the titanium rods.

"Ishido Takashi. Susan's cousin from Tokyo." He approached, extended his right hand. "You must be Stilt. She's told me a lot about you."

Stilt stared at him incredulously. "Great. Except we're a little pressed for time—"

Ishido lowered his hand, still smiling. "Good. Where are we going?"

"You're not going anywhere, except back to the armory to remove that suit."

"Ahh, yes. The *yin-yang* with compass points." He gestured toward the reflective symbol on the armored breast. "*Shihodo.* The way of the four directions. I assume that means you are willing to accept ideas and assistance from all sources, and may be able to use a 10th-degree black belt in Shaolin *kenpo.* Therefore, I ask you again: where are we going?"

Cuda tapped Stilt on his armored shoulder pad. "He's right, y'know. That's always been our way. But you can drop the way this time. No one'll question it. If you don't want him taggin' along, just say so. But let's get the fuck going."

Stilt sized up the young man with a teacher's eye. "*Kenpo,* huh?"

Ishido sighed. "Yeah. And my father taught me a fair piece of *kenjutsu.* He fought in Taiwan in '47."

"Yeah, yeah, alright." Stilt waved an impatient hand. "Down to level eight. We got us some heavies sent by Selby. Look like the ones we partied with at the Jet house in Daly City last week."

The Circle found their way to the maintenance elevator and Stilt pushed the down arrow. "And there's one condition. You do as I say. Live by that, and nobody gets killed." The lift began to approach, and they waited patiently, watching the numbers on the level indicator light up.

Somebody whistled an old TV theme. Van chewed his toothpick.

The vault door imploded in shredded bits of steel and titanium, looking for all the world like an abstract metal sculpture by Charles Manson. Kuvalda lowered the weapon and smiled. "Boom."

Harlot pulled her fingers from her ears. "Alright, let's get a move on. They'll be down here any second." She made her way cautiously into the smoke and debris, scanning the wreckage with a variety of optical enhancements. Thermo, UV, HD telescopic. She found the plastic clamshell case on a metal shelf in the back, below a box full of Euro bonds. There was nothing else in the vault. She was tempted to grab a few of the notes, but decided they were much too easy to trace. Besides, they were getting two mil apiece for The Circle. She grabbed the card and dropped it into her cleavage, stepping quickly back into the smoky office. "Done. Let's jet."

Kuvalda chuckled sarcastically. "Ha. Funny girl."

"Security now monitors invaders leaving the eighth level via stairway." The words buzzed into Stilt's ear over the mastoid commlink.

"Shit." He reached for the panel and hit the parking level button. "Have you ID'ed the getaway vehicle?"

"Affirmative. Black Lexus AV-50 registered to Monoped Systems. Driver could be Bartak. There's a *ronin* with him. Looks like a superjack."

Stilt nodded, scanning the interior of the lift car. Everyone was silent, listening to the exchange in their own headset in bursts of comm static. Stilt tilted his neck, hearing the vertebrae crack. "Keep track of 'em, security. We'll pursue by car."

"Roger that, Mr. Tokura. You sure you boys don't need any extra muscle?"

"Make a token show of force, see if you can knock out the vertical thrusters. It'll be a lot easier to catch 'em on the ground." He paused. "But don't overextend. These guys are heavy shit."

Cuda smiled. "There. I knew there was a reason you get to give the orders."

Van clenched his jaw. "Aside from the fact that he can kick your ass?"

"Aside from that, yeah."

Ishido wrinkled his forehead in a bewildered mask. "Is this The Circle, or fucking Abbot and Costello *Meet* The Circle? You guys always like this?"

Creep flared his dark nostrils and ran a claw through his flowing, heavy-metal hairdo. "Actually, we're the Teenage Mutant Ninja Circle. I'm Raphael."

The military construct shook his head. "I'm Raphael," he grunted.

"You're Donatello," Cuda explained, pointing an enormous dark finger at the former Arena Champ.

Van shrugged. "Who am I, then?"

Creep glanced up with fiery eyes. "You are Pezzoni, the fifth Beatle."

Stilt scowled. "Would you please shut your mouths? All of you."

Van could tell he meant it. "Cool. Cool cool." His hands dropped to his sides, and he turned to look at the closed elevator doors. Stilt did the same, and the rest of the group fell silent as the lift came to a halt at level P1.

The doors opened, and Larry was waiting with the Honda limo. The motor was whining louder than any of them had ever heard. An enormous blower vibrated majestically from a hole in the center of the hood. The rear airfoil was much larger than they had remembered. He'd been doing *something* during the past week. The driver shouted over the echoing din of staccato gunfire from the street outside. "Come on, they're getting away!"

Van blinked at the amazing vehicle before them. "Fuckin' ay, Larry." He ran to the front passenger seat. "Shotgun!"

They piled in, and suddenly the cement beneath them was a blur. The ear-blasting squeal of rubber on slick cement pierced the dark garage.

Stilt reached up and pressed the sunroof control. The tinted armorglass slid back with a servo whine. He poked his head out just as the limo pulled into the sunlight.

The security guards had done their job: The AV was no longer an AV—just a four-wheeled sports limo, riddled with bullet holes and unable to fly. Sparks trailed from the pulverized vertical thrusters, and the vehicle swerved and screeched in the wild semblance of a right turn onto Battery Street.

An old one way sign hung halfway up the hollow metal tree of a traffic signal. As the light blinked yellow, Larry yelled, "Hang on!"

Van grabbed the passenger side "Oh-Shit" handle, and Stilt dropped from the sunroof. The light flashed red.

"Jesus, Larry! It's red!"

"It's orange!" Larry set his jaw, hauling over on the wheel. The Honda fishtailed into the intersection in front of a scooter messenger. KML grunted. Creep tumbled into Asano's lap, looked up at his cowled comrade and smiled.

Ishido righted himself as the Honda regained its traction and accelerated down Battery. "Well, if this is any indication..."

The construct grinned thick white teeth. "Gets better." A ratty mop of blond hair found its way into the KML unit's face. He wiped it back with a single, graceful motion.

"Oh I don't doubt it," Ishido blinked. "Susan knows how to throw a party."

Stilt pushed forward to the partition window. A portion of the backseat had been altered to provide better access to and from the cockpit. "Larry, come on, man. Punch it."

Larry frowned and stared intently at his rocketing target. "Shut it, Stilt. I'll catch him. You boys get ready to do the freight-train jump."

"Straight up, *amigo*." Stilt turned to the group. "Alright, boys. Get ready."

Creep slid forward, blue eyes intense and full of vengeance. "Let me go over, mate. I want those motherfuckers so bad I can taste it."

Stilt balked. "I dunno, Creep. Can you handle yourself? I don't want a fucking suicide move."

"No way, mate. I'll be good."

Larry gestured with his elbow. "Van. Get the light."

Van reached toward the dash control and flipped the switch on a cycling blue strobe mounted to the limo roof above the center windscreen. "Shit, man. All you need now is a siren."

Creep grinned. "'E's got one." The hirsute gladiator winked at Stilt. "Goin' up!" Reaching through the sunroof, he grabbed the sides and pulled himself up. He crawled to his knees, surfing the steel of the Honda's roof. The wind rushed through his silky hair, and he let out a long, oscillating howl.

Larry breathed hard, tracking the Lexus as it squealed into another hard right turn at the intersection ahead. "Hold on!" he warned, blinking nervous sweat from his eyes and hauling over once more. Good thing he'd lowered *and* widened the suspension.

Creep howled again as the Honda flipped up on two wheels, forcing him to grab onto the open sunroof. His feet kicked out into the air and he was sure the damn car would flip, but the occupants in the back threw their weight against the right side at the last moment, and Creep suddenly found himself staring down Market Street, furry hands still gripping the sunroof opening.

The Champ slid into a ready crouch as the Honda began to close on the target. He scanned ahead and could see movement within the car. Suddenly Kuvalda appeared out the Lexus sunroof, hefting the enormous grenade launcher toward the Honda.

"Oh shit," Creep muttered. "Forgot about that."

Van cringed. "Shit, Larry!"

"Quiet," the driver urged. "It's under control." Larry moved his left thumb to a green button on the side of the steering wheel and pressed down hard. There was an electronic clacking sound as twin housings opened under the front bumper and two tiny missiles launched into the air in front of them.

The payload exploded on impact with the trunk and rear window of the Lexus, lifting the entire rear end two meters off the asphalt.

Kuvalda ducked, faltered, and fired a wild shot into the air as he fell below the sunroof. A medium-sized chunk of the Powell Street Tram Station blew out onto the sidewalk in a popping, smoldering mass. Streeters screamed and ducked away, fell to the ground or ran for their lives.

"Okay! Now!" Stilt pulled himself up to the sunroof and scurried out.

Larry floored the accelerator and the Honda closed within five feet. "*Larry?*" It was Stilt's voice, buzzing over his headset. "*You hear me, pal?*"

Larry squinted. "Yeah."

"*Get closer, man.*"

"I'll try." The electric motor buzzed as the Honda inched closer, closing the gap, tires spinning. The Lexus swerved to avoid a tram, and Larry followed the move instinctively. The horn from an old Ford Paragon blared at the vehicles as they careened by. On every corner, pedestrians turned to watch with wide eyes.

Ishido propped himself up through the sunroof. He crawled forward, and that's when Bartak slammed the brakes on the Lexus.

Larry stomped down hard, sweat beading on his forehead, but the Honda plowed into the rear of the first vehicle. There was the deafening crunch of metal, and Ishido launched forward onto the trunk. Creep saw the impact coming and leaped gracefully into the air, landing on dexterous feet, directly atop the Lexus roof. Stilt grabbed the sunroof opening on the Honda and braced himself as the cars collided.

Tires screamed as the Lexus shot forward on a fresh burst of acceleration. Larry followed suit, only losing a meter distance.

Creep looked down to see the pale face of the IRK soldier staring back at him below the sunroof. A chrome hand shot up through the opening, and Creep rolled away onto the windshield.

The soldier burst through, quickly leaping the tiny gap between bumpers. Stilt met him with both sticks cleaving the air, rubber *tabis* gripping the Honda's hood. The blower surged with life as Larry edged closer to the Lexus, and the pallid soldier snapped the blades out from his metal fingers. The hiss of autoinjectors in his battle harness was drowned out by the whine of engines and the whistle of air down Market Street. He struck out, and the bladed hand met the blunt metal of a titanium fighting stick.

Ishido crouched on the mangled Lexus trunk, gripping the steel with rubberized feet. He reached over his shoulder and drew the translucent *monokatana* from its scabbard, slowly inching to the rear window.

"'Allo, love," Creep smiled as Harlot poked her face over the roof from the passenger window. The cockiness lasted until he saw the suppressed barrel of the Brigadier level at his head. He swiveled his body at the last moment, wincing as he felt the armor-piercing slug enter his left shoulder. "Aww, fucking 'ell," he roared. His foot shot out, clipping the weapon from her hand.

The Lexus swerved by a pedicab, and Creep lost his balance, falling to his back on the roof, sending him toward her. Thinking quickly, he locked his legs around her upper torso, forcing her backwards so that she hung horizontally from the passenger window, with Creep riding her middle. The tight fabric of her outfit stretched across an ample chest, and Creep saw something nestled in her cleavage. "So *you've* got it!"

The IRK soldier staggered as the other stick met the left side of his bald skull. Another quick pummeling, and the soldier stepped back away from the hood of the car and toppled to the ground. Stilt was in the air and on him in an instant. They rolled to the sidewalk, scattering suits, streeters and pigeons in a tumbling frenzy of flesh and steel.

The soldier snapped his knee upward, and Stilt's face met concrete. He was on his feet at the speed of instinct, dropping into a defensive *kenpo* stance. His left hand clutched one of the metal poles in an upright block, his right arm cocked back to his side, second pole ready to strike. His feet spread naturally apart, his weight lowered on his knees. He watched the soldier from a narrow sideways posture.

Bystanders and hovering surveillance drones documented the conflict. Someone nearby yelled, "Hey! That's Stilt!"

Ishido braced his knees and swung the monomolecular sword in a downward arc. The cry of severed steel met his ears with a pitiful squeal, and the bulletproof glass of the rear window came away in tempered squares.

Creep shot a furry hand down the front of Harlot's suit and he grasped the small plastic case. The assassin's fingers tenuously clutched the side of the door to keep herself from falling headfirst to the thrumming concrete below. Creep let himself fall forward, spinning away onto the street. He tumbled and rolled with the impact of 45 miles per hour, grunting as his armored limbs met the asphalt in a flurry of Kevlar, carbon fiber and fur.

Stilt blocked the incoming roundhouse kick with a blur of metal. He let out an ear-splitting kiai and struck back with his right arm, the rod making contact with the target's armored rib cage. The soldier spun away, whipping his right hand in a flash of gleaming blades toward Stilt's head. A quick block with the crossed poles diffused the strike, and Stilt brought his right leg up into the soldier's groin. Not that such an obvious move would do any good. And it didn't.

The soldier pulled back and Stilt heard a metallic click as the cybernetic left arm raised toward him. There was a puff of compressed gas, and Stilt felt his stomach split in front of the long flechette spike.

"Stilt's been hit!" someone observed.

Stilt staggered back and grunted as he violently yanked the metal shard from his gut. "No shit," he answered the random bystander. The flechette fell to the sidewalk with a metallic *tink* and a spatter of crimson.

The soldier was relentless. A flurry of *Muay Thai* kicks and slices from the metal claw sent Stilt reeling backwards. Blood seeped from cuts in his face and jaw. Another swipe and his lip split from chin to nose. He cursed and tried to plant in a stance, but the barrage kept coming. Another kick to the left side of the head, and Stilt reeled in a complete three-sixty.

Somehow, the pole in his left hand found the back of the soldier's extended leg. The assassin stumbled, and Stilt heard the wheeze of the autoinjectors as they filled the soldier with a new boost.

Stilt scanned down his opponent's armored front and found what looked to be a digital display in a box-like apparatus on his hip. A quick blow with the titanium rod sent the unit tumbling to the sidewalk.

The mercenary cast an anxious glance down at the fallen bio-monitor. A sudden strike to the back of his head sent him stumbling forward. The optical unit cracked and fell to the ground with another head shot. He spun to face Stilt, and gasped in horror as one of the metal poles pierced his chest. Injectors spat and wheezed again as an unrestricted supply of chemical boost glutted his veins.

Stilt pulled the rod from the soldier's chest and backed away a couple of paces, watching cautiously. The man inhaled, lungs sputtering as they rapidly filled with fluid. He reached out once more with the razor-hand, and Stilt spun a flying roundhouse at his head.

The assassin flew sideways, propelled by the attack, into a small plum tree staked in a square of open earth by the street. He twirled clumsily into traffic, and the Market Street tram hit him straight-on. The soldier's limp body landed face-up in a bloody heap on the sidewalk.

Stilt watched as the armored chest rose and fell for the last time. He heard the dying hiss of the injection system shutting down.

"Ishido, jump back now!" Larry burst over the comms.

Ishido looked up in horror as the Lexus appeared set to collide with a Peterbilt sixteen-wheeler making a left into the intersection. The young suit vaulted into the air and came down hard on the front bumper of the Honda just as it screeched to a halt. He rolled forward onto the warm asphalt, coming to an upright position as the Lexus managed a last-ditch boost from the vertical thrusters. There was a sick whine from the engine as the crippled sports limo sailed forward into the air, barely clipping the cab as it sailed over.

The truck driver had thought it prudent to slam on her brakes as well, and the thirty-foot double trailer came to a stop without jack-knifing in the middle of the intersection.

The hollow wail of a police AV came wafting down out of the sky as the flashing vehicle zoomed overhead. Van, Cuda, Asano and the KML unit spilled out of the Honda limousine, sprinting at top speed to skirt the giant trailer as the driver leaped from the cab, yelling, "Hey! What the hell? Shit! It's The Circle!"

Ishido was right behind them.

Larry pulled to the curb and stepped from the door, thumbing his earpiece. "Stilt, buddy. I'm out of it. Blocked by a big rig at 14th. Police on the scene. Team in foot pursuit. I'll wait here."

"That's cool. I'm out of it too. Way back at...8th Street. Superjack is flatlined."

"Copy," Larry nodded in response, and saw the blur of Creep hightailing it past the limo. "Be careful!" he warned the furry bullet.

KML029 rounded the rear of the trailer and the sun hit him as he emerged back onto the sidewalk. The Police vehicle came down in a roadblock position across Market. The Lexus looked like it had been hit by a giant baseball bat: the front end was crunched upward with the force of the landing, and the right rear wheel rolled away down 15th Street. The motor still clicked and hummed alternately, steam shooting up from the cracked liquid cooling system.

Three occupants ran at high speed toward the police vehicle, weapons blazing. Bartak let loose a volley of pumped shotgun blasts, and the cop splattered against the side of the black and white, portions of his face and head falling to the pavement in a wet mess. Harlot peeled the cop away from the vehicle and climbed in, Bartak heading directly for the driver's seat.

Creep shot past the hesitant group of enforcers by the truck, screaming at the top of his lungs. "Motherfuckers!"

Kuvalda turned, and Creep instinctively ducked and crouched as the first explosion tore a hole in the sidewalk next to him. A shower of concrete dust covered him and he dared to peek from behind his upturned arm guards. There was another blast, and another. KML029 hit the ground and rolled away underneath the enormous trailer. Ishido flinched and fell prone, as did Cuda. Van swore and jumped into the air as a fourth blast hit the side of the trailer. He fell to the sidewalk, praying and covering his head. Asano turned away and retreated down Market, back toward Larry and the Honda.

The police vehicle roared to life, and the street was suddenly full of dust and litter. It hoisted into the air and banked away to the east, gone in a matter of seconds.

Cuda stood, stomped angrily on the torn cement. "Damn! Muthafuckas got away!"

The careworn group staggered to their feet, and Creep turned to them, smiling. "It's okay, mates." He held out a furry palm. In it was the plastic clamshell case, covered in cement dust. "I got the card."

41

SUSAN TURNED to the assemblage of board members. Fifteen people, gray suits, white shirts, trendy lenses, finely-tuned bodies. Their faces were sculpted copies of Greek and romantic art and celebrities from television. Women or men, short hair or long, every affectation was meticulously tailored and manicured. Each stared at her in a quizzical tableau.

Susan's hair was loose around her shoulders, her attire casual—they'd never seen her like this, ever. She approached the head of the table, and Love gave her a friendly smile of concern. She blinked and looked away.

"Certain events of late have led me to a decision. And it's not a decision you may be happy with." She frowned. Why had she said that? Any one of these backstabbing shits would absolutely covet the idea of taking over as CEO of the second most powerful megacorp in the US. She swallowed hard, forcing herself to make eye contact with the double row of artificial empathy before her. "Let me cut to the chase. I hereby resign my position as President and Chief Executive Officer of Kitayamacorp, effective immediately. I name Mr.Love as my successor." She turned to the astonished man, offered a shaky hand. "Congratulations."

He stood. "Susan, what are you doing?"

A female executive stood at the far end of the table. "Yes, Ms. Kitayama, what is the meaning of this?"

Susan glared down at her, the Tigress returning stronger than ever before. "It was a difficult personal decision, and mine to make." She turned to Love. "But don't think you can lead us to ruin, Love. I'll remain on the advisory board, and I'm not selling my stock." She backed away from the table and turned to leave.

Love hailed after her. "Susan!"

At the tinted glass doors, the Tigress stopped and gave the assembled suits and corporate suck-ups a final glare, then she stepped away into the hall.

Michaels rubbed his jaw with uncharacteristic nervousness. McDowell stood perfectly still, hands deep in his pockets by the dark office door. Dr. Blake sat at her immense desk, quietly surveying yet another news article about The Circle, and their use of a mysterious genetic construct. They hadn't mentioned the specific lab. Until now.

"Well," Blake grunted, sitting forward uncomfortably, "they've done it."

Michaels stepped closer. "Done what, ma'am?"

"Released our name to the press. GBE is now under federal investigation. And you can bet Dr. Ridley didn't just have an accident in the elevator at Monoped. Selby had him flatlined." She stood, the weight of a hundred small but significant issues hanging heavily on her face. "We're fucked, gentlemen. The only way out is to immediately dismantle all of the military construct projects and trash all related data."

Michaels blinked. "Ma'am?"

"Michaels, I want you to cover the Selby connection. Erase Ridley's data, wipe Jorgenson from the database. In twenty-four hours, neither of them should have ever existed. Understand?"

"Crystal clear, Dr. Blake."

"McDowell, you work on your own division. I want everything gone."

McDowell nodded compliance, enormous sadness in his eyes. "Yes, ma'am."

Blake leaned forward on slender arms over the desk, her eyes red with fatigue. "God help us," she mumbled.

Michaels frowned. "Ma'am?"

"Nothing." Blake waved the two scientists away. "Nothing."

"How did it go this time?" Frank Selby slumped in his leather chair. A very attractive woman entered the office and set a tray of coffee paraphernalia on the desk blotter. He gave her an appreciative wink. She smiled and left.

Kuvalda's frustrated visage filled the giant telescreen. "Not good. We had the card, but they retrieved it."

Selby winced, flipping the portable Matsushita screen to an upright position. The motion powered it up automatically. He brushed the designated icon for the Newsnet. "How the hell did they retrieve the data?"

"They pursued. We had a rough time of it. Bartak lost Irk, we wrecked the Lexus, had to jump a cop AV to get away."

Selby fought the urge to smack his forehead, not wanting to deal with the resulting wrinkles. Instead he seethed through a clenched jaw. "Jesus!"

The screen blinked and came up with the front page news. There was still a big deal about Senator Means' philandering drug overdose in the Washington D.C. hotel. Another news article extolled the virtues of The Circle as a corporate law enforcement organization affecting positive change in local neighborhoods. A related story consisted mostly of an interview with their military construct, and named Genetech Bio-logical Engineering in Climax, Colorado as its birthplace.

"You *stole a police car?*"

Kuvalda cringed. "Yeah."

Selby was beside himself. "The fuck is wrong with you, Kuvalda?"

"I know, I know. And believe me, it's just as baffling to us. That Stilt guy, he's fast. And the rest of 'em, they fight like sons of bitches. Should've seen their fucking limo."

Selby breathed, reigning in his emotions. "Oh, have a neat car, do they? Fight like sons of bitches, do they? That Stilt guy's fast, is he?"

"Look, Mr. Selby, we can do it."

"At this point, Kuvalda, I doubt that very highly. Notify Bartak I'm flying in tonight. Tell him to inform the Bitch."

"Really, Mr. Selby, that isn't necessary..."

"Kuvalda, you want to do me a favor, finish up with The Circle. Our original contract is now null and void, but I'll pay you a million to clean up."

Kuvalda paused, turned and mumbled something to the side. There was a brief exchange with an off-screen voice. He turned back to stare frustratedly out of the wall at Selby. "Done. Like I said before, it's a matter of pride."

Selby laughed viciously. "Yeah, Kuvalda. Sure. End call."

The video screen went black.

He leaned forward and gently rubbed his eyes, pausing to marvel at the colors the pressure of his fingers on his eyelids made. Finally, he leaned back and let out a long sigh. "God-damn amateurs. Gotta do every little thing."

"You did what?!?" Stilt stood, gobsmacked by the news. Clad in cotton baggies, his half-kimono hung loose and open in the center. A cicatrix had formed over the wound in his stomach where Asano had worked his magic. "Susan, we need you where you are!" The ferns wafted in the artificial breeze of electronic climate control.

Susan sighed, her eyes shiny and full of excitement. "Stilt, I don't want to be a prisoner anymore. I want us together."

"Holy shit, Susan. This war with Selby is getting hotter and hotter, and you're abandoning the position that can help us the most!"

"Love's taken my place. He's completely loyal. He'll still help us. And I still have my stock." Her voice was anxious.

"I don't like Love, Susan. I don't trust him."

The ferns rustled again, and Love strode into the office. "I don't like you either, Mr. Tokura, but I have to agree on that point—we are better served by Susan being in the CEO chair."

Stilt glared at him. He hadn't heard the elevator. "Who invited you?"

"It's my office, Mr. Tokura."

Stilt rolled his head. "Oh, man. You're fucking kidding me!"

Susan sighed, grabbing Stilt by the arm. "He's right. And we were just leaving." She gave Love a quick, casual smile. "I'll get my stuff in a couple of days."

Love had never seen her like this—or close to this—ever. "You are absolutely sure about your decision, Susan?"

"Absolutely," she winked.

"Then, by all means, take your time. I'm in no hurry to chuck you out."

"Thanks, Love." She squeezed Stilt's arm and urged him toward the lift. "Come on. We haven't finished our discussion."

"Discussion? As I remember, I was having a complete seizure over this incredibly short-sighted decision."

The elevator doors were still open from Love's exit. They entered, and Susan pressed the floor indicator for the executive suites. "Now I'm short-sighted? Never been called that before."

"Am I wrong?"

"Fucking hell, Kai Tokura. I just want to get out of that glass coffin and fight with the big boys."

Stilt shook his head, laughed, his voice dripping incredulity. "Now you want to fight? This is just wonderful."

"You think I can't hold my own with you manly men?"

"I know you can *absolutely* hold your own. That's not the issue. We need you in that top position."

"Stilt, look. The CEO draws a lot of fire. Literally. It's not a conducive atmosphere for child-rearing."

"So? You're not a child."

Susan giggled. "You missed the point, big guy. I want to be out of the hot seat so I can be with the father of my child."

Stilt winced, his face crumpling into a mask of utter desolation. He had no idea she had a child. He should've expected something like this. There were no good relationships between streeters and suits. It was all a fun fling to her, and now she was dumping him for some Tokyo *Yakuza* or corporate samurai. "Who's the lucky guy?"

Susan couldn't believe her ears. "Stop sulking, you fucking imbecile! I'm trying to tell you we're going to have a baby!"

Stilt swallowed. "What?"

"I did a home scan last night. I'm pregnant...with our child." Her eyes were wide and bright green with enthusiasm, but she was disappointed she couldn't see his. She couldn't read his expression, and it bothered her. But when he spoke, all doubts were put aside.

"Wha—er, um. You're serious." He nervously ran a hand through his hair.

"It's not the kind of joke I'd pull, Stilt," she said, smiling, cradling his face gently in both hands. "I want this. Very much. And I hope you do too."

Stilt inhaled deeply. The elevator door slid open on the hundredth floor. He stepped out and she followed, watching him carefully. Stopping at one of the huge windows, he pressed his forehead to the armorglass, gazing out from the towering arcology into the city. A seagull winged by on a shifting air current.

He could see a police AV in high speed pursuit of an early model Nissan Vector Thrust Vehicle with Ohio plates. Angling down, he could see the roofs of the shorter, older buildings, a vast expanse of uneven checker-squares, most of them sprouting gardens and penthouse lawns, littered with people.

This was the world they'd be bringing a baby into.

A baby.

Stilt had never thought of himself as a father. It was likely no one else had either. He was wonderful with children, a firm but loving teacher. An easily-adopted big brother. But a baby. A real child of his own.

Whew. It would be...different.

Susan edged up cautiously behind him, reaching a hand out to delicately tap his shoulder. "Hey. Is there any room in there for me?"

He laughed. "Susan, you're all that's in there right now."

"Well. I'm flattered."

"It was a dirty trick."

"Oh, go to hell. I didn't know my implant was expired. It just happened. Why didn't you have one?"

"I'd always assumed I was sterile. That's what all the doctors used to tell me."

Susan smiled, moved in slowly to embrace him. "Well they were wrong, 'cause I haven't been with anyone else for almost a year before we met, and this kid's brand new."

"You really want this, don't you?"

"Yes. Is that okay?"

"Do I have a choice?"

"Yes," she said softly. "You absolutely do. One hundred percent."

He sighed, wrapped his arms around her and planted a soft kiss on the top of her head. "Alright. Let's do it. I'm game if you are."

She let out a joyous laugh and nuzzled into his chest. "How about lunch?"

"Sounds good. You buying?"

"Don't look at me," Susan winked. "I'm unemployed."

They strode arm in arm down the pale white hallway of the Kitayama arcology, passing Van and Cuda going the other way.

Stilt slapped his giant friend on a broad shoulder. "Guess what, bro? I'm gonna be a daddy."

"Cool cool," was the absentminded response.

Stilt and Susan were down the hall and around the comer before it sank in.

Cuda gasped and Van halted in mid-step.

"—the fuck?"

42

"**They're coming**, aren't they?" Creep crumpled the empty beer can in a furry fist. KML029 occupied his usual spot by the tinted window, and Asano sat regally in the big armchair in the corner of the common area.

Ishido leaned against the back of the soft couch, and sipped from a gold can of Kirin Ichiban. "Probably."

Creep nodded, painfully aware of this new morbid understanding. "That's it then. It's over for us."

The construct grunted viciously, turning away in disgust. "No way."

Asano glared at Creep in surprise. "Nothing is ever certain, even when we consider ourselves silly for thinking otherwise. The odds are Selby's guns will come back for the formula. We just have to be prepared."

Creep tossed the crumpled can to the plush carpeting. "Aww, bloody 'ell. It was a stupid idea in the first place. Why'd Susan have to tell Selby about it?"

Ishido sat forward and set his beer on the glass coffee table. His voice was halted, as if he were trying to piece his words together. "To solve the problem with the least amount of bloodshed."

"That's bollocks."

Ishido scowled. "Let me tell you something about my cousin, Champ. When all the major corporations were duking it out with private security forces and hit squads, Susan held off. Because she hated what it represented—the decline of society so far that corporations could only do business with a sword or a gun."

He sat back again and drummed nervous fingers on his thighs. "She's not a violent person, Creep. And one of the things that attracted her to you guys in the first place is that you were using your brains and your natural skills, and the guys with the guns were running the other way. She saw something dishonorable in the thought of privately funded corporate wars. Kind of old school, that way. But it is a respectable position to take, nonetheless. She can be one hell of an atomic bitch in the boardroom—there's no place for slackers or below-the-board deals. It's the way her father worked, and he got his brains blown out by a Selby *ronin* six years ago. That's what he got for his trouble."

Asano shook his head angrily. "Bad call, *Ishido-san*. Akio Kitayama built one of the most profitable companies in the world. His employees loved him, and his enemies respected him. *That's* what he got for his trouble."

Ishido bowed his head, acquiescent. "Forgive me, *Asano-san*. I stand corrected."

Creep stood. "Don't matter," he mumbled, ambling away from the group. "See you at practice." The door shut quietly behind him.

Asano folded his fingers together in a meditative pose as the construct sighed and stretched out on the carpet.

"Lose somebody?" Ishido asked.

Asano watched him curiously. "Who?"

"Creep. He lose somebody?"

Asano let out a quiet chuckle. "If only you knew, Ishido. I think everyone in this group has. Cuda lost his wife and son, our construct was alone to begin with, and the first person to show him kindness was nailed to a cross and burned to death."

The KML unit rolled his head from the window to deliver a sharp, "Feh."

Asano watched as the construct's gaze returned to the glass. "When Kelly was killed, we all lost a good friend and Creep lost his love. And then there's Stilt..."

"Yes," Ishido mused. "Tell me about Stilt."

Asano leaned his head back and closed his eyes, recalling the story. "Stilt's father was a soldier in the North Korean conflict. Superjack. He lost his mother, his *sensei*, his school, his neighborhood, his friends, his students. All of it. All he's got now is Susan. And us."

Ishido mulled the data over in his brain, nodding mechanically. He didn't know this Stilt person very well at all, but he knew his cousin. He knew her priorities, knew what was important to her. For that reason at the very least, he silently promised to look after them. "I understand," he said.

The door flew open. Van and Cuda entered, arms laden with Mexican food from the old neighborhood.

Cuda was grinning comically. "Lunchtime! *Casa de Tacos* for everyone! And gather 'round, boys and girls, 'cause ol' Uncle Cuda's got some news for y'all."

The construct was first into the big canvas bags. The smells were wonderful: Spanish rice, beans, chilis. His mouth watered automatically and he began to drool on the carpet.

Van shoved a burrito into the construct's wide mouth. "Somebody feed this guy quick, before we have to row to our bedrooms!"

Asano stood, intrigued. "What's the news?"

Cuda smiled, and his teeth glowed brightly in the mute sunlight through the tinted window.

Ishido peered close. "What, you get dental work done?"

Cuda disregarded him completely. He glanced at Van who was unwrapping the construct's third burrito. "Should I tell 'em?"

Asano sighed impatiently. "John. What."

Cuda blinked, his smile still broad. "Stilt and Susan, they're gonna have a kid, *amigos!* We're gonna be uncles!"

Ishido wrinkled his tan forehead. "Sorry?"

"Uncles, man!" Cuda repeated, pointing at each of them in turn. "Uncle Cuda, Uncle Daisho, Uncle Creep, Uncle Ishido, Uncle...um, whatever you are..."

The KML unit looked up blankly with the wet burrito mess dripping from his wide mouth.

"...and Uncle Shithead." He cocked a thumb at Van, and received a sharp slug in the arm. "Ow! I'm telling!" Cuda grinned at Asano, rubbing his stinging shoulder. "Uncle Daisho! Uncle Shithead just hit me!"

Asano shook his head, bemused. "You deserve it."

Stilt and Susan, having a child. This could either be very good, or very bad. He watched Cuda stuff half a soft taco in his gaping maw.

Uncle Daisho. Hmm. He didn't hate the sound of it.

"Mr. Love, I have a Mr. Bartak on line two for you. He says it's urgent." The young male voice blared from the air in front of the short executive.

Love glared at the console speaker on The Desk like a primate seeing television for the first time. "Bartak? What does he want?"

"I'm sorry, sir. He didn't say precisely. Just that it was important."

"Alright, I'll take it." He punched the button for the Sony, and Bartak's face suddenly filled the wall.

"Why, Mr. Bartak. What a pleasant sur—"

"Cut the shit, toady. Where's Kitayama?"

Love blinked. "Not here. I'm CEO now, Mr. Bartak, and if you have business to conduct with Kitayamacorp, you may do so through me."

The face was red and angry. Bartak paused momentarily. "Alright. I don't give a flying rat's ass what you're up to, friend. You tell Susan Kitayama that Frank Selby is coming up to your HQ tonight to pay her a visit. You should have the card ready and available, and no tricks."

Love blinked again, bewildered. Two tiny reflections of Bartak's digital visage moved and shifted on his thick glasses. "I'll be ready, Bartak. No tricks on either side."

"Right," said the reddened face.

"Right," said Love. "End call."

The screen buzzed a quick moment of grainy static, and went dark.

Love's expression soured immediately. "Well, Mr. Selby. Looks like I'm in check, doesn't it." He reached forward and picked up the open card case. The plastic data card sat safely inside. "You can just keep thinking that."

43

Van entered the lavish exec single room condo. It was smaller than the multi-room suites, but it was the most luxury Windy had ever seen. Potted green plants hung everywhere, some climbing plastic latticework. Windy sat wearing jeans and a loose T-shirt. She appeared to be reading a coding manual on her tablet, and Van had to laugh aloud when he saw the strange scene.

She smiled and rose from the futon sofa to meet him. "Stilt told me about Susan. It's wonderful."

Van pointed at the open file on her tablet. "*Zen and the Art of Net Piracy?*"

Windy gave an awkward laugh. "I got Pick's cybersuit. Wanted to see if I could be useful."

He reached out to hug her. "I think you'll make a great hacker."

"But that's not why you're here."

"No."

She pulled away, locking eyes with him. "Come on, Van. Don't hedge."

He broke away from her stare and looked down. "Okay, I won't. Let's put it this way: Stilt's just informed us that Selby is coming here. Personally. To retrieve the data card."

Windy's face wrinkled in shock. "Here? Selby's coming here?"

"That's what we're hearing. I'm scared shitless, Win. I really don't know if we're gonna make it this time. He's bringing the war here, to us. I just have this feeling—"

"Van, no. Stop it." She squeezed him tightly around the middle. "Don't talk like that. It'll be fine. You have nothing to worry about."

"I can't help it, Win. I'm still small-time. We came into this way too fast. Christ, I'm just a motorcycle mechanic!"

Windy looked up and found his eyes again. They were red and glassy. "Hey. Take your mind off it?" She tilted her head toward the bedroom.

Van shook his head. "Can believe I'm saying this, but...no. Thank you, though." He pulled her back, wrapping her in a strong embrace. "Just be with me for awhile."

Windy blinked back tears. "Jesus, Van. I wish there was some way I could help."

"There is," Pezzoni spoke softly through her hair.

"What?"

"Leave before he gets here."

She pushed away to arm's length. "You can fuck all the way off with *that*."

"I'm serious. He's gonna bring all sorts of *ronin* and guns and shit. This whole building is gonna be a fuckin' war zone. Do us both a favor and let Larry drop you somewhere back in the neighborhood." He gazed sternly at her. "Do it, Win. I want you to be safe."

She sighed, well aware that once Van Pezzoni set his mind on something, it became the proverbial immovable object. She also knew he was right. She was no fighter. And there was no reason for her to be caught in a violent crossfire and die meaninglessly. Ironic that retreating to the hood was safer than holing up in a corporate palace.

"Alright, alright. I'll do it for you. But if I come back and you're not here, I'll never forgive you, Van."

He smiled and blinked a tear away before it could escape the corner of his eye. He pushed away and rubbed the bridge of his congested nose. He was developing one hell of a headache. "Thanks, Win. I appreciate it."

"I know." She laughed. "I'm only doing it to impress you."

Stilt paced the *dojo* floor, solemnly folding his arms and rubbing his itchy beard. The black armor suit creaked and rubbed as his legs continued in the elongated figure eight he was marching.

Asano stood motionless by the city-lit window, clad in his dark uniform. The cape and cowl hung loosely over his shoulder, the red *monokatana* and *wakizashi* sashed tightly to his slender waist.

Susan knelt near Asano's window, head bowed, hands upturned in her lap. Her dark hair was pulled back into a utilitarian ponytail, draped casually over the black canvas shell of Shihodo armor. A transparent blue monoblade lay unsheathed in front of her.

Cuda leaned against the far wall, centering his thoughts with a furrowed look of intent. His almost-shaved head sported one of the blood-red headbands Ishido had given everyone. Armored fists pressed together at the knuckles.

Creep alternated between clenching his hands, flexing his bare toes and sighing heavily, his vocalizations laden with impatience. His armor itched. He wanted to go break something, just to keep his mind off it.

Van just needed the whole thing to be over. He nervously chewed through his third toothpick in half an hour.

KML029 twirled an elastic sling around and around, the whistle of air filling the darkened room as he aimed at the practice dummy and let his projectile fly. The steel ball bearing smacked the matted wall to the left.

ERROR.

RE-ACQUIRE TARGET.

Ishido entered, eyes roving from person to person. No one made a move to greet him, and he wasn't expecting them to. They were clearly lost in their own thoughts, and deserved the peace in which to do it. Ishido was a veteran of corporate warfare. As someone familiar with a variety of enemies—including and perhaps especially *Yakuza*—he knew what it was like to await an attack. They didn't even know whether Selby would take hostile action, although it was a good bet he would. It was the waiting that drove everyone crazy. He sympathized with them.

Stilt turned and Ishido's red headband caught his eye, a stark contrast to his black armor and long raven hair. The visored leader strode forward, silent except for the slight grip of *tabi* soles on laminate. "Alright, everybody. Huddle up."

This was the sappy part—the circle before the show, the drink before the war. They knew it was a cliché, a relic of human kindness and bonding, and they knew how desperately important it was. They stepped together, standing in a circle in the dark. The very embodiment of the *Sakuru*.

Stilt.

Tigress.

Daisho and Creep.

Van and the military construct.

Ishido and Cuda.

Stilt cleared his throat. "You know what's going to happen." There was a general murmur of acknowledgment. "Then I don't need to tell you things are probably going to get extremely dicey. But nobody panic. We've been through a lot. Been through some changes. But everybody in The Circle tonight has earned the right to be here, and don't ever forget that." He turned to Susan. "That's my inspiring speech. Your turn."

Susan smiled halfheartedly. She couldn't deny the fear that had unwound in her stomach. "When I first contracted you all," she said, almost a whisper, "I didn't know how close I would become to you. Didn't want to know you. Only use you. I'm sorry for that, but I can't lie—it's what you were for. Now our positions are somewhat reversed, and I'm so grateful that you have accepted me into your family. I can truly say I know what it's about now. Thank you all for showing me what is important." She closed her eyes and leaned her head back toward the ceiling. "And Dad, I hope it won't come down to violence, but I won't hesitate to take a shot at Frank Selby if he gives me half a reason. Love you, *Papa-san*." She opened her eyes and nodded at Asano.

"To quote a brilliant colleague of mine, Kai Tokura, 'stay alert, stay alive'. You don't know how much you have affected me. All of you. I feel like I have a family, if you can understand what that means." He wrinkled his patchwork face and turned to David Maddock.

Creep smirked that familiar, toothsome, savage half-grin. "Wot's this? Kung fu therapy?" He chuckled and mimed wiping a slate. "Wait. Okay. I have a four-point agenda: One, we're gonna kick some Selby arse tonight, mates. Two, maybe then Kel won't have died for nuffin'. Three, I wish I'd met you blokes ten years ago. And four, be careful. Not that I will."

Van spat the worn toothpick from his lips. "I wanna do well. I wanna come out okay. And Mama wants to have you all over for pasta." He ran a gloved hand through the construct's thick tangle of hair, patting him squarely.

The construct grunted, holding up his wide, three-fingered pads. His voice was low and gravelly, as usual, with the familiar slow pattern. "Ah, thanks. Fun...riding...in...the car." He beamed happily, enormous white teeth flashing as he winked at Ishido.

The young man inhaled, letting out a slight laugh. "I have to admit, this is probably the most bizarre gathering of martial arts talent this side of a Jackie Chan retrospective. But you're all good. Hell, I've seen it. And if Susan likes you, that's cool with me. As for Stilt, I'm very pleased to have made your acquaintance. And if you don't take care of my cousin, you'll have me to answer to."

Stilt smiled. "What an attitude. You'd make a good *jonin* for this group."

Ishido laughed. "We'll talk later." He glanced at the large man next to him.

Cuda paused briefly before speaking. What he said was passionate and eloquent. "Don't forget what it's about, *mi amigos*. It's about keepin' things like Jet off the street, and it's about maintaining your self-respect. Most of all, it's about the *kids*, man. The *kids*. Don't ever forget that. I'm proud to be a part of this team, man. And I ain't never gonna forget any o' you."

Creep saluted. "Cheers, mate."

"*Mia famiglia*," added Van.

Stilt stepped into the center. "Alright. Selby's gonna be here any minute. We have to expect a fair number of *ronin*, some hired guns, maybe even ninja. From what Susan tells me, he's used 'em before." He turned to Cuda, giving his old friend a stern look. "We're gonna need to split. I want you to take a group to the ground level and guard against street entry."

"Why?" Cuda folded his arms. "Why don't we just wait 'til they show up?"

"You wanna wait?" Stilt barked, taking a tone. "Then wait! But I need somebody to guard against street entry!"

"I didn't say I wouldn't do it!" Cuda spat, eyes hard with a growing fear. "I was just askin' why!"

Susan stepped between them. "Drop it."

Stilt bowed his head, reached out his hand. "Sorry, brother. I didn't mean anything."

"Ain't nothin, *amigo*." They bumped fists and suddenly it was over.

Stilt turned back to the middle. "I want Daisho with Cuda's group. The ground assault's likely to have the big guns. Creep, you go too. And the KML. I'll take Van and Ishido, and we'll need Susan to make the deal. Each group take a unit of

K-corp security." He slowly turned, examining the granite expressions on his comrades' faces. "Let's get it."

As if on cue, the alarm sounded from the wall panel by the door, and Love's voice echoed from the corner. "Susan, I think he's here. Security's picked up at least two approaching AVs and ground traffic like Iraq."

Stilt lifted his eyes toward the ceiling, as if he could hear the approaching aircraft. He glanced quickly at Cuda. The blinking strobes from the Bay Bridge cast an eerie dance of light through the window onto Stilt's visor.

Cuda looked at him, watching his intermittent reflection flash on and off in the chrome surface of the eyepiece. Their silent communication took only a brief moment, but it was the most important exchange in the world.

Yes, Cuda thought. Yes, he'd do it. He'd look after Susan and their child, if it came to that. It was the least he could do. "Let's get a move on, *amigo.*"

Stilt hugged him quickly. "Be careful, or I'll have to kick your ass."

"Ha," Cuda laughed. "You can try."

44

FRANK SELBY came with three AVs, each setting down in turn atop the concrete roof. Susan stood armored with the grip of the blue *monokatana* poking out of the scabbard on her back. The new cowl was a blend of ballistics weave between a lattice of thin titanium "ribs", and looked like the face-mask of a videogame ninja. The nose-and-mouth air filter was still part of the design, and a small, round pad over the right ear linked up with the user's mastoid implant, connecting them with the local audio network. A tinted filter shield covered the eyes, offering protection from dazzle grenades or laser light.

Stilt and Ishido stood within two sword lengths of each other, armored cowls up, watching cautiously as the air cars came to a billowing, whooshing stop on the LED-lit landing pads.

A fifteen-person armored security team crouched ready on the hidden steps to the roof reception area.

Van scurried to the concrete wall between the miniature green-space and the landing area. He slid into position and swung the canvas bag of incendiary toys around in front of him. Flipping it open, he pored over the contents: a dozen dazzlers, half-dozen smoke bombs, ten concussion grenades and a dozen frags. A one-kilo block of EPX-2 rounded out the collection, looking like a brick of gray government-issue cheese.

The first AV began to power down, and the passenger door flipped open in hydraulic slow motion. A young Thai with long hair stepped out, clutching a SP5K submachine gun in his gloved hands. Stilt recognized him immediately. Quan. He nodded at the thug, the AV headlights reflecting off his visor in an array of silver halos. "Isn't that a parole violation?"

"Fuck off, asshole," was the curt reply. The young Thai stepped to the side as Frank Selby emerged from the car.

He was clad completely in black, and clutched a steel briefcase in one hand, a sheathed *katana* in the other. He was draped in a gray Armani overcoat. Synthetic hair blew and ruffled in the strong wind.

More doors opened on the vehicles, and a variety of hired guns and *ronin* stepped out into the chill night sky. Susan estimated about ten, no problem for the waiting security force. Stilt squinted through the visor. Shadows, moving between the west wall and the AVs. He grunted and whispered into the built-in mic. "Heads up, people. Looks like he brought some boys in black."

Frank Selby smiled, holding his arms out to the side like a long lost relative. "Susan? Is that you?"

She stayed put, content just to stare at him, feeling the Tigress paw impatiently in her chest.

"I didn't know you liked the commando armor thing, Susan. But it's you. Don't change a thing."

Cuda flinched as the armored truck rammed the security gate. The air in the garage was filled with the scream of spinning tires, the whine of electric motors and the repeating *pop-pop-pop* of automatic gunfire. The security team moved forward, out of the shadows, returning fire. An urban camo APC was next, followed by a black stretch limo, sporting thick ballistics armor. Employee cars ruptured as they were blasted aside by the incursion. Cuda breathed into his mask. "Alright, KML, let 'em eat balls."

The construct peeked around from a concrete pylon near the employee lifts. His squat, armored form was almost invisible in the darkness. He pulled a golf-ball-sized clump of the clay-like plastic explosive and delicately pressed a tiny impact detonator into the center. Gingerly placing it into the sling, he stepped out from the column and began to whip it around and around, over his unarmored head. The small black tube of the headset radio wiggled against his furry cheek as he twirled the device in a slow buildup.

ACQUIRE TARGET.

ARMORED VEHICLE APPROACHING. RANGE: 25 METERS. SPEED: 42 KPH.

GAUGE TRAJECTORY. COMPENSATE.

RELEASE.

The tiny bomb shot from the sling and hit the armored windshield dead center. It exploded on impact, the bulletproof glass rent away from the frame with an ear-shattering thunderclap, thick flames coating the cab. It swerved, clipping a steel-concrete column, flipping over in a mass of smoldering metal.

Suddenly, Cuda felt a tap on the shoulder. Who was that? Creep was supposed to be waiting in the access ledge above the main security gate. Daisho was supposed to be clear across the parking garage. He turned and saw the blue SFPD riot armor, the familiar scraggly face and buzzed blond hair.

"Dennis! What the hell, man?"

"I was in the neighborhood."

"Get the fuck outta here."

"Really. You guys did great snuffing Bug, so I thought I'd lend a hand. Need some help?" He pulled his sidearm from its belt holster.

Cuda laughed. "I don't know yet. Keep an eye on the heavies in the black stretch."

"You got it. By the way, I took the liberty of inviting Cheryl and her gang to the party. Should be here soon."

Ishido watched the collection of corporate *ronin* with cautious eyes as Frank Selby strode forward from the pulsing LED landing lights.

The corporate *shogun* quickly appraised Stilt, then went back to the Tigress. "Susan. This case contains four million dollars in hundred-gram gold bars. It's yours if you give me the card." He paused, nervous. Sweat began to break on his forehead. "You do have the card, don't you?"

She nodded silently.

Stilt raised the small card case. "Your boys just crashed the street-level security gate. We give you the card, you call off your dogs?"

Selby smiled unenthusiastically. "Of course, Mr. Uh, I'm sorry, I didn't catch your name."

"Stilt."

Selby's eyes widened with amazement. "Stilt. Why this is indeed a pleasure. You know you saved me about two million dollars by being too good for the guns I put on your ass."

Stilt glared at him from beneath glistening chrome. With the hood up, he looked inhuman, like an armored android. It had the added benefit of not telegraphing any facial expressions.

Selby's eyes narrowed. "Hell, I'll give you a percentage."

Ishido snapped his head to the side as a shadow passed in front of the lead AV's headlamps. The woman from the Lexus yesterday. The one who'd shot Creep. The bullet removed from Creep's shoulder had been a 40-caliber armor piercing round, the same that had been found embedded in the street-lamp in Daly City, according to Stilt. Ishido was almost glad Creep wasn't here to confront the woman who'd killed Kelly. He was unbalanced enough as it was.

Stilt angled his head, still holding the sleeve firmly in the black, rubberized mesh of his gloved fingers. "If we give you the card, you're going to set up a new Jet operation, aren't you?"

"Smart man," Selby observed. "You seem to know a lot about the stuff. I could use you on my crew, you know. Very bright, indeed."

Stilt stood unmoving. "You'd sell out a generation of children for money you could easily make in other ways. Ethical ways."

"Slower ways." The smile dropped from Selby's face, and the metal briefcase suddenly felt very heavy. "Look, if you're talking about the kid in the video, it was an overdose—"

"Stop pulling my dick, Selby." Stilt's voice was hollow, angry. "I know what an overdose looks like. I've lost a student to this shit. I've seen what it does to a community."

Selby spat. "Shit. What do you care about community? You're a fucking suit like me. The costume's different, but you and me, we're the same up here." He leaned forward and pointed at his head.

"Now, maybe." Stilt thumbed his breastplate. "But not in here. You saw the kid as one less customer."

"It's a fucking military drug, man! What do you want? It was untested in an urban environment. The new variant formula on that card will reduce the harmful side effects."

"Reduce the harmful side effects? Well." Stilt turned his head toward Ishido. "That makes all the difference in the world." He glared at Selby, the reflecting circles of light from the visor casting tiny stars on the face of the mogul. "You saying 'New Jet' will be a safe drug?"

Selby grinned broadly. "That's right. A *safe drug*. You got it. Very smart. What do you say? The bullion, plus, say, a five-percent cut? Nobody dies, we all go home happy and rich.

That's a lot of money, *amigo*. And you can sleep with a clear conscience, because it's safe."

Stilt sighed. "No such animal, Selby. And you're not my *amigo*." He tossed the plastic case to Ishido.

Selby dropped the corners of his mouth in a mask of disappointment. "So, basically, what you're saying is, no deal."

Susan's breath filter emitted a puffing sound that might have been considered laughter. "No, Frank. Basically what he's saying is, fuck off." Her weight shifted imperceptibly, and her hands rested together in front of her crotch.

"You do realize I am prepared to take the formula by force."

"Oh yes, we've expected that."

"You realize that I have nothing to lose at this point, and everything to gain. With you out of the picture and your board and headquarters in disarray, I can have the buzzards picking over your company's assets by tomorrow morning."

"That scenario goes both ways," Ishido shot back, shaking his head. "You've got a lot to lose, chief. If you're smart, you'll pack up and go home, write off the loss, and get back to jerking off your shareholders on Monday."

"Nobody wants this, Frank," Susan urged. "Walk away now."

Selby closed his eyes for a moment and caught a whiff of salt air coming in off the Bay. "Oh, I think you want this, my dear. I think you want this almost as much as I do."

Stilt rolled his left shoulder, loosening the muscles. His next words could mean death for several people, including himself, his partner, and the new life growing inside her. He found his heart softening and realized that when dealing with Selby, sentimentality could only contribute to failure.

He had to be Selby to fight Selby.

Susan was here of her own accord, and Stilt wouldn't have been able to keep her away if he'd tried. The security team was well paid to put their lives in danger for Kitayamacorp. They knew what they were doing.

His gaze returned to Selby, who stood, arms at his side, waiting for an answer. Time to call his bluff.

"Let's do this. I'm curious to see if you've got the spine to do the dirty work yourself."

Frank Selby smiled, and this time it was a look of grim, evil intent. His sparkling white implants bared, and he gave a short chuckle. "You have no idea what I have the spine to do." He raised the sheathed sword with his left hand, signaling the gathered *ronin* with a twist of the scabbard.

The armored limo came to a screaming sideways halt, its left side smacking hard into a line of parked company Acuras. KML029 flung splat after explosive clay splat, until his supply was reduced to a plastic bucket full of steel ball bearings. The parking garage was a mountain of sundered vehicles and burning consumables. The APC plowed through the carnage, 50-caliber machine gun clearing a gruesome trail of torn security personnel. Those who fell were crushed under its massive wheels, screams cut silent with a motorized whine.

Cuda headed past the rampaging tank. "Creep, man. Take out that motherfucker." Dennis followed, helmet and visor locked in riot position.

They made it to the side of the halted limo and were amazed to see two enormous hulks stepping to the smeared cement. Cuda had to laugh. "Aww, man."

Dennis grinned. "Well, is this a reunion, or what?"

Biggs moved forward, unhurried, staring down the barrel of the cop's sidearm. "Pay's good, *amigo*."

Cuda drew the *monokatana* from the sheath on his back. "I don't get it. Shouldn't you guys be pickin' up soap down at Solano?"

Johann reached into his jacket, producing a set of *nunchaku* from the breast pocket. "Someone who didn't work for Frank Selby probably would." There was a slight whistle of air, and the blunt metal handle whipped out at Cuda's head. The sword blade met it with an echoing *TINK!*

Dennis fired at Biggs, and the large thug grunted as the shoulder of his jacket opened in a spatter of nylon, Kevlar and carbon fiber. He scowled and released the magazine, left hand probing desperately over his armored uniform. "Where the hell are my APs?!"

Biggs took two steps and flung Dennis against the crashed limousine.

Murray coughed as the wind was knocked from his lungs. He tried to stagger to his feet, but found a pair of tree-trunk arms latched via thick hands to the front of his uniform. He gasped unsuccessfully for breath as he was hoisted into the air, then vaulted headfirst onto the limo windshield. The glass parted, and the riot helmet thumped as it hit the steering column inside.

Johann whipped and smacked the flail with a masterful instinct, and Cuda was glad he was wearing the armored hood. He backed against the cold, round surface of a concrete pylon and prepared for Johann's next move. It was a high shot to the head, and Cuda dropped in place, sweeping the thug's legs from under him. The giant met cement with a *thud*, and Cuda stepped forward, opening Johann from groin to chin in a lightning flash of plastic and muscle, his *kiai* lingering above the violent din.

Creep let out his siren wail and dropped to the roaring metal of the APC. Like the construct, he did not wear the hood, letting his long hair stream out behind him. A quick slap of EPX with a timed detonator on the 50-cal, and Creep dived from the moving tank, onto the back of a corporate *ronin*. The APC gun exploded in tiny fragments of ruined steel, the vehicle's massive tires squeaking to a stop. Creep rolled the thug onto his back and slid down fast, crushing the *ronin*'s windpipe with his knee. The top hatch on the APC swung open, and Creep spun to look.

"Oh," grunted Kuvalda as he leaped to the roof of the vehicle. "It's you." He flashed a sinister grin, lowering his enormous grenade rifle at Creep's head.

"Do it," ordered Selby with the wind in his hair, and the *ronin* opened fire. The Kitayama security force took the cue, storming up cement steps onto the landing zone.

The night was suddenly full of rocketing lead, empty casings and the jackhammer sound of submachine guns spraying the open air. Selby's force pressed forward toward the roof entry.

Susan whirled on Quan and with one fluid movement cleft the gun from his hands, taking two of his fingers with it. He flinched, but didn't cry out. Clenching his teeth, he leaped into the air and delivered an astonishing Taekwondo kick to the side of Susan's head. She gasped, feeling her brain jar inside her skull as she spun away from the blow.

This guy was good. She hadn't expected it from a wheelman. Continuing in her three-sixty spin, she adjusted her wrists, and the neon blue monoblade came out. It entered the right side of his body, between his third and fourth rib, and exited on the other side. She watched, tense, as the young Thai dropped, his chest opened like a bloody smile. His nerves twitched in spasm, and she followed through with a second swipe. Quan's head rolled away, leaving a crimson trail.

Susan had potentially been responsible for deaths in the past—her record in the course of corporate oversight certainly wasn't spotless—but something about this was different. She inhaled sharply, realizing her fear for the first time. It hadn't bothered her at all. Suddenly the burning sting of an AP round in her right thigh sent her crumpled to the ground. She tore the cowl from her head, gasping for breath amid the dust and smoke.

Four security soldiers dropped to the bloodstained cement. There was a sound of concentrated thunder from Selby's car, and a flash of high-intensity light. The AV burst into metallic shreds, sending a handful of *ronin* over the edge of the building along with the ruptured motor.

Stilt crouched, hissing into the commlink, "Good work, Pezzoni."

Frank Selby dropped his briefcase and started to duck away behind one of three giant air processors that lined the south wall.

Ishido ducked, watching Selby with partial attention as he tried to follow Harlot's movement in the other direction. This was not turning out as promising as he'd hoped. There was a small park up here—trees, grassy hills, 'synth machines and walls and all sorts of fun places for them to hide. But they were all directly across from the landing pads. He'd assumed they could drop Selby's grunts before any of them scattered. There was another explosion to his right, near Harlot's last position. Another AV ripped apart. He realized he'd lost track of her, and decided to head after Selby.

Stilt scrambled forward, knocking two *ronin* to the concrete with a flash of red plastic. He'd not used a sword in a long time, never as a neighborhood vigilante—but he'd been practicing. He tapped a finger against his right ear, barking into the comms. "Talk to me, Cuda. What's going on down there?"

"We're in some deep shit, brother. Get back to ya." Cuda sucked in air as Biggs swung a deadly-looking blade at his head. His own sword came up in a strong parry.

Biggs smiled and Cuda backed away, gripping the *katana* tightly in front of him. There was a sudden blast of hot air as one of the company delivery vans blew to pieces behind Biggs, and the giant man fell forward onto Cuda's sword, two jagged shards of steel lodged firmly in the back of his skull.

Creep rolled away as Kuvalda opened fire from the top of the APC. The cement opened around him like a dozen collapsing gopher holes. Years of gymnastic evasion skills, honed to theatrical precision in the Arena, surged through his body like a possessing entity. A vault into a handspring, a full back flip, another spring, a cartwheel into a somersault—all the while screaming, "Somebody. Take. That. Thing. Out!"

Then, a flurry of gray and black.

The billowing wing of a dark seraph.

An answered prayer.

Daisho strode from the smoke and swirling propellant-fueled flames like a masked, vengeful rider of the Apocalypse. Explosions erupted from craters in the concrete as the floor was torn asunder. Kuvalda followed Creep along the floor, blasting away with the automatic fire of explosive shells.

He paused when his target sight found the gray ghost.

Suddenly it was gone. Then it was back, fifty feet closer than before.

Kuvalda took aim and fired. The ghost was gone.

He looked again. It was now only twenty feet away, giant cloak flaring in the smoke and dust. He pulled the trigger again, looked down at his silent weapon. He checked the digital ammo counter on the side: 00.

Oh shit.

His eyes grew wide as the gray curtain of night opened in front of his terror-stricken face. He saw a brief glimmer of light within the blackness. A red moon, glinting coldly in his eyes. He screamed in mortal terror for the first time in his life. A scream lasting only a second before it was cut short.

Then a loud blast, and Daisho slumped over Kuvalda's body, his ribcage full of buckshot.

45

THE NINJA swung up over the edge of the cement rail, smacking something on his concrete perch. Van glanced up, but the acetylene flare was already in the canvas pyro bag.

The explosion rivaled any single blast seen in a military conflict.

Van Pezoni was vaporized in a brilliant, flowering whiteness of chemical superheat. The ninja was blown a hundred feet away into the sky above the city. The cement retaining wall ruptured completely, showering the entire landing area in small chunks of steel-reinforced concrete. The dazzlers whistled and flashed, a psychotic display of lightning and chemical strobe. The remaining EPX tore a hole in the roof, sending giant slabs of pavement, grass and soil into the tech access four floors below. The entire southeast corner of Kitayama headquarters was transformed into a living, breathing organism, a maelstrom of thunder and hellfire, bellowing savagely through the smoke and flame and flashes of dazzler.

Stilt looked up from the pavement as he was showered with dust and metal. He scrambled to his feet and sprinted toward the angry wall of fire. "Oh God!"

Creep tumbled through the airless smoke, through the wreckage of the security gate, into the street. The black pavement flickered with orange and yellow, a white-hot spectrum of reflections from the firestorm above. He could see a great cloud rising like purple ink into water, from the roof into the limitless sky.

He came to a halt and lay still on his back, breathing hard, staring up at the inferno, bright flashes in his clear blue eyes. There was the sound of a shotgun being pumped, and he could see Bartak standing above him. A faint smile of satisfaction painted on face—the smile of a man who knew he'd won. Creep spat blood from his mouth. "Go ahead, you fuck. Blow me away like you an' your mates did Kelly."

Bartak grinned, lowering the barrel to Creep's forehead. Creep stared at him, not bothering to close his eyes. Bartak breathed, his finger twitching on the metal trigger.

The construct hit him from behind, a flying cannonball kick to the small of his back. Bartak felt a pop in his lumbar spine, and the shotgun flew from his hands. He landed face-down in a stagnant puddle of rainwater and transient urine, his face scraping the outer wall of the parking garage as he fell. Creep was on him in an instant.

"Tag, you're it!" A dull thud, and Creep buried a hairy fist in Bartak's kidneys. The blows that followed were brutal and savage. "How many times I gotta tell you not to point guns at people!"

Bartak rolled, knocking Creep into the construct's legs. The series 29 stumbled and fell forward. Bartak was instantly on his feet. A snap kick with the cyberleg to KML's head, and the construct tumbled to the ground, blood streaming from his broken nose.

Creep let fly a truck-stopping spring kick from the ground, missing as Bartak ducked to the side. He landed in a crouch, preparing his next move. Bartak moved in, Nikons scanning and twitching as Creep pivoted on his heels. Contact—the cyberleg impacted an armored thigh without damage.

Creep spun away from the blow, and was clipped again, in the face. He felt his jaw give way, and spat blood into the air. Another roundhouse to the head sprayed more blood. Creep grunted and his vision shifted, cloudy black moving in around the edges. Somehow, his left arm found its way up to shield the next kick. He snarled, launching his right palm into the bottom of Bartak's nose, forcing the cartilage up into his brain with a vicious scream.

The startled weapons designer stumbled back on limp feet, his face radiating an elliptical burst of red from the center. He fell, brown Nikons still locked open, purple lips pursed together in confusion. The servos in his leg hummed their automatic shut down sequence and went silent.

Creep hauled the construct to his feet. 029 shook the fog from his head, looked up at the flashing reds and blues of police AV strobes as the cops descended from above. Cuda's voice screeched into their headsets. "Come on, guys! Double-time! Head to the roof!"

Ishido leaped from behind the processor, and Selby clipped the air with his chrome blade. The young swordsman swung again, and Selby was waiting, blade angled up, as if he instinctively knew Ishido's movements before execution. Ishido cursed, sure he couldn't be broadcasting that much. An inside fake only served to push his opponent back, toward the billowing, bursting fire.

Stilt rushed up behind Selby. "Ishido! Get rid of the card!"

Selby spun, his blade arcing up in a backhand strike.

Stilt met the attack with enthusiasm. "Run!"

Ishido blinked beneath the hood. He tore the stuffy armor from his head, backing away toward the cement stairs. The security detail were dead. All of them. And the *ronin* too. Most had been impaled by rocketing shards of steel from the explosion.

Everything was burning.

Suddenly the woman was in front of him, her armored jumpsuit dancing with firelight. She held some sort of canister in her right hand, aiming a flaming trigger unit. The industrial acid was highly concentrated, volatile in the open air. Searing flames melted the armor over his outstretched sword arm. He screamed as he felt the hot singe of a military-grade chemical weapon spray his eyes. There was an agonizing twinge of bitter pain from his hand, then he could no longer feel it. He collapsed, unconscious to the simmering roof.

"Ishido!" Stilt only turned his head for a split-second, but it was enough for Selby to get through. Grafted, steroidal muscles bulged beneath the custom armored Armani suit. The chrome blade surged forward.

Stilt inhaled a desperate breath, dropping his *monokatana* in a helpless spasm. He looked down to see the glittering weapon embedded in his chest.

Selby grunted, hauling down on the sword. Stilt tensed as the blade perforated his lungs, his liver, his stomach, finally lodging firmly in his spinal cord.

There was a scream from behind, and Selby turned in time to see the stained blue glow of his death arriving by messenger in black armor.

Susan swung hard, and Frank Selby's head spun away from his body, landing and rolling with a grotesque, wet *splat* near the wreckage of the first AV. His headless body slumped to the ground. The sword pulled from his hands—still embedded in Stilt's torso—and Susan's own blade clattered to the ground.

Stilt faltered dizzily, his mouth agape in complete astonishment. What the hell had he done? He'd only broken concentration for a brief moment. Selby would've never bested him otherwise.

"Fuck," he cried, chest sucking air from the smoky sky around him. Susan ran to him as his legs gave way. His breathing was shallow and labored. She pulled the armored hood from his head. Sweat-soaked dark hair fell into her hands as she gently helped him to his knees. "S-sword…" he gasped. "God…take it out." Blood gushed from the ghastly rip in the armored shell, leaked from his mouth, stained his gloved hands.

Susan's forehead wrinkled in abject shock, tears streaming silver down her cheeks. "Oh God," she winced, pulling hard on the hilt of the chrome *katana*. It ripped partway out. Stilt cringed, letting a tortured whimper escape his blood-stained lips. Pulling again, the weapon came away and she tossed it angrily aside. "Oh God, oh God, Stilt." Susan steadied him, gently lowering him to the scorched concrete. "No no no, hang on, love."

He grunted, let loose a sputtering cough. "Oh Jesus," he whispered, the air hissing from his ruptured lung.

Harlot dropped the micro-flamethrower next to Ishido's body, knelt and grabbed the plastic case, singed but still intact. She scanned the area with boosted optics. Stilt: dead or dying on what was left of the south landing pad. The Tigress: kneeling wounded over him. Frank Selby: decapitated body lying in a pool of scarlet gore. She was not going to get paid now, that was for sure.

A sharp noise from the roof reception office caught her attention. She let her cyber-optic implants zoom in through the broken glass. The rest of The Circle were arriving. Grasping the data card in her fireworn hand, Harlot sprinted to the third and final AV, leaping inside with little grace.

Cuda scampered up the cement stairs, dodging slumped bodies in black and others in shredded blue security armor jackets. Creep was next, and the KML unit limped up behind them.

Susan held Stilt's head in her lap, softly caressing the matted hair from his face with a gloved hand. The AV's engine roared to life, and suddenly the air was all smoke and dust, a whirlwind of debris. Susan held him tightly, shielding his face from the roaring wind, sobbing quietly as he exhaled something that sounded a lot like "love you," and died.

Cuda stood helplessly, watching as the AV rose into the night sky and banked away to the south.

The construct was the first to see Stilt's crumpled body in Susan's lap as she tenderly cradled him on the red-stained concrete. He approached, hearing Creep's expletive behind him, and Cuda's desolate moan. He'd seen this reaction before. When Father Fisk and Kelly had died.

If anyone was more surprised than Stilt at his passing, it was the stocky military construct with the serial number tattoo. He shuffled to where Susan knelt, large blue eyes welling up again. He tried to breathe through ruptured nasal membranes, but got only the sharp sting of smoke. Kneeling by Susan, he ran a thick, nailed digit across the gaping wound in Stilt's armor, managing only a guttural, "Ohhh..."

Creep flew into a rage, scurrying almost on all fours to Frank Selby's headless corpse. He attacked it, tore it, rent it apart. He ripped the clothing from the bloodied torso, gouged his claws deep into dead flesh. He leaped on it, kicked it, ground it to pieces, left only a grim pile of grafted meat. He found the head near a sputtering tongue of fire in the landing circle, lifted it, screaming at it as he gripped the open-eyed artifact by its flaming hair. Cocking back his arm, he launched it over the edge of the roof. It plummeted down into the city, flame streaming out behind it.

Cuda stood back, watching the scene with wild anger in his eyes. There was no one to pay back for a transgression this dire. He wanted to kill someone, and he wanted to kill no one. He wanted to punish the world, and he wanted to protect everyone in it. He wanted to go home and put his old gun in his mouth, pull the trigger, just to spite his best friend. Some fucking nerve, to keep a guy from blowing his own head off, become his ally, his brother, and then let some corporate asshole with some store-bought muscles and a sword take everything away. What the hell did he think he was doing, leaving in the middle of the revolution? What did he gain from this? As if he had a choice.

It was just so fucking senseless.

He saw the severity of the gutting Selby had performed. It was far beyond anything Asano could've fixed, even if he were here and not headed to San Francisco General in a meat wagon. "Aww, damn, *amigo*." He slumped to his knees and watched Susan helplessly.

It was like she was rocking him to sleep.

Harlot inhaled, blinking cautiously. She checked the mirrors. Nothing. Switched on the radar. No one in pursuit. Yet.

She set a course due south, engaging the autopilot. Sliding the vinyl package from her jumpsuit, she opened the flap, coaxing the tiny card from its sleeve. Inserting it into the reader under the dash screen, she pressed a couple icons, opening the contents: A small text file simply labeled JET V2...

Her electronic eyes scanned the screen as the data came up.

. . . .

GUAIFENSIN 100MG

PHENYLPROPANOLAMINE HYDROCHLORIDE 12.5MG

DEXTROMETHORPHAN HYDROBROMIDE 10MG

ALCOHOL 4.75%

. . . .

"—the fuck??" she gasped. "Cough syrup? Fucking cough syrup?" She blinked, slamming a hard fist into the steering wheel. "Shit!" She slammed it again, then twice more in rapid succession. "Shit! Shit, shit!"

The dash radar blinked and emitted a two-tone warning beep. Her eyes shot to the rearview mirror. The flashing strobes and wailing sirens of three police AVs pierced the still night behind her.

She hit the wheel again. "Shit!"

CODA

THE DAMAGE to Kitayama headquarters was significant, but Love had it repaired and brand-spank-
ing-new-looking in less than six months. I have to admit he
made us all proud. I never really thought he had what it took
to run a megacorp, but he surprised me.

He funded the repair activities with some of the proceeds
from the Selby liquidation. Didn't actually cost Kitayamacorp
dollar one. Once he'd acquired the Selby stock at their bargain basement rate, he parted out the subsidiary companies,
raking in literally billions from international competitors.

He kept Monoped for himself. K-corp stock skyrocketed
when word of the Selby takeover hit the news. My shares split
twice, and I daresay we will be able to live quite comfortably
on the dividends. But I'll get to that later.

The one escaping AV was found abandoned in a rail yard
near Bakersfield. No one fitting the fugitive's description was
ever located. According to Pick's findings just before his un-
timely death, the woman's trade name is Harlot and she's
made quite a rep for herself in the hit biz. As long as she
doesn't come back looking for payment or revenge, I think we

should be fine—but to tell the truth, she's the one I'm most worried about.

Special Agent Dennis Murray was hospitalized briefly, his arm set and cast, his neck braced. Captain Bonner, John and I went to visit him at General when he was well enough to have visitors. He took the opportunity to announce his retirement. Cheryl was sorry to see him go, but she could understand how shit like that could get to him, getting injured all the time.

The SFPD threw him a party, bought him a new Rolex, filled him with Cesaro's pizza and champagne, and tried to raise his spirits. I remember the triumphant footage on the evening news. They all gathered on the steps in front of the precinct to bid him farewell, cheers and shouts in the air, almost like a wedding or graduation party. He waved with his police-blue sling, stepped happily into the driver's seat of his classic 2018 Corvette.

It exploded on startup.

No conclusive evidence was recovered, and the case remains open.

John tried valiantly to track down Windy. Larry said he'd dropped her at her old place in SoMa, and she'd called him once to find out about Van, but that he hadn't seen or heard from her after she received the news of Pezzoni's death. I wish her well.

Asano was treated for the gunshot wound to his ribs, the steel shot extracted, his torso slapped with collagen, bandaged securely. He called me once to say goodbye. I can only assume he returned to Japan, though to what kind of life I'm not sure.

Far be it from me to judge such a man. I feel honored to have known him at all. We miss him terribly.

The military construct KML029 suddenly found his family severely reduced in number. That, coupled with a natural curiosity, prompted him to bid us farewell and head to the Southwest in search of the one man who could answer his questions: Dr. Noah Jorgenson. None of us begrudge him the knowledge he seeks.

Although K-corp techs were able to access the formula stored in his DNA, the storage card had been a decoy—a ruse thought up by Love to draw Selby to our doorstep. And it worked. At great cost, to be sure. Love used the formula as leverage to have the feds look the other way while he picked over the carcass of SelTech.

I don't know how many Selby's *ronin* lost their lives during the attack on K-corp headquarters. We lost twenty-seven security personnel. And of course losses among the *Sakuru*.

David "Creep" Maddock retired from sports and security work. At my urging, Love grudgingly let him out of his contract. The former Arena Champ managed a few sportswear endorsements, then disappeared completely from society at large. He hinted that he might join the KML unit in his search, as he could drive and the construct has certain physical limitations where that's concerned.

I can't help but think what an interesting pair they'd make, roaming the desert roads. But I do wish them luck in their search.

Ishido was treated for major burns to the face and right arm. The limb was unsalvageable, as were his eyes. Both systems were easily replaced with cyberware, and he soon found himself in physical rehab and psych sessions with a so-called "sinister dominatrix" he referred to as Ilsa. He came by a few times to talk before disappearing with Larry about two months before the birth of the baby.

The girl's name is Kelly Tokura. My pregnancy was closely monitored, and no defects were found initially. I felt good about the process. The only traits she seems to have inherited from her late father's altered DNA are a quick mind and keen observational skills.

And she's strong.

John fulfilled his silent promise to Stilt and took care of me from day one of the aftermath. During the course of my term, I began to grow closer to him, and our lives eventually branched together, whether out of genuine love or just shared grief and exhaustion. It is said that a relationship based on mutual need cannot work, but ours seems to function pretty well. The bond of shared crisis is a strong one, as it turns out.

He is truly a remarkable man, caring and genuine. He is a compassionate teacher and father figure, a gentle and intuitive lover. I can readily understand how he earned Stilt's unconditional trust and bond of brotherhood.

We left the Kitayama arcology for the spacious warehouse apartments above the new Shihodo School of Martial Arts. The sound, modern building sits on the old site, at the northwest corner of 15th and Irving. It really is beautiful, and we're a lot closer to the street.

Funny. I never thought I could be comfortable below twenty floors of glass and chrome. Strange how life works out. Now I can't imagine living anywhere else.

A new bunch of kids has returned, and Jason and Elizabeth were given teaching jobs. Cuda teaches evening classes, and I do tutoring when I can. My main priorities, however, are advising Love, running the business-end of the school, and helping John raise our daughter.

Mike McCann, Jesse Hawkins and her infant daughter have also returned to the apartments, where they currently live rent-free. Jess and Mike once put their faith in Stilt. I want to try and win it back.

The Pezzoni family took some time recovering from the loss of their son and brother, but they have gradually warmed up to us again. I think there was probably a lot of blame placed on us for Van's death, and I truly can't condemn their thoughts on the matter. When I'm not waking up in a cold sweat from the nightmares, I'm usually crying myself to sleep, or John is.

I guess we have each other...

...and the good memories to keep alive.

Stilt was cremated, the ashes spread on the rose bushes in the park—as his will requested—and his visor mounted on the mantle above our apartment fireplace. The titanium rods hang on the wall, on either side. Some would call it a shrine, I guess, but it's our way of remembering. I don't know what we'll tell Kelly when she asks about her father. The truth, I expect.

In time, the neighborhood returned to its diverse normalcy, and people almost forgot that there had been a terrible corporate war fought through these very streets. The community had been used as a battleground, its citizens as pawns in a much larger game.

An inexcusable crime, I now realize, but Ishido told me once before he left that we must not blame ourselves forever if we are to move on. Self-incrimination is like an anchor dragging from place to place.

I didn't have long with Kai Tokura, but count myself blessed for the moments we did have. Holding him as he took his last breath was both my greatest trauma and my ultimate privilege. Stilt never saw the world with the same vision the rest of us do, both physically and emotionally. It makes perfect sense that having him briefly in my orbit helped me see with a different vision. And for that I will always be grateful.

Where the rest of the Sunset is concerned, John keeps remembrance a high priority, and I convinced Love to erect a small memorial across the street in front of Huey Newton Park.

It was a war, after all.

The End

ABOUT THE AUTHOR

Todd Downing's love affair with genre fiction dates back to his consumption of classic radio dramas and comic books as a child in the 1970s, which broadened into a general appreciation for scifi and fantasy media of all kinds.

He grew up in the greater San Francisco Bay Area, writing and drawing from a young age, his works ever-present in school literary journals and newspapers, and eventually on film. He married his high school sweetheart and moved to Seattle in 1991 where he began to write professionally, and worked as an artist in the videogame industry until his publishing company became a full time operation, while raising two children amid the chaos.

As the co-founder and creative director of Deep7 Press, Downing is the primary author and designer of over fifty role-playing titles, including *Arrowflight, Grimmworld, Airship Daedalus*, and the official *Red Dwarf* RPG. He continues to write genre fiction for stage, film, comics, audio, and adventure gaming products.

Widowed to cancer in 2005, Downing remarried in 2009 and currently lives in a three-generation home in Port Orchard, Washington, with his wife, her mother, their daughter, and three cats. Thankfully, he has an office with a door that closes.

Join the author's mailing list:
www.todddowning.com

Read the *Airship Daedalus* series:
A Shield Against the Darkness
Assassins of the Lost Kingdom
(By E.J. Blaine)
The Golden City
Legend of the Savage Isle
The Arctic Menace
Raiders of the Red Storm

Plus:
AEGIS Tales
(volumes 1 & 2)

Primordial Soup Kitchen

Calico Kids

The Parish

AVAILABLE NOW
in ebook and print!